LUCRETIA:
BADDY TWO SHOES

Lucretia:
Baddy Two Shoes

STAN KENT

BLUE MOON BOOKS
NEW YORK

Lucretia
© 2002 by Stan Kent

Published by
Blue Moon Books
An Imprint of Avalon Publishing Group Incorporated
161 William St., 16th Floor
New York, NY 10038

First Blue Moon Books edition 2003

ISBN 1-56201-357-2

9 8 7 6 5 4 3 2 1

Printed in the United States of America
Distributed by Publishers Group West

DEDICATION

This book is dedicated to anyone who has given or had taken their family jewels in the misguided course of religious fervor. Take General Kang Ping Tieh, "the Iron Duke," patron saint of Chinese eunuchs. Kang earned this lofty honor as a result of being left in charge of the imperial concubines for a long weekend while Emperor Yung Lo was off hunting. Knowing his political enemies would plant rumors that he had enjoyed sexual dalliances with the emperor's chicks, Kang chopped his genitals off and hid them in the Emperor's saddle bags prior to Yung Lo leaving the Forbidden City. When the emperor returned, Kang's fears were realized. He was accused of frolicking with 73 concubines. With a smug smile Kang retrieved his black, stinky and shrunken, but still recognizable family jewels and showed the emperor where they'd come from. Yung Lo was so impressed with the sacrifice that he promoted Kang to chief eunuch, gave him a truck load of gifts and jewels to make up for the loss of his fleshy jewels and proclaimed him a holy man.

Not so exalted were the thousands of young boys castrated by early 17th century Catholic Italy in the name of maintaining their cherubic vocal chords since women were forbidden to sing in church or on the stage. Boys with the slightest bit of a voice were sold off to the

Church by poor families at such a rate that within a few years every adult male in the Vatican choir was a ball-less soprano, and Bologna became known as the castration capital of Italy.

Kang Ping Tieh and thousands of young boys deprived by a religious nut of the ultimate feel of a really good wank, suck or fuck, this book's for you.

THANKS MUCH

What can I say to the woman who enjoys receiving luscious foot massages from me and has over one hundred pairs of really cool shoes and still doesn't mind shopping for another pair of heels, including letting me help her try them on, much to the dismay of all those attentive sales associates? What can I say to the woman who enjoys reading and editing my work and making cool suggestions to improve my plot ramblings? What can I say to the woman with the most perfect ankles ever situated between a gorgeous pair of massageable legs and feet? Only "Wow, I'm the luckiest author and man in the Shoeniverse. I Love You Much, my muse Cyn. Mega-thanks for being my inspiration, friend, lover and solemate."

To all my other readers I say mega-thanks and drop me a note at stan@stankent.com and tell me what you think of Lucretia. To see what's next for me you can visit www.stankent.com.

To all those that helped me write this fourth and perhaps final installment in the Violetta Valery Cutrero Shoe Leather saga I say Thanks Much. You know who you are, but my readers don't, so here goes.

Randy Rocket Scientist Tom Wunderlich for the Git Lekerk character the naughty notion of a perverted version of "These are a few of my favorite things," and for attending the Hustler readings, even when we don't go out drinking afterwards.

Satellite Repair Man and all around Renaissance Guy, Jack Vaughn for all the books he's read, including mine, and the discussions and suggestions for future plot developments.

The hundreds of shoe shops, women, men and websites the world over who've unknowingly contributed shoe designs and inspiration to Violetta's tales. The best new shoe shop in Los Angeles is Diavolina on La Brea. Thanks to them for all their cool sales and cooler styles. The best shoe cocktail bar and vintage shoe salon anywhere is Star Shoes on Hollywood Boulevard. Shoes and alcohol—what a dangerous concept. And those of you into shoes and feet and doing kinky stuff with them have to check out www.abusedshoes.com.

Teresa Flynt-Gaerke, Gary Sunshine and all the staff of Hustler Hollywood for hosting my monthly Naughty Bits and Bites Nights erotic discussions where much of Violetta's character has been developed and field tested.

Dita Von Teese for teaching me how to spank Cyn at Hustler Hollywood on Sunset Boulevard, especially the snapping of suspender straps against the butt as a lovely means of warming up her ass. Mistress Isabelle Sinclaire (www.isabellasinclair.com) for letting me review Lucretia while a training session transpired. It was good inspiration. Thank you, much mistress.

Cid and Kiki the cats for their love of rubbing on shoes and us and being the inspiration for Spykes. Note: No animals were injured in the writing of this book. I'm a card carrying PETA member.

Author and distinguished Ripperologist Donald Rumbelow for his authoritative work on Jack the Ripper, and for the rainy, foggy night tour of East End London where my great, great, grand-aunt, Catherine Eddowes, the fourth victim of Jack the Ripper was murdered. Mr. Rumblelow gave me the facts. The extrapolations surrounding the crimes are mine and should not be judged as his opinions.

Authors and Ripperologists Stewart Evans and Paul Gainey for their book, *The Lodger,* and the intriguing theory suggesting American physician, Dr. Francis Tumblety was Jack the Ripper. As with Mr. Rumblelow's work, the extrapolations on the Tumblety character were mine and should not be judged as their opinions.

Dan and Lucy Walker for help with Spanish translations.

Ginni Machamer for liking the Johnny Gianni character and mentioning it to Cyn at just the right moment when I needed inspiration, for the www.abusedshoes.com referral and for making some of the coolest jewelry and earrings imaginable that Violetta would just kill for. You can get info about Ginni's Beadwerkz by emailing her at blinni@attbi.com.

Rosie Duenas and Ruhi Logan for last minute help in moving armoires, for the lively discussion about cock and ball shaving, for looking after Cid and Kiki at the last minute so Cyn and I could enjoy a much needed vacation in France and Italy following the finishing of this book, and for coming to the readings.

Reader Jason for his kind words about Violetta, the third book in the series. His suggestions made it in to this book, so see, we authors do listen to reader footback.

Reviewer Gary Adler for a great service in exposing erotica to a wide audience. Gary reads and writes about more smut/porn/erotica/one-handed reading material than anyone I know, and he hasn't gone blind yet. Check him out at http://bestpornhost.com/sfmaster/

To all my friends and partners in crime at the Boring Silly Satellite company who do more for me every day than they'll ever realize, especially the ones who cover for me while I'm off writing books—Julie Perkins, Greg Mc Donald, Dean Yamanaka, Patti Procter, Layne Silva,

Erica Roesler-Wong, Chris barsamian, Linda Kong, Diane Partsch, Cynthia Austin, Orv Hett, Danielle Corso, Jon Fish, Jacqueline Hoang, Sheldon Epstein, Felix Okpala, Phil Donatelli, Jerry Salvatore, G.P. Purohit, Bill Heckeroth, Mark Rookwood, Denny Ertsman and William Prophet.

Barney Rosset, Neil Ortenberg, Dan O'Connor and the Blue Moon staff for continuing to publish my porn with a plot—especially Mike O'Connor for the opportunity to make the much needed corrections.

Claudia Menza, friend, agent and great shoe conversationalist. Thanks for giving me the time to write the books I want to, and the suggestions to make me a better writer. No author could enjoy a better agent. I've said it before, and in a grand demonstration of implied redundancy and wordiness, I'll say it again. "Here's to many more nights when we can reach that state of perfect equilibrium—half man, half whisky." Cheers, Claudia.

THE FIRST PAIR:
BOVVER BOOTS

CHAPTER ONE

I'M VIOLETTA VALERY Cutrero, and if you've read *Shoe Leather, Shoes Your Weapon* and the humbly titled *Violetta* then you know all about me. Sort of, because I'm not sure even I know all about me. Much has happened in the few years since my Roman Holiday that was the subject of my eponymous volume. Remarkably it doesn't involve killing anyone, although someone very dear to me died, and after the funeral I cheated on my lover, who I'd just reconnected with after saving her from a date with the Big House and maybe the Big Injection while being strapped into the Big Gurney.

Call my transgression the byproduct of too much grief and too much temptation, and generally being an Avenging Angel Sex Goddess who's above the restrictions binding mere mortals like you, dear reader. I know, call me Ms. Rationalization. More about that later—later being throughout the next couple hundred pages of this latest installment in the ever eventful, star crossed, fate-fucked story of my life.

One thing you should know. Remember this well. You'll hear it many times throughout these chapters: The Feet Cannot Be Denied. That's my excuse—the ultimate rationalization for all my actions that some of you might find objectionable, and that includes my foul mouth, cocksuckingmotherfuckers.

Okay, here's the set-up. I'm twenty, and I got a kid, a cat, a lesbian life partner, a supernatural Guardian Angel, and a house on Stinson Beach in Northern California's Marin County, just forty-five minutes north of San Francisco for those of you that are geographically challenged. For this neck of the woods—okay, so wait a minute, like what the fuck does that mean? When do woods have fucking necks? Excuse me, I mean, what the heck does that mean? When do woods have darn necks? Since having Luc, even though he's only eleven months, I've tried to watch my language. Honest, I fucking have, but it's frigging hard. Ellen, my lover, friend and worry-wart earthly Guardian Angel is doing a pretty good job of reminding me to keep it clean. I don't want Luc growing up with my kind of foul mouth.

Or feet.

There—the cat's out of the bag—the jism's out of the cock—the juice's out of the cunt, and I can't finish my neck of the woods comment in good faith because I've mentioned my feet. I was going to say, "For this neck of the woods, we're pretty darn normal."

Not.

I mention my feet, and all thoughts of saying we're pretty darn normal evaporates like a warm fart on a cold day—whoops—sorry Luc, sorry Ellen—like a, like a, like a, oh what the fuck, like passing gas on a cold day. Damn, that's lame. This good-mouth shit and using politically correct speech is fucking—messing—up my brain. I feel like a retard on my guard. I mean a mentally challenged—oh shitworms—enough of the speech angst. I'm talking about my gifted, cursed feet. They're the reason I have closets full of previously fucked-in shoes. They're the reason why we have a house on the beach. They're the reason I have a kid from fucking my half-brother Tony. They're the reason I have Ellen. They're the reason I lost her and got her back. They're the reason Ellen blew Tony's brains out. They're the reason I saved Ellen from a certain date with the death penalty or at least life behind bars. They're the reason I cheated on her by fucking the brains out of Johnny Gianni—this really dishy Italian guy from my Roman Holiday who I just happened to run into right after the funeral of my aunt Crista. Hell, they're even the reason why we've got a cat called Spykes.

Spykes the cat—and Spykes the shoe fetish nightclub in New York—belonged to aunt Crista Cutrero. She was the last of my relatives left alive. She survived the Cutrero Curse by chopping off her feet, but she was still way into shoes and kink. She made some of the hottest, perviest footwear imaginable. She never really recovered from the uptight Feds and tight-ass Mayor closing down her club. She died in her sleep in her shoe-shaped bed on Halloween, handing the government a big ole trick since they planned to indict her the next day under trumped up porn trafficking charges. She handed me a big ole treat with hundreds of pairs of shoes and Spykes the cat, plus the opportunity to get my rocks off with Johnny.

Thanks, Crista, you knew more than anyone of us that the feet cannot be denied. I know you believed in reincarnation. I hope you come back as a really cool pair of fuck-shoes, or at least a really nice, normal pair of feet that enjoy lots of sex in really cool fuckshoes.

My feet are not normal, nor nice; the things they've seen and done would curl your toes. My gifted and cursed feet are the reason why locked away in my closet there's a pair of caliges—ancient Roman lace-up, thong sandals that allow me to invoke my supernatural Guardian Angel, Lucretia Cutrero. She's my great, great, great a bunch of times aunt who dabbled in some pagan rites, ended up being made to fuck her brothers, Crispinus and Crispinianus, by this sick Roman fuck, Rictius Varus. The Crispies went on to become the patron saints of shoe repairers, and Lucretia went on to give birth to a son and the Cutrero curse.

It's been footed down through the ages according to Lucretia's spell of incestuous sex. It's why I had sex with my half-brother, Tony, just before Ellen killed him. It's why I can put on a pair of fuckshoes—shoes that have been fucked in—and I'm there inside the fucker or fuckee, having his or hers sex, living, coming, and if I'm not careful, dying like the original wearer. It's called shoesex—the Cutrero curse, blessing, and gift.

Shoesex is a jealous mistress. I learned the hard way its cardinal rule—the feet cannot be denied. After numerous people I cared about met nasty, premature deaths because I diddled away my responsibility to be the serial killer of serial killers, I went to Rome by way of New York city and Crista to see how to ditch my curse. I came back with Lucretia, or rather, she came back with me. I'm supposed to be able to invoke her with the caliges, but as I found out on my way out of Rome, if I'm threatened, she comes running to my aid uninvited, claws bared, cannons blazing, torpedoes damned, and she doesn't take prisoners.

In that regard she's just like Ellen.

Jeez, between my earthly and supernatural Guardian Angels and me I'm a walking death sentence for whatever stupid fuck gets in my way.

So now you know why I can't really say we're pretty darn normal. Shoesex and its consequences are anything but pretty darn normal. I've used it to have amazing sex, learn all the dirty stuff I could about people's kinks, including some celebs' mega-weird peckerdilloes, as well as receiving many a rude and fatal reminder of its main purpose—to track down evil fuckers and execute them. I sliced and diced the Dildo Killer and did away with an uncle of mine who was doing in little kids. If you'd been cursed/gifted with shoesex power you could put on the shoes I wore when I carried out these obligations and see/feel/hear/taste/smell exactly as if you were me, but since you don't have the Cutrero curse you'll just have to read my other books if you want to know what it's like growing up to be the Avenging Angel Sex Goddess of shoes.

One thing you don't need shoesex power to know is that having a kid is pretty funky. It's a trip. It's so weird to have him sucking on one tit and Ellen on the other with her hand up my cunt.

Attention Right-Wing Prudes, Religiously Uptight Individuals, Justice Department Jerk-offs, Fraidy Cat Publishers, and Censorious Booksellers—this is not kiddie porn. This is a mother's description of what it's like to nurse a kid while having sex with her life-partner-lover, okay. Luc isn't being abused or even used. He's actually happy that he doesn't have to wait to be fed, and you know what, I bet he'll develop a healthy sexual attitude being around so much love and lust at such an early age.

So what if my son and lover sucking on my tits at the same time turns me on. If you're a tight ass prude stop reading now because it's gonna get worse. Way. Much. I'm a fucking Cutrero and proud of it. "Incest Shoe Us" should be our family motto. I can just see the coat of arms. Right under the Cutrero name is a pair of crossed stilettos under which is emblazoned in Latin "Incest Shoe Us" with "The Feet Cannot Be Denied" under that for good measure. Okay, having said that, this little scene with Ellen and Luc is not kiddie porn or incestuous sex. Not at fucking all. It's convenience. He needs feeding, and I need fucking. Not keeping him waiting is a good mommy thing to do, and the feeling I get by looking at my son and feeling him suck on my tit while Ellen does me is not kiddie porn. It's love in all its greatest majesty.

Get the picture? If not, here it is. I'll paint it for you with my fingers. Imagine this scene, and do me a favor. Really get into it. Jerk your cock or rub your cunt and make yourself come or jerk your lover's cock or rub her cunt and make each other come while I tell you this, and yeah, wear shoes. I might just come across them someday and it'd be nice to know what my words made you think and do as you came like a burst fire hydrant.

So here we are, Ellen, Luc and me. We're lying on our bed. We're all naked. I'm propped up on a mountain of comfy pillows. The ocean breeze blows a saltwater tang through the lace curtains. It mingles with our wet cunt smell. I cradle Luc to my right tit. He sucks away, happy and contented with every gifted drop, like a government contractor milking a federal contract. Ellen does likewise on my left, making sure I'll never need to use one of those pump things to remove the excess milk from my tiny tits which have grown about two cup sizes and are oh so fucking sensitive. My boobs feel like I'm on a permanent period. Ellen knows this and so she sucks and bites like a wild animal at a feeding trough, driving me crazy with milky lust. It's a two-way cunty highway. My moans and groans and writhings work her up. Her hand forks between my thighs, parting the flesh, rotating her finger on my clit, while another finger flits in and out of my cunt, rubbing on the G spot. I'm turning to cream, literally. I never knew nursing could be such fun. This they don't tell ya in all those books and birthing and babying classes.

I'm not just a passive mommy. My free hand snakes around Ellen's shoulder and toys with her nipple. I rotate the taut flesh between my finger and thumb, first one way and the another. Ellen moans. She has very sensitive nipples. Always has. Man, if she got pregnant and had a kid and was nursing, California would slide into the ocean from the shockwaves. Perhaps that's why she's into this nursing scene so much. She knows how good I feel having her and Luc latched on to my nipples with their limpet lips.

Prompted by my squeezing she sucks harder on my nipple, and it seems Luc does likewise, the naughty little Cutrero that he is. The milk flows, fountains and drains out of me. I feel like I'm coming through my nipples and my cunt.

Yup, I'm turning to cream.

Ellen wraps her self around me, enjoying the mess, snuggling her body up close to me, grinding her cunt against my hip, her leg thrown over my pussy, adding extra pressure to the crush of her hands. I hear my wetness slip, slide and slap at her fingers, mixing with the sucking slurps of Luc and Ellen on my tits. It must sound like a lollipop convention in here.

I like this attention big-time. No post-partum depression for me. Fuck no. Being a mommy has made me hornier and more attractive. Ellen says so, and I believe her. We've had the best sex since Luc came along.

Speaking of which, he's curled up tight, still sucking away, happy as a little boy sucking on his mommy's tit while she gets fucked by her lesbian lover. Fuck Murphy Brown, Ellen, Luc and me, we define true family values, Dan-boy Quayle.

Ellen twists her hand and one of her fingers toys with the bud of my asshole. My juices have dripped down between my legs and made the rosebud entrance all slippery wet. Ellen twirls her fingers in the goo and spirals the slippery digit into my butt. My hips lift off the bed and with a little push she's inside and there's enough lubrication to give me a good ass finger-fucking. She slides another finger inside my cunt and this one massages the skin wall between my ass and my cunt while her other digit doesn't miss a beat on my G spot or clit. The woman is fucking ambidextrous or whatever the correct term is— vagina virtuoso and an anal artiste combined. She's got one finger on my clit, two up my cunt, and one up my butt and they're all working me into a slathery symphony of superfine sex.

I'm moaning and groaning and my hips are undulating. Luc's sucking and rocking in my arms like a regular little happy camper. Ellen squirms against me. I feel the slick trail of her juices on my hip. She's close to coming. I'm close to coming. Luc, well, he's close to dozing off.

Like I said. This ain't kiddie porn.

Ellen starts to come from her grinding, so I squeeze harder on her nipple. This drives her insane, so she stops sucking on my tit and smothers my mouth with hers and screams into me as her tongue pounds away like a little wet jackhammer. I taste the sweetness of my milk on her lips, and I feel a deep connection between her, Luc and me. Ellen's fingers go crazy up my cunt and ass, dancing and rubbing and flicking about like a hummingbird on speed. I'm over the edge, come-cream churning out of me. I feel like everything from the waist down is melting. Ellen keeps kissing me, and Luc keeps sucking on my tit, and I feel all warm and happy that we're one big happy family.

Ellen grinds into me, and I twist and her hand gets caught at a funny angle. She tries to be careful pulling her fingers out but the one furthest up my cunt scrapes a little. I scream from the sudden shock, pulling my mouth away from Ellen, my eyes tearing. Luc wakes into a crying fit, and as my eyes clear and focus I see Lucretia standing at the foot of the bed, wild-eyed staring at Ellen. I scream, "Luc—" catching myself before adding the "cretia." I knew I named my son after his great, great, great a bunch of times aunt for a reason.

Ellen leans over me to stroke Luc's head, comforting him on her way down between my legs. Luckily, she's occupied by my son and my cunt and doesn't see Lucretia.

"He's okay, V, don't worry. I'm sorry. My hand was twisted," Ellen says as she heads south to summer in my pussy regions. "There, there, let me kiss it all better," she adds between the first few licks.

Oh yeah, she will make it better. Ellen munches cunt but good. She drops her face deep between my wide-spread legs and plants firmer kisses on my sore pussy. Luc sobs himself back to sleep with a few tit sucks. Lucretia disappears, leaving me with the memory of her menacing smile. I breathe a sigh or relief and enjoy Ellen's tongue licking my pussy.

I close my eyes.

That was close. Lucretia looked a bit on the green side of jealous. I'm going to have to score some quality calige time so she knows that I've still got the hots for her and that Ellen is no threat, no matter how much screaming and moaning there is from the bed, bathroom or kitchen table. I have been kind of neglecting Lucretia ever since Luc was born. Ellen is so attentive and always there. It's hard to get the time to do some shoesex without Ellen wondering if I'm up to my catching-another-killer tricks. Ellen's still scared of shoesex and super protective of me, and I can't say I blame her. She still blames herself for leaving me alone when she went on her book and movie tour, and I went after the Cinderella Killer, only to find it was my half-brother, and then Ellen killed him, and I went missing in search of why my life was so fucked up, and she rotted in jail until I sussed out it was all the Cutrero curse's fault, and I came back and saved her.

Ellen's tongue slides inside my pussy and the warm softness feels so good. I can tell she loves me.

"All better," she says, in between licks, her hot breath painting my pussy. I feel so good being loved by her, being lusted by her, and I know I can't keep Lucretia a secret from Ellen much longer. It's not fair to her or Lucretia. I've been putting off telling Ellen about her supernatural counterpart because it was tough enough for Ellen to get over the whole Tony thing. She's done really well adjusting to life with a fucked-up Cutrero and all the baggage my family shoetree brings, but Lucretia would have been too much. I think our relationship is now strong enough to take the initial strain that finding out there's another woman in my life will cause, even if she is seventeen hundred years old and technically dead.

No problemo. Like I said, we're not your average, normal New Agey family living an oh so groovy life in Marin County's neck of the woods. Oh no. I have to tell Ellen soon because Lucretia is getting stronger and doesn't seem to like staying in the closet. One day they're going to meet and it would be best if I introduced them rather than these two powerful women with protective mean streaks meeting by accident. Which is what almost happened.

Okay, I consider my self warned. It's no big deal. What am I worrying about. They'll get along like a dick and a cunt or a cunt and a cunt. I can be the go-between. I can do it. I killed the Dildo Killer. I am the Avenging Angel Sex Goddess. I can do anything. I can make them see that it'll be best if all my Guardian Angels could just get along.

Yeah right, dream on, Violetta, dream on.

Ellen's tongue feels so good snaking in and out of my cunt and my ass. Luc has dozed off. He's satisfied and has a little hard-on, bless him. That's my boy, a true Cutrero.

I'm happy. I'm contented. Ellen's munching is going to make me come. Oh yeah. Oh yeah. I'm melting again.

Hmmmmmmmm. I'll tell Ellen about Lucretia tomorrow.

Honest I will. Trust me. By now I really do know that the feet cannot be denied.

CHAPTER TWO

WELL OKAY, CALL me a candy-ass, procrastinating, conflict-avoiding wimp in love but I don't talk to Ellen the next day about Lucretia.

I have every intention of doing so, but how can I dump on her after she ate my pussy for hours last night, and I munched on her twat for a couple more until we both fell asleep in a swampy bed of girl juice. Waking up in post-cunnilingual bliss wasn't the right time. We both had pussy breath. And neither was it the right moment after we'd showered, eaten breakfast and were taking Luc for a beach stroll.

There I am, staring out at the ocean, listening to Luc's attempts to match seagull cries. Ellen's holding my hand. I'm summoning up my courage to spew confessional when she grabs my other hand, gives both of them a shake and says all girlie gigglelish, childishly enthusiastic and oh so sweet, "There's a flea market for a bunch of AIDS charities in the Mission. It's such a gorgeous day, V. Why don't we drive into the City, do some shopping and take Luc on his first big expedition. I want to find him the perfect present for his first birthday. It's two weeks away, and I have no idea what to get him."

How could I tell her about Lucretia after that dollop of lovey-doveyness? I may be the Avenging Angel Sex Goddess, but I'm not heartless. I'm also in love with Ellen, which makes what I've got to tell her about my relationship with Lucretia all the more difficult. So I smile and say "cool" and hug Ellen. Trying to salvage a semblance of self-respect I go through the mental gymnastics of setting myself a deadline for The Talk. I look at Ellen twirling Luc around, chanting in a singsong voice, "we're going on an adventure. We're going on an adventure," and I know I should wait until after his birthday to do an emotional Enola Gay on Ellen. I don't want anything to spoil Luc's Big Number One, especially a spat between his mom and her lesbo life-partner. Right after his birthday would be too obvious, telegraphing I'd been putting it off until the festivities were safely over, which would piss off Ellen even more than she will already be fuming much to the max, so I decide that within one week after August 29—no—two weeks—three at the outside—definitely before the end of September—I'll tell her.

Yeah, candy-ass, procrastinating, conflict-avoiding wimp in love, that's me.

Despite my feeling like a shitty wimp for keeping Ellen in the dark because I don't want to risk disturbing the domestic bliss we've bathed in since we got back together, we have a blast in the City. We do veggie burgers at

Hamburger Henry's, and the flea market isn't bad. For forty bucks we find two really cool old rocking chairs that'll be awesome on our patio. Maybe we'll be able to rock away the angst of me telling Ellen that I have an evil Guardian Angel who likes to have shoesex with me and kills anybody who just so much as looks at me or Luc funny. Maybe I'll tell Ellen when we're on the chairs, you know, all that rocking being good for the soul and the soles. Maybe Ellen will actually like Lucretia. Maybe Ellen won't worry that she's got to be so protective of me. Maybe Ellen will win the Nobel Peace Prize.

Luc is a good little boy through all of our flea market shopping, gurgling at all the trinkets and people from his stroller. This bodes well for the future. Ellen and I love to shop. We really do lose ourselves. Even going to the grocery store is fun, but clothes and shoes, that's where we go to town. When she was a cop, Ellen subjugated all her normal shopping urges to climb up the police ladder. I'm helping her make up for lost time. We can kill so many hours enjoying retail therapy, and lately we haven't done much. That's why this jaunt was a major mega-cool notion timed to perfection.

I'm having such a blast that I'd almost forgotten about my impending confessional. I'm way lost in our stall perusing when a rude reminder slaps me upside the head. Ya know, I should have known, the feet cannot be denied.

Ellen's rummaging through a box of junk and pulls out a pair of tiny cowboy boots sized for an infant. She holds them up, waving them at me, shielding them from Luc's inquisitive gaze.

"These would be ideal for Luc's birthday. He'd look so cute."

The blood rushes from my face into my hands. My world spins.

"No," is all I can manage through clenched teeth.

"But they'd look so cute. They might be a little big, but he'd grow—"

"No fucking way. Are you crazy?"

It takes Luc's crying to make me realize I'm shouting.

"Take it easy, V. You're scaring Luc. And me."

"And you're scaring me. No way will he ever put on used shoes, especially ones I can't test out cause they're too small."

It's Ellen's turn to go white faced.

"Oh, Violetta, I'm so sorry. I didn't think."

"Well you should. I'm not taking any shoesex chances with him."

"But I thought you said that according to the curse he wouldn't have the power. That it skips a generation. That Luc would be a carrier, not a practitioner."

"Yeah, but my fucking power is always surprising me, so I'm not taking any chances. I told you already. No used shoes for Luc."

Ellen drops the boots and puts up her hands in surrender.

"I know. I know. I know. I forgot, okay. I got carried away finding him a present. I know how you love shoes, and I thought—"

"Yeah, well, get him a teddy bear."

Luc hasn't calmed down. I hold him close to me and feel the squish of a full load.

"He needs changing."

"I'm sorry, V."

"Don't be. I'm used to cleaning up shit."

"I meant—"

"I know what you meant. I'm trying to make a joke. I'm sorry for snapping. It's just the Avenging Angel Sex Goddess Mom coming out of me. Let me go change his diaper and then let's head back. Cool?"

"Cool."

The drive back to Stinson is done in awkward silence. Luc snoozes. Ellen pretends to be paying close attention to the road she knows like the inside of my pussy, and I stare off into space knowing that the real reason I yelled at Ellen was because I felt bad about not telling her about Lucretia. I could have easily said no to the kiddie cowboy boots and explained why, but I lashed out. The feet cannot be denied. How the fuck am I going to wait to tell her?

Still in a funk, I take Luc in the house while Ellen unloads the chairs. She tells me she's going to the hardware store to get some sealer to coat them so the saltwater air doesn't damage the old wood. I say all pouty faced, "Cool, go look after your old wood." Ellen gives me a pout back, a kiss on the cheek with her pout becoming a smile, and I know she's really off to get a bit of space and to let me cool down.

Smart woman that Ellen.

I decide to use my space to have a sole-to-sole with Lucretia.

Making sure Luc is tucked in his crib all asleep, I put on the caliges.

Two people, one body, that old familiar feeling.

"Violetta," Lucretia says, slamming me down on the bed, pushing up my tee shirt and pulling down my shorts, ramming her fingers into me like a train. "What an unexpected pleasure to be called when you're not in danger."

"We need to talk."

"Yes, my daughter, we do, but we also need to fuck."

I try to tell her that I need a serious chat, but she's all over me, her tongue fucking my mouth with the urgency of a rarely blown cock. Oh fuck, I'm getting horny, horny, horny. She knows me too well.

"We can talk after I make you come," she says as if

sensing my dissolving resolve. I moan a response that qualifies as something more like encouragement than protest.

Lucretia smiles, "And after you make me come."

"Oh yeah."

"Yes. I've got centuries of limbo to make up for. You've neglected my needs. You've been cruel, bringing me to life then keeping me locked up in a closet while you have all sorts of fun being a mother and a lesbian lover. You don't want to neglect your Avenging Angel Sex Goddess mother, Violetta."

My juices coat her fingers. She snakes one up my butt and slides it in and out in rough rhythm with the two assaulting my cunt. Coherent thought becomes all the more difficult with each juicy thrust but Lucretia's mention of motherhood sparks my protective instincts.

"What about Luc? He's asleep in his crib. What if he wakes, and I'm lost in a shoefuck with you?"

"I'll keep an eye on him, and you. That's what I'm here for—to protect my heirs. Now shut the fuck up and trust me. I can't wait any longer."

Lucretia slides deeper into every one of my orifices. Being supernatural she's not bound by physical limitations. When she fucks me it's always deeper and more intense than any human could. It's like she's flowing inside me, like I'm fucking myself, which in reality, I am. Lucretia is I, and I'm her. But fuck all this metaphysical crap. It's good sex. I feel like I'm being fucked by a horny octopus. She fucks like she's trying to even her lost sex balance sheet in this one session. She makes me come so many times it's not fair to call them multiple orgasms— just one big rollicking juicer turned up to ten, that's me.

I'm catching my breath as Lucretia squeezes my come-sensitized nipples, enjoying the little deaths that shudder through my body with every touch. I'm wondering if I'll ever walk again when Lucretia makes it clear that I'm not getting off that easy.

"Do me with that big black strap on thing. The one you use on her."

"Her has a name. And how do you know about that strap-on?"

"You may keep me in the closet, but I'm a part of you, Violetta. I see and feel through you when your emotions run high, which they do when you make like a boy and do Ellen from the rear and the front and the side. Like when that delightful Johnny did you from the rear right after we'd laid poor Crista to rest."

"Don't bring that up."

"Sorry to touch a sore nerve, my child, but as I remember it was your nerves that were sore for days after. He is so well endowed."

"Lucretia!"

"I just want you to know that there's a lot I know, but to shut me up, for now, just do me with that artificial cock. It has been ages since you or I had a real dick. I miss it. You miss it. Come on admit it. You like dick."

"Some dicks."

"Yes, I agree, some dicks are better than others. So do me with some dick, my daughter. Fingers and fists aren't quite the same as a cock, and while this strap-on isn't as supple as a real dick, it'll do for now. It is very well made. The veins and bulges are so life-like."

"Yeah, sex toy technology has come a long way in a few thousands of years. Ellen got it for me from Good Vibrations."

"Well isn't Ellen ever so thoughtful."

"We have to talk, Lucretia. About Ellen. About us."

"After you fuck me like a boy."

She lies back on the bed and spreads her legs, parting her swollen pussy-lips. She's pink enflamed, sodden and ready for penetration.

She reads my mind, sliding her finger inside of her, slowly, in and out, the slippery slurp noise smacking around the bedroom. She chuckles.

"You won't need all that messy lube that Ellen requires."

I sneer.

"Green doesn't suit you."

"Moi, jealous? Never, my child. Just making a factual comment."

"Well enough with the snide comments if you want a fucking."

"I won't say another word. I'll just scream."

As we've been pre-fuck bantering I've been stepping into the strap-on's harness. With a slight squat I snug the nubby pad against my clit and fit the mound into my lips, snapping the strap snug at the back.

Lucretia arches her back, spreading legs so long so wide I feel like I'm being drawn into her, that I could fall inside the glistening vortex of her pussy. She smiles.

"You look so sexy with a cock. Kiss me."

I kneel between her widespread legs, which snap rapidly behind me, locking behind my waist. She grabs my strap-on dick and pulls me to her. Our lips lock and our tongues flick. She pulls the dildo to her and rubs the tip up and down her pussy, moving it in circles around her clit until the gyrations it causes work the artificial dickhead into her vagina. The dildo slides into her cunt with all the ease of a warm knife spreading butter. Her hands grab my skinny ass and I feel her nails bite into my flesh and she pushes and pulls me in and out of her.

"Fuck me my daughter, my brother."

I think back to the first time I donned Lucretia's caliges and found out where the Cutrero shoesex curse came from—of Lucretia being made to fuck her brothers, and I'm tempted to make a reference to it, but I don't. We all have our baggage.

I wouldn't be heard anyway. Lucretia's screaming. I'm pounding, ramming into her. Each thrust pummels my clit, sending shudders of lust up my cunt, mainlining through my spine, pausing to titillate my tits before splattering my brain.

"Ram your cock into me," she hisses. I grab her long black hair and pull her to me with my thrusts, brushing my clenched fists across her engorged, darkened nipples, rubbing her hair into the hardened nubs. Lucretia tosses her head from side to side, gyrating her Sophia Lorenesque tits in that enticing way that only large, natural boobs can move. It's hypnotizing. She looks fucking hot.

"Yes, yes, yes," she says. "It's been so long. Make me come, Violetta."

It's not like I have to try very hard. I'm shaking and flailing and thrusting as every delicious lunge of the strap-on is like I'm being fucked too. This is way better than having a dick. It's like having a dick and a clit. I'm convinced if guys could feel what I'm feeling right now, they'd line up around the block to have their dicks cut off in exchange for clits and strap-ons.

Lucretia's coming, and it's all I can do to hold on to her bucking and writhing body. Her machinations send me over the edge. I feel like I'm being swallowed into the strap-on, disappearing down that big black shaft into a never-ending tunnel of sexy feelings.

Somewhere at the bottom of the tunnel I splash into a warm wet mess of come. It's all encompassing, swallowing everything I am. I feel like a baby in the womb.

Thanks Mommy.

"You're welcome. The pleasure was most definitely mutual. You fuck good, my daughter."

She's licking her juices from the strap-on. The sight is intoxicating. It feels like I'm really getting a blowjob, as if I've got a cock and it's getting sucked. It's as if all the times I've experienced fellatio through footwear now coalesce into actually feeling the real thing in real time, but then I'm snapped back to the amazing reality of the moment when I realize I didn't say Thanks Mommy. I thought it.

"You can read my thoughts."

"And this is a surprise? We are one. It's why I'm able to make you feel as if you really have a cock and are having it sucked. I'm able to draw from all the times you've experienced blowjobs through shoes. Our power has so many facets. You will enjoy learning. I will enjoy teaching."

So I was right about why the feeling was so real. Still, I'm not thrilled at the one-sided nature of this relationship.

"I can't read your thoughts."

"In time you will. We will become closer. We will truly be one."

"And what of Ellen?"

"We will all become closer, but it will be difficult for her. She's not of our flesh."

"I need you to promise to give me the time to get her used to the idea of you."

"Take all the time you need."

"I mean, I don't want you making any surprise appearances."

Lucretia kisses me and holds my face close to hers.

"Then don't neglect me. I have needs, just like Ellen, just like you, and better than you, I know your needs and am honest about them. When are you going to invite that delicious young boy from Rome over? That strap-on whetted my appetite for a real dick, and I think I did like-wise for you. Judging by his post funeral performance he's over the loss of his trollop girlfriend by now."

"I'm not going to hurt Johnny any further."

"He loves you."

"Yes, and so does Ellen."

"But he's a good fuck."

"Okay, Lucretia, that's enough. It's Luc's birthday in a couple of weeks. Promise me you'll be good."

"I promise, but you have to do something for me."

"What?"

"I want to feel Johnny's dick inside me. I want to feel the sex you had after Crista's funeral."

"And if I put on those shoes you'll be good."

"I'll be as good as you would under these circumstances."

"Okay," I say, wondering what the double-edge of her last comment meant.

"I meant, that the feet cannot be denied. They are our masters. We do their bidding."

I point to my feet.

"Yeah, well, these feet bid you to not spoil Luc's birthday."

"As long as you let me be a part of the celebrations."

"I'll find a way, but for now I don't want Ellen finding out about you. I have to do this in my way. Don't force things."

I take the funereal shoes from the closet as Lucretia runs her hands down my back, whispering in my ear, nib-bling on my neck.

"I don't have to Violetta. The feet cannot be denied, and right now, my feet won't be denied Johnny's dick."

I have the shoes in my hand. They're classic Gucci black stiletto heels. I bought them especially for the funeral from their high-priced store in Union Square. What can I say? I splurged a grand on shoes. I wanted to say goodbye to Crista in the best of shoe styles. I got my sartorial priorities right. I scored a simple black A-line dress, overcoat and veiled hat from A Faded Star thrift shop—less than a hundred bucks. I already had the black-seamed stockings and gloves. I was tempted by a five-grand Mikimoto pearl necklace from a ritzy jewelry store who had guards following me around in case I made a smash and grab, but I headed a few blocks south and bought a $20 pearl strand from a much friendlier Chinatown shop. I remember as I dressed that I thought I looked like a gothed Audrey Hepburn.

"Beautiful," says Lucretia, feeling the shoes through me.

I stroke the shoes, admiring the exquisite work, thinking of the exquisite fucking that they enjoyed and my reaction afterwards. I never wore them again after the funeral and the surprise sex with Johnny. I took a cab back to the hotel in my stocking feet and never put them on again. Back then I didn't think it was fair to Ellen.

But this is now, this is okay. This is all in the cause of keeping the peace in my bizarre love triangle. I'm not sure whether those are my thoughts or Lucretia's, but I give in to the moment. She was right. I do want to feel Johnny's dick and the urgent way he fucked me that night.

I have missed his dick, and more, I have missed him.

I bend my knee back and slip on one shoe. I'm about to put on the other when I realize I'm still wearing the strap-on. Balancing on the skyscraperish Gucci stiletto heel by extending my bare foot, I reach to unlace the fake plastic dick.

"Don't," says Lucretia. "The black of the stilettos matches the dick. Leave it on. I'm sure it'll feel good as you're being done from the rear, two cocks grinding into you."

"Lucretia, you're nasty," I say with a wicked smile, slipping the other shoe on, bracing myself against the bed.

Two people, one body, that old familiar feeling . . . .

Hello, Johnny.

I'm bent over in the dark of a decrepit restaurant's patio. My hands brace my body against the window frame of what was once a bustling place to eat called Anacapa. It's a dark, cold November evening. There are people walking along the Soho streets, separated from us by thin sheets of blacked-out heavy plastic, broken glass windows and warped plywood boarding. I hear conversation—the honk of horns—the jingle of keys—the unlocking of car doors—the fall of footsteps—Johnny's heaves as he grinds into me—my moans as he fills me full of his lovely cock—the scrape of my stiletto heels as Johnny's lunges lift me off my feet.

Every sound is amplified, adding extra frisson to this hot, sexy moment. The noises are like little whiplashes to my libido. It's an exciting soundtrack of sex in public for us, two people who met by accident sometime ago, became separated on purpose and now reunited by sad fortune, we just don't care if the world watches us celebrate the impossible passion that is our common bond. All that matters is our raw fucking, and that we could be discovered just makes it all the more visceral. This is the kind of sex normal people have fantasies about experiencing but never have the opportunity or balls to try.

It's hard to believe just a few hours ago I was shedding tears for Crista. Ellen cried her fair share of rivers too. Luc bawled, mostly because being a couple of months old is what he does when he doesn't get tit-on-time, which pretty much puts him squarely in line with most straight males much older. Mistress Vamp streamed so much her makeup made her look like a melting wax figure. Salvatore Donatelli, who'd flown over from Rome as the Lowest Soles representative, choked back tears as Crista's coffin descended the way hell infernal, and we all tossed shoes into the hole, covering her coffin with shoe leather before they covered it with dirt—ashes to ashes, shoes to shoes, dust to dust.

It was in the limo on the way back to the hotel after the farewell meal at Sal Anthony's S.P.Q.R. in Little Italy that Salvatore leaned over to me and spoke in hushed tones as if he were reassuring me. He handed me an address and told me to get out of the car and walk down the street to the location, telling everyone I wanted to be alone and would make my own way to the hotel.

Pacifying Ellen's concerns, asking her to look after Luc, I got out of the limo and walked down a fashionable Soho street past glittering art galleries.

Art galleries . . . ?

No. It couldn't be.

It was.

Johnny Gianni had flown over with Salvatore, and was waiting for me, minding some art opening at his parent's place. I was overjoyed, overwhelmed, and I babbled. He dispatched my "why hadn't he got in touch with me" questions with explanations that he didn't want to intrude on the privacy of the funeral. He added that he only had one day before he had to fly back. We kissed as if we hadn't ever stopped our Italian Affair, and after he'd ordered some minion to close up once all the wine and cheese had been ligged, we were running down the street hand-in-hand. It was like a scene from a movie.

We didn't know where to go and couldn't take the time to consider the options. We paused in a doorway to kiss. It was Anacapa's doorway, and it didn't take any words to decide this was where we would fuck. Johnny pushed through a boarded-up door and we were in the patio.

"How?" Johnny said, pausing between kisses, and for a moment I thought of wrapping my legs around him like on the plane and in the Colosseum, but I wanted it different and there wasn't any convenient place to prop up against, and the floor looked too major skanky for rolling around.

Necessity is the motherfucker of invention. Inspiration comes from a yapping dog someone is walking down the street not a few feet from our kissing bodies. I bend over, propping my hands against the window ledge. Johnny lifts up my coat and my skirt, pulling my thong down to mid-thigh. He whistles a "Mamma mia" at the sight of my perfect ass and runner's legs framed by stockings, illuminated by yellow streetlight shafts intruding through gaps in the boarding.

"Fuck me from the rear." The words are superfluous given my pose, but it's exciting to say them loud enough for a passer-by to hear. Johnny's answer comes from his fingers. He pulls the black suspender straps away from my butt and snaps them back into place against my skin. The snaps feel like tiny little finger spanks all up my ass. I utter a tiny ouch of excitement, and he rewards me with more snaps—over and over, and my ouches turn to constant moans of randy pleasure as my butt warms from the whip-like attention. I imagine the tender little ripples the suspenders make on my butt, seeing the thin red lines emerge from the snowy landscape of my soft ass skin. I must look so fucking hot bent over like this. It doesn't take long, and I'm dripping from this lovely, horny, sexed-out foreplay. I can't wait. This teasing is too much. I'm gonna come soon, and I want to be taken hard as I do. My hips rock towards Johnny, inviting him to up the stakes from foreplay to fuckplay. He diverts his attention from the straps to part my thighs, stroking from the black stocking tops, up the suspender straps still warm from his snapping, around the curve of my tensioned ass to my already sticky cuntlips, rubbing his finger between my labia as he alternates slapping and rubbing my butt full on with this other hand. Spanking me, whether with his hand or the straps, comes natural to him. I don't have to tell him how. He knows. He starts slowly, warming me up until it builds and then it sounds and feels so magical, so powerful—the thundercrack of the slap and the lingering warmth as if his hand was still planted there and the sudden sting as he glides his fingers across my glowing skin. It's too much and not enough at the same time. I teeter on the stilettos with every slap, but Johnny keeps me steady.

"Fuck me, Johnny," I say. "Fuck me hard. I haven't had sex since Luc was born. I don't like being a virgin. Fuck me, Johnny. Take my mommy virginity."

"Violetta, you are so, so naughty. I have missed you."

"And I have missed you. And I've missed this."

Keeping myself braced with one hand I reach between my legs and unzip his trousers, hefting out his solid cock. I rub my hand up and down the length, marveling at how alive and urgent it feels. It pulses in my fingers. His cock is ravenous for my cunt. I pull him towards me and he spreads my labia and rubs his swollen cock head up and down as I push my ass backwards and sink him in my cunt so deep it feels like he's in my throat.

Our moans grow with every thrust and push. His body slaps into mine and he grabs my spiky hair and pulls my head back.

We don't speak, we just fuck and moan and groan and yell and scream.

Johnny is the gentlemanly master, rubbing my clit hard and rough as he thrusts with his dick, his voluminous head and shaft tickling my G spot as he drives in and out of me, driving me crazy. I feel my wetness dripping down the soft flesh of my inner thighs, soaking my stocking tops. Johnny's balls slap into those dampened thighs making rudely delicious smacking sounds, reminding me of how he spanked me to begin this lovely fucking. We're so sexually in tune that he senses my recognition, or perhaps it's that the sound likewise reminded him of the way he loves to make my ass jiggle under his hand—whatever—he lets go of my hair and slaps my ass in time to the slap of his balls and my skin stings pink again in the cold air.

He releases my clit and with both hands grabs my ass and pulls himself into me, down the entire length of his shaft until I feel the brush of his pubic hair on my butt. He lunges and pushes me forward, almost to the end of his dick, only to slam me down again with his hands as I push back from the window ledge. This fuck me, fuck you jackhammering continues at a frantic pace. I feel little drops of Johnny sweat rain down on my back. The boy is working hard and we both work in sexual synchronicity, every in and out journey rocking me off my feet. With every one of Johnny's lunges he hoists my body off the ground so all my weight presses me down on him, forcing his cock in deeper and deeper.

The string of pearls bounces upwards with one of Johnny's lunges. I catch them in my mouth, running the shiny, smooth objects over my tongue and against my teeth. I feel Johnny's cock arch tighter, swelling and he bellows like an animal as he comes into me, thrusting deep, pushing me hard so I push back. He fills me so full his come oozes out and warmly spreads between our meshed bodies. He reaches around and palms my clit, pressing and rubbing my swollen bud in tight circles. I come, and all the strength in my body melts and my arms collapse and Johnny crushes my body against the window, continuing to rub my clit into sensory overload. I bite through the pearl string sending the little beads spilling around the dank surroundings flowing from me like my dripping pearls of come.

They shine in the dim light.

As Johnny comes down from coming he cradles me close to him, lifting me into his arms and the stilettos dangle off my feet.

"What happened after?"

Lucretia holds me tight. I'm shaking. I'm soaked. I'm exhausted. She was right. Keeping the strap-on attached during that shoesex escapade was wild. We came just like when Johnny fucked me, only more, in different ways.

"Johnny got me a cab. I went back to the hotel. Ellen wanted to know where I'd been. I made excuses and went into the shower. Luckily she was caught up looking after Luc and playing the perfect hostess to Mistress Vamp and Salvatore, who did his best to keep Ellen occupied while I cleaned up. I fobbed her off with the story about how I needed to be alone, to take care of some family business. She knew better than to pry."

"What about Johnny?"

"He flew back the next day."

"And you haven't spoken since?"

"We've exchanged some letters. He wants more than I can give him, but he's happy to exchange the occasional fuck when our paths cross. I told him I was involved with Ellen. I couldn't dump her after all we'd been through. He was hurt, but he understood."

"But you wanted to leave Ellen for him."

"No I didn't."

"I know what you feel, Violetta. You wanted Johnny."

"Yes, but it wouldn't work out."

"Why not?"

"Once he found out I was involved in his girlfriend's death he'd hate me. And he would find out."

"He's forgotten her."

"No he hasn't. A few weeks after our encounter he sent me her shoes, asking me to tell him what she saw when she died, whether she was thinking of him."

"Was she?"

"I don't know. I didn't put them on. I told him I did, and there was nothing sexual involved so I couldn't detect what she was feeling."

"Aren't you curious to see me in action through Gina's eyes? To know what she thought of as I killed her?"

"Not really. I saw you in action. That's enough for me."

"Well, maybe one day curiosity will get the better of you."

"I'm not a cat. Those shoes will stay in the box."

"Along with your true feelings. It's sad, Violetta. You and Johnny belong together. Luc needs a father."

"Don't give me that crap. You didn't need a father for your incestuous offspring."

"I had the Lowest Soles."

"And so do I, and I have Ellen, and I have you, and I have Johnny. We know there'll be other encounters. After sending me Gina's shoes he sent me his shoes—the ones he wore that night at Anacapa—with a note that if ever I felt the need of his dick, but couldn't go for the real thing because of Ellen, that I was lucky enough to have the next best thing—his shoesex, but if ever I changed my mind to call him."

"What did you tell him?"

"I told him he'd be the first to know."

I hear Ellen's car in the driveway.

"Fuck—"

I barely have time to get the caliges off and throw on a robe before Ellen's in the room all smiles. I'm still wearing the strap-on, which I angle upwards so it's not poking out of the robe, feeling like a teenage boy hiding a hard-on from mom after she's entered my bedroom without knocking.

Ellen holds out her hand.

"Hi, come with me. I have a surprise."

She notices the disheveled bed.

"I took a nap," I say all preemptively guilty.

"Some nap."

"I was restless. Bad dreams."

Ellen smiles.

"Well, come with me. I've got something to make you feel better."

She's tugging on my free hand so I have to follow, cradling the strap-on against my thigh. Somehow I'm going to have to avoid hugging her or it'll be Excuse City.

She leads me out to the rear garden, telling me to close my eyes.

We stop.

"Okay, you can look now."

I have to laugh at the sight. Ellen bought the little cowboy boots and another pair of really ancient looking men's lace-up ankle boots, Victorian in appearance. She's planted them in the garden as pots, the bigger boots in the center, with the little cowboy boots on the side. Each one has golden yellow daffodils growing in them.

I laugh.

"They're so cute."

"They're a peace offering. I found the other boots at the same stall while you were changing Luc. I just wanted to say I'm sorry and maybe this is the best use for them, to put them and all this tension to rest."

"Oh Ellen, that's so sweet."

I kneel down to look at the flowers and the robe slides open and the strap-on pops out. Ellen's eyes widen.

I think fast.

I roll over on my back onto the grass, opening wide the robe. The strap-on stands straight up. I stroke it.

"I'd planned a make-up session too."

Ellen smiles.

"I'll get my lube."

As Ellen trots off to get her Astroglide I sigh a huge exhale of relief. The feet may not be denied, but they sure can be danced with.

Silly Violetta, the feet cannot be denied.

It's Lucretia's voice I hear echoing in my head, reminding me of the Cutrero truth, then I hear Ellen scream, then there's a crash and then Luc cries, and I'm running as fast as I can into the house, the strap-on slapping from one thigh to the other.

CHAPTER THREE

ELLEN'S SPRAWLED NAKED on the floor. Luc's crib is knocked over. Ellen's holding him.

"He's okay, V. I caught him."

"What about you? What happened?" I say as I take the bawling Luc from Ellen's arms.

"I was stupid. I grabbed the bottle of lube, but it was open and a jet of it shot out and I stepped on the puddle and my foot went out from under me as I turned the corner. I demolished Luc's crib, but I caught him as he rolled out."

I can't help laughing.

"Are you okay?"

"I think I sprained my ankle, but my pride's damaged more. Sorry to ruin your romantic make-up plans."

"Oh don't worry," I say, eyeing the closet. "It's not your fault."

*   *   *

Ellen's ankle is better in time for Luc's birthday. The same can't be said for the daffodils in the big old Victorian men's boots. The flowers wither and die almost immediately, but the blooms in the little cowboy boots do great. Ellen feels mega-bad and wants to throw the men's boots away. I say no way. They're a gift from her. I'll just plant something else. Maybe the bulbs were rotten. Maybe the soil was crap. I tell her not to worry. It's worth one more try. I empty out the dead flowers and potting soil and put the boots in the garage. While Ellen's out picking up groceries for the birthday party I decide to plant something new. As I walk into the garage I find Spykes rubbing up against boots, spraying cat pee over them. Shooing the hissing little pussy away I'm tempted to throw the boots in the trash, but I'm a sucker for distressed footwear. I can't help feeling sorry for the old boots. I care about shoes the way some people are with stray animals. A cleaning and a polishing will take care of the fresh cat pee stench, but time and using them as a planter has warped the once sturdy soles, so more radical shoe surgery will be needed. So I take the dust covers off my shoe repairer machines and give the boots a good Cutrero going over. I'm proud to say I haven't lost any of my old touch, and I need every bit of those years of accumulated shoe repair experience to rescue the Victorian clodhoppers. Holding them up to the light they sparkle, and the creases give them character. I'm impressed. They are very well made. If I had more time I'd completely refurbish them. With new laces, soles, heels and a re-stitching they'd be as good as new, maybe even wearable, but they'll be fine as planters, or . . .

Old habits die hard.

They've got to be fuckshoes. Somewhere in the life of these boots they must have been fucked in.

Feeling the same naughty rush like when I sneaked my first few fuckshoe tests in my dad's shoe repair shop, I slip the boots on my sensitive soles just itching to feel that two people one body rush.

What'll it be? Some guy scoring a blowjob from a prostitute in an alley? Buggering a boy in a coal mine? How about a priest taking much more than confession while his anal rosary love beads are deep up his butt, popping them out one Hail Mary at a time? Hopefully it's not a sicko chopping someone up while jacking off.

How about a horny little cat?

Oh shit, I'm inside Spykes. Well this is a first. Not two people one body, but two beings one body. Does this qualify as bestiality? I've often been inside a female pussy, but now I can say I am—literally—inside a feline pussy.

I should explain about Spykes—aunt Crista's constant companion, he was named after her foot fetish club in New York. He often curled up around Crista's ankles and purred up a storm, rubbing himself silly on her shoes and stumps so it shouldn't surprise me that this cat has a thing for footwear.

Meoooooooooowwwwwwwwwwwwwwwwwwwwwwww wwyowwwwwwwwwwwwllll.

I feel my body vibrate like it's being excited by a tiny electric current—not a shock but something totally pleasant. Like the most exquisite of fluttering tongues on my clit. Oh wow. So that's what it feels like to purr.

Meow, it's cool. These boots feels so good to wrap around. They're so big and rough with all kinds of neat hard parts to rub against. I just love baring a tooth and digging it into the shoe leather, dragging my lip from gouge to gouge. It's been awhile since I had a new old pair of shoes to play with. Violetta doesn't seem to understand that I need my human footwear the smellier the better. Hopefully she'll get the message if she finds me playing with these crusty old things. I'm so happy my whole body shudders from deep within. My tail stiffens and judders. I let go a little yowl of contentment.

Meooooooooooowwwwwwwwwwwwwwwwwwwwwww wwyowwwwwwwwwwwllll.

Even though I'm inside a male cat all this purring feels so damn good on my clit. It's like I swallowed a vibrator and it lodged in my pleasure nub. Yummm.

I put my paws inside the boots and I'm kneading and paw-popping the soles, licking and biting at the worn laces, and the tang of the old shoe leather tastes so good. My super-hyper-cat-sensitive nose picks up hundreds of scents, some of which are recent, some way old. Hmmmmm—that little whiff belongs to the little tortoiseshell cutie from two houses down who comes over at night while I'm locked up, the little tease. Wouldn't I like to slide my spiny dick into her and bite her neck and make her howl at the Moon as I fuck her like the panther I look like.

Meooooooooooowwwwwwwwwwwwwwwwwwwwwww wwyowwwwwwwwwwwllll.

I got a kitty hard-on. The pointy thing is sticking out from my black fur, wiggling all around, and it feels so darn good to rub the tip on the rough ankle bulge of the boots.

Meooooooooooowwwwwwwwwwwwwwwwwwwwwww wwyowwwwwwwwwwwllll.

I'll give that little tortoiseshell cutie something to sniff.

I bare my claws and dig into the grungy sole, ripping through the decades of moldy lining, unleashing all kinds of pungent odors. I sniff and rub and purr, pausing to let rip with a few throaty yowls as my kitty coming rushes nearer.

My tail fur fills into a big ole brush and the fur along my back stands on end. My back arches, and I squirt kitty jism on the boots. For good measure I spray my scent—whoops—busted—here comes Violetta.

"Shoo, shoo, shoo."

Better scram. Hope she gets the message that I'm into shoes as much as she is.

I have a new admiration for Spykes. He'll get an extra dollop of cat food tonight and his choice of shoes to play with. Crista would be proud of her old kitty. I can't wait to tell Ellen. Wait up. Fuck telling her. I'll show her as we turn them into proper fuckshoes. That's it. That's how I'll bring a smile to Ellen's face. After Luc's party I'll get naked, slip these big old clodhoppers on and enact Spykes' Puss in Boots performance for Ellen. I'll jump up on the bed and do a kitty dance in the boots, and then I'll do Ellen with the strap-on imagining she's the tortoiseshell. We never did get around to doing the strap-on after the slip-and-fall on lube disaster. It'll be a great way to celebrate Luc turning the Big One after he dozes off by turning these old pair of cat-fuck boots into new fuckshoes.

With a big, naughty smile on my face I stash the boots in my closet.

Detective Michael Donovan takes the afternoon off and comes up from the City to celebrate Luc's birthday with us. He's kind of like Luc's godfather. Which is a kind of funny thing for a gay cop to be, but he's so cool, and Luc really digs him. Ellen and I owe Michael a bunch. If it wasn't for him brokering the deal for me to testify on Ellen's behalf in the killing of my half-brother, Tony a.k.a. the Cinderella Killer, and getting me immunity, even though I did flee the scene, both Ellen and I might be lesbo lovers behind bars, taking turns to look after Marge the butch guard.

Luc is spoiled silly. He scores more presents for his first birthday than I got in my entire life. In addition to a bunch of games, Michael bought him an awesome dragon kite from Chinatown. Luc loves all the bright colors. Ellen bought Luc some brand new red, tiny hightops, which pleased Mom immensely, and some coloring books. I splurged on far too many cute clothes that he'll soon outgrow, but he'll be way stylin'.

The party starts around noon. We barbecue veggie dogs and us adults drink bottles of Grgich Hills Violetta dessert wine. Ellen presented me with a case for my last birthday—our first one reunited following her trial. We've been saving it for a special occasion and this is about as special as it gets. Even though I'm still nursing I figure I haven't had a drink in almost two years, so it's about time Luc got a taste for the good stuff. Way diluted with mama's milk shouldn't present a problem to the growing lad. With the Cutrero curse lurking in the background, alcohol will be the least of his worries. I intend to keep those demons at bay as long as I can. Forever, if I have my way. That's the present I'll keep on giving him every day, birth or otherwise.

So I drink away, rocking-on on our rocking chair, putting heavy thoughts at the bottom of an empty glass, and befitting the occasion of his first birthday, Luc doesn't have a care in the world or an inkling of the curse. He's a happy little dude, giggling and sputtering and screaming with delight. With much help from three rapidly inebriating, slightly silly adults, he gets to blow out the single proud candle on a chocolate fudge cake sending many gooey splatters over all the guilty parties and the patio. After we gorge ourselves, and I clean up, we take Luc for a walk on the beach to fly the dragon kite. He's all ooohs and ahhhhs and with Michael as hidden backup we let Luc hold on to the string.

Luc's asleep before we head back. I'm really thrilled. My son's first birthday party was a mega-success and nothing bad happened. I just wanna hug everybody, including Lucretia. Since she says she can hear or feel or whatever she does when my emotions run high I whisper a big thanks to her and hug myself, figuring she'll feel the good vibes. I know it can't be easy for her, being brought to life after all these centuries by her destined true daughter and then asked to hang out in limbo in a closet. Not fun for a powerful pagan Avenging Angel Sex Goddess's self-image at all, but she's a trooper and she has Luc and my best interests at heart, witness that she didn't do anything to ruin the party.

I got a funny feeling things are gonna work out for the best for all of us. Hell knows, we all deserve it. We've been through more in a few years than most sad fucks suffer in their lives, including those that believe in reincarnation.

Once Luc's all tucked in we drink more wine sitting in our rockers. I'm on Ellen's lap, enjoying the ride as Ellen and Michael exchange SFPD stories about so-and-so doing you'll never guess what to so-and-so. Michael's on the fast track to the top, so he's full of hard-to-come by gossip. It's good to see that a nice guy can win, and having a good gay cop in charge can't be bad in a City with so many fags. More wine flows and before we know it we're all completely soused. We watch the sun set into the Pacific and our eyelids follow its course. Michael can barely stand so we insist that he snoozes this one off until the morning, or at least until he feels better. He at least agrees upon a nap. No need for the best cop in the City to be driving the winding road to the highway in a completely shitfaced condition—just not good for Just Say No publicity nor his fast track. We pour Michael into the guest bedroom and give him a couple of bottles of water and make sure he knows that he has a bathroom adjoining the room.

We stumble our way to our bedroom and there's much kissing and rubbing and fondling as we get naked.

Ellen's lying on the bed looking exceptionally fuckable.

"Just a minute. I have a surprise for you. Close your eyes," I say all cock-ate-ish.

"What? What? Just fuck me."

"I will, but first you're going to get some pussy."

I can hardly say the words without sputtering giggles.

"Well, I hope so. Come on, quit fooling around. I'm horny and close to passing out."

"Me too, and I'm hurrying, but you have to promise, whatever I do, you have to let me fuck your pussy, okay?"

"Like you have to ask, V."

I reach into the closet and snag the strap-on, wriggling into the harness, making darn sure that all the rubbing bits are in exactly the right position. Next I grab Spykes' Puss in Boots, careful to give Lucretia's caliges a fond little touch and wish her well. Stumbling a few times I angle my feet into the boots, lacing them up past my ankles. I leap up onto the bed, that not so familiar feeling of two beings, one body tingling up from my soles. Soles to paws.

"What the fuck," Ellen says as she opens her eyes, incredulity turning to laughter.

It's just turned eight in the evening, August 29, and I'm on my hands and knees on the bed, pawing on the mattress. I'm Spykes and I got a kitty hard-on. The shoes feel oh so good. The smells, oh the smells as I wrap my furry body around them, nibbling on the old shoe leather, wrapping my furry body around Ellen, rubbing on her soft skin. As she slides under me, I feel reality and the kitty shoefuck merge. I feel her tugging on the strap-on, and I feel me inside Spykes rubbing my spiny little cock on the bulge of the boots. I flex my claws on the soles, and I'm squeezing

Ellen's breasts, pinching the nipples. She moans, stifling a scream. I purr, and Ellen vibrates with me.

Far in the distance I hear a bell chime.

There are no churches around here.

And where did Spykes go?

Who am I in now?

It's not feline. It's a human. Who am I? Where did this shoefuck come from?

And what's with all these cobblestones?

And funky gas lamps?

And that stench of urine and horseshit and cheap beer and stale vomit and nasty cigarettes? This place reeks to Hell and back.

I'm in an alleyway. There are horse drawn carriages clip-clopping by in the distance. Wait a minute—nah—this isn't Central Park in New York where Luc, Ellen and I did a tourist horse ride last year to make up for my walk-about and guilt over my surreptitious sex with Johnny.

This isn't San Francisco.

This isn't even now.

Where am I?

No, Spykes, we're not in Stinson anymore.

Where the fuck am I?

And who is that under the lamplight?

I see her teetering. She's drunk and she looks like the perfect victim. How pathetic.

I stay hidden in the darkness, my boots protruding into the light, catching her drunken whore gaze. She stumbles up to me. The sight of her helplessness makes me hard. I stroke my cock underneath my cape.

Whoa, the strap-on ain't a strap-on any longer and it's way bigger than Spykes' little pointy kitty dick. Sorry, Spykes, I'm sure you're well endowed for a cat, but to me it's still a tiny cock, okay, and what I have pulsing between my legs—jeepers.

"Fancy some company, dearie?"

Okay, so we're in England or in on some movie set with people faking English accents, cor' blimey. Maybe I'm 'enry 'iggins and this is Eliza Doolittle. All I wants is a room somewhere. The rain in Spain falls mainly on the plane. Yeah fucking right. Somehow I get the feeling that I'm not too interested in improving this tart's vocabulary.

I nod ayes to her question about company, smiling at the silly euphemism for cheap sex, not even asking how much. I pull out a few coins and flash them under her nose. It's more money than she sees in a month of back alley East End hurried and diseased copulations.

"Ooooh, big spender aintchya."

She grabs the coins and stuffs them into a ratty velvet purse between her surprisingly fair bosom. She smiles a missing tooth smile and grabs my crotch.

"Ooooh, big down there too. Ready as well. Been saving it up for me havya. Gonna give Polly summathat, are ya luv. Let's get down to the business, lovey. Don't have all night you know, even for a toff likes you."

She hikes up her mud splattered skirt and her bushy sex glistens under the gas lamp. She's dispensed with the inconvenience of knickers. She's dripping wet from the Lord knows how many cockfull of sperm she's had tonight. Well, this will be her last. For tonight. Forever.

She fumbles with my trousers, unbuttoning my erection.

"Come to Polly, lovey."

She puts one hand around my neck and pulls my entire body to her, using her other hand to guide my erection into her. I admire the way she balances on one leg, the other hiked up like she's a dog about to piss. I rut into her, thrusting into her vagina, banging my body against her pubic bone. I enjoy the sound of the slap of my thighs against her, knocking her backwards.

"Likes it rough does ya?" she says as I knock the breath from her.

I don't say a thing. I use my body to communicate. Words aren't required when dealing with lower forms of life.

"Quiet one aintchya? A bit shy maybe. Give us a kiss. You're getting me all worked up you are with that big dickie of yours."

She plants her lips on mine. She tastes foul, sour. Enough of this. I reach around her body and grab her ass, pulling her bucking body hard against my loins. I smile to myself. We're in Bucks Row, and she's bucking like a horse, grinding against me as I subdue her wildness. How appropriate and quaint are these street names. With my thrusts I'm lifting her off the ground. She's sweating. I dare say this is the best and most energetic fucking she's had in a long time. I feel my cock stiffen. She does too.

"Come on, lovey, give it to me. Give it all to Polly."

I'm never one to refuse a lady of the night. I slide my hands up her back from her ass and latch them around her neck. My thumbs press tight against her windpipe and she sputters and struggles, but I have her impaled on my cock and my hands are strong. She's unconscious in a matter of seconds.

I drop her limp body to the ground, cushioning my fall upon her sack of bones. From within my cape I extract the surgeon's knife. It's a quick slash across her throat severing the carotid artery. She dies as I come.

Waves of anger wash through me. She's stolen my life-seed. I must get it back for it is my precious juice. I slash at her sex with the knife, cutting deep into her abdomen. I fancy more bloodsport, but I hear voices. For now this must do. There will be more before I'm done.

* * *

"Violetta, Violetta. Stop it."

Ellen's fighting me off. She has a scratch across her neck and her pubic mound looks a bit on the ravaged side. She's holding my hands, coughing. I'm impaled in her with the strap-on. I'm thrusting like a pile driver. She's hanging on with an expression that looks fearful for her life.

Where am I?

What was that killing?

Oh shit. I'm in Spykes again. I wiggle my ass, and spray, marking my territory.

"Oh fuck, Violetta, what are you doing."

I guess I just peed on Ellen.

"Shoo, shoo," I hear myself saying to me, to Spykes.

What the fuck am I doing?

It takes a while for us to calm down. I'm explaining to freaked Ellen what happened, how a shoefuck came along that wasn't there before when I found Spykes' shoefuck. We're both shaken, but when there's a knock on the door we leap off the bed.

"Must be Michael," says Ellen, stating the obvious.

"He probably heard all the commotion and wonders whether we're all right," I say, also stating the obvious as we pull our robes around us.

Ellen opens the door.

"Sorry if we dist—" she says as Michael interrupts her apology.

He looks like shit, but he's fully dressed. The pale green of his suit matches his face. The circles under his eyes are as dark as the cup of coffee he's clutching.

"What, no, I'm sorry for disturbing you. I just got paged. Of all the days to take some time off and tie one on. There's been a murder down in the Tenderloin. Some sicko sliced up a hustler in a very nasty way. The press are all over it. I gotta go. I didn't want to leave without telling you I'm off and thanking you for a great time. We'll have to do it again."

Ellen looks at me. I look at Ellen. We both look at the boots.

I look at my feet.

So much for that funny feeling I had earlier today about things working out for all of us.

Fuck my can't be denied feet to hell and back.

CHAPTER FOUR

WE DON'T SLEEP much the rest of the night, kicking around ideas, literally. I put the fuckboots on again, but there's nothing out of the shoesex ordinary other than me inside of Spykes fucking Ellen. The murder shoefuck isn't there and neither is there a record of me experiencing it as a shoe-fuck, which is kind of weird. There should be one or the other, especially since I was having shoesex with Ellen at the time, but no, there's no record other than what's in my head or perhaps buried somewhere in those boots.

"Chalk one more shoesex surprise up to the Cutrero curse," I say, examining the mangy soles.

"Maybe our mad passionate sex let loose whatever's hidden deep in the boots? Maybe the murder doesn't come out just by putting them on," Ellen says all detective and thoughtful. I can't resist a little jab in a haughty English manner.

"Elementary, my dear Watson. By Jove, you've sussed it. You've cracked the case. If I follow your razor-sharp thinking then if we have mad passionate sex again in the boots then the damnable thing should come out, what?"

Ellen slips into English detective mode, pretending to puff on a pipe.

"You'd think so, Holmes."

"I say, care to give it a try, Watson?"

"Absolutely old chap. Purely out of scientific curiosity you understand."

"Of course. A controlled experiment. Let me rip off my deerstalker and shoot up some opium."

After a mutual chuckle at my knowledge of the escapades of Arthur Conan Doyle's characters, Ellen turns mega-serious.

"Then maybe we should do this right. Start by getting Spykes to do what he did."

"Yeah, we should try to reproduce the circumstances as exactly as possible. Maybe Spykes clawing at the soles helped free the hidden shoefuck."

"I'll get him."

Ellen yells "Spykes" as she runs through the house trying to find our shoe fetish cat. After a few minutes she returns with the struggling pussy. He sniffs at the boots and hides under the bed after much hissing. No amount of coaxing will tempt him into the open.

"That's weird," I say. "He was all over them before. Maybe he senses something."

"Maybe I scared him. I guess we can skip the Spykes part."

"Should we be drunk or skip that too?"

"I'm still a bit tipsy."

"Me too."

"Okay, no cat shoesex, kind of drunk instead of fully wasted, but what the fuck, let's give it a go."

Ellen closes her eyes, just like before. Déjà vu-ing, I strap on the strap-on and slip my feet into the boots. Spykes runs from the room as I jump on to the bed.

"What the fuck," Ellen says as she opens her eyes, doing a very good job of re-enacting her initial surprise of incredulity turning to laughter.

Two beings, one body, that old familiar feeling thanks to the number of times I've re-enacted my encounter with Spykes. It's just turned one in the morning, August 30, and just like a few hours earlier, I'm on my hands and knees on the bed, pawing on the mattress. Yeah, that part works okay. I'm Spykes, and I got a kitty hard-on. The shoes feel oh so good, just like they did before on my kitty body. The smells, oh the smells, they drive me yowling wild as I wrap my furry body around them, around Ellen. She's really trying to get into it as she slides her body under me. I feel reality and the kitty shoefuck merge. I feel her tugging on the strap-on, and I feel me inside Spykes rubbing my spiny little cock on the bulge of the boots. I flex my claws on the soles, and I'm squeezing Ellen's breasts, pinching the nipples. She moans, stifling a scream. I purr, and Ellen vibrates with me.

Far in the distance I do not hear a bell chime.

Fuck.

So I fuck harder. I pound into Ellen, ramming the strap-on deep in her cunt. She slides around the bed, doing her best to be mad and passionate. She reaches around my skinny hips and digs her nails into my ass, relieving the pressure at just the right time before it becomes too painful. She doesn't ease off in the ass play though, switching from grabbing to spanking, slapping me the way she knows I like it, building slowly from gentle pats on both cheeks into full fledged butt-reddening thunder-clap whacks. Alternating between these two titillating tush tortures drives me crazy. I plunge the strap-on in as far as it can go, as hard as it can go, knocking the wind out of Ellen and me. I don't pause. I press the dildo firm against her womb and grind my pelvis into her cunt, feeling the strap-on titillate my clit. I pinch her nipples, and Ellen rips one of her hands from my butt and squeezes my tit, arching her back to latch her lips and teeth to my nipple.

Still, far in the distance I do not hear a bell chime.

I'm still Spykes, and I'm rubbing my little, spiny, pink and slimy kitty cock on a pair of old and musty boots that right now I won't even go near.

I slow down.

"Don't stop. Don't stop."

Ellen's frantic, as if she's on the brink of coming like Niagara Falls, so I batter away with the strap-on until I'm sweating like Niagara Falls. Ellen's bucking and writhing slows. I realize that she wasn't near to coming. She was trying to get me going with all that mad passion that we had before.

Still, far in the distance I do not hear a bell chime.

Our eyes meet and we know that we're thinking too much to fuck with mad passion.

"Let's take a break," Ellen says.

"Yeah," I say, collapsing face down onto the bed. Ellen pulls the boots from my feet as I hear me say "Shoo, shoo," to me inside of Spykes.

Following our less than passionate sex Ellen has me spew all my memories of the murder shoefuck into a tape recorder. She plays it back over and over, looking through criminology books and making notes as I give Luc a tit feed so he dozes off again suitably placated. After I've tucked him back in his crib Ellen tells me her theory.

I go dumbstruck numb. I thought after all I'd been

through in Rome with the Lowest Soles and Lucretia, that nothing to do with shoesex could discombobulate me, but I should know better. What Ellen says makes sense, but it's almost too fantastic to take in. I sit in silence while Ellen makes coffee.

Downing mugs of bleary-eyed espresso, Ellen and I watch the early morning news for details of the Tenderloin murder. Not much hard info, other than a male prostitute was killed in brutal fashion with a knife, as best as we can tell, at the same time that I was performing Puss in Boots meets Jack the Ripper for Ellen's delectation.

That's right, Jack the Ripper. Ellen's enough of a criminologist to recognize the setting. From my verbalizing it didn't take her long to fathom the Polly and Buck's Row references. Polly a.k.a. Mary Ann Nicholls, the first victim of the first and most famous of all serial killers who was to become known as Jack the Ripper, never to be found, though theories concerning his or her identity have run rampant. Well, at least I can squash the theory that Jack was a Jill. Very definitely male and definitely educated, although there's a mean, mean streak and contempt for women and prostitutes especially. I sure don't think he's the Queen's Surgeon, Sir Edward Gull, as many conspiracy theories have promoted. No, this guy wasn't an aristocrat, but he wasn't some poor London butcher or Jewish tailor either. He seemed more American middle class to me.

These are all things Ellen and I kick around all espresso-buzzed by the dull morning light. I'm having a hard time with the fated implications of this revelation. Ellen's kind of excited by the potential these boots and my feet have unleashed.

"Do you realize, V, that we may be able to solve the most famous unsolved crime of all time."

"I'm not so sure I want to. It's not like we can bring him to justice. It's just morbid curiosity."

"Oh come on, V, you're dying to know. Think about it. Maybe this is another reason you have your gift. Those boots were worn during the murders and for whatever reason, they only play on the anniversary of the crimes. It's the only possible explanation. Think about it. Taking in to account the time difference, you experienced Polly's murder at the exact time it happened over a hundred years ago, and I'll bet that's why you can't get it to play now. It's got nothing to do with Spykes or our mad passionate sex. It only plays to your feet at the exact time it happened, which means that, if I'm right, you'll be witness to the next murder on September the eighth."

"As long as I have the boots on."

"Of course you'll have the boots on."

"Maybe not."

"You won't be able to resist. I know you and all that 'the feet cannot be denied' stuff. It's your responsibility. Maybe solving the Ripper murders will prevent more. Did you think about that?"

"Like the Tenderloin one tonight?"

"Exactly."

"What happens if we're actually causing these new murders?"

"Oh come on."

"No, you come on. My power always surprises me, and if it's one thing we've learned it's that there are no coincidences where my feet are concerned. You've as much as said that those Victorian fuckboots came into my possession for a reason. What if that reason isn't a good one? What if the evil that was Jack the Ripper lives on in those boots and I'm letting it out again. It's all too weird, too worked out, and it scares me."

I'm shaking, my jaw set in defiant mode. Ellen nods. She kisses my cheek and strokes my shoulder.

"I admit, it's strange. I'm freaked too, V. You know me—once a cop always a cop. Forgive me. I let my enthusiasm run away with me. You're right. We should think this through before putting those boots on anymore. Maybe you should talk to those guys in Rome, the Lowest Soles. Maybe they know something about this."

Fate forces my foot, whether it'll be in my mouth the next few minutes will tell. Well, so much for being a candy-ass, procrastinating, conflict-avoiding wimp in love who was gonna wait until the end of September to spill the Lucretia beans.

"You're right. I can't resist putting those boots on again for the next murder, and you're right that we need help from the Lowest Soles, only I don't have to call Rome. The most knowledgeable person about shoesex is right here."

Ellen chuckles.

"Modest aren't we?"

"I'm not talking about me."

"Who?"

"Lucretia Cutrero."

"Where? In San Francisco?"

"No, here."

"Stinson?"

"Yes, in the closet."

Ellen starts to laugh, her chuckle dwindling to a gaping mouth as she realizes I'm serious.

"You're not kidding are you?"

"No, this is kind of involved and may hurt you a bit, but let's just say I haven't told you the entire truth about Lucretia Cutrero. She is my Guardian Angel, and she's very much alive."

I spill the whole Lucretia story, leaving out the bit about her killing Johnny's girlfriend when she threatened to expose me to the cops. I know Ellen—once a cop, always a cop. I've learned that with my over-protective life partner it is often best to take the Fifth.

There are tears in Ellen's eyes. I hold her hands in mine, and I'm reassured when she doesn't pull away.

"Why didn't you tell me?"

"I was planning to. Only, we've been through so much. I couldn't tell you everything when I got back from Italy. We had to re-build our relationship so I gave you the PG-13 version."

"You gave me a lie."

"I gave you your life back, and I got the strength to do that from Lucretia. We both owe her our lives."

"Then I'd better drop to my knees and thank her."

"That would be a good start."

We both spin our heads around so fast at the sound of a different voice that we almost collide. Lucretia stands in the doorway, naked, legs astride. Her finger works between her legs. The slipperiness of her cunt sounds louder than the roar of the nearby Pacific.

"Well, what are you waiting for," Lucretia says as she walks towards Ellen and grabs her head. "On your knees."

CHAPTER FIVE

SUCH IS LUCRETIA'S power that the normally stubborn Ms. Ex-SFPD top-dick cop with balls bigger than the testicular sum of the entire male members of the Frisco-Crisco force drops to her knees and lets Lucretia rub her face into her cunt.

"Ellen, I'm going to make you see all I've done for you, and you will show me how much you value my efforts."

Lucretia blows me a kiss, stilling my desire to wrench Ellen away from my Guardian Angel's pussy. Desire to wrench is replaced by desire to fuck because with that kiss I feel Ellen's tongue on my cunt. It's amazing. I'm watching Ellen tongue Lucretia, standing a few feet from me, but I feel Ellen's tongue on me, as if she's kneeling between my legs.

What the fuck is going on here?

Lucretia looks at me with a smug smile that comes from coming out on top after thousands of years of paying major dues. It's the kind of look a supergoddess gives a trainee supergoddess who just failed supergoddess 101.

"Have no fear my lovely, naïve daughter. Ellen cannot see me. She sees you. You are talking to her as if you are I. You are standing here, against the doorframe. I only appear to you and you alone because we are connected through supernatural powers and are therefore above mere mortal limitations."

"You mean I pushed Ellen to the floor and told her to show her gratitude?"

"No, we did. We are one. When you summon me—"

"I didn't summon you."

"Not consciously. It's as I have explained to you before. When you are threatened or your emotions run high, the primal shoesex energy that flows between us sets me free. I can appear to you without you putting on the caliges. Of course, you can always summon me with the caliges, but in this case you were so upset and in difficulty as you explained our relationship, that I appeared for you, to help you, to form the right words and deeds, and together we pushed Ellen to the floor and spoke to her."

"So Ellen's licking me."

"Yes."

"Weird. Like Dr. Jekyll and Mister Hyde," I say thinking back to the book Salvatore Donatelli gave me, and I—or was it Lucretia—threw in the trash.

"I prefer a less melodramatic analogy," says Lucretia, displaying a not amused expression.

"Some might call it schizophrenic."

"I prefer to think of it in more superheroic terms."

"Avenging Angel Sex Goddess at your service."

"Exactly. Just think of it as a natural extension of

shoesex. We are connected through our power. I feel you. You feel me. We enjoy together. We fight together."

"Can Ellen hear us?"

"No. She only hears what we want her to hear."

"Her tongue feels good doesn't it?"

"Oh yes, she licks cunt so well."

We both look down between our legs. I watch Lucretia's head roll as Ellen's tongue rolls inside her pussy. Inside my cunt. Ellen's hands grab my ass. Grabs Lucretia's ass. Ellen's fingers bite into our flesh, kneading and squeezing, parting our butt cheeks so her widespread fingers graze our assholes, sending spasms up our spines.

The sensation arches my neck back, then my head whips forward as I stare down at Ellen's head being rubbed into my pussy by Lucretia's hands. Into Lucretia's pussy by Lucretia's hands. Into Lucretia's pussy by my hands.

My head spins with all the combinations and permutations and their attendant sensations; I rapidly come to the cunt slathering realization that this is a ménage à trois to top all threesomes. It's a threesome where one of the fuckers thinks it's straight ole monogamous sex. This isn't like when Johnny did me from the rear while Ellen worried where I was. It's cheating without cheating, and I'm not talking that old redneck rationalization, sucking ain't fucking. This is having your pussy and eating it too.

Ellen's middle fingers slides easily into Lucretia's ass. My legs collapse slightly as I settle onto Ellen's digit. She slides another finger inside Lucretia's pussy and massages the ass finger through our pussy wall while her tongue sucks on my clit—sucks on Lucretia's clit—sucks hard, like it is a little, erect, throbbing cock, pulling it into her lips, flicking my swollen bud. Flicking Lucretia's swollen bud, giving us clit blow jobs, our bodies melting over Ellen's hands and face. She has no choice but to keep going until we're coming, and she thinks she'll get some relief, but even then our hands won't let her free. We're teaching her a lesson.

"Keep it up Ellen, you suck and frig and fuck so good. Show me how much you appreciate me, how much you appreciate being forced on your knees and made to make me feel good for all the good I've done you. Oh shit. Oh shit. Oh shit, yeah, keep it up. Don't stop. Don't stop, you cunt, I'm coming."

I'm coming so much I wonder if I'm pissing, but then I realize it's because it's not just me that's coming. I'm feeling Lucretia orgasm, and she's feeling me and I'm feeling her feel me.

Fucking intense.

I wrap my fingers in Ellen's hair and tug at her head, treating her like a ragdoll. I watch as Lucretia yanks on Ellen's short blonde locks, squeezing her neck, pulling her face deeper into my cunt. It's amazing to watch sexy things being done to someone else and feel them being done to me at the same time. If the porno industry could sell this effect then smut tapes would be obsolete overnight. This is fantasy become reality instantly. I see sex. I feel sex. Monkey see. Monkey do. Monkey come.

Fucking awesome.

Ellen's coughing, sputtering as I juice into her face. Her sputtering lips send me over the edge of a cliff so high I fly. Her fingers go deeper into Lucretia's pussy as my legs shake from my coming. From Lucretia's coming.

Lucretia releases Ellen's head roughly, throwing her to the ground as Ellen falls away from my pussy. My legs collapse and Lucretia dives on Ellen, giving her no release, forcing her legs wide, latching on to my girl-friend's cunt like a ravenous predator finding downed prey. I bury my face into Ellen's sopping sex, trying to stuff as much of my head up her cunt as I can. Lucretia works her fingers into Ellen's ass. I watch as first one finger, then another, and another disappear into her stretching sphincter as I fold them together, working all my fingers into Ellen's butt, using Lucretia's dripping mouth as lubrication. Momentarily stalled at the knuckles, my hand pauses, but Lucretia's mouth doesn't. She sucks down on Ellen's clit. Ellen gasps and in her writhing my whole fist enters her ass and Ellen screams and moans as Lucretia fist fucks Ellen into delirium while I tongue her clit and stuff as many fingers as I can up her cunt and her ass.

Ellen's screaming, grabbing at her tits, squeezing her nipples red raw, pulling her small breasts into volcanic cones, releasing them to shudder on her heaving chest, pounding her hands on the floor as if she's a wrestler signaling submission, only to go back to torturing her tits once she realizes there will be no relief from my fist making those eruptions ripple through her body. My fist. Lucretia's fist. My fingers. Lucretia's fingers. My tongue. Lucretia's tongue fucking Ellen, my girlfriend. My Guardian Angel fucking my girlfriend. Me fucking Ellen nastier than I ever have.

Ellen comes like an epileptic having a fit while sitting on a bust fire hydrant. There's gushing liquid everywhere and so many limbs at odd angles that our kitchen floor resembles one of Picasso's worst bad dreams, but still we don't give Ellen a break, sending her into orgasm after orgasm, adding more pressure to already overly sensitive body parts. Fucking good job Ellen doesn't have a weak heart.

With all the flailing it's getting pretty skanky. Shit streaks Lucretia's wrist as I fist Ellen into oblivion and little bits of poo fly around reminding me of the times Luc struggles when I'm changing his diaper. Ellen screams, the yells turning into crying, tears and snot streaming from her face, begging us to stop, but begging us to go on in the same breath. She arches upwards and falls back to the floor, holding onto to her tits as if they're the only thing keeping her alive.

I pull my fist out of her ass and the sphincter stays distended, a huge gaping hole, and I swear I can see in to Ellen's soul. The huge flowering rosebud closes, winking at me in the process as if to say "good job fucker."

I crawl up Ellen's limp torso, grab her head, force open her mouth and stuff Lucretia's fist into the gaping hole that reminds me of her asshole.

"Lick it clean, Ellen, lick my fist clean of all your shit."

Ellen licks away, obedient, oblivious to the degradation foisted upon her because the pleasure of a swarm of total body orgasms has her dead to the real world.

"Beautiful," says Lucretia.

"Isn't she," I agree.

We kiss. Lucretia and I, and I wonder what it looks like to Ellen, through her delirium, watching me kiss myself as she licks my fist clean.

"So, what's with these Jack the Ripper boots?" I say to Lucretia as our lips part, keeping one eye on Ellen to make sure she doesn't choke on my shitty hand. Lucretia's shitty hand.

"They're an enigma."

I sense hesitation inside Lucretia. Inside me.

"What aren't you telling me?"

Lucretia looks away. She speaks solemnly. I've rarely seen her like this. She's about to dish out some heavy shit, and the thought makes me smile seeing how we've got Ellen poo on us, but my good humor quickly fades.

"There is extreme evil which lives on beyond its agent. It can imprint itself on any object. Shoes—boots—are perfect vehicles to hold such primeval energy—and shoesex can release it if the timing and circumstances are right. It's because of the very origin of shoesex. The evil foist upon me by Rictius Varus created the curse. Luckily he drowned, but maybe his footwear were found and that's where this line of serial killers began. Maybe it came from some other evil source. Who knows, but our paths have been linked and centuries of Cutreros have fought evil as a result. And there's a lot of evil out there. Jack the Ripper has surfaced throughout history as many killers, always evading justice. Most recently he was the Boston Strangler. It didn't play out like every one thought. The man who died in jail was not the real killer. The Boston Strangler was a traveling shoe salesman who gained access to women's homes by showing them his samples. I'll wager all the shoes I've ever loved and worn that some lesser Cutrero unleashed that evil from these boots, but didn't finish the job. Now it's your turn, and you, my daughter, will be up to the task because you have me."

"Are you saying that I unleashed Jack the Ripper on San Francisco."

"Yes, my daughter."

"Why didn't you warn me? You're supposed to be there when something threatens."

"Even I cannot fight the responsibilities of the Cutrero curse. It is why you have the power."

"But I caused a murder."

"Yes and no. It was always there waiting to be freed. The only way it could be killed was to free it so you could destroy it. The victim was a casualty of war, the war between good and evil."

"Are you saying it was destined that the boots would make their way to me?"

"Yes, as it was destined that you would meet and release me."

"But how did they make it here to the flea market at just the time for Ellen to get them for me as planters? Oh Jeez, that's why the flowers died, huh?"

"Yes, nothing can live where the evil lurks, and how the boots made their way to you isn't important. It was inevitable that they would."

"The feet cannot be denied."

"Yes, you are learning, my child."

Lucretia strokes my face. Her hand slips to my tit. She caresses me, and I feel extra safe and warm, some small part of me telling me that it's my hand touching me.

"Why not just destroy the boots?"

"Evil such as this is alive and will not die in flames. It takes someone with the good side of the power to neutralize it, otherwise it will live on to kill again and again. Rictius Varus, Jack The Ripper, The Boston Strangler— they are all one and the same."

"So how do I kill it?"

"Together we will."

"How? Do I go into the Tenderloin?"

"No. Remember back to the Rome Airport? How I killed Gina to prevent her threat?"

"Yes."

"You were not near her."

"No."

"Just like you weren't near Ellen a moment ago."

"But to Ellen I was."

"Yes."

"So, oh my God, Gina saw me killing her."

"Yes."

"Oh my God. So if I put on Gina's shoes I would see me killing her."

"Yes, my dear, you would. Just like you will be killing Jack the Ripper in his latest incarnation. Through me. I will walk the Tenderloin while you fuck in his boots."

"But here and with Gina we were in the same room. The Tenderloin is miles away."

"You're feeding me, Violetta. Each time you merge with me I grow stronger. Soon I will be powerful enough to walk miles from you. To kill for you."

"You will kill him while I stay here?"

"We—Us—will kill him. We will be together. It is the power. It is our destiny. We are the serial killer of serial killers."

Ellen stirs. I pull my hand from her mouth. She coughs. I look at her.

"We will kill him," I say, holding her head in my hands, squeezing her cheeks together, pulling her face to mine.

We kiss, and we taste shit.

THE SECOND PAIR: SPATS

CHAPTER SIX

ELLEN WALKS OUT of the bathroom after taking a very long shower. She walks like a woman who's taken a big crap after a month's constipation and boy did it hurt.

I pucker to kiss her lips and she gives me a glancing blow that's more like an air kiss. After that shot across my emotional bows there's no fucking way I can't resist resorting to my trademark quick wit.

"Hey, I brushed my teeth, gargled and chewed a bunch of Certs."

I exhale a breath blast at Ellen after which I smile a—dare I say it—shit-eating grin. Ellen doesn't respond. Well she does. She responds with no response; her expression remains stone face, speaking through the same rigid jaw.

"So did I. For a long time."

No smile. Not even a sarcastic one. Okay, Ellen isn't

amused by my 'isn't everything cool' flippancy. Well, fuck me, I'm not in the doghouse. I'm in the canine fucking slammer.

Ellen turns, stomps away to the fridge, throws opens the door and grabs a mineral water, wrenching the top off as if she were wringing my neck. Bad news. Not so much the violent opening, but her choice of beverages. I'd feel much better if she'd resorted to beer, or at least a junk soda of some sickly sweet kind. A decent glass of wine would have suggested she felt like relaxing. Fuck, a shot of vodka would have at least declared her intent to get wasted, after which she'd feel bad, and I'd get off much lighter, but mineral water is a way bad omen. It means she is thinking too healthy and wants clarity of mind to nail my ass to the wall.

Ignoring me, she walks to the living room, knowing I'll follow, like a lamb to the slaughter. I do, follow, that is, but no fucking way am I going to be anybody's sheep curry fodder. I'll allow her some ventage, but I'm not gonna take too much crap by way of balancing the heavy shit scales.

"So what went on back there?" Ellen says in a forced soft voice, so obviously trying to hide the rage she feels as she sits down. I sit crossed legged on the floor directly across from her, trying to exude an-everything's-Zen vibe.

"We fucked," I say, shrugging my shoulders, my face straining to maintain that forced mask of innocence.

Ellen slams her mineral water down on the side table. A big jet of liquid shoots out like a blob of jism. I can't resist giggling as it splashes on the floor.

"Oh come on, V," she says over my jocularity. "Be serious. Don't insult my intelligence as well as my body. You abused me."

"You seemed to enjoy it," I say, staying as infuriatingly

calm as I can, fighting my Italian genetic desire to gesticulate and curse.

Ellen furrows her brow. Her eyes look like they're throwing daggers. The phrase, 'If looks could kill,' comes to mind, but she relaxes her expression, and I feel way better. Maybe this won't be so bad after all. Maybe my being calm is diffusing the situation. Whoa, who'd have thought I could be so Newy Agey. I slide my ass across the wood floor towards her. I'm at the point of thinking that we're about to kiss and make up and maybe have a nice, cozy fuck when she goes off like John McEnroe in his prime. She rants about my insensitivity, scoring about ten words for every one of mine. All of her verbal blows center around how she's so shocked to have seen a new, frightening side of me after all these years and how inconsiderate I was of her feelings.

"That was not you back there in the kitchen. You've always been so considerate of me and my pleasure."

"What are you saying?"

I know what she's saying, but I figure that now I understand how she can't see Lucretia, I may as well not cop to the crime. Ellen doesn't need to know all the details. It'll be better that way. Less shit for her to deal with. I mean, look at her, she's having a hard enough time coping as it is. That I have a supernatural Guardian Angel with a mean streak who only I can see, who thinks she can project from me and kill people while I shoefuck would send Ellen running for an exorcist. No way.

"You were possessed. It didn't sound like you and it certainly didn't act like you. It scared me."

See what I mean. And I didn't even spin my head around and projectile vomit green bile and say her mother sucked cocks in hell. So I blow some smoke. The best offense is to be offensive.

"Don't refer to me as it."

"Oh for fuck's sake, Violetta Valery, quit being cute and tell me what is going on here."

Using my middle name reminds me of how my mom and dad would scold me when I'd been bad. For the longest time growing up I thought they'd given me a middle name not because of their love of opera, but because it gave them something to call me when I needed reprimanding. Ellen knows this bit of Cutrero family lore. I confided in her. I don't like that she uses it against me.

I stiffen my back and throw big fucking broadswords from my eyes at her emotional jugular. Fuck daggers. All's fair in love and war, right.

"Nothing is going on Ellen Anne Stewart, besides it seems you don't like role playing as much as I thought you would. Maybe you're getting old."

"Oh come on, V, don't stoop that low. You know this is way more than bedroom games."

"You're right."

"Thank you for that. Now we're getting somewhere."

"They were in the kitchen actually."

Ellen breathes in, stands with a resigned push of her hands on the couch, staring down at me in disgust. Her long tee shirt flutters in the breeze and I see up her legs to the new mown lawn of her trimmed bush. All the anger in me turns to horniness, but the same can't be said for Ellen.

"V, if you can't be serious then there's no point in talking. When you feel like being an adult, a parent, a partner, let me know."

She makes to walk but I grab her ankles, pulling her legs out from underneath her. She topples back onto the couch.

"What the fuck are you doing?"

"I'm being serious."

"I'm not in the mood."

She kicks at me, but I've got her feet held tight and

even though she tosses me around like I'm a nuisance dog that's latched down on her ankle, I don't release my grip.

"Let me go."

"No. The feet cannot be denied. You want an explanation. Fine, but we'll do it my way."

I see Lucretia standing behind me.

"Can you handle this?"

"Yes, I can. I know what I'm doing. Let me do this my way. Ellen's cool. She's no threat to me."

"Don't mind if I watch?"

"No, but no influencing me. I know Ellen better than you."

"I'll be as quiet as a two-thousand-year-old dead woman."

Ellen slows her kicking. She doesn't speak for the longest time, until, finally a "Well? I'm waiting," slips out.

"I'm going to give you a foot massage."

"Don't patronize me. It's not my feet that's sore."

"I know, but I figure you don't want your asshole touched anymore, so I figure I'll ease some of that tension through your feet. You know there are more nerve endings in your feet than anywhere else, and if I zone in on the right spot I can ease all your pains."

Ellen looks to the ceiling.

"V, I don't need this. I don't need comforting. I need answers."

"Shush, we'll do this my way. As I rub your feet, as I worship those divine digits and soothe your sole, I'll tell you everything."

"Be careful," says Lucretia.

"Shut the fuck up. Give me an ounce of credit. Of course I'm not going to tell her everything. Just enough so we can get through this. Okay?"

"You're wise beyond your years, my daughter."

"Well, I'm waiting," says Ellen.

"Let me get some lotion," I say, my head spinning from

keeping straight this bizarre three-way-two-way conversation. I trot off to the bathroom and return with a tube of massage oil that heats with rubbing. It's cinnamon flavored. I lay a towel on the floor and take off my old Fuck Me And Marry Me Young tee shirt, kneeling naked at Ellen's feet. I place her soles on my thighs, pressing her feet into my skin with my cupped hands.

"While you've known me a long time, Ellen, through much shit, you still don't know me that well. Don't feel bad. No one does, even me."

I pour oil onto my palms and massage it into my hands, after which I clasp my hands on Ellen's ankles, sliding my slippery fingers down, across the ridges of her feet. I trace the outlines of the bones, working outwards, circling back around the sides to insert my fingers between her toes, fucking those spaces, in and out, feeling the warmth of the oil soak into Ellen's feet. The cinnamon smell wafts upwards, intoxicating us like we're baking something sticky, sweet and oh so decadently good.

"Feels good," Ellen says. She closes her eyes. Her head lolls back. Her body arches and in doing so, her tee shirt rides up and I see the swell of her pussy lips rise invitingly.

This is excellent progress. She's not yelling at me. I'm horny, and I harbor a sneaky suspicion that Ellen is on the slow boat to horniness too. Feet are wonderful. I'm firmly convinced that there would be no more wars if opposing world leaders were made to give each other foot rubs and then enjoy the subsequent pleasure of a divine pair of feet massaging them or a divine pair of hands on their feet, depending upon their personal peccadilloes.

"I've told you that a lot happened to me in Rome. I've told you about how I discovered the secret to my power. In those caliges I was Lucretia. I endured all she did, and yes, part of me liked all the things done to her and that she then did to others."

I pour oil directly on to the top of Ellen's foot, letting it spill down and onto my thighs. I rub my fingers in the mess, scooping it onto Ellen's foot flesh. I arch her feet upwards and press my thumbs into her soles, following the outlines, curves and ridges, pressing hard into the depressions. I work my fingers along the bones, back up to the toes, each one of which I masturbate like tiny cocks, pulling them upwards, lifting Ellen's foot from my thigh until its weight drops it back down with a rude slap. I repeat this over and over. Ellen moans. Her head tips to the side. She's a ragdoll. I'm not sure if she's hearing me.

"By now you should know that life with me is never going to be normal. I know you think you can keep the wolves at bay, but you can't. And bad things happen when you try. Remember Tony?"

Ellen lifts her head and nods, but she keeps her eyes shut, her head falling back against the couch. I slide all my fingers between her toes, squeezing and pulling. The cinnamon smell is too inviting. I bend down, breathing in the delightful aroma that bears a slight tinge of Ellen's feet to it. I extend my tongue, running it up the bottom of Ellen's big toe until I reach the top, then I purse my lips and suck down like it's a dick, and I'm giving it a blow job. Up and down I suck, pumping the rich cinnamon vapors into my nostrils. Ellen squirms softly, slowly, undulating like she's fucking an unseen lover. I pause at the top, talking more to her big toe than her.

"In Rome I had things done to me just like what I did to you, and I liked it. I'm learning about me, about my power all the time. There's always something new. Like those boots you gave me. They're a new threat, and I have to rise to it."

I suck down again on Ellen's big toe, and I'm not sure whether it's my hand or Ellen's leg that's the instigator but her other foot slides from my thigh to between my legs, working its way to nestle between my pussy lips. As I suck down on one big toe the other big toe slides up and down my labia, flicking across my clit. This footsie play makes it harder for me to talk. Little shivers of delight punctuate my words.

"You know the feet cannot be denied. That's much more than a saying. Thanks to my connection with Lucretia I can summon all of her knowledge. I can fill myself with her supernatural power. She's my Guardian Angel. It sounds fantastic, but fuck, so is shoesex. To do it I need powerful, intense emotions of the kind that come when we're having sex, so don't feel bad about what happened. Feel good. You allowed me to discover the means to solve the Jack the Ripper crimes and prevent the latest incarnations of his evil that lives on in those boots."

I'm dripping pussy juice down Ellen's massage oil covered foot and her toe is spreading the heated mixture over and inside my cunt. I feel tingly and electrified from the cinnamon, almost burning, smoldering. I gnaw on Ellen's toe, opening my mouth wide to stuff all of her toes inside. I run my tongue around and inside her toes. She arches the other big toe and it slides inside my pussy while the others dance across my clit. I snake my arm up her leg, smearing massage oil streaks along her pale, soft skin. My cinnamon-lubed fingers slide effortlessly inside her sopping cunt. I arch my fingers to rub her G spot and we rock backwards and forwards. My lube-coated fingers slide in and out of her pussy as her lubed big toe does likewise to my cunt. If she's feeling half the tingle from the cinnamon that I am then the smolder is gonna ignite into a raging fire. It's almost too much, too sensitive, but we can't quit. We mirror each other's clit attentions, flicking our hardened nubs with fingers and toes. We come together, linked by Ellen's feet and my hands and mouth. I feel her shudder and release on my fingers as I do likewise on her foot. Locked in this climactic embrace for what seems like ages, I continue to massage and lick Ellen's toes as waves of coming wash over us, cresting, falling, but never quite dying down as I demonstrate the simple truth behind "the feet cannot be denied."

Quite some orgasms later Ellen stirs, her foot still in my cunt, prompting frequent little come spasms.

"I'm not sure if I can handle all this connecting with a dead woman, but I'll try."

"And I'll try not to freak you," I say after I take her foot out of my mouth, leaving my fingers flexed in her crotch, making Ellen enjoy the same little come spasms shuddering through my body.

"I just don't get how those boots made their way to you. There were so many chance events. We could have easily not gone to the flea market that day. We could have not gone to that stall. Someone else could have bought them. Buying them was a spur of the moment thing I did for you. There was no plan."

"The feet cannot be denied."

"You say that, and I know what you mean, but I have a hard time believing that it's feet at work here."

"Your foot wasn't denied my cunt. It worked pretty good there."

She slides her foot out of my cunt, but at least she doesn't have that mean expression on her face anymore.

"V, you know what I mean. You might hide behind your jokes, but I know that you know what I mean."

I slide my fingers our of her pussy, smearing my hands down her legs to her feet, which I keep massaging, now with a mixture of cinnamon massage oil and Ellen cunt juice.

"Feet. Fate. Same thing. It's what brought the Dildo Killer and me together. It's what brought Tony into my life. It's what brought you and me together. What were the odds of that chance occurrence? It's why those boots came to me and no one else. My Avenging Angel Sex Goddess destiny is at work here. Just like my actions were linked to the Dildo Killer, so too am I linked to this latest psycho. We've let loose the evil in those boots, and it's my job to kill that evil. What happened back in Victorian England with Jack the Ripper is part of my Avenging Angel Sex Goddess destiny, I'm convinced of it. Evil lives on in some killers' footwear and it's up to me to be the serial killer of killers, dead or alive."

"Even so, some very human beings were responsible for those boots coming into our possession. My cop training sticks with me. I'm going to trace where the boots came from. There's got to be a trail. All that stuff in the flea market originated in estate sales. There should be records. I'll contact the charity. I have the receipt."

I sense victory. Ellen's over her fistfuck snip, galvanized by the lure of good old-fashioned detective work devoid of all supernatural connotations. 'Once a cop always a cop' snooping through details will keep Ellen busy while I work on solving the real crime with Lucretia's supernatural powers.

"Cool, and I'll research all I can about the next Ripper crime so I'm ready for him."

"Yeah, you do that. Some good old fashioned police work dealing with 'just the facts, ma'am, will do you good."

Ellen's voice gets all smug. "Soooooooooo—I take it this means you are going to put the boots on despite what you said earlier."

I smile. This is the part where I make her feel real good about how much she thinks she knows me.

"Yeah, you were right, Ellen. You know me well. I won't be able to resist putting them on. And just like you also said, in stopping the Tenderloin crimes, we might find out who Jack the Ripper was. We can kill two sick birds with one pair of feet. And there are others—The Boston Strangler was not the man who died in jail. We can put right all those wrongs."

"How do you know all this? How can you be so sure?"

I don't say anything. I just stare down at my feet. Ellen smiles. She knows. Ellen leans forward and kisses me on the forehead. We hug each other tight.

"I love you, V."

"I love you, Ellen."

"I love you too, Violetta," says Lucretia from over my shoulder. "You handled that very well, my daughter. Now can we all just get back to fucking. You need to feed me all the sex you can if I'm to be ready for my date with Jack in a few days' time."

CHAPTER SEVEN

THE WEEK LEADING up to the night of September 7—early morning, September 8, 1888 London—is a whirlwind of shoesex and research. Reality blurs with fantasy. When I'm not fucking Ellen for Lucretia's benefit I'm pouring my way through a shitload of Ripperology to learn everything I can about Annie Chapman's grisly demise in the yard of 29 Hanbury Street a few minutes before sunrise. I become a fucking Saucy Jack trivia expert—I'll take Victorian England Serial Killers for a thousand, Alex. Bingo, lucky me, it's the daily double and I'm in big ass jeopardy all right, working round the clock, hoping to retire Jack before he becomes another five-time winner a century and a few years later in my—cough—cough—neck of the woods.

That I'm making reference to nerdy gameshows is no small indication of how demented this manic effort is making me. I feel like my brain and body are being pulled in a gazillion different directions at the same time. It's no slacking for Ellen either. When she's not being frigged, licked, fucked or returning the compliment, she's using her police connections to learn about the Tenderloin Ripper and to discover the identity of the boot donor.

During those times when Ellen's off being a dick—as in private detective, not a prick—I don't get to lounge in bed eating chocolate bon-bons. There's always Luc to look after, who is getting quite adept at sucking tit while Mom's attention is riveted to a Ripper book. I sure hope being exposed to all this murder and mayhem at such a tender and impressionable age when his brain and learning ability is supposedly developing doesn't turn him into a serial killer who then I'd have to slay. Fucking scary much. That I can even think such a notion is just another sign that too much killing work makes Violetta a demented sicko. Shit, that Mom kills Son Greek tragedy crap gives me the fucking chills. No fucking way. Hear this Fate—I'll kill myself before Luc turns bad. Whatever it takes, he's getting a normal life, and I've got more than the usual sneaking suspicion of Fate the Joker at work that this current episode has a lot to do with giving him just that.

So stop freaking me out.

Oh fuck, I shouldn't whine so much. Looking after my baby isn't that taxing. It's mega-fun—a much needed distraction. When Luc's not sucking tit he's peeing or crapping—both of which I've always been good at cleaning up. Then he's snoozing, and you'd think I'd get some rest, but noooooooo, then it's Lucretia's turn, and she is way taxing when she demands her equivalent of a Luc tit suck—shoefucks. She's insatiable, having me play through my collection of fucked-in shoes and boots. She says that experiencing as much shoesex as possible will help build her strength to walk farther from me and hence cut short the killing career of the latest incarnation of

Saucy Jack. Her rationalizing sounds like a vampire justifying the jugular feeding habit on the basis that there's not enough anemia going around.

To be fair, I think she's making up for all those dormant years by seeing how much kink has evolved while trying to learn as much as she can about me. Let's be honest. Sex is the best way to get to know some one. Forget all that 'so what do you like to do for fun' pleasantries crap and those subsequent strained conversational explorations simply to avoid the stigma and supposed doom of a one-night stand. Sex between two people interested in a long-term relationship is a way better foundation builder than endless cappuccinos and plastic chat. At least at first. There's nothing better than sex for bringing down the initial personality barriers, and then real communication can occur to see if this liaison will last. It's simple getting to the meat of the issue of do we really click and are we for real. During fucking the mask comes off and it's naked soul in more ways than one. A faker in the bedroom sticks out like a floppy cock or a dry cunt. The way we act in the boudoir says more about us than all those gut-wrenching heartfelt conversations when it is so easy to put up a front.

So I have no problem indulging Lucretia's desires. Man, it's funny the things she really enjoys, demanding them over and over. Whenever I press her about why a particular shoesex scene intrigues her she becomes evasive, waffling on about how she wants to explore some nuance she isn't familiar with. I think she's bullshitting, which, since she's inside me, she probably knows I'm thinking she's full of it. I let it ride cause I figure she's sussing out what makes me tick by seeing how I handled myself in tough sexual situations. I bet she's trying to see if I'm ready to graduate to the next level of being an Avenging Angel Sex Goddess, and I intend to pass with flying fucking colors.

Lucretia spends a lot time enjoying Johnny's view of my tensed ass in the boarded-up Anacapa restaurant, snapping my suspenders against my butt. She dwells on watching me take it doggie-style in near-public, screaming and moaning for all the world to hear, not a care in the world, devil and Johnny and her take my hindmost.

Beyond Johnny I indulge my Guardian Angel, taking her through my initial experiences with shoesex, exposing her to Mom's sparkly stilettos. She enjoys meeting the Dildo Killer, but for some weird reason she really gets off on when I lost my virginity to Jimmy Purcell in an alleyway behind the DNA nightclub. I'd relegated that little episode to the been-there-done-that category of my shoesex bin and hadn't put on those granny boots in years, but it comes right back, right there, right now. That's the beauty of shoesex—instant total recall.

"Take my fucking boots off, Jimmy. Take my boots off, please."

It's weird scary much to be me right now seeing Lucretia fucking Jimmy, feeling what I felt when this guy that I had such a crush on did me for the first time, knowing now what I know—that he'd die in a few months in this same alley, his eyes fucked out by the Dildo Killer, buttfucked and strangled by Mister Perfection.

"Do you feel any regret?" Lucretia asks me.

"Yes and no."

"I see," and I know she really does.

I soak it all in, letting Lucretia into my heart, head, and soul through my soles.

She's standing on one leg. As Jimmy came he hammered into me like a prize bull, replete with snorting sound effects. I toppled backwards into the wall and the heel caved in. I couldn't help smiling, thinking of the damage to my boots. If I'd have brought my busted footwear to

Cutrero's, I'd have been certain they were fuckshoes without having to put them on.

I feel Lucretia race with excitement as she relives the panic of the heel breaking, feeling the snap as Jimmy's dick pulses and throbs in me. She loves dick. Our cunts juice.

She's in a precarious position. I'm standing on the leg with the busted heel. My other leg is held up partly by Jimmy's arm, partly by the dumpster. My drenched panties are in my pocket. The cool night air blows hot across my formally deflowered cunt.

My shoe fucking powers take instantaneous effect at a level that turns my pussy inside out. The moment we finished fucking, Jimmy pulls out his condomed cock, leaving me propped up against the wall with my skirt above my waist, my cunt open to the night and my fishnetted feet in contact with the shoe leather of my granny boots. Thanks to my power, no sooner have we finished the deed than it starts again for me. Rewind. Replay. Instant total recall.

Now I understand Lucretia's fascination with this scene. In one shoefuck she gets the power of many. She feels me come a multitude. She enjoys tens of Jimmy cocks coming in her.

"You're learning, my child."

I smile as Jimmy stands there in awe of Lucretia's possessed gyrations, unaware of what is transpiring between my feet and my pussy, and now, all those years later, between my sexed-out Guardian Angel and me. He was always slow as molasses on a cold day. Super-cute, a good screw, a dishy dude, but dumb. I think he thought my moaning about my shoes was like a woman saying "No, no" when she means "Yes, yes." So the bastard just stands there, kissing me and fondling my tits, piling layer upon layer of sexual experiences as I relive the First Time.

"Take my fucking boots off, Jimmy. Take my boots off, please."

When it first happened I was pissed at him a little for not giving me a breather. Now I see it served a higher purpose. With shoesex there are no chance occurrences. Fate always plays its foot. Yeah, Jimmy, wherever you are, heaven or hell, the feet cannot be denied. Lucretia sends her thanks for all the fucking, and I just need a breather.

"Take my fucking boots off, Jimmy. Take my boots off, please."

It was at this moment in my multiple de-virging that Jimmy got the notion I had a foot fetish, because after much fumbling he unlaced my boots, pulled them off and sucked on my stockinged toes. Then and now and every time I've played through this shoesex scene I'm impressed with his boldness. Most guys on the first screw won't go for the feet unless they're really footfreaks themselves.

With my boot off my First Time replays cease. What a relief. I come back to earth. Jimmy must have enjoyed the stink of dancing feet cause he gets hard again as he sucks on my toes. Yeah, he was a footfreak all right. After all my shoefuck replays I don't want too much of a gang-bang night, so I give him a hand job while he sucks my toes. Man, does he nibble and shrimp away, giving each one a little blowjob, rubbing the balls of my feet as I squeeze his balls. He squirts into my palm in no time. It's a dreamy feeling to have real male come on my fingers as Jimmy slobbers on my aching feet. On Lucretia's aching feet.

You think we'd take a break after that lovely moment, but no. Lucretia let's me know in no uncertain terms that there's no time to rest or reflect upon the importance of Jimmy's multi-fuck moment. She next fixes on Marsha Sandowny, not just how she met her demise with the DK, but her relationship with me. She enjoys the murdered-in thigh highs and absorbs my fear at feeling Marsha die, but it's a different pair she focuses in on. They're the closest thing Marsha had to formal wear. They're opened toed purple satin high heels with ankle straps. She'd only worn them once. I didn't think they were fuckshoes since she bought them for her birthday when I took her to see *La Traviata* at the San Jose opera. I rented a limo, and we had a pizza dinner during the drive south, got drunk, Kleenexed our way through Verdi's masterpiece and bawled all the way from San Jose back to the Tenderloin, but we never had sex. Then or ever in our all too brief friendship, Marsha and I never fucked, and I didn't feel the slightest shoesex twinge when I tried those shoes on after I scored all of her shoes after she was killed. No two person one body old familiar feeling stuff. Not then.

But this is now.

Lucretia feels my surprise at the sudden rush of Marsha's horniness through shoes I'd written off as vanilla.

"Don't be shocked. I'm growing stronger. I'm able to sense Marsha's fantasy."

"Get out of here. No way. You're making this up."

"You know me better than that, Violetta."

"Yeah, sorry, Lucretia. It's just so fucking weird."

"Not really. It just a matter of degrees. What is the definition of having sex in shoes? There's not much difference between playing with oneself and fantasizing so much that one gets excited. Your power will eventually refine itself to be so attuned that you can pick up lustful thoughts and hear romantic notions without the need for overt sexual activity."

"Shit, yeah, but this isn't oneself. This is me and Marsha. I'm reading my dead girlfriend's mind through her shoes because she was turned on by me. It's freaky. We weren't dykes. We weren't even lipstick lesbians. We were buds. Well, yeah, I knew she wanted to do me, but I was scared to let her get too close in case she tripped on my power."

"She was tripping on you. Marsha was sexually imaginative."

"And active."

"Oh yes. Let's enjoy her. Let's enjoy us."

I give in to Lucretia's ability to attune to sexy thoughts had while in shoes. It's kinda neat to learn all this new stuff about shoesex. I thought I had it all sussed out after my experiences in New York and Rome with the Lowest Soles, but hey, just goes to show, a footfucker's never done learning, and a couple of thousand-year-old foot-fucker can always show a twenty-year-old footfucker a few things.

Two people, one body, that old yet now new familiar feeling . . .

So there I am, sprawled on the backseat of the limo, champagne bottle in hand, tears in eyes from that opera cry fest, chugging gulps of bubbly. Siouxsie's singing about kiss them for me, and man, there's a bunch of 'them' close by that I'd like to kiss and 'them' all do belong to that little tease Violetta. She's such a fox. My legs are spread, and my purple satin slip dress has inched up my thighs. Well okay, I inched it up to be more comfortable.

No. Not comfortable. To be more open for Violetta. That little tease has passed out, her head on my lap, her hands holding those cool purple strappy shoes I scored just to impress her since she's so in to shoes. They were my bday prez to me, and icing on the fucking cake would be if I got to lick Violetta's pussy and blow out her candles. Fuck, she's a hottie. She's drooling into my crotch and it feels so fucking good to feel her warm wetness on my wetness. It's easy to imagine her eating me. Her long black pencil dress has slid all the way up so I see her ass. Okay, I helped slide it up. I wanted to ogle her bod. Fuck, I want to fuck her.

She's not wearing panties since the dress was so tight and we hate VPL and couldn't be bothered with thongs. It felt naughty to go out for a fancy night at the opera without underwear. I see the pout of her pussy lips, the pucker of her ass, tufts of dampened pubic hair. I wonder what's she dreaming with her head inches from my pussy. Is she thinking of parting my sticky lips with her tongue, circling it around my clit while I wrap my legs around her neck. Is that why her pussy drips and her cunt hair is all sticky with promise?

Oh fuck, I'd love to finger myself, to flick my clitty while looking at Violetta's skinny little bare ass. It would be so easy to reach under Violetta as she drools and snoozes on my lap and bring myself off, but I can't risk it. I might wake her with my thrustings and probings and squirmings, and then I'd be busted, and I'd be bummed if she didn't want to play. Rejection—not me, not at all.

Better to live in my little fantasy world where we both munch each other's cunts but good rather than die in the reality of "get out of here." Fuck, reality bites. What if Violetta really wants me to make a move and figures I'm not interested cause I don't take the initiative. Oh shit, stop thinking, we're just friends. Better not fuck it up. Just birthday blues. Start having fun.

Violetta stirs and rolls a little and her spiky hair tickles my thighs. Oh that feels good. Just enough of a sensation to fuel my dirty mind. She squeezes my ankle, strokes the straps. Maybe, just maybe I should slide my hand between her legs, give her head a little nudge into my damp thighs. Fuck sweet Jesus she's close enough to my cunt to smell how wet it is. She's got to know. Maybe, maybe—uh-oh—she's waking up. I'd better pretend I've crashed.

My head rolls back. I feel Violetta lift her head. She smoothes my slip skirt down and strokes my shoes as she snuggles to my side.

I keep my eyes closed. We're just good friends.

I feel Lucretia stir as Marsha fades.

"What did you think when you woke up and saw Marsha's pussy just inches away from your face, wet with your drool and her juices."

"I dunno. It was so long ago."

"Violetta. I know what you're thinking."

"Oh yeah. Then why'd you ask?"

"It's the polite thing to do, and it makes you confront those dark rooms you hide in."

"I wanted to kick my shoes off, eat her pussy then borrow her shoes to see what she thought of me."

"Why didn't you?"

"I didn't think it was any way to treat my best friend. I thought I shouldn't involve her in the whole fucked-up mess of my life beyond the nice distance of just good friends."

"But she was involved."

"Yeah, and it killed her, and I'll always regret not doing her that night. Especially now I know that she wanted it too."

"So I hope you've learned not to think too much, but to trust your feet, your sex, your Avenging Angel Sex Goddess powers, your intuition, and not to worry about mere mortals' feelings."

"Yeah, right."

"Next pair."

I'm not sure I want to do this now that I know this shoesex mind thing. I'm kinda freaked because Lucretia really wants to get inside Ellen's feet. It seems too much like cheating to me, but I rationalize that it's all in a good cause so I go along with it because it helps me to understand Lucretia. The things she finds interesting tell me a lot about my pagan protectoress.

And me.

And that's the scary part, especially where Ellen's concerned. I'm not sure I want to know what Ellen thinks of me.

There's no denying Lucretia.

Or me.

At first it's all innocuous stuff. When there's real shoesex in the shoes it kinda masks all the other thinking stuff. We zoom through the standard shoesex shoes, reliving everything from those first few encounters where we used shoesex to send messages to each other when Ellen was busy taking the fall for me offing the DK. Lucretia's impressed.

"That was ingenious. I've used similar methods over the centuries, but you just picked right up on it."

"Actually, Lucretia, it was Ellen's idea. She sent the shoes to get repaired. Then we used it later when we were apart when she was traveling for her book. Sure beats a letter or a phone call."

"But not being together."

"No, there's nothing like real physical contact."

"No, there's not."

Lucretia's words and the thoughts behind their delivery chill through me as I sense all that she's missed in these centuries of being in shoesex limbo, trapped in a pair of smelly old sandals. There's more there, but she shuts me off. I feel a wall. She definitely has more power than she's showing me.

She senses it.

"In good time, Violetta. You will know all."

"Doesn't seem fair. You know all about me, but you don't pay me in kind."

"Oh but I do, you just don't understand the power in your feet and your destiny yet, but if it's payment you want then come, let me show you."

I put on the shoes Ellen wore when we first had sex after she was released. Actually, they're not fuckshoes at all. We both agreed not to wear shoes, and well, I gotta be honest, when I sneaked a peek in to them, and all of Ellen's shoes for that matter, she'd not been getting any while I'd been away, and she'd been in the slammer.

But now, thanks to Lucretia, I can see what Ellen's thinking. There's nothing much more than butterflies before we do the deed. It had taken awhile for us to get it on. Ellen had mega-rejection angst to get over, and I'd had to tell her my odyssey, and well, I was six months pregnant. Not exactly the most romantic ingredients for a reunion fuck. It actually took us about a week of tentative touches, pathfinding pecks and hopeful hugs before we got down and dirty and Ellen found out how big my tits had got being pregnant.

Post fucking-great-coitus I'm snoozing on the bed. Ellen wants to go to the bathroom so she's eased off the bed and slips her feet into her Hush Puppies since the floor's cold on the tootsies. The Hush Puppies are cute black loafers— not exactly classic fuckshoes, but sexy in a naughty librarian kind of way. It's amazing we've never fucked in them, but then again not so planet-shaking as they're so easy to kick off and we have so many other pairs of shoes crying out to be fucked in.

Ellen's sitting on the toilet having a good old pee. She wipes her pussy adding a few extra swipes to take care of the extra juice from our fucking and coming and fucking and coming *ad passoutium.*

Ellen spies me through the door crack.

Violetta looks so cute.

And she knows it.

And she thinks she's gotten away with it.

That everything is okay.

And it is. Really. Making love with her is so fresh. God, did I miss her touch, and I feel so alive and right now we're intimate again, but I'm so scared I'll lose her through some quirk of this Cutrero curse. That baby is her flesh and blood in more ways than the obvious, and I'm not. Is she always going to look at me as the woman who killed his father? What will she tell her child about me. Will she dump me at the first sign of conflict between us?

Well, she said our debts are paid. I saved her from the justice system when she killed the Dildo Killer and she exonerated me in the death of her brother. Half-brother. But is a debt like that ever paid? Sometimes Violetta and that power scare me. What if she's setting me up for some bizarre retribution? She's the serial killer of serial killers. What if she sees me as just another sicko to be executed?

Oh, Violetta's awake.

"Ellen?"

"Coming, V."

"Again? You maniac. Finishing yourself off. I thought I did you pretty good."

"Oh you did. You did. You got me good."

Violetta seems back to her old flippant self. I shouldn't worry.

I flush the toilet and wish my worries away with my piss.

Lucretia soothes my teeming emotions.

"Now you know why Ellen is on edge sometimes. She needs reassuring about her fate."

I don't have time to explore what Lucretia means because Ellen comes back from one of her snooping forays in the City much earlier than I'd expected. Even though the shoefuck with Lucretia had finished and I had time to put things away I feel rushed. It's silly, but as I hastily put her shoes away and untousle the bed, I can't help torturing myself with thoughts of what would have happened if Ellen had been fifteen minutes earlier and found me with her Hush Puppies on. What would she have thought about me sharing our most intimate moments with Lucretia? It's hard for me not to act caught cheating red-footed. I feel like I'm in one of those Victorian love triangle farces where my paramour is hiding in the closet.

Which in a way I am, and she is.

I fuss too much about the room, flitting from mess to mess, avoiding the bed. Ellen notices my edginess.

"What's the matter?"

"I'm just tired. I didn't get much of a nap. Luc was cranky."

"Oh, my poor baby. Just you lie back and let Ellen take care of you."

Now don't I feel the guilty sleaze. Why can't she be angry? I'll be more testy. Best to play the edgy bitch role to the max. Fuck reassuring. I stiffen my back, not my clit.

"I'm not in the mood for sex."

Ellen doesn't take the spat bait. She's getting to know me too well.

"Who said anything about sex? There's more than one way that the feet can't be denied. I'll give you a big foot rub and tell you all about what I found out in the City. Lie down, we've got to look after your gifted dogs so they're ready for their big date."

Ellen pushes me back on the bed, lifting my feet gently down on the hastily arranged covers where moments before I'd been shoesexing with Lucretia in Ellen's shoes. Ellen props pillows under my calves and knees so my feet are elevated. She pulls my sweaty tee-shirt over my head and covers my nudity with the softness of a sheet. I feel good already. She kicks off her Mary Janes, pulls off her socks by the toes and shimmies out of her jeans.

She grabs a bottle of lotion she keeps by her bed—peppermint-rosemary—and drains dollops of it onto her palms from quite a height as if it's pee streaming from between her legs. She's kneeling at the foot of our bed wearing just her white thong panties and a white blouse. She looks hot.

"Close your eyes," she says as she rubs the lotion into her hands.

"I want to watch."

"As you wish, Mistress Violetta, but before I'm done, your eyelids will close, footslave."

I chuckle at Ellen's submissive/dominatrix switch in the same sentence but the chuckle turns to a moan as I catch my breath when she cradles my feet, squeezing. The cool of the lotion tingles on my heated soles. I close my eyes. Her fingers work tight circles around the soles, winding out to my heels and my toes, masturbating each little digit as if it were a tiny cock. She presses in all the right spots, with precision firmness, just like when she works my cunt. I open my eyes to watch. Ellen's intent on her handiwork, her tongue protruding from between her pressed-tight lips. She looks so cute, as if all she cares about right now is making my feet feel good. I really didn't mean what I said about not being in the mood for sex.

"So what did you find out?" I say through a slurring, sleepy mouth, trying to sound sexy and conciliatory and yeah, reassuring.

Ellen doesn't look away from my feet.

"Nothing that can't wait until later. Suffice it to say I had a good day of snooping, so you lie back and enjoy yourself. No talking shop allowed, but you can whisper sweet-somethings and general moans of pleasure."

Now I feel really bad about being a bitch.

"You're too good to me."

"Shush, you deserve to be spoiled. It's tough to be a mom and an Avenging Angel Sex Goddess at the same time."

"And lover."

"That's not tough. You're easy to love."

"Yeah, and you're full of it."

"That's my Violetta Valery."

"Ooooooooooooooooooooooooooh."

Ellen's rubbing her knuckles up and down my soles, pulling my feet up off the pillow by my toes, letting the weight of my feet drop them down across her fists. It feels so darn good I could come. She cups the heels and pinches those tender spots behind the ankles before sliding her fingers around and down the top of my foot, tracing the bones, easing the tension to the outside. She slides her hands to my inner ankles, rubbing along the curves with her thumbs. It's like she's prying apart the sticky swell of my pussy lips, making my juices flow, easing my cunt open so she can slam a finger or two inside. I feel like my legs and feet are extensions of my pussy, that my whole lower body is one giant cunt with my legs being my labia and my feet my clit, and I'm not just saying that to be Ms. Oh So Fucking Literary Erotica Intellectual Snob. I really do feel like I've turned into a big cunt, in the best possible sense of the term. I feel Ellen's touch on my feet all the way up my legs, parting my thighs and up into my pussy, where her fingers work comely magic. I'm not sure whether Ellen's the instigator or whether it's me, but my legs spread slightly and I arch my back, pulling the sheet from my body. I'm naked, hot, and in heat.

I look down the length of my body through blurring vision and imagine I'm all cunt swallowing Ellen as she massages my feet. I'm really getting turned on by all this attention when it dawns on me that Ellen's been on her feet all day, burning the shoe leather, as they say in old detective novels, to zoom in on who she thinks is the prime suspect. Her dogs must be barking, so why not pet them like the good puppies they are.

Ellen's reclined on the bed as she kneads my foot flesh so it's a simple matter for me to reach over with my hand and stroke her nearest foot ever so lightly.

"What are you doing?"

"Fucking your feet like you're fucking mine."

Ellen smiles, pulls her blouse off and slides her panties off with a flurry of a kick so they sail through the air, much to Spykes' amusement as he bats the flimsy things around the skating rink of our polished wooden floor. Giggling, Ellen rolls her body close to mine so we're lying head to toe. I grab both of her feet and rub them like she's doing to me, trying to make the same motions, just like when we finger fuck each other.

I press Ellen's soles together and it strikes me how much like a pussy they look. Maybe I'm horned out but the arches so resemble a pair of cuntlips, I can't resist it. I run my tongue along the curve, tasting the tang of Ellen's all day pounding the pavement on her feet. She giggles louder, and maybe further, sending my tongue to her toes, licking them like clits, sucking them like cocks, and Ellen does the same to me and we foot sixty-nine each other into a frenzy, stuffing our feet into our mouths, chewing on our toes, tonguing the spaces in-between. We're locked together rolling around the bed, and I swear we come just from doing this but maybe it's because our pussies rub together as we frolic. Either way, it's fucking awesome total body fucking.

And yeah, even after we've come we have more sex, licking each other's pussies until it feels like we're coming out of our feet too. It's fucking great mind-blowing body-part dislocating fucking—the kind that comes after an hour or more of foot rubbing and sucking.

After fuck knows how many orgasms Ellen rotates, and we fall asleep, our pruned feet entwined, our tender pussies nestled together, our parched mouths locked in a kiss, tasting our cunt and foot tinged hot breath. I sleep restlessly. Between Ellen, Lucretia and Luc I'm exhausted and on edge. I can't rest, no matter how much good fucking or relaxing I enjoy. I feel like I've lived several lives in a little over a week, all to prepare for several deaths in a few wretched moments, and, shit, it bums me out, man. Being the serial killer of serial killers sometimes sucks. And this is one of those some times.

CHAPTER EIGHT

JACK THE RIPPER murdered Annie Chapman between 5:30 and 6 in the morning. To make sure we don't miss the big moment Ellen and I plan to fuck in the boots around 5 a.m. London time, 9 in the evening California time the night before, with Luc tucked safely in his cot, soundly snoozing away for the duration. We make damn sure there's none of that daylight savings time mismatch crap with the oh-so-proper-sun-never-sets-only-it-has-but-they-don't-realize-it-but-they-sure-make-good-music-even-if-they-drink-warm-beer-British. We even call a hotel in London earlier in the day and ask them what time it is in over-the-pond land just to make sure we haven't fucked up. We hadn't. Okay chaps, synchronize watches, tally ho . . .

Tally not. In the cause of preparing to snag Jack I've fucked so much with Lucretia in shoes and with Ellen *au naturel* over the last week that sex is getting to be like the daily grind. Nine-to-five—punch in—fuck—lunch—

fuck—punch out—dinner—overtime fucks—sleep—
wake—breakfast—punch-in—change shoes—fuck. My
cunt and clit feel like Hamburger Helper—Texturized
Vegetable Protein for all the vegans out there. Honestly,
after this marathon-fucking week I'm wallowing 1 e in
the Annie Chapman prostitute mindset than the Jack the
Ripper vibe. Dude, I know why they call hookers loose
women—it's got nothing to do with morals. I'm fucking
worn out—a hole too well traveled. No offense to Ellen,
but killing 30 minutes having kitty sex in the boots after
my week in the Land of Fuck just doesn't light my buttons, even with all the extra lube and candles ai 1 adrenaline flowing through my tired veins from the prospect of
snuffing out Jack the Ripper's eternal evil.

I actually snooze through some of Spykes' horny cat
antics. Ellen's way cool, cuddling me more than fucking
me, keeping things cooking until it's a few minutes before
the time when all the Ripper accounts says that a foreign
looking gent not much taller than Annie walked up to her
and said "Will you," and she said "yes."

Two people, one body, that really old, altogether too
familiar feeling after this week.

At first I think Luc's crying, and I start, like when he
wakes me from a deep snooze, but then I realize where I am.

London 1888. There's a baby crying all right, and it
makes Jack start from his deathly wait. Makes me start,
and I'm there inside him, the most famous serial killer
ever. I try to focus on the details of my feelings to get
clues to his identity but my heart races, and I curse my
luck that the place I'd staked out for a killing field was
ruined by some prostitute's brat screaming for an emaci-
ated teat. Muttering, I move from my hiding place and
ferret from doorway to doorway, looking from my
shadows for another likely victim.

There are many around, but I want a particularly sorry

one. I check my pocket watch. 5:26. It will soon be light. Maybe I will have to put off my retribution until tomorrow night if I don't find the perfect cow to slaughter in Margaret's name.

That sad state of affairs will not do. It's been too long since the last retribution. I clench my fists under my cape, but it does no good. I want to scream at the thought of passing another day without release from Margaret's torment. I break out into a cold sweat. I wipe my forehead with my handkerchief. As I do so I look up. I'm standing in a doorway of a particularly decrepit building. The sign says Mrs. Hardyman's Cats' Meat Shop. In the distance I see Saint Botolph's church. How appropriate. How jocular. My mood improves. This is a good sign. My hardyman will indeed make cats' meat out of some sorry trollop with God looking on and approving, and with any luck, by the time the sun rises over this squalor, Mrs. Hardyman will have plenty of new raw vittles to put in to her blessed pussy food.

I take a few moments to inspect the rear yard. Perfect. Walled in. Dark. A wretched privy. A door into the rear lane. Perfect. Now all I need is a slab of aspiring pussy meat.

I go back to the doorway and providence smiles upon my Divine mission. She comes stumbling up Hanbury Street. Ugly as this part of the town in which she peddles her body. Short. Stout. Sickly. Coughing. Drunk. She's missing teeth, and what's that—a black eye. Perfect. This one must not get away.

I step slightly from the shadows and intercept her progress. I let her see the glint of the coins as I tumble them in my palms. I swear she salivates as she stumbles to a drunken halt.

"Will you," I say.

"Yes," she says, and I lead the foul creature into the backyard of Mrs. Hardyman's Cats' Meat Shop.

Margaret, I will be doing this hideous world, this

hideous country, and this hideous woman a favor, and I do it all in your name.

Oh this is too fucking weird. I've gone schizo. All the while I've been stalking the East End of Victorian London I've been getting flashes of the Tenderloin of today. The feeling is exactly what it's like when there are two competing shoe fucks in one pair of shoes. I swear I just flashed a bunch of twenties to a homeless hustler and asked "Will you?" and he said "yeah," and now I'm leading him down an alley off Eddy between a peep show theater and the homeless charity of Saint Anthony's Dining Room. I'm thinking about Jimmy as I steer this young hustler down a path between porn and religion.

Why is Jimmy Purcell entering this scene? Yeah, we fucked in an alley, but it wasn't this alley, and he wasn't a homeless hustler. An asshole, yeah, but this doesn't fit. And who the fuck is this Margaret that Jack's tripping on?

So where is Lucretia? This mishmash of religious and sexual imagery has to have something to do with my Guardian Angel and her preoccupation with my past.

I'm here with you. I'll protect you. We are one. We're drawing strength from your past experiences. Trust me, my Avenging Angel Sex Goddess child, all will soon be clear. The feet cannot be denied.

I feel her words rather than hear them, and I don't see her. She's so far away. She may as well be in London.

Or Stinson Beach.

Or San Francisco.

I feel so alone.

I feel so full of hate for this ugly degenerate.

"What's your name, luv?" she says.

I don't answer.

"The silent type, eh. Old Mrs. Hardyman's Cats' Meat got your tongue?" She looks up at the sign and cackles, no doubt trying to impress me with her meager intelligence's reading ability. I hurry her along, not wanting to draw attention to us. Still she chatters, nodding at the shadow of the nearby church. "Or are we too close to God? Well, not to worry, me old cock, just let your money do the talking. Fork it over, Mister, because God looks after those that looks after the less fortunate, and in return the Almighty's given Annie the means to make your hardyman all soft, Mister."

She cackles again, and grabs for my crotch with her filthy fingers. As she kneads my cock and balls all I think of is how you did the same thing, Margaret, to countless men but you wouldn't satisfy my husbandly needs. I can't wait to silence this ugly bitch like I should have muted your duplicitous protestations of courtly love.

I give her the coins and she slips them into a pocket of her ragged dress. Her toothless smile tells me she thinks she's been overpaid.

"What's a toff like you doin' around here with the likes of me?"

She thinks she'll be rich for the rest of her sorry life. The thought makes me smile.

"Oawwh I see," she says. "Likes a bit of rough does ya?"

"A lot of rough," I say as I push her against the fence and hike up the tattered layers of her filthy skirt, thinking of Margaret and how she betrayed me.

"What's your name, dude?" he says.

I don't answer.

"The silent type. That's cool. Pussy Cat or God got

your tongue?" He looks up from the far away entrance of the alley to the Pussy Cat peep show neon flashing 'Talk to our Pussies for a dollar,' and the poorly lit sign of the Catholic Church charity and laughs that semi-retarded guffaw street hustlers perfect for annoyance.

"I'm Arnie," he says snickering, holding out his raised clutched palm in one of those awkward white kid-wannabe-black-street-dude motions.

I push him behind the dumpster so we're out of sight of passers-by, druggies, do-gooders, child-molester priests and other assorted Tenderloin denizens. He tries to maintain his coolness, but I can tell he's rattled.

"Hey, be cool, man, just let your money do the bragging, and I'll do whatever you want. Fork it over and I'll take care of your pussy, bitch."

He guffaws again and reaches between my legs and squeezes my cunt like Jimmy did. I give him the money. He releases my cunt and flicks through the roll of bills. He whistles. "What is it with you rich bi-dykes that you gotta get your dick from the likes of me?"

His familiarity breeds my contempt. His sudden wealth makes him think he'll be rich for the rest of his life. I smile. He smirks.

"Now I get it. You're slumming."

"Wrong. I'm slamming," I say as I throw him back into the wall and rip open his jeans thinking of Jimmy and how he screwed me over and ended up dying in alley at the sick fuck hands of the Dildo Killer.

Parting my cape, I unbutton my trousers and extricate my throbbing erection with one hand. The other hand holds this sorry Annie woman against the fence by the throat. The pressure of my grip forces her head back and she gasps for breath as I lift her off the floor. I part her swinging legs

– 106 –

with my knees as I stare from her to the outline of the church in the morning twilight and Mrs. Hardymans Cats' Meat Shop. The symbolism is perfect. With my free hand I rip off her disgusting bloomers and feel the hairiness of her musty bush. The cunt is damp from fucking countless other men, but that's no matter to me. I stick my finger in and thrust in and out, the struggling of her body aiding my penetrations. She lubricates well enough that my erection will find its plunderous way through her vile folds of flesh. I press my loins into her, wedging my body into hers, still holding her by the neck against the fence. Her eyes bulge. I thrust. My cock lunges into her cunt. Her tongue sticks out of her mouth and she clenches her fists. My body batters into her. I reach up with my free hand and squeeze her udderous teats, pulling and mauling at the saggy mounds, pinching her nipples so hard that if she could have screamed she would have. My release wells in me. I fuck her unconscious, pounding hard, relishing in the sad way her pliable flesh gives in to my hard, demanding body. She is a sack of flesh I bury my hatred of women in. I feel the pulse in her neck slow as my cock pulses its juices into her. She dies as I finish spending.

"Margaret," I say as I lay Annie down in the filth of the dingy backyard of Mrs. Hardymans Cats' Meat Shop. From the warmth of my cape I uncage my surgeon's knife so that I may complete my macabre tapestry dedicated to the evils of loose women.

"Margaret," I say as knife cuts flesh.

Arnie's surprised by my strength. I can tell by the way his eyes roll upwards. What's up, bro? It's not time to die yet. Okay, I get it. That stupefied look is definitely surprise and not the last pathetic look of the doomed.

That'll come soon enough.

As he struggles against my grip his dank jeans slide down his scrawny legs. I rip away his stained Y-fronts and squeeze his cock. It hardens. I cup his balls, squeezing, kneading, rolling the sacks, my middle finger flicking across his asshole, threatening to slide in.

"Jerk your cock," I say.

He nods, his head banging against the brick wall of the Pussy Cat peep show, his feet pointing towards the Saint Anthony's Dining Room. He grimaces in pain, but his hand grabs for his dick. "Be cool," he tries to say through a sputtering mouth. After several tries he snares his swinging dick and tugs at it like a pro. I relax my grip on his neck enough for him to feel that if he continues I'll let him live. After toying with his asshole and balls, I slip my free hand down my jeans and slide my middle finger between my moistening cuntlips, flicking my clit in time with his fevered strokes.

"Jerk your cock, Arnie. Make yourself come for me. I want you to squirt your load in my face. Do it."

He masturbates as if his life depended upon it—which it doesn't—there's nothing he can do to save himself by impressing me with his jack off expertise, but even so his jerk off efforts make my cunt drip over my finger. I love watching his cock bulge under the pressure of his fierce grip, his balls pendulating from the motions of his swinging body and fevered pumping. I increase the pressure of my finger on my clit, rubbing the swollen bud in ever tightening circles, up and down, up and down, round and round, round and round. His cock leaks that telltale drop of pathfinding jism.

"Come on, give it to me, Arnie. Come on my face."

His eyes bulge as he gasps for air, but to his credit he doesn't falter in the frigging of his cock. I don't falter in squeezing the life from his sorry body or from finger fucking my cunt. I grow juicier as his death grows nearer.

"You know that choking as you come is an intense high—they call it eroto-asphyxiation—and the trick is just to come before passing out. Many people don't get it right. They choke to death enjoying one killer of a final orgasm."

His tongue bulges from his mouth and his free hand forms a fist as tight as the one clutching his cock. He pummels my arm to let him down, but the blows lack force.

"Come—for—me—Arnie."

It takes supreme focus on my purpose to continue. Orgasmic waves wash over me, weakening my legs. I squeeze his neck tighter as my warm juices flood my finger.

"Come—"

I don't have a chance to finish my order. Arnie splatters come onto my face.

"Was it good for you, Arnie?"

He doesn't respond to my witticism. I doubt he heard my words. Arnie passed out as he came, his life leaving him with his shudders of jism.

"Marsha," I say as I lay Arnie down in the filth of the dingy alley behind the Pussy Cat peep show and the Saint Anthony's Dining Room. From the warmth of my leather jacket I uncage my shoe-trimming knife so that I may complete my macabre tapestry dedicated to the evils of hustlers who prey on loose women.

"Marsha," I say as knife slices flesh.

Hold the fucking phone. I want out of here. Lucretia, where are you? What is this with a leather jacket and a shoe-trimming knife? And who the fuck is Margaret and why am I mumbling Marsha and thinking of my dead stripper friend who I should have been able to save? No way. This makes no fucking sense. Flashing on Jimmy

Purcell was bad enough but now Marsha. No. Not Marsha. Who's playing foot games with my head? What gives? Annie. Arnie. Jimmy. Margaret. Marsha. What the hell is going on here? Lucretia, why are you playing through Violetta's Greatest Footsex Fuck-ups? Ellen, get me out of these boots.

I kick at my feet. It's moments like these that I know why Aunt Crista had her feet amputated.

My surgeon's knife works wonders, slicing through flesh like butter spread by warm steel on country bread or perhaps 'cuntry bread' would be a more appropriate simile. I chuckle at my wordplay wit. Entrails ooze out as if they know this is all they were created for. I place Annie's intestines over her left shoulder before slicing the source of all evil to pieces. I am hard again.

"Margaret, help me."

My shoe-trimming knife makes short work of Arnie's pale flesh. His insides leap into my hands as if they know this is their fifteen minutes of fame. I place his intestines over his left shoulder before slicing his cock in to ribbons of flesh.

"Ellen, help me."

CHAPTER NINE

LUCRETIA IS BFMIA—Big Fucking MIA—as in Missing In Action—as in lost without a trace.

It's as if she was never a part of me—nada—as if I'd dreamed or hallucinated the whole frigging Guardian Angel crap, and now, more than ever, I need a protector. I'm fucking wrecked. Ellen too. She took the brunt of my acting out the second Jack the Ripper murder and freeing my feet from the boots and trying to calm me down and understand what the fuck went on through all my blathering and thrashing. Honestly, it's at times like this that I wonder what she sees in me.

Ellen says I was rabid during the Ripper shoesex, and it didn't get much better afterwards. The notion that perhaps I'd wigged out and imagined all this Lucretia nonsense haunted me. Was I a cured schizophrenic? I could tell by Ellen's unbelieving reaction to my "Where's Lucretia," ramblings and frantic donning and doffing of Lucretia's caliges and attempts to get sexually aroused that my lesbian lover life partner thought me a tad bit disturbed.

Which didn't help at all, but I can hardly blame her as I rub my clit like Lady Macbeth trying to get that damn spot out. Again, again and a-fucking-gain I pull the hood backwards, exposing the swollen bud, flicking my clit to and fro, rubbing it up and down, up and down, up and down, as I work my other fingers in and out of my cunt, in and out—oh what the fuck—you get the picture. I'm masturbating to the max, like a teenage boy before a hot date.

"Take it easy," Ellen says, trying to hug me.

"I've got to find Lucretia. Help me. Finger my ass."

Ellen's bleeding a little from my scratches and the welts look ugly across her pale flesh, but she looks pretty damn good to me. I grow hornier. I'm juicing. All the frigging is working. My cunt's opening. My walls are melting with juice.

"Come on, Ellen," I say, gasping for air, reeling from the gut punch of cunty contractions. "Be rough with me. Make me come. Don't hug, fuck. I'm almost there. Don't stop it."

"Violetta, I'm spent. You should rest. Come on, let's cuddle."

"Fuck cuddle. I don't need cuddle. I gotta know I'm not crazy. I'm getting there. I don't want to lose this. Puh-leaze."

Ellen sighs. I know she can't resist me even though her heart and parts lower and above aren't in to it. I blow her a pouty kiss and make my cunt lips pout just as much. She kneels between my widespread legs and licks her finger, sliding it easily up my ass. My cunt spasms. I pull my lips back and apart, making my erect clit stand out just about as far as it can.

"Suck it, Ellen, suck it."

Ellen runs her tongue up from the finger that's reaming

my ass, up my labia, licking my fingers as they fuck me, encircling my clit as I finger it. Her lips wrap around my clit and my frigging finger and I feel her tongue dancing all over me, beating my nub in time with my finger. She draws her lips away, sucking as she draws back, latching on to my clit, releasing it with a pop. My clit vibrates as if it were a pager being beeped, and the vibrations feed each other until my clit makes like a hummingbird during hummingbird mating season.

These amazing sensations ignite a swarm of little orgasmic explosions that blast me over the big edge of a nuclear come, but there's no Lucretia anywhere, and I'm crying as Ellen keeps sucking and tonguing me into oblivion. That's when it dawns on me that perhaps I've lost my power. Could these Ripper boots be my match, the shoes that bested me? Was losing my power what this clusterfuck of a shoefuck was all about? No way. No fucking way.

I push Ellen away.

"Ellen, Ellen, quit sucking and get me a pair of fuck-shoes. Any fuckshoes. Maybe I've lost my power," I say because of the "I can't believe this is happening" look on Ellen's face.

Grumbling something that sounds suspiciously like "first you want to be fucked, then you don't. How am I to know what you want," Ellen retrieves my mom's sparkly stilettos from their pride of place in my shoe closet. I can tell she's exasperated by the way she holds them dangling above me with her fingers inserted in the toes. I owe her an explanation.

"Look, Ellen, this isn't me going through mega-PMS or being fickle. We talked about this. This is what it's like being the lover of an Avenging Angel Sex Goddess."

"A bratty twenty-year-old Avenging Angel Sex Goddess who could do with a spanking."

Ellen makes a light spank on my ass as I grab the high heels, smiling in my most winning of ways.

"Promises, promises," I say as I slip the shoes on in a flash and—

Two people, one body, that old familiar feeling.

Yes. Fuck me, yes.

With constipated shoesex relief I smile even as my dad comes in the bedroom and molests me. Or so I thought when I was ten and tried on mom's shoes and got a dose of my parents fucking like bunnies, only I didn't know that then. I thought dad was doing the nasty on me. It freaked me back then but never has it been so welcome as now. I relished in the scene and all its campy comments by mom and dad about love monsters and being as creamy as tiramisu and tight as a new pair of shoes, and I'm thankful to Ellen for not pulling me out of it. She knows me well enough to leave well enough alone.

I come out of my mom and dad's shoefuck happy as a well-fucked clam, and I bawl my eyes out. Ellen cradles me and we sleep, rest and doze for days.

I don't even dream of Lucretia.

But I do think of her when I'm awake, lying there listening to Ellen snore the snore of someone exhausted by the ponderous weight of simply getting by.

I've been stirring a few minutes, and she's still soundly out. One thing I'm sure of—no way could I have imagined Lucretia. No way was the end result of my Roman Holiday a stress-induced hallucination. The Feast of the Lowest Soles happened. Johnny Gianni had the sweetest dick I've ever fucked. It happened. We had sex in the Colosseum. Not just any sex but Colossal Sex in the Colosseum and follow-up sex right after Aunt Crista's funeral in the ruins of Anacapa. I have the shoes that Johnny wore at Anacapa when he did me from the rear and snapped my suspenders, and I have the plastic sou-

venir Roman sandals he bought to wear at the Colosseum
so he wouldn't spoil the blow job loafers that he wore at
Caffé Greco. They're in the chest in my closet, right next
to where I keep mom's sparkly high heels that I wore last
night to enjoy dad's dick going in and out of mom to
make sure I hadn't lost my power. They're part of my special collection of shoesex memorabilia. Now that I know
I'm not a wack job, maybe a bit of good Italian shoesex
dick will coax Lucretia out of whatever shoesex hole she's
fallen into. Maybe all that stuff that Lucretia told me
about how my power's getting stronger will tell me more
about Johnny. I miss him and I miss his dick. Maybe I'm
truly bi, cause there's times I need a dick, and this is one
of those Kodick moments. Lucretia and I have that much
in common. We both do like dick as well as pussy.

I'm horny.

Careful not to wake Ellen, I grab Johnny's plastic Roman
sandals from the chest, careful to avoid Gina's shoes. No
way am I going to try those Pandora's boxes on. I don't
need to see me doing the killing thing. The Colosseum sex,
these silly sandals, are my favorite, not because the sex was
so much better than all the other times but because Johnny
had to run out and find a pair of footwear so we wouldn't
ruin the imprint of our earlier escapade. It was so cute and
so sexy and so caring of him to accommodate my shoesex
demand in such a creative way.

Holding the sandals tight to me, I sneak into the bathroom, sit on the floor and slip the cheap, plastic fuckshoes
on—two people, one body—that old familiar feeling.

It's cool being inside Johnny looking at me. It is like
being there. We're in the Colosseum. I see me smile as he
dangles the sandals in front of my face, and I hear me say,
"Way to go, Johnny. You rule."

Then we high five, a loud, hearty slap, and I can tell
from the smile on my face that I'm thinking of Johnny's

balls banging into my ass. I know that because that's what I was thinking then, but now I'm seeing me thinking it and my dirty smile says it all.

I, that is Johnny, starts to say "Thank—" but I Violetta don't let him finish, and I'm totally there inside him, kissing me, experiencing me trying to rip his lungs out with my tongue.

Fuck do I kiss good.

Back to Johnny.

Violetta, she is insatiable. She's an animal. She's more Italian than American. She is more passionate than Gina. She is more passionate than anyone I've ever made love to. She is wild, wild, wild.

Her hands wrap around my neck and she's lifting herself off the floor by her hands and swinging, and I feel her heat and her body brush against my cock. I'd better put these shoes on, and fast. We'd better not get caught. What would Papa say? What would Gina say? It would be thumbs down and feed me to the lions, that's for sure.

My life is strange. A few days ago I simply tried to make the moves on an American hottie just to pass the time on a long, boring transatlantic flight, now here I am, fucking in the Colosseum, buying plastic fake Roman sandals to wear so she'll have a shoesex record of fucking me. Too fucking strange. Here we are, chasing around Rome for a shoe-repairer who will lead her to the secrets of this amazing power she has. It's almost too silly. No one will ever believe me.

I don't believe me, but what do I care if this is a Fellini movie gone out of control. It sure is fun.

Life is fun. *La dolce vita* for sure.

As we kiss I rip open the bag and manage to bend over to slip the plastic sandals on my feet. I don't bother lacing them up. There's no time. Violetta wants to fuck. She rips open my jeans, popping buttons all over the place like drive-by bullets. The stray cats scram. My dick dives into her palm and it's hard as the Colosseum pillars as she strokes it. I feel her mouth smile as we keep kissing, my cock pulsing to her squeezes. Violetta likes my dick.

She pushes me back up against the wall and lifts her skirt. She lost her panties somewhere back at the Caffè Greco so there's no more undressing required. She wraps her arms around me, hoisting herself on top of me, sinking my dick into her juicy cunt in one swift motion with her feet braced on the wall to the sides of my hips. It's kind of like the way we fucked in the airplane toilet. The woman is amazing—a sexual ath-e-lete—I'd give her a gold medal for fucking and style.

She pumps her pussy up and down my shaft and I feel her slight weight smack against my thighs. I help her squat with my hands on her hips, easing her up and down my erection. *Mamma mia,* it feels so wonderful the ways she slaps her ass into my crotch, squishing her juices onto my thighs, pressing my body into ancient stone that's seen so much bloodshed and fucking.

We kiss violently, drawing our own blood flow from nipped lips, thrusting and parrying like gladiators locked in combat. I pinch Violetta's tits through her sweater, and she pounds into me, slamming her ass down into my crotch like a train. I almost feel like a woman being fucked by a guy the way she pummels me, taking my fist of a cock deep in her cunt so hard I wonder if maybe, just maybe, I could hurt the little shoesex carrier lurking in her womb.

I'm tempted to tell her to take it easy, but her pussy shakes and her body spasms and she explodes. She comes as if it's her last breath, and she cries. She wails. Tears stream out of her like her cuntjuices. She's wet all over, from both ends, soaking me from head to cock. I kiss her neck, stroking her spiky hair. I whisper to her that everything will be all right.

She sobs against me and I hear her whisper "I hope so."

It's then that I know I love her and always have, from the moment I saw her on the plane, we were fated to do this dance.

This is a love to die for.

After it all there is still no Lucretia, just some tears for Johnny. I go back to bed and fall asleep next to Ellen, exhausted, and feeling guilty over my feelings for Johnny. I cuddle up close to Ellen. Her snores rumble through my body, and I feel like a baby in the womb. Maybe I should just kick all this Jack the Ripper crap in the head, talk to Ellen and Johnny about a three-way modern relationship and enjoy life . . .

The phone wakes us. The answering machine kicks in.

"Hello, Ms. Stewart, it's Git Lekerk. I'm the lawyer for the United Convent Charities fleamarket. I handle the estate sales acquisitions. My assistant told—"

Ellen de-spoons me in a flash and grabs the phone. She's all yesses and smiles and makes an appointment for later that afternoon somewhere south of the City. She scribbles directions, and I'm feeling a bit grumpy. Just when I was ready to punch out of all this serial killer of serial killers crap at maximum escape velocity the real world intrudes, just like it always fucking does, crash-landing me back to Earth.

Ellen grabs my hands and we kneel together, touching knees.

"So?" I say, trying to appear not too bummed.

"That was the lawyer for the charities who put on the flea market—"

I nod at the answer machine with a 'Yeah I have ears' look. Suspense I don't need. Ellen continues with a girlish giggle.

"Oh yeah. You heard. Silly me. Well, through all my ex-SFPD contacts I pulled enough strings to trace the paperwork for the boots. Where they came from."

"And, where did they—"

"It's not that simple. There's boxes of documents to go through. He's going to meet us at the document storage facility and we can sort through the records until we find the owner of those boots."

I'm not too thrilled.

"And this will do what for us?"

"It's basic police work. We've got to follow the trail. Who knows what it will tell us. Maybe whoever had those boots knows something about their purpose. It's worth a try."

"I'm not so sure."

"It's better than waiting for your mythical Guardian Angel to wave her magic wand and make it all better. In two weeks time there's supposed to be another two murders—on the same night—the double event. We've got to follow every lead."

Ellen sees my face tense. I set my jaw.

"Oh come on, Violetta. Let's make a day out of it. We can take Luc and have lunch in the City, spend a few hours going through boxes, and if it's a dead end what have we lost but a few hours. And if I'm right and we find out something useful then you have to be my love slave tonight."

Ellen rolls on top of me and tickles my sides. I scream "Uncle," adding "Okay, okay, we'll go." And the tickles turn to caresses and probings, and before I can giggle "Do me, baby," we're fucking again.

And still there's no sign of Lucretia, and I can't help wonder if I'm cured or am I sicker?

CHAPTER TEN

LUNCH AT THE Phoenix is pretty cool. For entertainment we play spot the just-waking-up-rock-star, and the food and drink around the pool is way good, even if the service is a bit 'tudish and slow to boot. Doesn't bother me. San Francisco's having one of those Indian Summer days when it's hot, no fog and we're all wearing light summer clothes that rarely get to go outside without a big heavy coat for just-in-case company.

I'm in no rush to resume my battles with the world. Ellen's bubbling with being hot on the trail of the Ripper boots and Luc's snoozing. I'm feeling pretty fucking mellow and it stays with me through the honk-honk-fuck-you-asshole-and-your-mother traffic to the warehouse in South San Francisco. It's amazing what clarity of mind, a sense of no purpose and a couple of glasses of wine and good food in the sun does for me.

What was it Oscar Wilde said? Looking good is essential in life. Having a purpose is not.

Right on Oscar. Life feels pretty cool. I figure once we're back at the beach and Ellen's got this detective work out of her system I'll spring on her the idea of ditching all this Avenging Angel Sex Goddess crap, with the caveat being letting Johnny into our lives. I'm sure she'll see the win-win side of things. What the fuck—if Lucretia can resign, so can I. Maybe we'll sell the beach house and move to Rome. I can see maybe living in a villa just outside of the Eternal City, eternally happy eating eternally good food and downing eternally good wine, having eternally good sex, between three eternally loving people raising one eternally great kid.

Doesn't get much better than that.

Until this fucking United `Charities' lawyer introduces himself.

"Hello, Ms. Stewart, Ms. Cutrero, I'm Father Git Lekerk."

"You're a priest," I say. "I thought you were a lawyer."

"I'm both. The one does not preclude the other, and truth be told, the one definitely improves the other."

"The lawyer or the priest?" I say, and Ellen casts me one of those "be good, Violetta Valery" glances.

Father Git laughs, and it's the kind of forced smile that gives me the creeps. It reminds me of the curl of a snake's mouth just before it strikes.

"Ladies, if you'll follow me I'll take you to the document storage area."

He ushers us into a corridor and speeds ahead to open another door, which he holds open with that same about-to-strike smile. We walk in.

It's dark.

Father Git says it'll take him a second to flick on the lights.

It does.

The snake strikes.

There's no boxes of documents. No file cabinets. Just a big old warehouse, a few packing crates, a limousine, a couple of priests, a nun, and several goons with guns.

I grip Luc's stroller tight. Where are you Lucretia? If ever I needed my supernatural powered Guardian Angel it's now. I look at Ellen. She looks at me. We both turn to face the door, which Father Git slams shut.

"I wouldn't try to escape," the lawyer-priest says, his threatening smile now wiped clean by a pursed set of lips. "We don't want to hurt you, but if we have to—"

He nods at the goons with guns.

"We will."

"What do you want?" Ellen says.

"The child," says Father Git, and it takes me a few nano-seconds to register that he means Luc. Then my maternal instinct synapses fire. I scream and strike out at him, lunging for his clerical collar. Ellen covers my back, but the goons are all over us, wrestling us to the ground before we can do any damage.

"Tie them up," I hear Father Git order as he straightens his robes and his shellacked gray hair. The goons proceed to rope us, copping many a good feel in the process. Thanks to the heat I'm only wearing a light dress, so it's nothing for the goons to feel my pussy and tits as they tie the knots. I wouldn't relish being left alone with these characters.

"You won't get away with this," Ellen clichés. "I have a lot of friends in the SFPD."

Ellen's wearing shorts, so they don't give her much of a feel, except they squeeze her ass, and when they tie her arms behind her back they rough up her tits, pulling her bra up and over her breasts so the underwire cuts into her flesh. These are not sensitive men.

Father Git looks on as if he's saying a great big thank you to the Holy Father, his hands pressed together as he admires what I hope isn't his goons' idea of foreplay.

"I doubt that you'll go to the police."

It's then that I notice that Luc's crying. Father Git notices it too and motions for the nun to go over to my son. She takes him out of the stroller and holds him close to her. He keeps crying.

I struggle.

"You're not going to take my son and molest him like you do all those other little boys."

Father Git gives an angry nod and a goon gives me a backhand across the face. I spit out blood, but I don't cry. I won't give them satisfaction. Ellen struggles.

"Leave her alone. You shouldn't—"

"Then she should learn not to besmirch the Catholic Church with her blasphemies, and keep her tabloid opinions to herself."

Father Git turns to me.

"Don't you worry, Ms. Cutrero, about Luc being subjected to sexual abuse. Sister Teresa will take good care of Luc. He'll be safer with us than with you and the world of depravity you would inevitably have exposed him to and perhaps already have. Indeed, given the evil toxicity of your power, the world will be safer with him with us rather than with you."

Sister Teresa? Sister Teresa? Where have I heard of Sister—?

"Since the unfortunate bride of Christ was defiled by the child's father she has been doing penitence for her sexual exposure and is highly motivated to see that the child does not follow in either his father or mother's lascivious ways."

Father Git motions to the limo. Sister Teresa nods, and her eyes meet mine, and then I put two and two together and come up with the size five ballet bondage shoes that sit in my closet.

She's the nun that seduced Tony, and I've been inside her soles many times playing through that shoesex scene. Fuck me, when Tony first exposed me to it I was tied up, and now here I am again.

The world does go in too small circles, and this is all too fucking weird. The circles are spiraling in. I'm reeling but I won't go quietly.

"He didn't defile her she defiled him. She and those nuns were charged with bringing up a troubled boy and they turned him in to their dildo. They were the rapists. As were the priests that came later."

"Shut up, Ms. Cutrero, and listen, and be careful. Your bodies could be put in those packing crates and shipped to some remote Catholic parish for burial. No one would notice. No one would care."

"Fuck you."

Ellen looks at me, as much to say cool it.

"We would be missed. Like I said, I have friends in the SFPD," Ellen says, emphasizing SFPD like it's a reminder she's not to be fucked with. Father Git nods at her.

"Ah, yes, Chief Detective Michael Donovan. A nice boy for a homosexual, but let me tell you why he wouldn't miss you, and why you will not run to him if we let you go unharmed. Let me tell you why you will keep quiet and let us take Luc away from your depravity, and why it is the best course of action for all concerned, especially Luc."

"I'm all fucking ears," I say.

"And you're all fucking mouth too," Father Git says. "Gag them both," he says to the goons, and they do their efficient best, enjoying much tit squeezing and cunt fondling as they silence our mouths.

"Pay close attention. I'll only say this once."

Through the gag I mumble "get on with it," which prompts one of the Father Git goons to force his hands between my bound legs, squeezing my cunt hard, sticking a finger into my asshole. Doesn't even wet his dirty digit. Ouch. I'm feeling a bit biblical—Lucretia, why have you deserted me so?

Father Git must be the real deal since it seems he can read minds, or at least has an uncanny sense of timing, or a direct line to the beings upstairs or downstairs that are privy to all us mere mortals' thoughts.

Notice I lumped myself in with the rest of you. Right now I'm not feeling very Avenging Angel Sex Goddess supernatural. I'm feeling very ordinary, especially after his next pronouncement.

"I wouldn't expect rescuing by your Guardian Angel, Lucretia, the mother of all this evil. She has been exorcised from the limbo torment in which she has reigned for almost two centuries. She has passed on, and we have you, Violetta, to thank for delivering her to us. We knew that neither you nor she would be able to resist the evil in those boots."

I feel very less than ordinary.

"It was a simple matter to make sure they came into your possession. It was just a question of time and being patient. We couldn't just send them in the mail or leave them on your doorstep. You would have been too suspicious. It took several tries until Ms. Stewart, rather than you took the bait at the flea market. Once in your hands we knew you wouldn't be able to resist their evil allure."

Ellen looks sorry. I try to give a 'don't be—not your fault' response.

"The Vatican Dark Museum and Special Investigations Protectorate houses quite a collection of instruments and accouterments of evil. The boots of Jack the Ripper—or should I say Dr. Francis Tumblety came into our possession when he died at St. John's Hospital in St. Louis—an institution run by the Sisters of Mercy. Tumblety was an American doctor with a pathological hatred of women, especially prostitutes, fueled by the discovery that his bride was and had been throughout their courtship and short marriage—a streetwalker. Tumblety confessed to the good Sisters of Mercy and they passed what belongings of his they couldn't sell to help with the running of the charitable hospital on to the Vatican along with his confession."

So that's who Margaret was and why Jack a.k.a. Francis kept invoking her name. Much makes sense now, although a lot of good it'll do us. Somehow writing a book revealing the true identity of Jack the Ripper doesn't seem so attractive anymore.

Father Git suffers from the verbal diarrhea afflicting most villains confronting their nemeses.

"Throughout centuries of battling evil we have learned that the most effective weapons against darkness are the very tools of evil—therein lies the means to defeat even the most pernicious force. As you have no doubt discovered, the boots contained Tumblety's evil essence, which as Lucretia no doubt explained is passed on and grows stronger with each new crime. That is why this shoesex power must be stopped. It grew out of a crime and has been sex and violence's unwitting accomplice for centuries. You might have thought you were fighting evil. Far from it. You were simply just another form of evil that we on God's side must stop."

I can't resist a snicker. Father Git raises his voice and points his finger in a way that makes me think he's been watching too much evangelical television.

"If you doubt our most righteous and earnest motivation then witness the crimes you caused and the murders you committed."

Ellen looks at me with wide eyes. I shrug my shoulders as best I can.

"I can imagine you're confused, and you, Ms. Stewart, are plotting how to invoke your SFPD connections as soon as we free you. Well, as I promised, you will not. Here is why."

Father Git snaps his fingers and the limo drives over to us. A goon opens the door. Inside sits Sister Teresa with Luc. Like this is news. Are they threatening Luc to keep us quiet?

Once again, Father Git displays that keen sense of aplomb that's obviously got him into the Chief Asshole position he so relishes.

"We are not so silly nor so hoodlum-like as to resort to simple threats on Luc's safety. I am a priest and we have and are bound by the laws of God, which transcend those of man."

Knowing I'll get more anal probing I can't resist a mumbled guffaw. It works. And I get a rough finger stuffed into my pussy as a bonus. The goon squeezes his fingers together, and I'm tearing and sniffling. I should learn to keep my mumbles to myself. Yeah, not me. May as well ask the Pope to sanction abortion and gay priests marrying.

"Please pay attention to the video monitor. Sister Teresa, please press play."

The goons prop Ellen and me up, and my goon keeps his fingers in my ass and cunt. I feel like a frigging finger puppet.

A video plays. It's a black and white surveillance tape.

"I'm sure you'll recognize this alley, Violetta. It is the alley in which you killed that young hustler. Watch carefully."

All fight flees from me as I see myself perform as I saw in the Ripper boots. Every detail, down to the ritual evisceration, in glorious black and white. Ellen flashes from the slasher movies scene to me and back.

Father Git enjoys our quaking foundations as much as any San Francisco temblor.

"I'll save you the pain of protesting that the video is a fake. It is from one of the Church's cameras—as you know the Saint Anthony's Dining Room abuts this alley. The police with all of their Silicon Valley technology would be quickly able to vouch for the tape's horrible authenticity, and I believe, Ms. Cutrero, you know that this tape is a correct record of your crime. There is also a tape of the first murder you committed on August 29."

I nod. I know it's true. It's why I saw it through the Ripper shoesex. The boots made me, through Lucretia, walk and kill. Ellen looks at me with something bordering on dismay and disgust.

Father Git presses his advantage. He's obviously a firm believer in the old adage of the ruling elite—'kick 'em when they're down.'

"Should you attempt in anyway to recover Luc or go to the authorities this tape will be given to the police. Ms. Stewart's testimony that you were involved in a passionate embrace at the time of the murder will hold little weight, especially when it comes to light that she has already covered up your earlier horrible and all too similar crime in the slaying of Randall Warren also known as Mark Dearside also known as the Dildo Killer."

How the fuck did he know that? I close my eyes. Father Git sniffs victory.

"I think they've seen enough."

I open my eyes as Father Git steps into the limousine and sits next to Sister Teresa. They make such a cute couple with my baby. My sniffles turn to full out sobs.

Father Git can't resist a parting shot.

"In time you will see that this is for the best, Violetta. Luc will never know his sordid origins. He will grow up as a ward of the Church and will lead a normal life in some faraway land. This hideous perversion of natural law that you call shoesex ends here, and with it further crimes. With Lucretia no more and all of your relatives deceased there can be no more heirs. Should you have another child, which we hope you do to replace this loss, he or she will be normal, conceived with someone not of your cursed bloodline. The Cutrero curse will die with you, Violetta. You should feel relieved. You are free. You still have your perverse power, but you don't have the worry of what will happen to your son. You can dabble if you wish, but I think after today you will have lost your desire to practice unnatural acts. You and Ms. Stewart can live happily ever after, although not in the confines of a wholesome, blessed Catholic marriage."

He nods at his goons and then at his driver. With a flash of that snakish smile he slams the limo door shut and the car drives off. A roll-up door automatically opens and then closes.

Ellen and I are alone with the goons. I wonder if they're going to kill us. I look at Ellen, my eyes communicating my concern. The goon with his hand up my ass and cunt answers my obvious worry by whispering in my ear, loud enough for all his goon buddies to hear.

"Father Git says you're possessed with a satanic power to feel people fucking in their shoes. That if you're wearing shoes when you're fucked that you experience it over and over until the shoes come off."

He laughs.

"So since you can't go to the cops and complain about anything we do, then you're gonna get the gangbang of your life, you little bitch, and just be thankful that we're connected to the Church wouldn't be right for us to kill you."

So I should be thankful for small mercies—makes me think of Sisters of Mercy. I hum Lucretia My Reflection as the big goon pulls his fingers out of my ass and cunt and stands over me.

"Untie her. Hold her arms and legs. I'll go first. We'll take turns. Do the same with the other dyke. Keep them gagged. I don't want them making too much noise."

In my years of experiencing shoesex I've footed my way through several nasty rapes. Perhaps the most notable and nasty was being inside Lucretia when Rictius Varus had his Roman way with her and her brothers. Then there were all the Dildo Killer's cruel escapades, but this is the first time it's been for real. Let's just say that it's true—the rape fantasy of being taken by an anonymous roughster is a big turn on—the gangbang scenario can also be cunt-wetting. Some women really get off on the whole being a slavegirl used and abused by a powerful lord thing. All good fun stuff. Works both ways too. I know some men get off imagining they're raping someone or being taken by a good strong Amazon woman. Again, harmless fun, because we all know it's fantasy and all's fair between consenting adults and their libidinous imaginations. In reality, rape is not about sex and coming and having a good time—it's about power and assault and is violence perpetrated on someone against her or his will.

All this goes through my mind as I lie there limply as the goons pull my panties off, rip open my dress and spread wide my legs, making sure they leave my Keds on.

The big goon slobbers like he's being offered a free beer.

"She's a real little cutie this one. Looks like she's all of thirteen. Nice little titties. This is gonna be sweet."

Nice to know I still have my youthful looks. I turn my

gagged head to the side and look at Ellen. She's struggling, which, when there's this many of them, only makes it worse. One goon slaps her, and she stops resisting, perhaps realizing it's gonna happen and may as well get out of this with as few bruises and scars as possible—at least on the physical side. Then we'll figure out how to get even, and retribution will help with the emotional healing. There has to be a way to get Luc back and make Father Git Lekerk, Sister Teresa and all their goon cronies pay or my name isn't Violetta Valery Cutrero—Avenging Angel Sex Goddess.

The goons rip Ellen's shorts and panties off. She's wearing the tartan Doc Martins I bought her for her last birthday so she swings her feet at the goons trying to kick the creeps away. They swat her legs down like annoying little insects and give her a slap for her efforts. Her eyes close screwed tight, but as they tear open her blouse she opens her eyes to look at me. Her face is a mask of misery and terror, so I try to give her a reassuring smile in between my sniffles, but I don't think it works. She closes her eyes and her bra is already pushed up above her breasts, so all the foreplay is over.

It's time to get fucked

My one consolation is that none of these goons will last very long. What is there—ten of them? I doubt they get much sex beyond the pumping of their hands. Should all be over with in twenty minutes—half-an-hour tops. I doubt too many of them will have the fortitude to do both Ellen and me, so it could be over quick. At least for Ellen. For me it will go on until the Keds come off or the cows come home.

The big goon drops his pants and pushes his underwear down to his ankles. He strokes his cock and tells me how good it's gonna feel.

Yeah, right, but then it also dawns on me—like,

Violetta, why make this so horrible? I hum the bassline from Lucretia My Reflection, and even though she's not with me, I hear My Lucretia whispering in my ear. She endured a rape and got the better of her attackers. So can I. I'll pretend that these goons are my fuckbuddies, and we're gonna have us a party. Shit, I've done enough shoesex scenes like this that it should be a nice, juicy piece of cuntcake to pull it off. I'll just pretend that these guys are my fuckslaves, and I'm making them fuck me. It'll get my cunt wetter and get them off faster. Yeah, big boy, it's gonna feel real good.

He kneels between my legs and instead of struggling I arch my back a little so my cunt thrusts forward. He licks his fingers with a big gob of saliva and rubs them up and down my pussy.

Doesn't feel too bad. His technique could do with a bit of refinement, but I've had worse. He's sure not up to Johnny's standard, but he'll pass in the juicing department.

"The bitch is a juicy cunt," he says to his goon buddies. They all chuckle, adding a few encouragements to get a move on cause they want some of that juicy twat. Ellen's goons note that she's not as ready, so big goon jokes that he'll be over to warm her up once he's done with me.

More laughing.

Big goon doesn't waste much time easing it in. He pries open my cunt lips and slides his cock in with a lunge of his weight, which knocks the wind out of me.

Enjoy it, enjoy it, enjoy it, I tell myself, thinking of all the good sex Johnny and I have enjoyed.

Big goon thrusts in and out and I wiggle my hips and clench my butt so that my cunt tenses and gives him all that extra stimulation.

"She's a regular little whore, this one. She fucks good."

As I work my body with big goon's thrustings his goon henchmen grip my legs and arms tight thinking that I'm maybe resisting. It's like being tied up and fucked, so it feels kinda sexy to have these strong hands holding me down and spread wide while being fucked so roughly. Yeah, it gets me wet. I hear my juices slopping around as big goon ruts into me. I'm slathering up a girljuice storm.

Big goon sweats like a steelworker, and it rains on my tits, big thunderspots. He looks at the drops and like the gentleman he undoubtedly is, he licks them off, taking the opportunity to give my tender tit flesh some bruising love bites. When he snaps at my nipples I can't help doing a muffled ouch, which makes my body buck and writhe, which certainly excites the big goon a lot, and makes his henchmen rough me down. He fucks me with short, rabbit like thrusts, and his balls bounce against my ass, slapping in my juices, and his thick cock swells, filling me solid, and he comes, lunging deep as he squirts, ramming his dick up into my cervix, giving my G spot a thorough bruising as his dick plunders by.

I feel a little coming coming on, which makes me feel good and makes the promise of more rough cock not seem so bad. My orgasm quickly subsides as he bites my neck and whispers what a great fuck I was. How he'd give me his number cause he's sure I'll want more someday, but it'll have to end here. Business is business, and he doesn't want to see my skinny little girl ass around here or the Church again or he won't be so nice next time.

He pulls out with a flop, and strokes his cock to try and keep it hard for Ellen.

Couldn't have been more than two minutes. Just like a minor penalty in hockey—two minutes in the box and then it's back on the ice to hit, shoot, and score again. One down, nine to go.

Not quite. This is where shoesex kicks in. I'm watching big goon tell the goon fucking Ellen to take a break while he warms her up but good, and there's another one taking his pants off to do me when I'm back at the beginning of my ordeal with them ripping off my clothes and big goon rubbing my juicy twat. Then there's another cock going in and more biting of my tits and I'm overdosing on dick and rough sex and I'm actually coming, not just little tremors but fucking great big cuntquakes that could topple buildings.

It never stops. Each cock builds on the last, merging with every fucking and coming and tit mauling, and it's like I'm taking ten cocks at a time, all up my juicy cunt, coming in tidal waves, and I understand how Lucretia was able to channel all of Rictius Varus' vileness into her single-minded determination to overcome her attackers through being an Avenging Angel Sex Goddess, and then it stops.

It takes me a while to catch my breath and figure out where I am.

I'm still on the warehouse floor. So is Ellen. We're both a naked mess. We're both tied up again. One of my Keds is off. Maybe it came off in all my thrashing.

Ellen sees me looking at the sneaker.

"I kicked it off," Ellen says. "I rolled on the ground and got next to you and suffered through all your contortions until I got lucky with my kicking to dislodge your tennis shoe."

"How long was I in the shoesex?" I say.

Ellen can hardly speak.

"Not sure. I passed out. A couple of hours maybe. Before they left I heard them say that they'd be back to let us go once you'd had enough of a warning. They don't want us being found here. Too many questions, so we can just wait until they return. Shouldn't be long."

"Fuck that," I say. "Let's try to untie each other. I'm not

sure I buy all this crap about how they won't kill us. It doesn't make any sense. Why would they keep us alive?"

"If anything happened to me Michael wouldn't stop until he found out what happened. They can't risk it."

"Any how are you going to keep what happened to you here quiet from him? If you're that close he'll sense something's up."

"I have to. It's part of the deal. We keep quiet—they leave us alone. I just want this to end."

"Well then let's end this now on our terms and not wait for those romantics to return. You roll on your side, and I'll do the side, sort of in a reverse spoon, and we can fiddle with the knots. I got enough finger strength to do it, and I know you do."

Ellen sinks to the ground. She's exhausted.

"Come on, Ellen. Let's not waste any fucking time. We gotta figure out how to get Luc back. If those fuckers think that one little gangbang rape by the Big Goon Gang is gonna stop me they got another thing coming. Lucretia might be gone, but she taught me well. Shoesex was born in a rape. It ain't gonna end in one. These feet cannot be denied."

Ellen bursts into tears.

CHAPTER ELEVEN

ELLEN'S A BASKET case, and I'm her basket. She's losing it bigtime.

I'm not surprised. Shoesex has seen me through some pretty fucked-up fucks. So this goon gang gangbang rape wasn't so bad.

For me.

For Ellen, the lesbian ex-cop, it had to have been just about the worst thing in the world.

She's hysterical, but I manage to get her to focus on untying my hands by kicking her with my bound legs while telling her I love her.

Tough love, yeah, that's my other middle name.

Once we're free I prop Ellen up with her arm around me and I steer her out of the warehouse until I realize I've forgotten something. Taking more time than it should to make Ellen realize that I'm not leaving her, I position her against the wall next to a file cabinet, and yelling that I'll be right back I run to the corner where we'd been raped and I retrieve what I'd never let those fucker steal.

Hear me well. I will need it again soon—very soon.

It's Luc's stroller. If it had been a bit bigger it might have been some use in getting Ellen out to the Jeep, because she loses it even more when she sees me coming over to her with the empty kidmover. It takes all my strength to lead the crying and shaking Ellen out and steer the stroller, and then it takes every ounce of concentration and determination to drive back to Stinson, while cradling Ellen to me, absorbing her shuddering sobs and muttering incoherences.

I soothe and Valium Ellen to sleep. As she's nodding out I tell her we can't go to the police or a hospital, so she's stuck with me as a nurse. She chuckles through her tears and I feel a bit better as her eyes finally close and she breathes deep.

I know we'll get through this.

Once I'm sure she's sound asleep I make the call.

It's early morning in Italy.

I don't waste time on pleasantries.

"Salvatore, we have big fucking problems."

Punctuated by a fusillade of Italian expletives and curses I clue-in my Lowest Soles contact as to the antics of the RCC Mafia.

"How do you feel?" Salvatore says.

"Pissed off. Really pissed off. You know, I'd almost got to the point of saying let's jack this shoesex thing in, move to Italy, and live a nice, peaceful life—Johnny, Ellen. Luc and me, with you dropping around for grappa in the evenings."

He chuckles.

"Yes, but the feet cannot be denied."

"Don't I fucking know it."

Salvatore's comment isn't lost on me. The nastiest things have always happened to me and my loved ones when I've been on the verge of—one way or another—quitting. Well, no chance of that now. The stakes have been upped. This is do it or die trying time.

"What are my options? Where would they have taken Luc?"

"The Lowest Soles have many contacts throughout Rome. We will go into action immediately, but the fact that we had heard nothing of this highly planned and coordinated action indicates that it is well protected. We usually know more than the Pope, but I fear our chances or finding out where Luc is are slim. We will try though. In the meantime you must concentrate on bringing Lucretia back. As suspicious as I am of her, she is our best bet."

"Hello, Salvatore, she is dead as a pair of Birkenstocks on a hippy."

"So says this Father Git Lekerk. They may have exorcised her into exile. They have not and could not kill her. Lucretia is a powerful pagan. That is why the Church is so scared of her and you. They may think they have killed her, but I will bet my best pair of shoes that she is waiting for you, her true and only descendant to free her."

"But the caliges are useless."

"Of course, and so they will forever be thanks to those Ripper boots. Whatever exorcism mass they used, those boots were the agent. It gave her the power to walk in your name and perform those murders—the trap for both you and her."

"Those boots are duds too until the time of a Ripper murder. Fuck, I don't have to wait until the next Ripper offing to free her, do I?"

"No, that self-same evil is exorcised with her."

"Wow, you mean Lucretia's locked in some shoe hell with Jack the Ripper and fuck knows however many other serial killers?"

"Yes."

"Fuck."

"Exactly. But all is not lost. Lucretia was not stupid. She will have left you a portal to her—an escape route—a safety line—a pair of shoes in which she appeared to you and no one else knows about them."

"Besides the caliges—"

"Think, Violetta, there must be a pair—"

"We spent weeks going through all my old shoes but there's nothing new that . . . "

My voice trails off. There is a pair. Gina's death shoes. No one but me, Lucretia and six-feet-under-joined-the-choir-invisible-pushing-up-the-daisies Gina knows about what's in them. Thank you Johnny. Thank you Gina. Thank you Lucretia.

"Thank you Salvatore. There is one pair."

"Don't thank me. It will be hard. The sex you have in the shoes will either free Lucretia or perhaps enslave her forever by writing over her experience. You simply can't put these shoes on and hope to free her. It will need much strong sexual energy. I'm sure Johnny would fly over in the blink of a wink. You will only have the one chance."

I could not involve Johnny in the shoefuck where Lucretia and I killed his girlfriend.

"No, Salvatore, I don't want to involve him in this right now. Please don't tell him. I don't want him getting hurt."

"But is your girlfriend up to the task after her ordeal?"

I look over at the darkened bedroom where Ellen sleeps.

"She will be."

And after I'd hung up the phone I spoke to the slumbering Ellen.

"She has to be. She'd better be."

I snuggle up close to Ellen's warmth and she doesn't resist. She doesn't jump away in fright. This is a good sign. Perhaps she's glad of the warmth. Perhaps she's just so out of it she doesn't know what's happening.

Okay, call me evil but I get horny.

I pull myself close to Ellen, stroking the violin curve of her waist to her hips, and I go from that delicious curve to the swell of my pussy lips and the bulge of my clit and I flick it to and fro as I rock Ellen in her slumber. I think of all that's happened and I figure this is my way of dealing with the gang rape—I make it a fuck fantasy—and maybe if I'm good at it I can absorb all Ellen's pain and make her see that things aren't so bad if we can just fuck our problems away. Sex solves everything. It really does. Sex heals

I imagine a time when I've got Luc back and Johnny is his dashing father and Ellen's my sexy partner and we enjoy great sex together in a big bed in a small Italian village where people turn a blind eye to such strange relationships. I feel Johnny's cock in my hand as Ellen slides her fingers inside me, and we alternate kisses. Ellen takes Johnny's cock and places it in my wetted opening and nudges him inside. She sits on my face and faces Johnny, who arches up from kissing my breasts to kiss her, and as he fucks me I eat Ellen, and we join as one coming sex machine, and Johnny's seed, full of all that love, gets me pregnant, and Luc will have a sister, and Luc and her will never fuck and the curse will end in a good way, killed by love rather than hate.

I come on my fingers, smearing my juices on Ellen's butt.

Wake up Ellen, the future's calling.

CHAPTER TWELVE

I'M VERY PATIENT. I let Ellen snore off the Valium. Truth be told, it's not like I have a choice. Honestly, I wasn't patient. Numerous times I tried waking her to fuck the living shit out of her but she was dead to the world, and I don't think necrophilia qualified under Salvatore's prescription for lusty sex to raise Lucretia from her shoesex limbo. No matter how many times I tried to pry Ellen's thighs apart or squeeze her ass and tits she remained clamped shut and sleeping. So, I said fuck it, she's just been gang raped, Ellen deserves her rest.

I kill the frustrating hours by examining Gina's shoes. I stare at my reflection in the black patent leather slip-ons but no fucking way do I put them on. Salvatore was very specific. The shoes need to be worn during hot and heavy sex to bring out Lucretia, and it can only be done once, since the sex will blend with and dilute the original experience. I know this is my one chance. I don't want to fuck it up, so I look at my reflection, remembering those few minutes in the bathroom at the Rome airport that seemed like a lifetime and were for Gina, trying to Zen my way through the wait for Ellen to wake up in a horny morning mood.

In between contemplating the reliving of Gina's murder I can't help thinking about Johnny. It was so tempting to take Salvatore up on his offer of dispatching Stateside the gorgeous Mr. Gianni. No doubt he would have fulfilled the hot and heavy sex prescription in the bob of his hefty erection. It would have also been nice to have him here, not just to fuck, but to friend, because I know it's gonna get very nasty and weird around me, and I'm not sure of Ellen's fortitude after what she's been through. I might be an Avenging Angel Sex Goddess, but I need the occasional shoulder to cry on and someone to hold me and tell me it will be all right. I also know I can't take the chance of involving Johnny too deeply. Too many people close to me have died or could die, and I want him around for the future. And oh fuck, yeah, here's the real reason. Let me be perfectly honest. I can't involve Johnny in the shoefuck murder of his old girlfriend. He'd ask questions about the shoes, especially since I told him there was nothing in them that I could sense, and I'm not sure I could lie to him face-to-face convincingly enough.

Thinking of Johnny makes me dreamy and exhaustion catches up to me. I sleep fitfully, waking often, looking over at Ellen, wishing her awake. I try every possible bed-terrorist technique—tossing and turning, figuring that the motions might disturb her, sighing loudly, pulling the covers, even farting. Nothing works. In one of my rotations I notice that it's getting light and my gaze falls on Luc's empty crib, and I choke back tears, tempted to shake Ellen into fucking so we can get to the business of getting my son back.

Frustrated, I shake myself out of bed and stomp to the kitchen, making as much noise as possible. I talk loudly to Spykes, making him yowl for his food. I fire up the cappuccino machine and steam the milk several times, making the biggest gurgling sounds I can in our echoy kitchen.

It works. Ellen limps into the kitchen, yawning. I pour her a coffee.

"How do you feel?"

"Like shit."

"We have to fuck."

"What?"

Okay, it wasn't the most enticing and romantic of approaches but I am way past lighting candles and sipping on fine wine listening to mood music. I put my arms around Ellen's neck.

"We have to fuck. I talked to the Lowest Soles. There's a way to bring Lucretia back, but it involves us having hot and heavy sex in a particular pair of shoes and—"

Ellen pushes me away, sits and stares at her cappo mug, sipping in between more unbelieving stares.

"Have you forgotten what happened yesterday? I was fucking raped. Many times. And you want me to have sex today. Are you crazy as well as insensitive?"

She slams her cappuccino down and it splashes over the table. I grab her shaking hand.

"I know it's a lot to ask."

"Damn right."

"But it's the only way to get Luc back."

Ellen breathes deep and locks her narrowed eyes on to me. It's that look of hers that I don't like seeing. It means trouble.

"You may not want to hear this, but maybe what has happened was for the best."

I know what she means but I'll be fucked if I play that game.

"Gang raped by a bunch of goons was for the best?"

Now it's Ellen's turn to squeeze my hand.

"No. The ending of all this shoesex madness. Lucretia laid to rest. Luc will never know."

I swat her hand away sending the coffee cup shattering against the wall. Spykes runs from the room yowling as I yell.

"Luc will never know his mother. Me. Whose fucking side are you on?"

"I'm on yours. I know what you're going through."

"No you don't."

"Oh I do. I love you, and I feel your pain, and I know you love me, but you can't feel mine. You want to have sex and hope that this evil ancestor will bring back Luc. It will just bring more killing. I don't want to see you in jail. I can't keep saving you."

"I don't want you to save me. That's the problem. I don't need saving. I don't need mothering. I need helping. I need hot and heavy sex to get my kid back."

"I can't give you that. Not now. You'd have to take it, and I don't think you'd want to see me raped again."

"No I wouldn't, but if you can't help me, I'll find someone who will."

I stand and head to the bedroom. Ellen comes in just as I'm throwing a bag together.

"Where are you going?"

"To get fucked."

"Please, don't. Stay with me. Hold me."

I stand my ground. No way am I giving hugs to make her feel better at having refused to help me. I gotta stay strong. If she puts her arms around me I might just melt and burst in to tears and lose my resolve. I gotta be mean.

"No way, Ellen. I have to go. I love you, but this isn't about love. It's about duty. It's about the feet not being denied. I hope you can see that. I've explained this to you so many times. You say you understand it but I don't know if you do. I want this fuck to be with you, but if you can't do it, shit, I understand, but don't stand in my way."

"How can you do this to me?"

"Don't play the martyr. I have to get my son back. You should be asking yourself how you can do this to me."

"Then let's try talking to Michael. We'll explain. He'll understand. He'll help us."

"And I'll end up in jail where I can do no good. No way. I can't take that chance. It's like you said. 'It's part of the deal. We keep quiet and stay out of jail.' So we do this the feet's way. My way. Lucretia's way."

"Violetta, don't walk out on me now."

"I'm not walking out on you. This is my duty as an Avenging Angel Sex Goddess. I told you when we got involved, and I've told you many time since. There are times I will have to do nasty and dangerous things. I don't particularly want to go and fuck a stranger for this important moment. I'd much rather it was you, but I know it's tough, and I understand. So why can't you? The feet can't be denied."

Ellen's in tears.

"Maybe it's time to hang up your Avenging Angel Sex Goddess shoes and try to build a normal life with me. We can start a normal family. I'm not too old and you can have more kids. Michael would donate his sperm."

"Fuck, Ellen, you got it all figured out, don't you, except go figure this. This—"

I point to my feet.

"These—are what I am and what I do. And you have my word that once this is done we will work on building a normal life. Maybe even get away from here. I've been thinking more and more about quitting, but not now, not like this. I can't just give up my son to a bunch of child molesting religious perverts."

Ellen's sobs shake our house. I put my hands on her shoulders.

"I've got to go now while I still can, but know I will be back to be with you. Luc and I and you will be a family once this is all over. But I have to do it my way."

I figure now is not the time to mention bringing Johnny into our lives, so I shut up and kiss Ellen on the cheek. She stops crying long enough to say, "I'm not sure I'll be here when you get back."

Far from wrecking me, her ultimatum steels me. My body stiffens but then I speak softly because I know Ellen's hurting. I squeeze Ellen's hand.

"I hope you will be. I love you."

I kiss Ellen on the lips. She reciprocates and pulls away. She cries. I walk away, petting Spykes as I leave the house. He purrs and rubs against my legs. He understands. He would. He's as much of a Cutrero as me. He's Crista's cat. He knows that the feet, or in his case, the paws, cannot be denied.

Crista would have understood too. I'm sure it was she that brought Johnny and I together for that amazing fuck in the deserted restaurant. She knew the value of sex as both a weapon and a shield. She's looking after me and will see me right through this ordeal.

I think of that fuck, of being bent over with people just a few feet away, Johnny's hard meat slapping into me, my ass cheeks shaking as he pulls me into him. It was so exciting. So intense. It was perfect, and I wish to Crista that she finds me something like that now so I can bring Lucretia back.

I feel my cunt juice at the thought of such sex, and I pause on our walkway, hoping I'll hear Ellen calling for me to run back and fuck the living shit out of her, but all I hear are the seagulls' maniacal cries, and I know I've got to find my fuck elsewhere.

I don't like doing this.

Ellen should understand my needs and not drive me to go looking for fucks. It's a dangerous world out there, and I don't have a Guardian Angel anymore.

I look back at the house one last time, wondering if I'll ever see it or Ellen again.

CHAPTER THIRTEEN

I'M SHAKING. I'M stunned. I'm a fucking zombie.

Thank the traffic gods that my little pink Bug knows the way to the City because I'm in the kind of daze where making turns, signaling, braking and mundane crap like that just doesn't seem so important. I really thought Ellen would see me right. I blast Sisters of Mercy's *A Slight Case of Overbombing* CD—the "Under The Gun" track over and over because the lyrics about love being strong enough when the road gets too tough really strike home.

Well, Ellen, is your love strong enough or are you just a pussy who won't give pussy when it's needed? Fuck, Ellen's tude just doesn't make sense, and don't give me that crap about her being raped the night before. We've been through worse in our shoesex life together, and it's not like she doesn't know the score. We both went through the ordeal of the goon gangbang, and I lost my kid, so who the fuck is more traumatized. At least I have a plan.

Do I?

Where am I going to get hot, intense sex and it isn't even noon yet? Since having Luc I've been so out of touch with the San Francisco sex scene. I'd be hard pressed to know where to go to pick up somebody but hey, bars are bars. Names and owners change but they're still the places people go to watch sports, make bets and connections, drown their sorrows and if they're lucky seek solace in the genitals of another. Yeah, Violetta, but think of the loser denizens to be found at this time of day in a bar—drunks—that's who, and those one step away from twelve steps aren't known for their sexual stamina, so despite feeling like I need a good stiff drink to go with a good stiff clit or dick chaser I resort to the old standbys.

I park the bug in North Beach and sip a mocha cappo at Caffe Trieste while I skim through the *Spectator* weekly contact newspaper purchased for all my stash of quarters from a skanky anonymous newsrack. I gloss over all the cheesy ads for strip clubs, massage parlors and dungeons because unless I'm extremely lucky I don't think I'll find extraordinary sex at the receiving end of a bunch of dollars.

No, I need someone who needs to fuck, who wants to fuck, and real soon to boot. I don't want a jaded professional. I want an enthusiastic amateur who gives it all and leaves all reserve at the door. In this Baghdad by the Bay, this Sin Francisco there has to be someone who is horny as all get out by noon on a weekday.

Someone? As I scan the contact ads I realize I don't even know what gender I want. A woman would probably be a safer bet, but fuck, thinking of Johnny really makes me want a good, thick, stiff dick.

As to be expected there's an overdose of Men Seeking

Women ads and since this home of the Forty Niners is the same sex capital of America there's almost as many Women Seeking Women and Men Seeking Men. The City should rename the football team the Sixty Niners.

I can't choose.

I'm on the verge of tossing the *Spectator* when I realize I don't have to make a choice. There's a bunch of Couples Seeking Others ads and midway down I find my Holy Grail.

KAMA SUTRA WITH US—ADVENTURESOME ATTRACTIVE COUPLE—HE INDIAN, SHE SWEDISH—SEEKS SLIM, GORGEOUS BI-FEMALE FOR INTENSE SPIRITUAL SEX. AFTERNOONS AND EVENINGS AT OUR TEMPLE OF SEXUAL WORSHIP. ENJOY NIRVANA ON EARTH THROUGH OUR POWERFUL TANTRIC ENERGY CHANNELING. NO PROFESSIONALS OR MONEY SEEKERS OR NEGATIVE ENERGY TYPES PLEASE.

Well fuck me, Ghandi. My lower chakras are definitely open. I dial the number feeling much that pretty soon I'm gonna be pumping my fist towards the ground screaming "she shoots, she scores."

The phone rings a few times. A sexy sounding Euro voice answers, slightly out of breath.

"Hello?"

"I called about your ad in the *Spectator*. "

"Yes, we've been expecting you."

"You have?"

"Yes, we were just relishing the crabbing lotus when you rang. We both said this would be the One. We felt it in our yonis and lingams. We felt your need for sex. We should meet to make sure our life paths are in tune."

"Right on."

It was all I could think of to say. I'm way out of practice on the Newy Agey speaky thingy.

She tells me to meet her in an hour in a nearby park in the Sunset District on the third bench from the street.

I ask her name. She tells me she'll tell me all if I am the one. If not it is best to remain strangers.

We say bye and I pump my fist and do a "she shoots, she scores" but my elation turns to anxiety as I realize I don't exactly look my hottie best. If I'm to be the One I'd better get gussied up in a hurry. But the clothes I threw in my bag are more slutty than hottie. Fuck. I slug down the rest of my mocha and am about to go blitzkreig shopping when I figure I oughta make a call just in case I really don't need to go shopping and meeting sexy strangers in a park.

Ellen answers quickly, as if she's been waiting by the phone.

"Hey, it's me," I say stating the greeting obvious.

"Hi, where are you?"

"In the City, having a coffee."

"Oh."

"Yeah."

"When are you coming home?"

"That depends upon you."

"Don't do that to me."

"What? It does depend upon you. You say the word, and I'll be between your legs so fast you'll think I was a body part."

She chuckles, which I think is a good sign, but perhaps it's an exaggerated sneer.

"Always the joker, Violetta."

"Yeah, but this isn't a joke is it."

"No."

"Look, if it's the rape thing, just say so and I'll wait a few days until you feel better and heal."

"You just don't get it do you?"

"I guess not."

"I see this unfortunate incident as a blessing in disguise. I guess I'm tired of fighting the good fight and worrying. I want a life."

"So do I. With my son."

"Then you've got to do what you will. I wish you wouldn't, but nothing I've ever said or done influences your actions."

"Do you still love me?"

"Of course I still love you. I always will. It's why I can see that losing Luc is for the best."

The tears that were brewing evaporate. I realize I have a job to do and time's a wasting.

"I gotta go."

"Be careful."

"I will."

"Be safe."

"You know me."

"I thought I did."

"I gotta go."

"Call me."

"I will."

"I'll be waiting for you."

"Thanks."

"I love you, Violetta. Remember that."

"I love you, Ellen."

I click off the call, sniffling back tears. Calling was a mistake. I'm fucking bummed. I need some serious retail therapy and fast. I spin by Betsey Johnson where I drop a bunch of dollars on something new-wave-hippy-funky. It's a knee-length, flared, purple velvet dress with long flared sleeves and a collar that cinches around my neck and a top that clings to my upper boney curves making me look more voluptuous than I am while swishing around my legs and arms all sexy. If I twirl around the dress flies up and shows my ass and pussy. It's a pretty stunning garment with thick red laces up the front and back that come criss-crossed down to my navel and small of my back. Sexy much. That I found such a number right off in my size speaks to me that I'm on a do right mission. I feel better, not thinking about Ellen. The clothing gods are looking out for me.

As are the shoe gods, right Lucretia?

It's a no brainer. Shoe-wise I know I'll eventually wear Gina's slip-ons, but for now I latch onto the cutest pair of black velvet lace up ankle boots imaginable. No stockings, no underwear. I do my make-up in the car and spike-up my hair, pulling my little ringlets down the side of my face to add a softer touch. I whistle in the mirror. I'd definitely fuck me.

I drive to the park listening to Lucretia My Reflection by the Sisters, and the song gets me hot and I'm ready to get down and get undressed as soon as I find parking.

Which I do right away—find parking that is—the getting down and undressed will have to wait for me to impress my kinky hosts. Even though I'm a few minutes early I figure I'm being watched so I sashay to the bench and spin around, crossing my legs in slow motion as I sit down, confident that somebody, somewhere just got an awesome view of the goodies under my dress.

I uncross my legs in the most exhibitionistic way I can and sit knees together, feet apart in a classic little girl pose. I alternate between this stance and the legs crossed one getting myself majorly turned on with every clench of my pussy muscles.

I clock her walking along the sidewalk at the far end of the park. She's as Swedish as meatballs and Absolut Vodka. She cuts across the grass and her golden blonde hair flows back in the ever-present breeze. She's backlit by the sun; her shapely curves peek-a-boo through her ankle-length skirt and filmy blouse. Energized by her long, athletic stride, her tits bounce like two pogoing punks. Her nipples seem to protrude through the thin material of her blouse, inviting pinches and sucks.

She sees me staring and smiles, extending her hand several yards before she reaches the bench.

I stand up and we shake, our eyes locked. Then we hug. Her nipples are bullet-hard and hot. They burn into my bosom, melting my insides into liquid sex.

"Hi," she says. "You're exactly as I pictured you. Delectable."

"Hi. You too."

"Sit," she says, motioning to the bench as if she owns it. She drops her purse to the ground and takes my hand and holds it in her lap between her hands. She massages my fingers and I imagine it's her pussy wrapped around me. I feel the heat of her cunt through the taffeta of her skirt. The woman is a sexual blast furnace.

"Tell me, why do you want to have sex this lovely afternoon?"

"I'm horny."

She laughs, inviting explanation with her eyes.

"And I don't just want ordinary sex. That I can get anywhere. I want the kind of sex that'll take me out of my body."

She nods.

"And you don't have a partner who gives you this?"

"No, I don't."

Hey, that's not lying.

"That's hard to believe that someone as beautiful and as radiantly sexy as you doesn't have a partner."

"I'm between relationships."

Okay, a white lie, but it could be true. Her eyes invite elaboration.

"They always fall apart. They say I'm too intense in bed. I just happened to pick up a *Spectator* in the cafe. Someone must have left it. It fell open and my eyes went right to your ad. I wasn't even thinking of fucking. It must have been fate."

"Fucking. How nice you say it. Say cunt."

"Cunt."

"Say I want to rub my cunt on your cunt and mix our juices."

"I want to rub my cunt on your cunt and mix our juices."

"Oh you are too perfect. I want you too, but first, you must tell me, are you clean?"

"Spotless. I even showered this morning."

She giggles and her tits jiggle. She watches me watching her bosom. She does likewise to me.

"Our bodies will fit perfect together."

"Do you object to drugs?"

"Nah. I don't need 'em, but I don't mind them, and I do enjoy them."

"We find they help liberate the senses."

"I'm all for that."

"Are you familiar with the Kama Sutra?"

"Some. There's some pretty crazy positions."

"Yes, and we're expert at them all. We've been looking for a woman to complete the posture of the gobbling fishes. I do believe you are divinely sent to us."

She looks towards the sky, and I figure she's having a spiritual moment, especially when she says "It is settled. You are chosen."

"Cool."

She nods and I follow her gaze to an apartment building across the park, top level. The curtains open and a naked statuesque dark skinned man stands stroking his cock.

"That is Kahn, and he approves."

"I approve of him."

She laughs and kisses me, all tongue going deep. She presses my hand deeper into her lap and I feel the brush of her pubic hair and the heated dampness of her cunt through her skirt. She shudders and pulls away.

"I'm Saffron."

"Lucretia," I say, not sure why, other than maybe the more I think I'm her the better my chances of bringing her back.

"How sexy. Let's fuck."

She jumps up, pulling me after her. We run across the park towards Kahn's cock, laughing. He watches us all the way—Saffron's tits bounce, and my skirt flies up. Kahn strokes his lingam in appreciation of what must be the sexiest sight since Eve decided to get it on with the serpent for Adam's voyeuristic pleasure.

Incense burns. Monks chant. Not that there's a bunch of monks in the pillow covered room. It's a CD of Tibetan chants, but it seems like we're surrounded by a monkhouse full of horny monk voyeurs cause we're all naked smoking joints. It's good stuff and we're high as kites.

I learned Saffron and Kahn's story. She was a hooker by night called Liz Stora from some small town called Torslanda near Gothenburg and a student by day at the university. Kahn came through as a guest lecturer in Eastern Philosophy and converted her from selling her body to slobs to giving it to him in the name of reaching Nirvana. He christened her Saffron and they've been Kama Sutra-ing ever since around the world. And they've gotten damn good at it.

Saffron's stroking my body, running her fingers over my hips, parting my ass cheeks to toy with my rosebud butthole. My hand slides between Saffron's legs. Her pubic hair is as golden as her long flowing headhair. Her pussy lips are plump and wrap around my finger, coating me with her musky juices. Her clit is hard, and each time I flick the sensitized nub Saffron makes this little ahhhh sound and arches her back. Kahn watches us with his deep, dark eyes, alternating between stroking his cock and making some pungent potion over a small candle.

Saffron kisses me, her smothering tits rubbing across mine. Our nipples brush, hard bullets against the softness of our silky breast flesh. My finger slides in her pussy. Her finger slides in my ass. Now it's my turn to ahhhhh, my moan reverberating around our locked mouths. We roll around the cushions, our naked bodies enfolding and merging. Saffron was right. We do fit together perfectly, and it feels like we're floating around the room. I know it's a byproduct of the weed but it's fucking good.

"The tea is ready," Kahn says.

Saffron and I brake from our liplock, but our hands continue exploring our bodies, our tits caressing. Kahn walks towards us, carrying three small ornate cups cradled in the triangle of his large hands. His cock bobs from side to side. He's lithe, his dark brown body glistening with a sheen of fine lotion that Saffron applied as I undressed. His shoulder length black hair makes him seem primal.

"It's made with the finest psychedelic mushrooms from deep in the forests of Sumatra. They are our passport to Nirvana."

I reach up to run my finger along the underside of Kahn's cock, running my fingers along that ridge of skin, the raphe, that separates his balls. His cock twitches, and a thin sliver of precome tears at the tip. I wipe it off with my finger and put it to my mouth tasting his saltiness. I can't resist adding my two cents worth of naughty narration.

"And this is our fuel, and this—"

I wrap my hand around his cock, stroking it.

"And this is our rocket."

"Drink," says Kahn, offering us the cups. Saffron takes one and I do likewise. We clink china and Kahn says a few works in Hindu, Urdhu or Katmandu—I don't know what the fuck du it is. My head swims. I just want to fuck.

We sip the tea in unison, our feet touching, our bodies nestled close in a triangle of anticipatory lust. The tea is sharp with fine bits of shroom pulp in it. It's hot, and each time I chew on a shroom bit it gets even hotter, releasing a flood of taste and temperature through my body. I feel the tea's glow radiate through my skin, and I feel it's heat through Kahn and Saffron's. I'm sweating and so are they, but it's not gross, it's like we're all coming through our skin. I zone fast feeling like my body is three or four sizes than it is. Everything seems small and distant and my body feels like it's closeted in cotton wool. I'm all sex.

"I want to fuck," I say, hearing the words echo in my head, thinking they're coming from somewhere else as Kahn takes the empty cup from my hands. To fill the heated void I slide my fingers around his warm cock. Saffron does likewise with her hands, and together we stroke his hefty erection, playing with each other's fingers as much as we're playing with Kahn's cock. He alternates kissing us, and we caress our breasts, marveling in their different sizes and shapes. I've never really dug large breasts but Saffron's are perfectly formed—firm, not fake. They're enlarged versions of mine, and in my high shroom state Saffron's tits seem larger and softer than they really are, almost floating into my hands. Her ample breasts remind me of Lucretia's bosom, and I think of bringing my Guardian Angel back through this sex-magick ritual so I can feel those lovely titties swamping mine again, and so I can feel Luc's mouth on my titties again.

Thinking of Luc and Lucretia makes me happy as well as high. It's easy for me to imagine they're with me, and we're all enjoying this dreamy fuck. I am so in to this scene, I'm not thinking of—well, you know who, at all. Luc and Lucretia—Saffron and Kahn—me—that's all there is, and I don't ever want to come down from this soft, sexy cloud I'm floating upon.

Kahn's hands slide from our necks, down our backs, around our waists and nestles under our sexes. He cups our pussies as he continues kissing us, alternating his lips from our mouths as his fingers undulate into our cunts, molding his hand to our labia. We match his motions, rocking on our haunches, working our clits into his palms like we're putting pearls back into their oysters.

"It is time for the posture of the gobbling fishes," Kahn whispers into our ears. Saffron smiles at me as she lounges backwards, pulling me with her, on top of her. She wraps her arms around me, pressing her breasts into me. I love the way her hard nipples burrow into my boobs and mine do likewise to her. It's such a turn on. We're kissing and grinding our cunts and tits together. Her golden blonde pubic hair brushes against my browny snatch and the two mesh as our clits dance a tango together. I feel Kahn's hands on my ass, positioning me above Saffron, working my body deeper into hers. She arches her back, thrusting with her pelvis and legs lifting me up, and even though I'm higher than the stars from the dope and the sex, I remind myself that Gina's death shoes are sitting in arms' reach next to my crumpled clothes, and that's how Lucretia and Luc will join me for real. Those shoes are why I'm here and not with Ellen, and once I put them on there will be no turning back.

Salvatore emphasized the need for intense sex while trying to resurrect Lucretia. What Kahn and Saffron are doing to me certainly qualifies and then some. I'm on top of Saffron, kissing her so deep we could be munching each other's twats through our bodies, our titties mashed together, our nipples diamonding hard, our pussies rubbing clit to clit, our legs spread wide, with Kahn kneeling between our legs, adding his purposeful manipulations to our natural feminine grindings. I feel his breath on my thighs and the brush of his long hair as his head nears our cunts. It must be an awesome sight to be so close to two dripping, sexing pussies.

Saffron shudders, and it takes me only a second to realize why as Kahn's tongue slides from between her labia, over her clit to my clit, massaging the two together, on up to my lips, spreading them, pressing them flat like he's licking an ice-cream cone, and after he's burrowed deep in there he slides out, tonguing my asshole, his fingers replacing his tongue inside our cunts. He rims me into a moaning fit, aided by the plundering finger fucking he gives us, the force of his thrusting hands pressing our bellies together, coaxing our clits to rub against each other. It's the most fucking amazing feeling I've ever had during sex. I wish I had shoes on to record this. It's so intense.

But not intense enough, I tell myself. Not yet.

Maybe it's the weed and the shrooms but I'm so high that my body can take more pleasure. I'm building a come so mega that the news tonight will report that the Big One finally hit San Francisco.

Saffron and I work together as if we'd been fuckers for life, Siamese twins joined at the cunts, our bodies rippling along each other like sea creatures. Kahn is a master, his tongue moving from my ass to Saffron's, to our cunts, always inserting a finger so we're never unoccupied. It's a sexy, wet mess down in the delta of our cunts but Saffron and I really gush when Kahn massages our G spots together through the thin walls of our tight pressed pussies, our clits licked together by his tongue. Doing something like that stunt that teenage girls practice where they tie a cherry stem together, Kahn entwines our hard clits. It feels like they're knotted tight, threatening to explode. I really come to appreciate the size of his hands as one of his fingers snakes up my ass. From the way Saffron jolts I guess he's doing the same to her, and it's simply the best fucking sex I've ever had. I've got to teach Johnny this trick. He can practice on Ellen and me when all this is over. Ellen will go for it. No way can anyone, no matter how tight-assed, not respond to this ultimate sex. A little weed, some shroom tea and three willing and able bodies and we can call Nirvana our home forever and ever, amen.

Johnny. Ellen. Gina. The shoes.

Not yet. Not yet, pretty please. I want to enjoy myself some before I rip this party apart.

Saffron starts to come. I feel it first in her mouth as we kiss, have been kissing through all Kahn's pussy tonguing and finger fucking. Saffron's mouth shakes and I feel her lips quiver. It's like she's nibbling on my lips, and I can't help giggling from the tickling feeling. It's that little laugh that seems to start it all because she clamps down on my mouth with hers and sticks her tongue in my mouth like it's my cunt and she's fucking me with her dick.

Kahn knows his girlfriend's body because as she does this he rams his fingers into our cunts deep, his tongue battering our clits, his fingers doing the same to our asses, it all merging together through the thin walls separating our asses from our cunts and our cunts from our cunts.

Saffron comes, lifting her body upwards and me with it. She collapses and I come down hard, and the blow sends me into comeland, and we're exploding and rolling together and it's like we're melting into each other. Two people one body in an altogether different fashion than I'm used to. Kahn pulls away for a moment, and as

Saffron and I remain locked in climax he fucks us with that huge dick, plunging first into her spasming cunt and then into mine, alternating pussies, one after another, and it's then that I understand where the position got its name —the gobbling fishes. Our pussies are down there, gaping wide wanting that dick, wanting to be fed, ready to gobble it down as soon as it has finished its stroke into the fishy cunt next to it.

If I thought the foreplay of Kahn's licking and finger fucking was hot, man, when he plunges his cock in deep, his hands on our hips, pulling us into him, it's fucking China Syndrome radioactive, melting down through the Earth's core, turning the entire fucking planet into come mush.

This is it. This is where I belong. This is the Universe of Fuck, and it's all I want and live for. It's like dying and being reborn with every fucking touch of skin on skin, cunt to cunt, cock inside fucking us both at the same time. Even when he's in Saffron I can feel his dick in me, my hole still ripe from the last plundering, sensing his mammoth cock through her skin and mine. It's like we're being fucked by two guys, only this is better, because it's like we're being fucked by every guy on the planet, by every guy that's ever lived, by one guy who really knows how to fuck a woman, two women, all women.

Man, I feel one with this fucking Universe of Fuck. It can't get any better. I'm coming and going and living and dying. My orgasm explodes from my brain, down my body, my nipples becoming so hot Saffron jumps as if she's been electrocuted by them. My orgasm rushes through my pussy, squeezing Kahn's cock so that the normally tantric man can't help himself, and Shiva knows how many restrained climaxes explode from him into my spasming cunt, and it doesn't stop there, his jism and my climax running down my thighs, the intense feelings melting into my feet, where I really enjoy its magic.

This cannot get any better.

Too bad it has to end.

Kahn's collapsed forward on top of Saffron and me, still thrusting into our cunts as his orgasm rubberizes his legs. Saffron's in some kind of come-drug-induced trance moaning a constant ohhmmmmmmm into my kissing mouth. I bend my legs at the knees and reach for Gina's shoes. I fumble a little as I have very little room for maneuvering, but after a few panicked pattings I find them and thankfully they're slip-ons so it is easy for my fingers to snag them under the bridge.

I swing on up and anchor it on my furthest foot and then do the same to the other.

How I managed all this in the midst of three orgasming locked bodies I'll never know, other than it is really true: the feet cannot be denied.

Two people one body, that very familiar feeling.

I'm in Gina and Violetta's standing in front of me in a bathroom at the Rome airport. We're alone, and this is as real as any shoesex fuck I've ever felt.

"Feeling ill are you, you boyfriend stealing bitch?" I—Gina—says.

"So it was you on the stairs," Violetta says. It's so fucking weird to see me speak.

"Yes."

"Then you know it's over between Johnny and me. He loves you. I'm going back to America."

I'm screaming, "Over. Over. Over."

"Yeah, over. Just like you should get over it."

My blood boils. I rage. I sneer. I spit.

"It's not over. I watched him hold your hand here today. He lied about coming to the airport with you. He said he had to pick up some artwork for his parents. Anyone can see he loves you. On New Year's Eve he pretended to be ill so he could leave me alone. He didn't go home. He waited all night outside that shoe repairer's hovel to make sure you were okay. He just waited there in the cold until you got home and left. He didn't even talk to you. He just wanted to see you for a few seconds, to make sure you were safe. How pathetic is that?"

"Actually, I think it's kind of sweet."

Now I'm really steamed. I shake my fist at me.

"He's obsessed with you, you cunt. He's already made plans to go to New York to see you. It's not over, bitch. Don't insult me by saying so. I know what you're doing. You're leading him on so you can have him all to yourself to make him a father to that bastard you're carrying."

"I honestly had no idea he was following me. I don't want him. I've told him so."

"Yes, as you fuck him. I heard you from the stairs. Not very convincing."

"Look, Gina, once I'm gone he'll forget me. He loves you."

"Oh, you'll be gone all right, but not in the way you think."

I edge towards me, pointing a long finger at my chest. It's so amazing to be in this drug-enhanced come state and to be inside someone attacking me. Fucking unreal. Fucking real.

"I know about the fake passport you're leaving on, and the one you arrived with. I know about the ancient shoes you're smuggling out of the country. Johnny's not too good at hiding things. The police will be very interested in your activities, Lucretia Cutrero a.k.a. Nicola Anderson a.k.a. Violetta Valery Cutrero."

"Hurting me won't make Johnny love you. It'll make him hate you."

"I'll have to take that chance. At least I'll feel better knowing I've ruined you."

"You're not going to do that. You're just angry. You

could have gone straight to the police. Johnny or I would never have known it was you that tipped them off. We'd have thought I just got unlucky. Now you've warned me, he'll know. You don't want that, Gina."

"Oh but I do. I want him to know I how much I love him. He'll eventually see I was right to turn you in. So don't think you'll be able to escape. There's a police office down the hall. I told you first because I want you to know that I'm better than you. When you rot in jail I want you to know it was me who put you there for trying to steal my man, and Johnny, he'll never stray again."

I, Violetta, laugh at Gina's, my, last comment. "Your man," Violetta says dripping sarcasm at my feet. I, Gina, turn to leave.

"No," I hear Violetta scream, and then she's on my back, spinning me around. I grab for her hair and the wig comes off in my fist. I stumble backwards and slip, sprawling unladylike on the floor. My skirt rides up my thighs. My white panties shine through my tanned pantyhose. I see Violetta smile, staring at the pantyhose.

My head rolls to the side and I catch our reflection in the mirror. Gina's lying on the floor and it's not Violetta that's pulling off her pantyhose. It's a woman with long black hair, tall and statuesque, big boobs.

It's Lucretia.

"Hello, Violetta, let's fuck."

She's baaaaack.

CHAPTER FOURTEEN

THIS IS WHERE it gets really fucking weird.

I'm sandwiched between Saffron and Kahn, getting fucked by his big dick as he comes, as Saffron grinds her clit into mine, only it's not mine, it's Lucretia's. I'm no longer inside Gina. I'm Lucretia. I'm Violetta.

"Lucretia, Lucretia," Saffron moans as she comes.

"Lucretia, Lucretia," Kahn moans as he comes.

"Lucretia, Lucretia," I say to myself as I come, as I become my Guardian Angel. I see her body in the mirror. She looks good. Lucretia, my reflection, looks back at me and speaks.

"Thank you, Violetta. You look as good as ever yourself. I'm sorry, my daughter, for deserting you. Thank you for rescuing me in such an inspired way. This is a fuck to wake the dead."

"Thank Salvatore and the Lowest Soles and Gina and Kahn and Saffron."

"I knew her death would serve a higher purpose."

"Getting you back is only part of the higher purpose. Much has happened."

Lucretia, since she's me, immediately knows all that I know.

"You poor thing. Poor Ellen. Poor Luc. I will not let them hurt him or you."

Kahn stretches upwards, and I feel his hands run up from my hips, up my spine to my neck where he pulls my long hair backwards, wrapping it around my neck with his fingers. He pulls it tight and squeezes, and Saffron wraps her arms tight around me so I can't escape. I'm choking. I panic, realizing it's not the Kama Sutra—it's the Killing Sutra. I can't move. Fear grips me, and with a burst of amazing strength Lucretia stands, throwing Kahn from my back, punching Saffron in the face as she does so. He falls on to the floor, stunned by little ole me's show of force. Saffron groans.

What the fuck is happening.

Lucretia bends to offer Kahn her hand to help him off the floor, and I notice it's me that's doing this. Two people, one body, Lucretia's body.

"You're not going to hurt Lucretia, Violetta or Luc," I say.

Kahn looks at me like I'm crazy. He mutters something like a bad trip, that's all, nothing serious. He didn't mean any harm. It's a big turn on to be choked while coming, it gets us all closer to Nirvana.

The fuck I like grunge I think. That Seattle sound sucks.

This is way too trippy for me. I should stay off the shrooms and pot. Too freaky of a combination if you add Lucretia and intense sex to the mix.

I'm conscious of Saffron stirring behind me. Rather than assisting Kahn to his feet, Lucretia and I lift him up, one strong hand under his neck. He dangles, his legs thrashing. Saffron charges at me and another strong hand grabs her throat and hoists her off the ground. The looks on their faces are priceless. They can't believe I have the strength, or the height.

Neither can I.

"Lucretia, what are you doing? These people haven't hurt us or Luc. They're not our problem. The Catholic Church is. Why are we wasting our time here? Let them go. Let's go."

"Oh no, my daughter, they're not so innocent. Are you? Are you?"

I scream at Kahn and Saffron. Held aloft by my hand, choking, Kahn's grown harder than when he was fucking us. It's that good old eroto-asphyxiation thang again.

"You're not so innocent are you?"

Saffron pees, a yellow stream fluttering down the wall. She blacks out. I let her drop. Kahn's still thrashing and getting harder by the second so I can't resist sucking him off as I choke him. The dirty bastard deserves to go out in style. I suck him dry, coaxing a final orgasm from him. He comes as he dies.

Just as Lucretia knew all I'd been through, I know all she knows about Kahn and Saffron. I was lucky. It was their kink to kill the third member of the gobbling fishes, strangling the little inbetweeny into Nirvana. They've done it many times.

We drag Kahn over to the stunned Saffron and wrap his hands around her neck and we choke her, sticking his death hard-on into her, fucking her to a final orgasm. She dies coming too.

"Okay, let's string him up. It'll look like he strangled her during rough sex play and out of sadness, remorse and guilt, hung himself. We'll fake a suicide note."

"Wow, Lucretia, you think of everything. How did you know they were killers?"

"When you brought me out of Gina's shoes, and I was free of the limbo of those vile priests and serial killers, my feet brushed Kahn's. That was all it took. My powers are heightened. I sensed him reliving all the kills they'd enjoyed. He looked to the mirror over there, where I'll wager there is a video camera and somewhere in here is a stash of videotapes of their other kills."

I go over to the mirror and pry it open, and yes there's a camera. I pocket the tape.

"Don't need another tape of me being a murderer."

"Or being a victim. You were to be the next, but you brought me back at exactly the right time and now there will be no more thrill kills for the Kama Sutra Killers. The feet cannot be denied. We are fulfilling our destiny as the serial killer of serial killers. You are an Avenging Angel Sex Goddess, and I am your Guardian Angel. Together we are unstoppable. Now let's get Luc back. There's not much time. Tomorrow is the Double Event when Jack the Ripper killed twice in one night, and I can think of a priest and a nun who have much to answer for. We need to get Luc back and their tape of you killing those hustlers. The double event will be the perfect opportunity. Those boots that the Papal bastards used to trap me were made for walking."

"And killing."

"And that's just what they'll do."

And I—we—me my bad self and I—Lucretia and Violetta—mother Guardian Angel and Avenging Angel Sex Goddess daughter—dance around a room where so much sex and violence had just erupted, singing Nancy Sinatra's "These Boots Were Made For Walking" to two dead serial killers.

Fucking trippy, man.

CHAPTER FIFTEEN

I'M NOT SURE whether to tell Ellen about Lucretia's return to life.

It's a subject of endless debate during the drive from the City to Stinson.

"Maybe it's best if we pretend nothing happened."

"No, Lucretia, we have to tell her. We need her for the sex in the Jack the Ripper boots tomorrow."

"No we don't. You are powerful enough now to do that on your own. I'm am powerful enough to walk with you alone. Being in limbo had its advantages. All those serial killers were much fun to play with. The Catholic Church actually did us a big favor. Thanks to them we don't need anyone else."

"Maybe you're right."

"I am."

"Ellen's been through hell. You and I can handle this."

"Yes, it's for the best. Maybe it would help you help her if we put on the shoes she wore during the rape. You'll know the horrors she felt and be better able to help her recover."

"That's a good idea. What do I tell her about Kahn and Saffron."

"Nothing. Say you couldn't go through with it."

"She'll know."

"No she won't. You give her too much credit, my daughter-in-love."

"She was a very good cop, and with her, I'm a very bad liar."

"Then tell her what you did but leave out the sex details. It'll be too much for her after the rape. Tell her that in trying to find someone to have sex with—something you had to do because she wouldn't—you were almost killed, and as a consequence you fulfilled your destiny as the serial killer of killers, and it made you realize how much you wanted to be back with her, to understand her problems and work it out so you can be together in all the ways a couple is supposed to."

"You're pretty slick, Lucretia."

"Yes, but I wouldn't tell her your plan to wear the rape shoes. Through several thousands of years of shoesex I've seen and felt it all. Don't forget, this all began with my rape. I know what Ellen's going through. I know what she needs to hear and doesn't."

"I couldn't go through with it. I love you too much. I tried. I tried, and it almost got me killed, but don't feel bad because it showed me how dangerous my power is and that's all thanks to you. I can't thank you enough."

Ellen's holding my hands, looking into my eyes. There's tears running down both of our cheeks.

"Be careful, don't rub it in too thick." Lucretia's voice echoes in my head.

"Sssssssssssh," I say out loud.

"What?" Ellen says.

"Sssssssssssh, just mumbling to myself," I say, regrouping, making more than a mental note to be careful about answering Lucretia out loud. "Ssssssssss, stop crying. I'm home to stay."

I wipe the tears away from Ellen's cheek.

"Where do we go from here?" Ellen says.

"To bed."

Ellen stiffens.

"I'm still not ready to have sex. If this is a trick then—"

"To bed—to sleep—perchance to dream or something like it," I say, raising my voice and hands. "Lighten up a bit, Ellen. Go easy on me. I'm exhausted."

"Sorry."

Ellen kisses me on the lips and leads me and Lucretia to the bedroom.

"Well done, my cunning daughter."

"Yeah, right," I say, making damn sure it's to myself.

It's about four in the morning. Ellen's out cold, snoring and cute, the sheets wrapped partially around her. Her trim body looks oh so fuckable. For the life of me I'll never understand people's hang-ups about sex. Humans are so fucked up. Fucking is good. Rape is not. So you've been raped. It's like falling off a bike or getting knocked off a bike by a road-rage driver. Why give the asshole driver the satisfaction of spoiling your enjoyment of something great and wonderful like bike riding or sex. Best way to fight a rapist is to laugh it off and have good fucking loving sex despite all the bastard did. Don't let them take your life or sexlife away. Take it back and enjoy it more. Don't wallow in the pain, regret or guilt. Get out there and fuck.

Good job I'm not a rape counselor. I'd probably be fired the first day.

I yawn my way to the toilet and enjoy a satisfying pee. Ellen's still asleep so I figure now's as good as any time to check out her rape shoes. Maybe then I'll understand why she thinks sex is such a no-no right now. I mean come on. It's not like I have to penetrate her. I could just lick her clit or she could do me. What's the big fucking deal?

I find the tartan Doc Martens under the heap of clothes that Ellen tossed by the side of the bed a couple of days ago when we came back from the warehouse. That she hasn't cleaned up is some testament to the mega-funk she's in. Maybe I kinda should be more understanding. Oh well, the boots will show me the way.

I take them into the bathroom and lock the door. If Ellen wakes she'll think I'm taking a big smelly poo and steer way clear. I pry open the laces and slide first one foot and then another down the throat and onto the soles.

Two people, one body—that old familiar feeling.

Very familiar as it turns out. I've been inside Ellen—literally and through shoesex—so many times that it's just like another of my moods.

And this one is full of fear, anxiety—and what's that—guilt? Oh come on Ellen. It's not your fault.

We're in the warehouse. Father Git Lekerk pontificates in more ways than one.

"It was a simple matter to make sure they came into your possession. It was just a question of time and being

– 176 –

patient. We couldn't just send them in the mail or leave them on your doorstep. You would have been too suspicious. It took several tries until Ms. Stewart, rather than you took the bait at the flea market. Once in your hands we knew you wouldn't be able to resist their evil allure."

Wow, I'm feeling way more anxious and tense than I'd expect. Ellen is really wound.

I look at me—Violetta—with an expression of sorry. I—Violetta—gives me—Ellen—her 'don't be—not your fault' response. But it is my fault.

It's always weird in a shoesex scene where I see myself as others see me. I'm really pretty darn cute, even when I'm being roughed up by a maniacal Catholic priest and his goon henchmen. And am I ever so considerate. That look to Ellen really said it all. Don't be sorry. Why the fuck is she feeling so guilty and worried. It's not fear for being held captive. It's something else. This is freaky. I told her then and so many times since it wasn't her fault. What gives? What have I done wrong?

"Pay attention to Ellen my daughter and what she says through her feet. This isn't about you. Concentrate on Ellen's feelings."

"Yes, Mother Lucretia."

And it's also weird having another person inside me giving me advice at the same time I'm inside another person's soles. Pretty fucking good job I have a strong sense of self or I could be burdened with bigtime identity problems.

"Concentrate Violetta."

"Oh, yeah, right."

Back to being awash in guilt-about-to-be-raped-Ellen.

Father Git's still rambling.

"Throughout centuries of battling evil we have learned that the most effective weapons against darkness are the very tools of evil—therein lies the means to defeat even the most pernicious force. As you have no doubt discovered, the boots contained Tumblety's evil essence, which as Lucretia no doubt explained is passed on and grows stronger with each new crime. That is why this shoesex power must be stopped. It grew out of a crime and has been sex and violence's unwitting accomplice for centuries. You might have thought you were fighting evil. Far from it. You were simply just another form of evil that we on God's side must stop."

Violetta snickers. Father Git raises his voice and points his finger at her. I wish she'd for once not be so flippant.

"If you doubt our most righteous and earnest motivation then witness the crimes you caused and the murders you committed."

I look at Violetta—me—with wide eyes. She shrugs her shoulders as if she doesn't know what he's talking about. It wasn't supposed to be this way. What is going on?

What indeed, Ellen. What the fuck is going on? Now I'm really concentrating. I'm feeling every little nerve ending in Ellen's body tingle. I'm focusing on the pounding in her stomach and the cold sweat trickling down her back and the angry, jumbled thoughts playing through her mind. And where does she get off wishing I wasn't so flippant. I'll give her fucking flippant.

Violetta.

Okay, Lucretia. I know, focus on Ellen. Well, here I go. I'm all feet.

If they hurt Violetta so help me I'll see them all in hell. If they play games with me I'll have them all in jail. They can't fuck with Ellen Stewart and get away with it. There's nothing I won't do for Violetta. Look what I've already done for her. I've covered up murder. I've killed. These guys should know better.

Thanks, Ellen. Too bad you rolled over and wouldn't help me when I needed you most recently.

Stay calm, Violetta. Your anger will mask Ellen's feelings. Control yourself. Be a sponge and all will be revealed. You can be angry later.
  A sponge, Lucretia? Man the things I do for shoesex. I just can't believe this. I'm a sponge . . . I'm a sponge . . .
  That's better, Violetta. Now concentrate and get back to Ellen.

Father Git reads my mind. It feels strange. Am I that obvious? He must be able to read my confusion on my face. There weren't supposed to be any murders. Violetta hasn't done anything wrong.

"I can imagine you're confused, and you, Ms. Stewart, are plotting how to invoke your SFPD connections as soon as we free you. Well, as I promised, you will not. Here is why."

Father Git snaps his fingers and the limo drives over to us. A goon opens the door. Inside sits the nun with Luc.

Lekerk continues proving he's been smarter than me all along. What a fool I've been.

What kind of fool have you been, Ellen? What the fuck do you mean, all along? Oh yeah, right, sponge, sponge, fucking sponge.

"We are not so silly nor so hoodlum-like as to resort to simple threats on Luc's safety. I am a priest and we have and are bound by the laws of God, which transcend those of man."

Violetta makes some sarcastic sound and the goons rough her up. Oh, Violetta, I'm sorry, but you bring these things on yourself. We should just play along and all this will go away.

Whose side are you on, Ellen?
Violetta, pay attention.
I am, Lucretia. Oh I am. Ellen is under my microscope.

"Please pay attention to the video monitor. Sister Teresa, please press play."

The goons prop up Violetta and me. A video plays. It's a black and white surveillance tape.

"I'm sure you'll recognize this alley, Violetta. It is the alley in which you killed that young hustler. Watch carefully."

I can't believe Violetta did this. My eyes go from the horror of the tape to Violetta. Now I know I have to stop this thing. It is evil. I was right to go to the Church. Violetta is at best sick. At worst she's possessed with that demon relative of hers. In time she will see that I've done her a big favor because I love her so much.

If I could scream right now I would. It's a fucking good job we're not having sex or Ellen would see just how sick and possessed I can be. How could she set me up? Fuck the sponge. I'm ready to kill.

Patience, darling daughter. I know this hurts to find out these truths about someone who supposedly loves us.

She does love me. She's just fucked up.

She's also jealous.

Of you.

Of me. Of Luc.

I feel so bad for her, but maybe Lekerk is doing the right thing. There's no way I can control Violetta. The threat of the tape could just be the thing to make her see sense. I wish Lekerk would have clued me in more. We were supposed to be in this together. He looks at me as though he's doing me a favor by acting as if I'm one of the enemy. When this is all over he's going to hear from me. We had a deal.

I feel so fucking sick. How long has this been going on? How long has Ellen been leading a double life? How long has she been betraying me? For fuck's sake, a deal! A deal to sell out me and my son and Lucretia. Is this payback for leaving her to face the charges in Tony's killing? Is it payback for getting pregnant and having his child?

Violetta, try to stay calm and feel. It's the only way to fight this. Knowledge is the ultimate power. Ellen can't hide from you as long as you keep your emotions in check.

I'm Italian. So are you. Don't tell me to control my fucking emotions.

Listen to all that is said and save your anger for later. We will use this scene to our benefit in tracking Luc down, but if you're ranting you'll miss important clues.

Okay, I'm all feet.

Lekerk is all mouth.

"Should you attempt in anyway to recover Luc or go to the authorities this tape will be given to the police. Ms. Stewart's testimony that you were involved in a passionate embrace at the time of the murder will hold little weight, especially when it comes to light that she has already covered up your earlier horrible and all too similar crime in the slaying of Randall Warren also known as Mark Dearside also known as the Dildo Killer."

I watch Violetta close her eyes. She's defeated. She'll need me to see her though this.

Her sniffles turn to full out sobs. I hope she never figures out that it was me who told them all about her. I needed help when I was in jail and they were there for me. I agree with Father Git, and that's why I did what I did. Violetta can never know. It'll all be for the best. We could never have been happy with Luc in the picture. What would have happened when he found out that I killed his father? Violetta would have favored him over me. Blood is thicker than water. I can't give her all these years just to have it all thrown away when her son decides he hates me or wants revenge. I hope Violetta pays attention to Father Lekerk and sees through her anger to his wisdom, like I did.

"In time you will see that this is for the best, Violetta. Luc will never know his sordid origins. He will grow up as a ward of the Church and will lead a normal life in some faraway land. This hideous perversion of natural law that you call shoesex ends here, and with it further crimes. With Lucretia no more and all of your relatives deceased there can be no more heirs. Should you have another child, which we hope you do to replace this loss, he or she will be normal, conceived with someone not of your cursed bloodline. The Cutrero curse will die with you, Violetta. You should feel relieved. You are free. You still have your perverse power, but you don't have the worry of what will happen to your son. You can dabble if you wish, but I think after today you will have lost your desire to practice unnatural acts. You and Ms. Stewart can live happily ever after, although not in the confines of a wholesome, blessed Catholic marriage."

Lekerk nods at his goons and then at his driver. He slams the limo door shut and the car drives off. A roll-up door automatically opens and closes. Violetta and I are alone with the goons. They should let us go now and let me get down to the business of making Violetta feel better. It'll take a long while and a lot of love, but I can do it. We can do it. We love each other too much, have come too far to fall apart now.

Sponge, sponge, sponge.
Well done my Avenging Angel Sex Goddess daughter. I know that wasn't easy for you. You are growing.

One of the goons holding Violetta speaks as he's whispering in her ear, but loud enough for all his goon buddies and me to hear. She looks at me, worry wrinkling her face. She's concerned for me, for her, for Luc. I wish I could tell her that they won't kill us because of my deal and how they fear that Michael would be all over them.

Yeah, like they were all over us.

"Father Git says you're possessed with a satanic power to feel people fucking in their shoes. That if you're wearing shoes when you're fucked that you experience it over and over until the shoes come off."

He laughs.

"So since you can't go to the cops and complain about anything we do, then you're gonna get the gangbang of your life, you little bitch, and just be thankful that we're connected to the Church and so it wouldn't be right for us to kill you."

He stands over Violetta.

"Untie her. Hold her arms and legs. I'll go first. We'll take turns. Do the same with the other dyke."

No, no, this wasn't part of the deal. Father Git promised there would be no violence. No harm to us, especially Violetta. He said they might have to rough us up a little to make it look convincing, but not this. I look at Violetta trying to reassure her but I can't even reassure myself. She's lying limp as the goons pull her panties off, rip open her dress and spread wide her legs, making sure they leave her tennis shoes on.

The big goon slobbers.

"She's a real little cutie this one. Looks like she's all of thirteen. Nice little titties. This is gonna be sweet."

Violetta turns her gagged head to the side and looks at me. I struggle, hoping to convince her that this is none of my doing. It was not supposed to happen this way. I know lying still is the best policy but I can't let Violetta think I'm going along with this vileness. One goon slaps me, and the shock makes me stop resisting. They rip my shorts and panties off and in another show of resistance for Violetta's benefit I swing my feet at the goons trying to kick the creeps away. Hopefully they'll pull my boots off because I don't want Violetta ever putting them on and catching any inkling of what I'm thinking.

Too fucking late for that now. You should have been your usual anal-clean-everything-up-right-away Ellen. You should have burned these boots with you in them. Now I'm a sponge, sponge, sponge and wringing you dry. Preferably by the neck.

They swat my legs down and yank them apart, but they leave the boots on and slap my face. The pain stings and I close my eyes screwed tight to empty my head of the guilty thoughts I feel at having caused this mess, but as they tear open my blouse I can't help opening my eyes to look at Violetta. I'm so scared. This wasn't supposed to happen. Violetta gives me a reassuring smile in between her sniffles, and it only makes me feel worse. I closes my eyes again. The goons squeeze my breasts, having already pushed the bra over my nipples.

I'm going to be raped. Violetta's going to be raped. And it's all my fault for thinking that the feet could be denied.

"The bitch is a juicy cunt," the goon fondling Violetta says to his goon buddies. They all chuckle, adding a few encouragements to get a move on because they want some of that juicy twat. I wince. The goons holding me feel my pussy, their rough hands prying apart my lips.

"This one's not so excited about getting fucked," the one between my legs says, licking his fingers and coating his cock and my vagina with his spittle, spitting on my pussy as well, more times than is necessary.

The big goon between Violetta's legs jokes that he'll be over to warm me up once he's done with Violetta. There's more rude laughing.

The goon between my legs doesn't waste much time easing in his prick. He pries open my cunt lips and rams his cock in with a lunge of his weight, which winds me, but I still manage a scream against my gag.

I lie as still as possible as he works himself in and out, moaning about how good my cunt feels. It's been so long since I had a cock in me. A real cock. Violetta's done me with that strap-on—Violetta—I look over at her when I hear her assailant say "She's a regular little whore, this one. She fucks good."

They're holding her legs and arms tight to stop her from resisting. She's struggling—wait—no it looks more like she's fucking him. She's fucking her attacker. She's moving that little ass under him to make him come. Over the goon's grunts and groans and rude comments I hear Violetta's juices slathering between her thighs. The big goon on top of her sweats on my love's breasts. I watch it drip down like it's raining. He licks the spots off, biting Violetta's tits as he does. He snaps at her nipples and she screams a muffled ouch. Her body bucks and writhes and the big goon makes his henchmen rough her down. He fucks her with short, stabbing thrusts, and his balls bounce against her ass, slapping in her juices. His thick cock swells, filling her more than I ever could, and he comes, lunging deep as he squirts, ramming his dick up into my Violetta as far as it can go.

She seems to go through the throes of a tiny orgasm and he bites her neck and whispers loud enough for all of us to hear what a great fuck she was. How he'd give her his number cause he's sure she'll want more someday, but it'll have to end here. Business is business, and he doesn't want to see her skinny little girl ass around here or the Church again or he won't be so nice next time.

He pulls out with a flop, and strokes his cock, looking at me.

"You're next, bitch. Enjoyed watching did you? I saw you staring. You want some of this don't you? Well, I'll be right with you, just look after my boy real good or I'm going to have to be rough with you."

I realize that I've been concentrating on Violetta rather than the goon raping me. It was a distraction to dull the pain, but it's served no purpose besides delaying the inevitable. I turn my face away from Violetta as another goon mounts her, and I know that the shoesex replay kicks in because I can hear her thrashing and moaning and bucking on the cold concrete as new men fuck her as she relives the most recent fuck over and over. It must be a hell I can't imagine.

Oh no, Ellen, this now is hell. The gangrape was a breeze compared to your violation of me.

Violetta.

I know, sponge, sponge sponge. It's just tough to soak up acid-toxic-shit like what's inside Ellen.

The big goon that had just raped Violetta tells the goon fucking me to take a break. Before he stops he rams into me as he kisses me, forcing my mouth open.

I hear the big goon bark orders.

"That's a good idea. Roll the cunt over. I'll fuck her doggy style while she sucks you off."

"No way, man, the bitch might bite my cock off."

"She won't do that if she wants to live. She'll suck your dick good. Won't you, whore?"

I nod because I just want to get out of this alive. Father Git will take care of them after this is over. He'll see that they're punished.

Stupid, stupid, stupid. Sponge, sponge, sponge.

The men holding my arms and legs roll me over and the big goon grabs my hair and pulls me backwards, angling my head towards his friend's cock. The man facing me pulls the gag out, grabbing my cheeks, forcing open my mouth into a pucker.

"Listen, bitch, do as the boss says and suck me good. One little nick and I'll cut you into little pieces and feed them to your girlfriend. So don't tempt me cause I'd love to watch one dyke eat another."

As he says this the big goon behind me sticks his cock into my pussy and thrusts, slapping into my ass.

"Whoooweee, look at the way her ass jiggles all nice. She got some tasty little booty on her."

The men holding my arms and legs take every opportunity to slap my ass and play with my tits, making jokes about how they swing backwards and forwards, pulling on them, leaning under me to suck and bite on them amidst much laughter.

I can't help myself. I get wet from all this forced sexual attention. The big goon is pleased.

"See," he says to his henchmen, "the dyke bitch is enjoying herself now. She's wet but good. Learn from me you assholes. You gotta be understanding of what a woman wants. See, she's a dyke and doesn't like this straight sex stuff. She likes it doggy style."

"I bet she likes it up the ass."

The big goon slaps my butt. It stings, even more when he pulls my cheeks apart and fingers my sphincter.

"Now there's an idea. Her cunt is a bit on the looser side of sloppy. Not enough dick, but I bet her ass is sweet."

"You like to swallow?" says the guy in my mouth. "Cause if you don't—too fucking bad cause here it comes."

His cock hardens and his balls slap into my chin as he forces himself deep into my mouth. His cockhead pulses on my tongue and he spurts into my throat. I swallow as much as I can, but some trickles out of my mouth as I cough.

"Next," says the big goon as he inserts a finger up my ass, getting my sphincter wet with my juices. He pulls out of my cunt and I hear him licking his fingers, rubbing them on his cock. He nudges the end of his dick at my butt.

"Hold her tight," he tells his goons, spitting onto my ass.

He grabs my hair and wraps his fingers tight around my short locks. He pulls me backwards and thrusts into my butt.

I'm not gagged and there isn't yet another cock in my mouth. I scream the kind of wail to wake the dead.

"Jeez, will someone stick a dick in her mouth. She's hurting my eardrums."

He fucks my ass with long pounding stokes and it hurts so bad, but since I've been so bad it feels good, and I find my pussy getting wet and wetter, and when another dick is stuck in my mouth I suck it hard and fast. The big goon up my ass reaches under me and feels my pussy. He sticks a finger inside my cunt and rubs his cock through the wall.

"Oooh that feels good. Don't it feel good bitch? You gonna want nothing but real men after this."

He makes me nod my head and in doing so the cock I'm sucking springs out just as it comes and it sprays on my face, and the big goon comes up my ass and they push me down on the floor, roll me over and there's another one on top of me, fucking me missionary style, and some how it seems fitting, and I can't believe it because I'm coming.

Then it stops.

We're in the here and now of real time Stinson Beach. Ellen's standing in front of me holding the Doc Martens. The bathroom door lock is busted. There are tears in her eyes. There's anger in mine.

"I'm so—"

She drops the boots and heads towards me with her arms open in hug mode. I'm not letting her say she's sorry. No way. Not in a million years. No fucking hugs and everything is okay. I put my hands to stop her advancing and guilt assuaging.

"Don't speak. Don't say anything. You know, Ellen, I've been wracking my brains trying to figure out why you wouldn't help me. I thought if I put those boots on I might find some way to help you, and what do I find? You wouldn't help me because you set it all up. You set me and Luc and Lucretia up. And why? All in the name of love? You don't know the meaning of the word."

"I just wanted to protect you from harm. When Father Git approached me it all made sense. He made it seem so reasonable. They helped me so much in jail when you were gone."

"Don't you try to make it out that this is my fault. Don't you dare justify anything that happened that way."

"I'm not. I'm just trying to explain. I'm sorry we were hurt and raped. That wasn't part of the deal."

"Fuck that. There shouldn't have been any kind of deal. You don't get it do you? I didn't mind the dicks and being fucked. What I can't stomach is having my son taken and being set up by my lover for a crime they made me commit. Raped? Fuck it was fun. All the more fun now that I know what they put you through. I don't feel bad that six guys fucked every one of my holes and thanks to my power it was like six hundred. I feel really bad because you fucked me over. You violated me and my trust and it hurts worse than a million rapes."

"Violetta, I know you're angry."

"You don't know the fucking half of it. I've been so stupid. It really bugged me that it made no sense that they would let us go. I figured they were just being stupid moralists, but in reality it was because you'd cut a deal. Fuck, Ellen, how could you?"

"In time you'll see it was for the best."

"Just fucking stop there. You want to know the fucking irony here? Just before we went down to the warehouse I was thinking of saying maybe we should just quit all this serial killer of serial killer crap and move away somewhere quiet. You'd have had what you wanted if you hadn't meddled."

"As long as there was Luc there would always be the threat. He's the means to continue the curse."

"I could have kept him safe."

"Oh yeah, just like I can keep you safe. No, what I did, while it may seem cruel and horrible, was for the best."

"Well it was for nothing because I'm getting him back, and since I can't trust you you're out of here."

"This is as much my place as it is yours."

"Not anymore it isn't. It's neither of ours. There is no ours anymore. There could have been. We could have had a life together. I wouldn't have set Luc up against you. He'd have loved you like I have, but you were so consumed by guilt and jealousy you betrayed all I held dear."

"We can work this out. Just give me a chance."

"No. Just go. Don't make me throw you out saggy butt naked, Ellen. I'm going for a walk on the beach. When I get back I want you gone. We'll sort out the details later. I ain't keeping this fucking place. If you want it you can buy me out, or we'll just sell it and split the bucks because when I get Luc back I'm going away somewhere where no one will find us, especially you. You'll never know where we are or how we're doing but you will be haunted by the knowledge that you could have been with us and forever happy if you'd just had faith in me and my fucking cursed and gifted feet."

In tears I push past Ellen, grabbing the Doc Martens and head out to the beach. I run to the wave line, up to my knees in the surf and hurl the boots out to sea.

"You knew, didn't you?"

I feel Lucretia's answer.

"Yes, I did. I may have been in limbo, but I wasn't totally dead. I felt her betrayal even before the warehouse, when we enjoyed her in the kitchen, I knew then she'd been compromised by the Church. She couldn't hide the guilt she bore, that those Christians made her feel."

"Why didn't you say anything? All of this could have been avoided. You're my fucking Guardian Angel mother."

"And you are my headstrong young Avenging Angel Sex Goddess daughter who wouldn't have listened to me. You needed to find this out for yourself and see the consequences of trusting normal humans too much."

"Fuck."

"Exactly. It's a hard lesson to learn, but I had faith in you to bring me back, just as I have faith we will find Luc. I wouldn't have let them trap me if I wasn't sure you could figure this out and save me and your son."

In the distance I see the lights of Ellen's Jeep as it swings out of our driveway. I hear the screech of its tires over the ocean's roar, like a pained seagull. I spit into the ocean.

"Then what the fuck are we waiting for? I want my son back. Let's go on a Double Event rampage and kick some papal butt."

THE FINAL PAIR:
SLIPPERS

CHAPTER SIXTEEN

LUCRETIA AND I have a scant day to prepare for the Double Event. It's good that I'm so rushed—I don't have time to think of Ellen and how angry she made me and how hurt I feel. I can't afford a moment to feel like a victim. I focus on other victims instead, spending the day researching Jack the Ripper's third and fourth slayings. He struck twice in the early hours of September 30. Long Liz Stride and Catherine Eddowes were murdered within forty-five minutes of each other, their bodies a mere fifteen minutes walk apart. Jack was nimble and quick that night, and he had to be. Ripperologists generally believe and debate endlessly that Jack's mutilations of Liz Stride were disturbed and he went off into the night to find another down and out woman to fulfill his need for bloodlust and vengeance. The Double Event wasn't a planned event, unlike ours, which will be executed to perfection.

It's a bit freaky when I find out Long Liz Stride was really named Elisabeth Gustafsdotter and she was from Sweden—same as Saffron—same hometown—Torslanda near Gothenburg. Okay, there's lots of people from there but how many of them are prostitutes named Liz, one of whom I killed yesterday.

"Could this fuck up the Double Event thing?"

"No, my worrying daughter. It simply shows how connected and pervasive evil is. The boots were not involved, but I'll warrant that it was Saffron and Kahn's destiny to die at our hands so I could be reborn. Their slayings shows we're on the right path. It was not a coincidence. It was a bonus."

I'm sure Saffron and Kahn think so—some bonus. Another bonus will be tonight we'll find out just what disturbed Dr. Francis Tumblety, and why he didn't proceed to slice and dice Liz Stride after he'd cut her throat, thereby putting to rest all the Ripperologists' conjecture. Some have suggested Liz wasn't even a Ripper victim but just one of a bunch of East End Victorian London brutalities. Well, yawn, to be brutal myself, this morbid curiosity of crime geeks is not on my fucking priority list. It's a nice benefit—a piece of witty conversation guaranteed to break the ice pick at crimesolver parties—but right now knowing the identity of Jack the Ripper and all of the circumstances of his bloody reign doesn't amount to a hill of beans in my world.

Getting my son back does amount to a fucking great big Mount Everest of beans, and with just a few hours to go to re-enacting the Double Event I'm getting *nerviousa mucho*.

"So how do we know that we'll be able to control what goes on in the boots? How do we know that we'll be able to confront Father Git and Sister Teresa and not just end up killing some more unfortunate street people?"

I feel Lucretia deliberating, hesitating.

"Come on, don't hold back. We don't have much time."

"You have one way of finding Sister Teresa. She will lead us to Luc and Lekerk and the tape they hold of you."

"The bondage ballet boots. The ones she fucked Tony in."

"Yes, there are no coincidences."

"But how can I wear those and the Ripper boots? I can't wear a Sister Teresa boot on one foot and Ripper boot on the other. My power has never worked unless I have both shoes in the pair."

"That's right. There must always be a pair."

"But—"

"And there will be. You will wear Sister Teresa's boots, and I will wear Jack the Ripper's boots."

"But—"

"You're beginning to sound like an asshole with all those buts."

"Quit fooling. What aren't you telling me? Coyness isn't becoming of the Guardian Angel mother of an Avenging Angel Sex Goddess."

"I am strong enough to walk free of you. It took tremendous power to imprison me. When you freed me, that energy was like a million fucks mainlined to my soles. I felt it as soon as I killed Kahn and Saffron. That wasn't you. It was me. If you watch the tape you'll see."

"No way. I felt it. It was me."

"No, you felt the connection between us. It was me in Gina's shoes. There was no way you could have held Saffron and Kahn up. You're just not tall enough. You felt me do it and thought it was you, just like you will feel me wrench the truth out of those Catholic cunts. See for yourself. Watch the tape."

I put the tape in the VCR and hit play. I fast forward through all the preliminary foreplay and to the killing time. It's pretty hot stuff. We made a good threesome. Whoa, scratch that—foursome.

It wasn't me that pushed Kahn off my back. Lucretia pulled him off and punched Saffron and she held them both up until they died. I'm lying on the ground rolling in sexual ecstasy, coming like a mad woman. And I'm not wearing shoes.

The look on my face says it all. I'm totally numb-dumbfounded-discombobulated-stunned-amazed-agog-nonplussed-at-a-fucking-loss-for-words-other-than-duh.

"Don't ask how, Violetta. It is the way of the curse. You've brought me to life. My daughter has given birth to me. It was always meant to be ever since the caliges brought us together."

"So how do we do this?"

"You will first wear the Ripper boots. You'll put them on before the time of the murders so as not to be trapped in them at that time. You'll play with yourself, invoking me through danger, like you're choking from say hanging yourself while masturbating."

"Wait a fucking minute? You said you could materialize to me without the danger—even before you went away."

"Yes, materialize to you, but remember we're not just talking about me appearing to you. It's me appearing as a separate entity capable of existing independent of you. In time I will have the power to do so, but for now it needs you to be in danger."

"Fuck, Lucretia, this is getting scary much."

"To realize your destiny you must face your fears. Winning Luc back is worth it."

"So I do this and you pop out of me and save me and you put on the Jack boots and I put on the bondage ballet shoes and—"

"We fuck, and at the time that Jack walks our shoesex

will merge, and I'll walk to wherever Sister Teresa is, and I'll take it from there."

"Lucretia, why do I think you're making this up as you go along?"

"I am learning too, my child. Where something as fantastic and as mystical and as powerful as shoesex is concerned, there is always something new to be discovered. It is the fun and attraction of what we do, and for these risks we take there are also unimaginable rewards."

"Like we will actually touch and fuck, not just as a shoesex scene, but in reality."

"Yes, we become two separate beings so we can become one."

When it comes to the time there's one fucking great big problem. The last shoesex that occurred in the Jack boots was Ellen and me trying to resurrect Lucretia. Experiencing Ellen sexually is teensy-weensy-fucking-great buzzkill right now. Being inside me doing Ellen isn't exactly on my top ten list of turn-ons, but then again maybe it's the best way to kiss off our relationship—you know—strangling myself while jerking off to an Ellen screw and having Lucretia come to my rescue. Then again, if it doesn't work and I kill myself do I really want my last sexual gratification to be with a shoesex Ellen?

Not an option. This had better work.

I strip butt naked and stand on a chair, my robe belt knotted around my neck and hooked over the door. I test it out with a trial swing. It'll hold my skinny ass but good, and as long as I don't wait until I'm blacking out and have no strength left in my arms, I can pull myself up if Lucretia somehow gets waylaid again by the Catholic Church. So I slip my feet into the boots, and yeah, it's there, that two people one body familiar feeling only, dude, this is not a body I want to be familiar with because I'm too fucking familiar with it and right now, I don't want to be too familiar with it.

It is between my legs eating me, and I'm running my hands through its hair and even though I'm experiencing this I imagine it's not it. Yup, I pull the age-old trick of bored lovers the planet over—I pretend I'm fucking someone else besides the person I'm fucking right there and then. I don't go for a star or a fantasy stranger—oh no—I've experienced enough of that stuff in shoesex. I go for Johnny since he's the one I really wish was here right now. I imagine it's his head between my legs and his tongue up my cunt circling my clit like only a good cunt-muncher knows how.

My hands fall between my legs, slipping from my twatlicker's head to my cuntlips, parting my labia with the up and down motion of the inverted vee of my fingers, exposing my tender pink flesh to his tongue. He circles my cunthole with his tongue, spiraling inwards like he's bathwater being sucked down a plughole, sliding his finger in to replace his probing tongue, curling his finger backwards like he's calling me to him as he licks my exposed clit with the tip of his tongue.

He doesn't miss a beat. He presses in all the right places, with just the right amount of pressure. He presses his finger on my G spot and he presses his tongue against my clit, pressing it against the G spot, against his finger, and he works his fingers in and out, inserting two and then three, always making sure one is pressing on the G spot and he's doing all this as I'm rocking my hips around his face, but he doesn't let my motions distract him. He keeps in perfect sync, like he's part of my body under my intuitive control, and it feels so good, all this pressure in all the right places with exactly the right amount of friction to make me ever so wet. I'm melting, and I'm crying out because it's almost too much to bear.

It's when he somehow manages to find the dexterity to slide a finger up my ass that I've got it all, feeling his fingers and his tongue all working inside, separated by my thin juicing walls of flesh, and I start to go over the edge into orgasm land.

Go over the edge . . .

I do. Literally in both worlds. I come, going over the edge of orgasm, and I go over the edge of the chair, toppling it over as my creaming legs buckle. The belt tightens around my neck, and I'm swinging and no way do I want to take my hands from my coming cunt, but my windpipe's collapsing and I'm blacking out and it's a rush of fear and fucking, the ultimate frisson of two extremes combining into the best and worst of all worlds when I realize that my coming is a few muscle spasms away from making me going. My body has no strength. There's no energy left to lift my arms even if I wanted to. I'm gasping for breath and without oxygen to feed my dripping body it weakens and I'm on the downhill spiral to oblivion twisting to and fro, experiencing the real little death in tidal waves of agony and ecstasy that would blow Burt and Deborah clean off the beach and all the way from here to eternity.

Which is where I'm fast heading until strong hands hoist me upwards by my tiny waist, and through tearing eyes and blurring vision I see Lucretia holding me aloft, unhooking the rope from the door frame, breathing life into me with her kisses as she carries me over to the bed and unlaces the boots. I recline, my head cocked to one side, coughing. Lucretia kneels over me, and I am in awe of her ethereal beauty. Her skin is so pale she glows like pearls. Her hair is coal black, long, cascading down like an underground waterfall. Her eyes shine equally as dark and as fine. Her breasts are large yet firm, with dusky nipples standing out from golden brown aureole contrasting richly against the snowy valley of her bosom. Her pussy pelt is an inviting, dark, wiry vee highlighted with her musky scent. She is all angles and curves, shadows and clear, tall and lean and explosively muscular, like some ghostly jungle cat.

She places her hand underneath my pussy, sliding up between my legs, pressing hard all of her fingers one by one over my clitoris. She tastes me, licking those fingers one by one.

"You are exquisite, Violetta. You've given birth to me. I'm free."

"And I'm fucked. I'm exhausted. That was close."

"No closer than when your parents died and you tried to kill yourself by hanging from the door of your earthquake-wrecked house."

"You know about that?"

As soon as I've spoken I realize how silly it was. Of course she knows. She's as much me as I am her. Two people, two bodies, one person, that old familiar feeling. She smiles, acknowledging my blunder as I realize my blunder.

"Yes, when you showed me the shoesex in your mother's sparkly high heels that episode was deeply hidden in there, but I sensed it and understood that it was the pivotal moment in your shoesex life, when you learned that your power had a destiny."

"I thought it was just to kill the Dildo Killer."

"It was, and so much more. It was why I suggested the same method to bring me fully to life. I knew it would take you to the next level and to your ultimate destiny."

"And what is the next level after this? Where will this all lead? What is my ultimate destiny?"

"I don't know, but as with all journeys, it begins with the first small step."

Yeah right. I'm not sure she's telling me the complete truth. I think Lucretia knows more than she's letting on about my destiny, but she's better than me at hiding her thoughts. Before I can pump her for more information she looks at the bedside clock. focusing on the glowing digits, obliterating all other conjecture. We're fifteen minutes away from Long Liz Stride's murder.

"It's time," she says. "Lie still. I'll put your shoes on first. I'll angle the soles so they don't make contact until I make contact with the Jack boots."

I part my legs slightly and Lucretia slides the bondage ballet boots on to my feet. I watch my Guardian Angel bend to lace on the killer footwear that had almost claimed my life. She looks up at me, brushing her long, black hair from her pale face. I watch her muscles tense in her legs as she angles her feet into the boots. I see the full swell of her breasts against her thighs as she pulls the boots on, arching her soles from the killer-fuck-footwear. The flushed aureole peeks at me and the dark hardness of her nipple presses into her leg. She smiles at me, blows me a kiss and slams her feet down into Jack the Ripper's boots, smacking her hand on to the soles of the ballet bondage boots.

Two people, one body, that old familiar feeling.

Two bodies, one person, that new familiar feeling.

Lucretia's between my legs, licking my cunt as I imagined Johnny would while the Sister Teresa shoefuck of Tony plays through my reality. It's a trippy experience where there is no here and now, just Lucretia and I existing in a hybrid universe of fucked-in-footwear.

This is one of the scenes. I've played it through many times before. It's when I found out that Tony had the power. When I found out he was my half-brother just before it—Ellen—killed him because he was also the

Cinderella Killer. Tony's fucking me. I'm tied to the bed. Only it's not me. I'm Teresa. Sister Teresa. I'm a fucking nun. One of the slutty nuns from Saint Aldopho's where Tony was sent for being a bad boy after his Mom was killed. The nuns knew how to treat bad boys—by being bad themselves in the time honored Catholic nasty nun's tradition. Sister Teresa likes to set an example for Tony of what will happen to people who're naughty. They have to be punished.

"Tell me how bad I am, Anthony."

"You're a slut, Sister Teresa."

"Call me that word."

"You're a cunt."

"And you're punishing me for being a—"

"Cunt. You're a dirty cunt who makes young boys fuck her."

"Yes, that's right, I'm so awful."

I playact struggle to incite him. "No, no, you must stop, Anthony. I don't want this. Let me go," I say in my best defenseless voice, comfortable in the knowledge that he will be relentless, immune to my pleadings, playing his punisher role to perfection.

"There's nothing you can do, Sister Teresa of the Horny Cunt Church. I tied you to the bed like you told me to. And you're wearing the punishment shoes."

"And now you're raping me because I'm a—"

"Say it."

"I cannot. It's filthy."

"Then you're filthy, because you're a—say it."

Tony takes his hand from mauling my breasts through my disheveled habit and grips my chin and cheeks between his thumb and fingers. He squeezes my mouth open.

"Say it."

"Cunt."

"I didn't hear you."

He takes his hand away and thrusts it up my habit, rubbing my sex as his thing batters my—my—cunt. "I'm a filthy cunt. Sister Teresa is a filthy cunt."

I feel so free, so dirty now that I've said the C word and it wasn't Christ. Anthony is amused by the blissful look on my face. For a young boy he is truly perceptive.

"That's better. That's what you want isn't it?"

"Yes, yes, I'm a filthy cunt who wants Anthony to—"

"Fuck her."

The wetter he makes me the easier the dirty words flow.

"Yes, fuck me, Anthony. Fuck me hard. Punish me for thinking impure thoughts about you and all the other boys here in my care."

He sings his response like a proud schoolboy.

"I'm fucking Sister Teresa. I'm fucking Sister Teresa."

"And you're going to come on my habit."

"And you're going to come too. I'm going to make you come, just like you showed me."

His fingers play with my clitoris. He fumbles, not knowing exactly where to touch, but remembering the vague area I showed him the first time I seduced him. Anthony's so young, so inexperienced, but so eager. He learns well. Oh, dear Lord, that feels so wonderful. Thank you God for punishing me in this way. It's true. You do work in mysterious ways.

I see Anthony Anderson's face grimace above me. His body arches. His young cock stiffens. His teenage balls bounce against my bottom as he pounds into me. I feel his shaft pulse.

"Pull out, Anthony, pull out."

He does as commanded, and I feel the warm jets of his release splatter on my thighs and drip down onto my habit. My orgasm rises. He slows. It slows. I snap at him and he responds. Despite my being bound, despite my submissive role, Anthony knows who's in control.

"Don't stop you lazy boy. Now you're free of temptation for another week, play with me. Play with my cunt and set me likewise free from such nasty, impure thoughts."

He slides his finger in me and rubs my clitoris with his thumb, pushing back the hood, smearing his heated come over my sex. I melt onto his hand and begin to cry. Holy Father, forgive me for I do know what I'm doing.

I'm coming. I'm coming. Jesus Christ forgive me. But he doesn't. He punishes me for being a slutty cunt. My climax subsides as my temptation flows out of me, soaking my thighs and my habit.

The original shoesex likewise subsides, to be replaced by the reality of Tony fucking me. Bye-bye Sister Teresa, hello Violetta Valery Cutrero, new memories over old.

"You're a slutty cunt, Violetta Cutrero," he says. "A slutty cunt."

Tony's on top of me pounding into me like I'm his well-lubed fist with that super-tight grip. I'm tied to his bed in a weird reconstruction of his kinky scene with Sister Teresa. The ballet shoes are still on my feet. My leather jacket's hanging on the bedpost. My tee shirt is pushed up to my neck so my tits are exposed. He's biting them as he slobbers his insults. He thrusts hard into me, and I like the urgency because I'm so horny from the shoesex with Sister Teresa.

He bites my nipple and his hand clutches my cunt. He's rough with my pussy, pressing my clit against his grinding body. Sister Teresa taught him well. He's good.

"Oh, Anthony—Tony, that feels so good."

He looks up at me with that dirty sneer.

"You're a cunt, Violetta Valery Cutrero."

"Correction. I'm a horny cunt."

"You're a horny cunt with a big mouth."

He pulls out. He straddles my tits. The cold heat of his

sweaty thighs presses down upon me. His balls slide up my micro-cleavage as he pulls my head to his cock.

"Suck it, you horny cunt, suck my cock."

Tony's an adventurous dude. With his cock in my mouth he rotates his body around mine and falls between my legs. He licks at my pussy. I gnaw at his cock. I feel the cool metal of the cross around his neck press against my stomach. It doesn't feel like a crucifix. Feels much bigger and chunkier. The chain tangles with my pubic hair as he works his face into me. The room fills with slurping noises. It sounds like a lollipop tasting convention. I laugh at the thought, and my spasming throat does all the right things to Tony's cock. It steels and his balls contract. He bites my clitoris, just like he did my nipples. I scream, my tongue battering the pulsing head of his dick.

He stops biting. He pulls out. My scream subsides. He spins around and plunges his cock into me and before the tip hits my pussy walls he's orgasming. His mound smashes against my clitoris, and I come as my body arches off the bed, pulling tight against the ropes until they burn my wrists and ankles. Tony collapses onto me, and his cross burns into my cleavage, but I don't relax against the rigor mortis of coming. He kisses me and I taste my cunt on his face.

"Tell me how bad I am, Anthony."

"You're a slut, Sister Teresa."

"Call me that word."

"You're a cunt."

Oh fuck, I'm Sister Teresa again. Our sex and the previous episode blur together and repeat. Tony's on top of me, mauling my breasts through my habit. The hem is pushed up to my waist and he's slapping his skinny-boy body into my pale thighs.

"Oh, Anthony—Tony, that feels so good."

I playact struggle to incite him. "No, no, you must stop,

Anthony. I don't want this. Let me go," I say in my best defenseless voice, comfortable in the knowledge that he will be relentless, immune to my pleadings, playing his punisher role to perfection.

"There's nothing you can do. I tied you to the bed like you told me to. And you're wearing the punishment shoes."

"Tell me how bad I am, Anthony."

"You're a slut, Sister Teresa."

"Call me that word."

"You're a cunt."

"And you're punishing me for being a—"

"Cunt. You're a dirty cunt who makes young boys fuck her."

"Correction. I'm Violetta Valery Cutrero, and I am a horny cunt."

"Correction, I'm your Guardian Angel, Lucretia Cutrero and I'm inside you, and I will look after you, and we will find our son. I'm sorry I wasn't there to protect Tony, but he died for a purpose, for our greater good."

"Lucretia," I say as her tongue licks my—Sister Teresa's—pussy and she's fingering my cunt and my ass and I'm going over the edge. The world spins, and I'm inside Lucretia eating me—Sister Teresa—on the bed, and I see her pussy, and I taste my pussy, and I feel Lucretia's strength in my arms and legs, and as I rear up I love the feel of my long black hair lash my nipples and I'm looking down at this sexed out nun being alternately fucked by me and by Tony and by Lucretia then suddenly I'm walking down a dingy alley and it could be the East End of London in 1888, and before I have time to check my spinning head I'm walking down a hallway of a fancy house and it could be the San Francisco Catholic Archdiocese mansion in 1992.

It's both.

I turn the corner onto Berner Street and hear a moan

between the numbers of 40 and 42. I enter a small carriage business called Dutfield's Yard. There's a woman lying on the ground in the dank darkness. Stepping over fresh clods of horse manure I approach. This is altogether too perfect.

I turn from the hallway and into another shorter passageway. All the rooms have numbers. Between 40 and 42 I hear sobbing. This room's called The Archbishop Dutfield's Suite, so I enter and find a woman lying on a bed in the cloistered darkness. She's dressed in a nun's habit. It's Sister Teresa. Stepping over the handcuffs and whip lying on the floor I approach. This is altogether too perfect.

By the light of the single gas streetlight I see she's wearing a black bonnet, a check scarf, a long black jacket trimmed with fur, a long black skirt and a dark colored velvet bodice. As she fell to the ground her skirt rode up her legs to reveal white petticoats and stockings and black boots. I feel lust stir. She is a prize prostitute, one that would no doubt lure many men with her rough street prettiness. The site of her so disheveled, waiting for me like manna from the heavens, is a sign that my mission is divinely guided. I shall enjoy defiling this one.

She stirs as I approach and speaks with a foreign-accented English.

"Oh thank you, sir, for scaring him off. I thought my time was done. He must have been the Whitechapel Murderer. He took my money. All of it. He'd have taken my life if you hadn't happened by."

What a pathetic creature. She thinks I'm here to save her. I offer my hand to lift her from the ground. I seethe that some small-time thieving hoodlums are mistaken for me by wretches such as this useless piece of human packaging, but I hide my anger so as not to alert her. I offer her a consoling, reassuring look. I pull out some coins.

"Will these make up for your loss?"

She counts them, eyes widening and her face filling with smiles as she realizes how much money is in her hand.

"Why yes, sir, and more so. You're such an angel—my guardian angel. I'm Liz Stride. Long Liz Stride they call me—nots that I'm that tall but on account of my last name being Stride. One of these funny English things that they do with names—Long Stride—Chalky White, but after tonight, thanks to you, sir, I thinks I'll be called Lucky Long Liz Stride and no mistaking that."

She pops into her mouth some of those hideous breath mints called cachous that prostitutes use to sweeten their breath so as not to offend customers with the rancor of foul gin and rotting teeth. Margaret followed the practice before she kissed me.

Margaret. Margaret. I still taste your tainted kisses. My eyes flow red, knowing how this Long Liz Stride plans to repay my kindness, my tightly wound anger uncoils.

"More of an avenging angel I'm afraid."

I spit the words out as I push Unlucky Liz Stride on her unsteady feet into the wall and hold her against the cobble bricks with my gloved hand, lifting her off the ground. She gasps. I grab the scarf, pulling it to the left side and twist so it constricts against her thin white neck. She struggles, but thanks to her scarf my other hand is free to roam up her dangling legs. I run my gloved fingers up her thrashing stockinged legs, enjoying the sudden jump from stocking to flesh. She wears no knickers as is the uniform of her profession. I rub her sex, feeling the wiriness of her cunny through the leather of my gloves. I ram my finger into her and she struggles even more, impaling herself on my hand.

What a delicious creature she is. So afraid, so at my mercy. So near death. Her eyes roll back so I penetrate her cunt vigorously with my finger, making her start awake. She bangs her head against the wall, and with each thrust of my hand inside her she hits her head, as if she wants to dull the pain by the anesthesia of unconsciousness.

"Oh no, no, no. We'll have none of that," I say with a chuckle. "You are to feel my pain."

I slide her to the ground, pushing her petticoats above her shapely hips. I press wide her legs with mine, extricating my sturdy penis from its cage as I do so. I pull the scarf tight to keep her voice quiet. Her cunny is wet from my probings so I don't need extra spittle. I nudge my cock to her opening and lunge inside her, thrusting as fast and as deep as I had with my fingers. My vigorous fucking pushes her into the wall and with each thrust she bangs her head again, and this annoys me, so before I reach fruition and give her my benediction I reach inside my coat for my knife and slit her throat. That'll stop her head from bobbing, and she'll be alive enough to feel me spurt.

I'm contemplating the perversions I'll foist on the tapestry of her soon-to-be lifeless body when there's the clatter of a horse and cart entering the yard. I'm close to coming but I can't take the chance of being discovered. This prostitute will remain an unfinished work.

I spit at this Lucky Long Liz who was short on her luck tonight.

"It seems you weren't as lucky the second time around. My regrets that I did not have sufficient time to make you fully my own. I do hope they realize that you were one of mine."

I pull out my cock, wrap my cape around me and head into the darkness passing an old merchant and his cart. Cursing my luck I head towards the river. My cock is hard. My knife is sharp. I need another victim before I can rest my bloodlust and bury Margaret's ghost until she returns to taunt me again.

Sister Teresa's habit is torn open and pushed up at the bottom to reveal a candystriped ass and back. She's lying face down, breathing heavy. She's out cold. I run my fingers across the welts. They're fresh, pulsating, tender. Her naked pussy oozes cuntjuice, filling the heavy atmosphere of the closed room with her musk. My hand drops from the stripes on her back to the ones on her ass, and as I go lower, she starts. Her eyes fasten on me, and in an instant I see that she fears more beatings, but then as she recognizes that I am not her punisher she breathes a sigh of relief and sobs.

"I thought they were back for more. I can't take much more."

"Who?"

"Father Lekerk and Alras."

"Alras?"

"His chief enforcer. His brutalizer. Ed Alras. He does all the work while Lekerk watches."

Lucretia and I recognize the description. Alras must be the big goon who enjoyed gangraping Ellen and I. We nod. Sister Teresa shakes our arms, pleading.

"You've got to help me. I've got to get out of here before they come back."

"You have to help me."

The look of recognition on the dazed face of Sister Teresa during the short time of that particular exchange gives away that she's sussed that she might have jumped from the frying pan into the fire. She regards me from head to toe. I'm naked, flesh glistening, black hair falling like a mask, large boots on my feet, boots she no doubt recognizes. She pushes back to the edge of the bed but I grab her leg and pull her to me.

"Who are you? What are you doing here?" she says, wriggling in my grip.

I don't answer, content to let Sister Teresa squirm. Using one hand I take off the Ripper boots, not because I'm polite, but because I don't need an immediate foot-fuck replay. I climb on the bed, pushing her down into the dampened bedclothes, my arms spreadeagling over her, touching her fingers, my body swamping hers. I feel the lined heat of her beating radiating like the sun through venetian blinds. I whisper into her ear.

"I'm Lucretia Cutrero, and I've come for my daughter's son, Luc."

Sister Teresa stiffens and struggles, reciting some silly prayer. I tire of these games. With one hand I squeeze her neck, pressing her face into the bed. The other hand I direct between her legs. She's sodden from her beating. I reach under and slide my parted fingers around her clit. I stroke backwards and forwards, pulling the flesh away from the swollen nub, twisting it from side to side. She moans. I whisper into her ear, biting at the fleshy lobe.

"Where is Luc?"

"I don't know."

I bite harder into her ear lobe. I taste blood.

"Not good enough."

Sister Teresa screams as I bite into her neck. I slide my hand out of her cunt, up between her ass until I find one of the welts. I pinch the wound. Sister Teresa screams more but I muffle the emission by pressing her face into the mattress, biting her neck as I go.

As her cries turn to whimpers I slip my hand back down to the nun's ass.

"I will get the truth out of you. I'll eat it out of you. You can't hide from me."

"I'm telling you the truth. I don't know where the child is."

I try a different approach. I push three of my fingers in and out of her cunt, twisting with every plunge into her sodden opening.

"Why was Lekerk beating you? Have you been a naughty nun?"

"I tried to give the baby back to his mother. They took him away from me. I was being punished for disobedience."

I ram my thumb up the naughty nun's ass. She's very wet in there, no doubt Alras, or perhaps Father Git or maybe both, enjoyed a buggering. I slide my fingers in and out of her cunt, rubbing them to my thumb along her sensitive separation between ass and cunt. She groans and arches her ass into me. The woman is a horny bride of Christ cunt. She can't deny her body's urges.

"You lie. Violetta never heard from you."

"I didn't get far enough. They stopped me with the baby before I'd gone a few blocks."

"We'll see if you're telling the truth."

I knot the sister's wimple and cape around her mouth, gagging her. There's a pair of slippers on the floor. I put them on her feet and turn Sister Teresa on her back.

"I told you I'd eat the truth out of you."

I dive between her legs and lick her pussy. She flails her arms trying to beat on my head but I'm too powerful for her. I kneel, almost standing and lift her body, flopping her legs over my shoulders, holding her thighs in my vise-like grip, keeping her cunt attached to my mouth and my probing tongue. Her upper torso falls backwards and she's unable to muster enough strength to hit me. It's goddamn obvious—and a darn good job—that vertical sit-ups aren't on the nunnery exercise routine.

I work my face into her pussy, pressing her ass and cunt into my mouth like I'm devouring a mushy tropical fruit.

I lick from the clenched tight rosebud of her ass to the pulpy pinkness of her cunt. After the working over from Lekerk and Alras she's ready to pop, so it only takes a few well directed suckings on her clit to send the dear little Sister Teresa into lusty spasms.

I throw the convulsing woman onto the bed and roll her over. I lay on top of her, my body smothering her like a second skin. I kick off her sexed-in slippers and maneuver them on to my feet, and there I am, two people, one body—or in this case—three people, one body—Sister Teresa, Violetta and Lucretia—and now the truth.

"I tried to give the baby back to his mother. They took him away from me. I was being punished for disobedience."

I say this with all the conviction that I can muster, that I can believe. It was true. I never wanted to take the baby away from his mother.

She's lying, Lucretia.

Yes, she is, Violetta.

The difficult thing is, she's lying to herself, so it's going to be hard to get to the truth, especially after the Catholic guilt trip and beating Lekerk and Alras laid on her.

This demonic Lucretia rams her thumb up my bottom. I'm wet in there from that brute Alras's sodomizing of me. How Father Lekerk would allow him this perversion just because I wanted to help the child. I've always only wanted to help the children, like the boy's father, Tony. I only wanted to help him.

* * *

Oh fucking shit, if what she did to Tony was called helping, then fuck, Luc is in big trouble.

Don't worry, Violetta. I'll get it out of her. Luc will be safe.

The Cutrero demon slides her fingers in and out of my pussy, rubbing them and her thumb along the sensitive skin between my openings. It is too much pleasure to bear. I am so excited. Why do I enjoy the pleasures of the flesh so. I can't help it. I want more. I groan and arch my back, thrusting my bottom to my attacker. You can have me. You can do whatever you want with me. Punish me. Make me pay for being so bad.

"You lie. Violetta never heard from you."

She needs to understand. I wanted to free the baby from its confines.

"I didn't get far enough. They stopped me with the baby before I'd gone a few blocks."

"We'll see if you're telling the truth."

Oh I am. I am.

She doesn't believe me. It's obvious. They never believe me. They always accuse me of molesting the children when all I want to do is free them from the confines of a religion that denies sexuality. Why can't they see that? Why do they punish me for being good, for doing the true God's work. He moves in mysterious ways. He moves through me and my fingerings.

"Oh please, please, don't hurt me anymore. Those two men have taken all I can give. I am yours, but don't hurt me anymore."

Ouch.

She knots my head covering and cape around my mouth, gagging me. Now she can't hear me beg for mercy or explain. Why?

What is she doing with my feet. She's putting my slippers on me. Is she going to take me somewhere? No. She rolls me onto my back.

"I told you I'd eat the truth out of you."

No, no, she's going to use her evil shoesex powers to read my thoughts, to find out why I am the way I am. Teresa, try to think of nothing but the moment now.

She dives between my legs and licks my sex. Not my sex, but my pussy, my cunt, my horny cunt. That's it— just think of my horny cunt pussy and how good she's making me feel by eating me. Oh that is so good. What is it about those Cutreros and sex? Tony was so good a fuck, and this woman is the sexiest bitch alive. Who knows what that Luc will grow in to. He's already a horny little boy with that cute little hard cock poking at me when I changed his messy underwear.

No, no, don't think of that. Stop it. Stop it. Stop making me feel so good. You're destroying my barriers. You're melting my mind. Stop it. Holy Father help me. I flail my arms like windmills trying to beat on her head but the woman is too strong for me. She kneels and lifts my over-sexed body almost off the bed, flopping my legs over her shoulders. I try to squeeze her head, but her hands hold my thighs apart, keeping my cunt attached to her mouth and her probing tongue. I fall backwards, and I can't strike out anymore. I can't resist.

She works her face into my pussy, pressing my ass and cunt into her mouth like she's devouring a succulent fruit. She licks from the clenched tight rosebud of my ass to the pulpy raw pinkness of my cunt. After the working over from Lekerk and Alras I'm ready to explode after just a few well-directed suckings on my clit.

She sticks her fingers into my pussy. Oh how wonderfully dirty this feels. It's like she's holding me up by those fingers, pulling my pussy to her mouth like I'm her perverted finger puppet slave. She presses down on my clit and presses hard on my inner pussy walls with her finger, sliding across my G spot. I come. I come so hard my legs straighten as if I'm filled with rigor mortis. My toes point and it feels like my orgasm shoots from my head to my tits to my tummy to my pussy to my thighs to my feet and toes and shoots out of my body.

Along with my thoughts. I can't help it. I feel so good. So right. There's nothing wrong with sex. I'm a bride of Christ. I was simply anointing the boy. So what if I did it with my lips. These are the lips of Christ. So what if I sucked the baby's hard, little penis. He laughed and chuckled. He enjoyed his very first blowjob. I did no harm. I didn't penetrate his little body. His penis was already hard. He is a horny little boy.

Sister Teresa is fucking toast, Lucretia. Fucking molesting my son in the name of some sick view of her sick religion. She is toast.

Easy my daughter. We still need information. Then we shall exact our punishment.

Yeah, well, let's get it out of her because all that stuff I said earlier at the beginning about it not being child pornography when I let Luc suck on my tit while Ellen and I were fucking. That still stands. But a fucking nun stealing my kid so she can suck his cock just lights my moral minority buttons.

The Cutrero demon throws my convulsing body onto the bed and rolls me over. She lays on top of me, her body smothering my like a second skin. She kicks off the slippers and it's over. She shouts in my ear. I jump. I'm still blissful from my release. Such harshness slaps at my face.

"Where's Luc now?"

"Lekerk took him. I don't know where. I wanted to give him back to the mother. He does belong with her."

"I know what you did to Luc."

"Yes, I know you do. I couldn't hide it. When Lekerk found me orally worshipping the young boy he was furious not so much at me but at the boy. He ranted about how the baby was demonic. How Luc corrupted by his mere presence. How the baby must be sent away to some country where there are not so many rules and civic watchdogs—sent away to be castrated."

"NO."

I put my hands around Sister Teresa's neck and press. She gasps.

"Don't—don't—I didn't want to see the child hurt like that. He is so beautiful. I tried to sneak him out to be with his mother, but they caught me. That's why I was being punished. They felt they had to cleanse my disloyal, dirtied soul of the impure thoughts and the temptation to stray that the demonic Cutrero baby gave me. I'm on your side. The baby doesn't belong with the Church. Don't hurt me."

"Where's Luc?"

"Lekerk has sent him away. I don't know where."

"Where's Lekerk?"

"Upstairs in the Mitre Suite."

We all start as we hear noises in the hallway—the mutter of voices—muffled laughter—heavy goon-like footfalls. Sister Teresa panics.

"They're coming back. Alras said he'd send some of his animals to have fun with me. You've got to help me."

"Oh, I will."

With one firm twist of my powerful hands I snap her neck.

"Now you won't feel any more pain."

I look around the room, quickly figuring how to make my escape. The door opens and in steps two of the goons who raped Ellen and me.

"Unlike some people," I say as I pull my shoe leather trimming knife from my boot.

CHAPTER SEVENTEEN

I WALK INTO Father Git Lekerk's Mitre Suite room muttering the Last Rites. I'm amazed at how no one locks doors in this place. Probably the same in the Vatican. They're so sure no nasties could sneak in that what's the point of deadbolts when we're all bosom buddies and equal in the eyes of God and the prying Pope and his ever-vigilante-up-to-no-good priests. I surmise it's also a major case of shit flows downhill. No locked doors makes it easy for the likes of Father Git to catch and punish wayward acolytes like Sister Teresa.

And for me to catch and punish Father Git and all his nasty big goons. This open door policy of the Church works both ways. Shit does flow downhill and right now I'm on top of the frigging mountain taking a big, smelly, currified crap on the Catholic Church.

Father Git's wearing a bathrobe—slicked back wet hair—rosy skin—sipping a glass of what looks like expensive cognac, brandy or whisky. I doubt he'd be drinking anything but the best. The Catholic Church knows how to spend its alms for the poor very well. He looks like he's just showered the sweat of punishing Sister Teresa off his Teflon skin.

I mumble some more of the Last Rites.

"What? Who are you? What are you doing here?"

He reaches for the phone. I assume he wants to call for security not a pizza delivery.

"So many questions. I'll save you the trouble. Alras is on his way up with the bad news about Sister Teresa. She's dead, Git, as will you be in a few moments if you don't give me what I want. And in answer to your first question I was practicing the Last Rites to make sure I get it right when I kill you. I didn't do it for Sister Teresa, and I'm sure it made her feel bad that she's gonna rot in hell now, but that's what she deserves, right, that child-molesting bitch."

"You know? How? Did she confess?"

He's edging to the door. I edge faster, meaner.

"Don't bother—I'd snap your neck in two before you got your hand on the knob. Now just sit down and let's wait for Alras."

I deliberately don't say anything about the two carved-up-dead gang-raping goons adorning Sister Teresa's death scene. I don't want Father Git to know his forces have been diminished. I want him thinking I'm limited to killing in parallel with the Jack boots. I want him thinking there's a way out of his pre-dick-a-mento.

It's working. He's not so cocksure anymore. He settles uncomfortably into his big armchair, like he's got enflamed hemorrhoids. He crosses his legs and sips on his drink. He looks at my Jack the Ripper boots trying hard not to look scared.

"Did that Cutrero whore send you?"

"You are inquisitive aren't you."

Father Git shrugs his shoulders.

"You barge in here, somehow passing our very capable security guards and systems, claiming to have murdered one of my nuns, threatening to do likewise to me. Yes, I have questions."

"Then shut the fuck up, and I'll give you some answers, and if you give me one, then I'll let you live."

He casually rolls his hand in my direction in that infuriatingly dismissive 'go on, get on with it' gesture. I'll give the devil in Father Git his due. The bastard is smooth.

"In no particular order, here's the answers. Sister Teresa didn't confess in so many words. Her feet told the tale of how you found her pleasuring herself at Luc's expense."

That soundbyte ruffled Father Git's demeanor so much he spit out his high-priced booze.

"Yes, Father Git, the feet cannot be denied. And no, that Cutrero whore didn't send me. I am her. She is me. We are Lucretia Violetta Cutrero."

The bad father crosses himself and mutters "Help me, Holy Father."

"Sorry, he no can do. Your stupid little exorcism couldn't hold me. In fact, it helped me. I had some very nasty assholes to feed off."

Alras bursts in.

"Father Lekerk, Sister—"

He doesn't get another word out. I'd stationed myself behind the door anticipating the big goon's entrance. From my vantage at his rear I kick him in the balls, as hard as all of my combined Guardian Angel Avenging Angel Sex Goddess prowess can muster. The sound he makes as he collapses forward is like a balloon blowing itself around the room. I kick him two more times in the balls and once in the gut and once in the head, putting him out for the count.

I look at the seated Father Git. Fuck ruffles, there's definitely some major cracks in his Teflon smooth exterior.

"And neither can Alras help you. It's just us and Jack the Ripper's boots and the clock.

He crosses himself again.

"Yes, in a few minutes these boots will begin their second murderous walk of the night. They've already killed Sister Teresa, paralleling Liz Stride's death, the third victim, so whomever's around me when the clock strikes Catherine Eddowes will be the fourth. But what am I saying? You know all since you've had those boots in your custody since Tumblety left them to the good Sisters of Mercy. That's very ironical I think, very funny too, since the Sisters are just about my favorite band. They even have a song named for me—"Lucretia My Reflection." You know, the more I live and kill the more I see that there are no coincidences. Everything's connected in some bizarre way, and in about five minutes I have to kill again as Jack slices up Catherine Eddowes in—surprise—Mitre Square—"

I wave my hand around his palatial abode.

"Like I said—no coincidences. Now, who is it going to be—you or Alras."

Lekerk watches the clock tick around as I rip off Alras's clothing.

"What do you want?"

"Right now, your robe belt."

"Excuse me?"

"I need to tie him up. The big goon will wake up soon, and if I'm killing you I don't need his interference."

Lekerk stands and undoes his robe. He tosses me the belt, pulling the robe demurely shut around him.

"Oh don't bother with such modesty. Take your robe

off. I might just make my decision based upon who's got the biggest dick."

He drops the robe around his ankles.

I snicker.

"Or the littlest."

Lekerk's male ego snaps. He shouts, his fists clenching. He might be a priest supposedly denying himself the pleasures of the flesh but let me tell you, his testosterone flows mega-free.

"What in God's name do you want?"

I finish trussing up Alras, gagging him with his boxer shorts stuffed in his mouth and his shirt knotted around his neck to hold them in place.

I walk over to Lekerk and put my hand on his throat.

"In God's name I don't want a fucking thing. In the Cutrero name I want two things, and there's no negotiation and just a few minutes to decide, or you'll feel the same pain as Catherine Eddowes. She was butchered, dismembered horribly, in a ghastly ritual by some sick woman-hating shit who couldn't handle a dent to his male ego. You know, Father Git, Tumblety slashed her face, removing part of her nose and ear, cutting her eyelids in two."

I trace the cuts with my finger held out like a knife blade. Lekerk flinches.

"He ripped her from her asshole to her throat rearranging her intestines around her neck. Some Ripperologists think Eddowes was a preface for his final, most grisly decapitation of Mary Kelly. Funny how each murder escalated in bloody horror and then ended. What they don't know is that they didn't end—they just moved venues when Tumblety fled Scotland Yard's custody to America to kill again and eventually die in your care. Two minutes."

"What is it you want?"

"Oh yeah, that. Well, you know. Of course you do. You're a smart guy. Do I have to spell it out? I guess so."

"What?"

Lekerk shakes in my grip as I tap my Jack the Ripper booted foot louder and louder counting down the seconds. His eyes go from the boots to my face to the boots.

"Ninety seconds. I want to know where is the master tape and all copies of Violetta being tricked into committing those first two murders, and I want to know where is Luc and in all cases, I want them back."

Lekerk shakes his head. I lift him off the floor. His legs dangle. His skinny little dick shrivels.

"Don't give me that 'I don't know' bullshit. For a smart, powerful guy with maybe just one minute to live you're acting really stupid. Did I tell you I have a very sharp shoe leather-trimming knife slid into my boots. The more you piss me off the more I'm going to enjoy chopping off your ear and rearranging your intestines to match some bizarre Masonic rite that Jack did on Catherine Eddowes. I might even slice out your kidney, fry part of it up for my dinner and send the other to the *Chronicle* with my regards for you, from hell. I can see the headlines now—'Modern day Jack the Ripper stalks the City. Respected priest killed in bizarre reenactment of Victorian crimes.' "

I look at the clock.

"One minute—or thereabouts—you know they weren't too precise in the time of the murders back then. Could happen any SECOND."

Lekerk practically saves me the trouble of slicing him up the way he almost jumps out of his skin. I'm tempted to laugh, but instead I press my advantage and reach for my knife, doing my best to maintain my most demonic-spastic-Linda Blair-eye-contact-possessed stare.

It works like a charm.

"Okay, okay, put me down, and I'll get the videos for you. They're in my safe."

"Father Git. I'm not stupid. Where's the safe?

"Over there, behind the picture of the Pope."

"I should have known. What's the combination?"

"I'm not telling you."

"Forty-five seconds, and you've still got to tell me about Luc."

Git rolls his eyes.

"Sixty-nine right, ninety-six left, sixty-six right."

"Cute."

"Hurry."

Holding the panicking priest by the neck I spin the dials, deliberately fumbling the combination for effect.

"Sorry, I'm a bit excited by all this. You could calm me down by telling me what you know about Luc."

"Nothing, I swear. I don't know where he is."

"I'm getting excited again, and you know, it wouldn't be much fun slicing up a big fat blob of passed out flesh."

I look at Alras and then back to Lekerk.

"Where's the fun in that?"

Lekerk eyes Alras predatorily as I open the safe. I see the video cassettes, which I snag. There's a shit load of cash and some airline tickets which I snag, and a gun which I leave. I slam the safe shut and spin the dials, rearranging the smiling Pope picture back into place.

"You bad boy, Git. You were going to shoot me."

He sputters.

"No I wasn't. I'd forgotten the gun was in there."

"Just like these airline tickets. I wonder where they're to? Twenty seconds."

Father Git looks down. Scared shitless and crestfallen comes to mind as an apt description of his mien.

"Luc's been taken to Mexico City. After the incident with Sister Teresa we thought it best if we sent him to a remote location. Many here believe the child to be possessed of unusual, corrupting sexual energy. Luc left today with Father Ritchie and Sister Maria. They're meeting a trusted local priest, Father Jesus Lopez at a small church—Our Mother of Guadeloupe—and will review many distant locations deep in the jungles or high in the mountains where there are few people to provide distractions or attractions for Luc. I'm leaving next week—you can check the itinerary—to meet them when they're done and provide the official blessing."

I look at the clock.

"Time's up. We need to see if you're telling the truth. You left out the bit about castrating my son so I don't trust you even as far as I could throw you."

I carry the struggling priest over to the bed, kicking the groaning and stirring Alras in the head for good measure as I walk by. Adding a physical punctuation to my last pronouncement I throw Lekerk onto the sheets and ram his feet into his dress shoes.

He's stinking hard before I even touch him. He clutches at his cock, trying to cover the evidence of his lust. I can't resist ridiculing him.

"You faux-celibates are all the same. In all my years of shoefucking I've seen it all. The men of God who condemn the evils of the flesh are always the ones most up for enjoying it. Ole Marquis de Sade got it right in his writings and look where all that literary priest-bashing landed him—the Bastille. While I admire de Sade in some things, I don't plan to emulate him when it comes to spending my days in captivity, and my priest-bashing won't be literary at all. Far from it."

I put my hand on Lekerk's throat, pinioning his writhing body to the bed, adding that extra frisson of asphyxiation to our fucking that I so enjoy. His cock noticeably stiffens to the point it looks like a frying sausage ready to burst. I hold his kicking legs down with my knees, spreading him wide so I see the hairy pucker of his asshole. I reach down with my free hand and cup his balls, hefting them in my palm, rubbing them around my fingers like Captain Queeg nervously juggling his ball bearings. I toy my middle finger across Lekerk's puckered rosebud.

Twisting his balls, I stuff my finger, pointy nail first up his dry asshole and give his prostate a good vigorous scratching. If Father Git could scream with pain and then pleasure he would, but since I'm throttling him all he utters are spitty-sputters and guttural moans.

I fuck his ass with my finger, careful to gouge the priest's prostate with every thrust. His cock steels and twitches and drips pre-come, and I can tell Lekerk is no stranger to ass play. I wonder how many altar boys he's had up his ass or vice versa. No doubt I'll find out. The feet cannot be denied.

I know I don't have much time before Jack struts his stuff so I go to work on Father Git's twitching cock. With his balls still in my twisting grip and my finger up his ass I bend my head and capture his bobbing cock. I suck like I'm licking out the last drops of a damn fine chocolate shake through a straw. I nestle his cock head at the back of my throat and let my gag reflex massage his cockhead down my throat. I am a perfect cocksucker, matching the arch of his dick to my mouth, guiding his shaft deep down my throat with his tongue. Lekerk is in heaven by way of hell when after several suckings I feel his balls swell with release so I withdraw my mouth and kiss him on the turning blue lips. I bite at his skin, drawing blood.

I look him in the bulging eyes as I nestle his cock against my pussy, rubbing the sensitive head up and down my labia, running circles around my clit. It feels good. It feels even better when I say, "So you thought you could have my son castrated? Any idea what that feels like?"

I sink his cock into my pussy, but I don't relinquish my

grip on his balls. I twist them even more as I ride up and down slowly, tightening my grip with every delicious thrust. I want Father Git Lekerk to think I'm going to tear them off, and I can tell from the horrified look on his purpling face that he fears the worst.

"You fucker," I say. "Jeez, you religious sickos are the worst. I thought the Jews were bad enough, lopping off a bit of the cock in the name of some strange purification reason, but, Father Git dude, castrating, turning my son into a eunuch, now that's taking Catholicism to the extreme. Why couldn't you just stick to molesting young boys instead of maiming them? But then again, the whole castrati thing is nothing new to you Catholic sadists, is it. Fuck, it was to please your Popes that the whole business started in the first place. You wouldn't let women sing in church so you encouraged poor families to sell their sons to the Church to be castrated so their voices would never break and the Popes would hear lovely little angelic tones in their services. Well, kiss my feminist ass, Father Git, that's two sins—discrimination against women and child abuse. You all should rot in Hell for what you've done, and don't dare tell me that the Church outlawed castration because you're planning to do it to my son right now, and don't tell me that Rome knows nothing about this."

He tries to shake his head in protest, but there's not much strength in him. I fuck him harder and I twist harder and I probe harder with my finger. Lekerk bucks on the bed adding more pain and pleasure with his writhing. He feels pretty fucking good underneath me.

"You're not a bad fuck, Father Git. You'd have made someone an excellent wife."

This is where it gets weird.

I'm riding Lekerk into oblivion. I notice him shaking his head, so I tell him, "Hey, don't bother denying anything because I'll know everything you're thinking from your shoes. There's no way you can hide from me."

He tries to say something, but I make it difficult by squeezing his cock with my pussy. Combine this lovely sensation with his ball torture and ass probing and Father Lekerk is not long for this world, literally. His orgasm is going to be his final because I don't need him alive. I'll know what he knows and with any fucking luck I'll be there to rescue Luc before those Catholic assholes down south of the border can chops his family jewels off.

Still, I can't resist toying with Lekerk. I'm still smarting from the supercilious way he treated me in the warehouse. What's the fun in letting him die happy. Now I know why all those serial killers love to rant. Torturing the victims with mind games is so much fucking fun.

"You could have saved yourself a whole lot of pain if you'd just told me the truth. It could be Alras who'll know what it is to relive a Jack the Ripper murder, but instead, you're going to join entrails with Catherine Eddowes. That was one of just a long line of mistakes you've made in this whole tawdry affair. Your biggest mistake was thinking you could exorcise as powerful a pagan as Lucretia. Your second biggest mistake was not having the balls to kill Violetta at the warehouse, precipitated by your third biggest mistake—joining forces with the spineless and unstable Ellen Stewart and then thinkng that the threat of police retribution would stop us. That's a lot of big fuck ups for a smart man, Father Git. How silly."

Lekerk pleads with his eyes. I can't resist. I loosen my grip on his throat. He coughs. I look over my shoulder at Alras.

"Will you tell me the truth," I say.

"Yes," he coughs, obscuring his answer, averting his eyes from me, perhaps more from his jealous and judgmental god. His transparent little obfuscation tactic doesn't fill me with the confidence that he means what he says.

"Will you?" I say, my voice growing sterner and more sinister.

"Will you?" I say in a voice that doesn't feel like my own.

"But of course, dearie. Catherine Eddowes will fuck ya for the price of a kip," she says as she leads me into the darkest corner of Mitre Square. Towing me along her drunken path this pathetic creature of the night drones on and on.

"Oawh it's been a horrid day it 'as. Got meself turned out of the Shoe Lane Workhouse and had to pawn me love's boots to get the money for our breakfast and drink. And for the love of it all I gots meself arrested for imitating a fire engine and falling down dead drunk. I'll get the hiding of me life from John. He's Irish and don't truck with me being unruly none. He's a bit poorly and my drunken ways don't do him no good, but he loves me cause I looks after him well, if ya knows what I mean, sir."

She winks at me. I register no reaction. Her familiarity breeds my contempt. I care none for her tales of being poor and the ridiculous script by which she and her 'love' live out their wretched existence.

"Ya sees I wouldn't being doing this normal as like. Specially with that madman murderer roaming the streets. I know who he is, so I'm going to tell the coppers tomorrow and gets the reward money so me and John we cans live the life of Reilly and show those stuck up so and so's from Wolver-bloody-hampton who's the better. Turned me out they did. Relatives! Burn the bleedin' lot of 'em. Sod 'em I says. So until I claims the reward I needs a bit extra for a bed for John and me, so I looks for a gentleman like you to look kindly and generous on me. You'll be kindly and generous won't you, sir? I'll do you a treat."

I nod, suppressing a smile. Irony of ironies, God is smiling upon me tonight. Providence washes over me with a purging bath. Imagine, if I hadn't been disturbed with Long Liz I'd have never met this Eddowes creature.

"So you know the identity of the Whitechapel murderer," I say to disguise my jocularity. This wretch is amusing with her stupidity. I shall take great pleasure in revealing how wrong she is.

She smiles all cat-that-ate-the-canary smug. She touches her nose and nods.

"Yes, I do, but mum's the word, but go on, you're a gentleman. Let me just says the name Lipski and no more, knows what I mean?"

"Indeed I do," acknowledging the East End slang for a murdering Jew.

Despite her supposed need for secrecy she can't resist divulging more. The woman is incorrigibly stupid and as a consequence, terminally gossipy.

"One of them tailors. I shan't say which. I asked him for a few pence for a drink and he chased me from his shop with a pair of scissors raised to slice me to pieces. I saw the look in his eyes. I knows it was him—the Whitechapel murderer."

I nod, knowing that I'll be saving some poor soul from police persecution by stopping this finger-pointer in her tracks. I shall silence her soon enough, and it shall be a welcome quiet that regards my ears, but I shan't be satisfied until every such whorewoman on this wretched planet is similarly still. A plague upon them from my hands. Tonight I do God's work. He guides me and delivers them to me.

She stops in a corner of Mitre Square.

"Here ya are, darlin'. This'll do nicely. The copper won't be back for another fifteen minutes or so. You'll be quick, especially once you feels me treats."

She places her filthy hands on my still engorged member. I haven't softened since leaving Stride's still twitching body.

"Ooooh, you've been saving a lot up haven't you? A nice hard one has you got."

"I will be quick," I say, throwing her against the wall as I pull out my cock and my knife.

I hop off Lekerk and kick Ed Alras's unconscious form around a few times. I pull my shoe leather trimming knife from my boot and flash it at Lekerk who's barely able to prop himself up on his arms. I sink below the bedframe and slice through Alras's throat and while the pain jolts him momentarily awake I look in to his dying eyes and say, "this is from Violetta Cutrero. Your raping days are over, fucker."

I slice off his cock and balls and the beauty of it is he can't scream since I'd slit his throat. He just gurgles himself to death. In a shining moment worthy of Jack the Crazy Nicholson's famous "Here's Johnny" scene, I peer over the footboard of the bed in to Lekerk's almost relieved eyes and toss Alras's bloody genitalia at the priest.

"So you thought you'd castrate my son did you?"

Lekerk scrambles away from me and Alras's dismembered member. By the look of horror on Father Git's ashen face I can tell he's no longer relieved. Good, I want the fucker scared. Time to rub it in.

"You might be tempted to think you're safe since I just sliced up your big goon henchman, but guess what. There are two dead goons in Sister Teresa's rooms. That's right you stupid fuck, do the arithmetic. I'm not limited to what dastardly deeds the original Jack did in these boots. Thanks to you and your stupid exorcism where I got to spend quality time with some very sick, murdering bastards, I'm living Nietzschean proof of what doesn't kill you makes you stronger. I put all those bastards out of their misery and now I'm more capable and ready for more. I'm the real evil fighter here, the serial killer of serial killers. You created me and now you're going to die by me because I hear the bells toll for you, Father Git. There's the chimes of Saint Botolph's church. It's 1:30 am in the morning in the east end of London. We're in Mitre Square."

Catherine Eddowes' impact upon the wall knocks the wind from her. I catch her by the throat before her legs buckle. Her eyes bulge.

"You do know the identity of the Whitechapel murderer, Catherine," I say, my eyes and teeth glistening under the dim light. "But it is not some poor Jewish tailor who refused you some change for another drink and chased you off with his scissors. It is I, and you will not be collecting any reward tomorrow. You are my reward."

I pull apart her ragged clothes and push my fingers between her legs. I rub my hands across her pussy, parting the lips with my fingers. I spit down onto my hand, working my saliva into her cunt, rubbing my cock to a shiny wetness. In I lunge, fucking her with long, deep thrustings that threaten to impale her heart with my steely dick.

Excited by my dual killings I am on the brink of relief in just a few travels of her juicing canal. I come and slice her throat as I ejaculate her life away.

*　　*　　*

I leap onto the bed, my hand clutching Lekerk's throat. I stuff his softening cock into my sopping pussy and ride it to full hardness, resuming my twisting of his balls and ass fucking with my finger.

He screams the usual platitudes.

"Don't hurt me, don't hurt me. Oh dear heavenly Father protect me. Don't hurt me. I'll do whatever you want of me."

"Too late. You already gave me everything I want and you already took everything I want."

Lekerk cries like a baby and half of his misery has to be that he can't deny his bodily urges. I'm fucking him but good, the likes of which I'm sure he usually only fantasizes about. None of the nuns or choir boys can give him this kind of raw fuck because he's always in control. Now the tables are turned. It's the best fuck of his life, and of his death.

I feel his cock stiffen in me. I bounce up and down on him harder and harder, pummeling his lower body with my lunges. I dig my knees into his chest. I squeeze tight on his neck, giving him that lovely head rush. It pushes him over the edge. He comes in me as I reach around with my knife and run the blade across his balls. I allow him one scream before slicing his cock off inside of me and then running the ball-bloody knife across his throat, silencing his scream into the same burst pipe gurgles that Alras still makes. With Lekerk's wide-eyed face a twisted mass of pain paying tribute to the vengeance I crave and the retribution I deserve, I kiss him once on the lips, rotate my body into the traditional *soixante-neuf* position and disgorge his cock and balls and the orgasmic cocktail of his last ejaculated load and my come onto Lekerk's face. Emptying myself of every drop, I pee on him for good measure and good riddance.

Hopping off the bed I admire my handiwork. Not bad,

but there's more to do and not much time. I pry open Lekerk's mouth and stick his cock and balls inside giving him a deep-throating. Drawing from my Dildo Killer dispatching memories I do some hasty slicing and dicing and insert Alras's cock up the enlarged sphincter of Lekerk's messy asshole. After some further symbolic organ rearranging designed to keep the police confused as to my motives, I gather up the booty, including Lekerk's confessional shoes, and head to the door, using a portion of his fluffy bath robe to wipe my hands of his blood and shit.

I exact a pretty tapestry on Catherine Eddowes' body. She deserves nothing less. I disembowel her completely in a matter of minutes. I slice off her nose and ears and carve up her face because she so offends my sense of beauty. I split her like the pig she was, carving out organs and arranging them in neat piles to confuse the police as to my perverse purpose. As a parting gift from the stupid woman I tear off a portion of her ragged apron and walking quickly from my stage, wipe my hands of her blood and shit.

As I make my way out of the East End I can't help but celebrate myself. A perverse sense of humor makes me laugh out loud. I feel so jolly tonight. Why not give fuel to the fire? Why not make use of Catherine Eddowes' belief that she had identified the killer. I ditch the apron in a doorway and scrawl on the wall with chalk "The Juwes are not The men that Will be Blamed for nothing."

Skipping lightly I head to my rooms, laughing. That should put the riotous cat amongst the pious pigeons.

Before Jack's boots transport me back to my bedroom in Stinson Beach I look around Lekerk's Mitre Suite and announce to the dead bodies, "The feet cannot be denied, and neither can a mother from her son." Using the blood and shit soaked apron I scrawl on Lekerk's bedroom wall "The Priests are not The men that Will be Blamed for nothing."

That should keep the SFPD busy for a while researching child molestation records from way back, and as I'm walking out I can't resist stopping by Sister Teresa's room to rummage through her closet for a useful disguise I can use in Mexico City.

Celebrating our night's work, Lucretia and I laugh and hug on my couch, watching the videotape burn in the fireplace. We've replayed Lekerk's death shoefuck to confirm the sorry bastard was telling the truth.

I also recount some of the Jack the Ripper details.

"Funny isn't it. The day of her death Catherine Eddowes was turned out of the Shoe Lane Workhouse and she pawned her lover's boots for money. Then all those years later it is another pair of boots that tells the tale of her death and commits another."

"Yes, my darling daughter, the feet cannot be denied and shoes play the scribe's role for us to learn from."

"And it all began with you."

"Yes, and now it ends with me and you."

Lucretia leans over and kisses me as the dying flames of the burning videotape flicker. We fuck, our bodies wrapping around each other like those flames. As they extinguish, Lucretia settles back into her hiding place within me.

I make the calls, check flights, book a hotel room and buy my ticket because I'm not so stupid as to try and use Father Git Lekerk's. I pack light, taping my shoe-trimming knife to the back of a huge crucifix which goes in my checked baggage along with Sister Teresa's nun uniform. I take a taxi to the airport, not knowing how long I might be gone, or if I'm even coming back.

I make a call to the number Ellen left me and ask her to look after Spykes until I get back. She's kind of cold, but agrees. I tell her I'm going to New York on family business. She doesn't believe me, but she wishes me well and says that maybe we can talk when I return. I say yeah, and go along with the idea cause I really need her to look after Spykes. Yeah, it's a calculating presumptuous imposition but I know Ellen wouldn't be able to resist coming to my rescue in one way or another.

As the taxi winds its way to the highway I hum a tune as I watch the sun rise.

"South of the border, down Mexico way."

I hum loud enough so I don't have to hear the radio's breaking news reports of the grisly apparent hate crime slayings of a priest, a nun and several church workers at the Catholic Archdiocese mansion.

The news was right about my motivation—hate, but it wasn't a crime. It was punishment. I am an Avenging Angel Sex Goddess and it's my job to punish child stealing molesting asshole mothersonfuckers wherever I find them.

And if I'm too late and they castrate Luc, Mexico is gonna see a Catholic Church bloodletting to make the Aztecs proud.

CHAPTER EIGHTEEN

IT'S MUGGY HOT and smoggy stifling. I'm sweating, and I haven't even left the terminal yet. So much for air conditioning, and by the sharp aroma, so much for deodorant. I'd kinda planned to change into my nun's disguise in the airport bathrooms but somehow I can't see wearing that sweatmaker until I absolutely have to. I'll stick with the long purple slip dress, my purple patent Mary Janes and not much else.

My first task is to stash the bulk of my cash into a locker for safekeeping and then change a reasonable amount of left-over dollars for gazillions of ready-to-use pesos which I hide in my shoulder bag. I exit into a killer heat that feels and smells like I'm a burning cake in somebody's dirty oven. I can't catch my breath, and to make overheating matters worse I'm pounced upon by a swarm of stinky taxi bandits offering a ride for senorita. Fuck me are they pushy. I feel like a female officer at a Tailhook convention. I figure the safest bet is to choose one taxi bandit, and he'll keep the others away from his prize. Who'll be my knight in not so shiny armor? They're all so sleazy, but sleaze is my biz so I go for a shady looking young guy who points towards a Bug taxi. I choose his ride since it reminds me of my Bug, only it's painted green and black. The guy is kinda cute too—the best of a rather skanky looking lot. He's rangy and wears tight black jeans, an equally skin tight Hugo Boss knock-off tee shirt, black cowboy boots, and is forever brushing long stringy black hair out of his eyes.

I point to him and he carries my bag and asks me where I want to go in an English that is very Latin suave. It's clear this dude fancies himself and his chances with me. I'm in no mood for a fuck right now since I've got my son's dick and balls to save, but I don't mind the flirting. I tell him the Hotel El Presidente—where the late Father Git was supposed to stay. I figure from there I can change into my disguise and raid Our Mother of Guadeloupe church once I suss the lay of the land.

My green and black bug driver tells me his name is Miguel Cruz and that the fare is so many pesos. I say no problem, not bothering to haggle like I think I'm supposed to. Thanks to Father Git's wad of Catholic cash I figure paying an exorbitant fare without quarrel is doing my bit to redistribute the Church's wealth where it belongs. Besides, I'm so fucking hot I just wanna get into a shower and plan my attack.

I'm also fucking tired. The adrenaline of offing a bunch of people ran out on the plane. I slept through the crappy breakfast and don't have the stomach for lunch. I know I should eat to keep my strength up, but I gotta be careful with the food and drink. Don't need old Montezuma claiming his smelly and debilitating revenge when I'm here to claim mine. Fuck, am I exhausted. Lucretia too. I can feel the energy drain from her, draining me. Doubleo fucko, it's hard keeping two people alive inside one, especially when one is me boiling over with all my natural angst. Kinda like being pregnant with an adult.

I try to doze, but in this heat—the Bug doesn't have air conditioning—and *Mad Max* meets *Bullitt* traffic there's not much opportunity to rest in between lurches, swerves, sudden stops and a near constant barrage of honks and insults. Even so, I'm nothing if not adaptable and what the fuck, I'm beat, so I actually do manage to close my eyes by resting my head on my shoulder bag. In my dopeyness I figure I'm either getting used to all this traffic or we've bust out of the worst of it because we seem to be flowing pretty smoothly. Either that or I'm so out of it I just don't notice the hassle anymore.

After how long I have no fucking clue I roll forward and backwards as the Bug brakes and the engine dies. I tell myself I should get up because the hotel doorman will be opening the door soon, and I should pay the driver when all my shoulds become irrelevant because I'm shaken out of my grogginess by the door opening. I sit up but I'm pushed down again, and I'm thinking, fucking rude doorman, he won't get a tip, when I feel warm sharp steel against my neck and hot sour breath against my face and a pulsing bulge between my legs as my dress is pushed up my sweat-dampened legs.

That's my tip, I guess. It's not the doorman. It's Miguel Cruz the taxi bandit, and guess fucking what, he's a real bandit.

"If you keep quiet you might even enjoy it, and I will let you live. Either way *mi corazon,* I am going to rob you and fuck you. Welcome to Mexico City. If you scream or struggle I will cut your throat and serve your body to the wild dogs."

You know, statistics say there is a woman raped every two minutes, and I'm beginning to think I'm her. I yawn. I feel Lucretia stir inside. We both feel in that kind of bored mood like we don't have the energy to swat this really annoying fly, but if we must, we must.

"Whatever."

I yawn again, figuring my breath must be way rank by now. I've got morning, noon and evening before breath. Miguel shrinks back a little. He looks almost hurt, as it turns out, not by my halitosis but by my lack of hysteria.

"You are not afraid?"

"No. Look in my bag."

He pulls the shoulder bag from under my head and I flop onto the hot vinyl of the bug. He unzips it and sees my wimple and habit and the crucifix.

He crosses himself and mutters skyward something that sounds vaguely like the Mexican equivalent of Homer Simpson's "Doh!" I guess Catholicism does have some uses.

"Mother of God forgive me. I had no idea. You do not look like a nun."

I can't resist laying it on thick with a shovel.

"My son, underneath our bride of Christ adornments we are normal women, with normal bodies. In the eyes of God, we are all the same. That is why we wear our robes, so you do not see the flesh that tempts you to attack poor, defenseless women."

"Sister, can you forgive me? I am not a bandit. I needed money to pay off my gambling debts, and—"

"Two wrongs do not make a right."

"I know Sister . . . "

"Lucretia. Sister Lucretia."

"I know Sister Lucretia, but the gangsters, they told me this was the easiest way to pay off my debts. Tourists, forgive me Sister, but they are so stupid. I rent this taxi for a few hundred pesos a day. I do not need a license."

"How does raping me pay off your debt?"

Miguel screws up his face. He punches his head.

"Oh forgive me Sister but I did not mean to rape you, but you looked so sexy lying there with your skirt riding up your legs. I watched you in my mirror, the wind fluttering up your dress. I did not know nuns wore thong panties."

"What did you expect? Sackcloth?"

"No, but nothing so sexy. You turned me on."

"So if a woman excites you this gives you call to attack her? So you thought you may as well rape me in addition to robbing me. You are despicable. How many poor women have you done this to?"

"A few?"

"How many?"

"Ten, maybe twenty."

"Oh Holy Father thank you. I arrived in time to save you from eternal damnation. The Lord works in mysterious ways. Take off your clothes."

"What?"

"Undress. I am going to purify you."

I pick up my crucifix from the open suitcase and hold it out at Miguel as if he were a vampire. I mumble some Latin-sounding jumble all the while making damn sure I can pry out my knife in a heartbeat.

"How much do you owe?"

He quotes a figure. I do the math. He's been a very bad boy, but I can afford it many times over. I figure I'll need a driver, and what better than one with questionable morals in my debt as a doting sex bunny.

"I will see that the Church pays your debt, but first I must purify you. Take off your clothes."

"Why would you pay my debt? I was going to rape you."

"I am not paying your debt. I am a poor bride of Christ, but on my word the Church will pay your debt. I am part of a very secret, select group of nuns who undertake undercover operations for the Church. We often travel in plainclothes to avoid attracting attention. I am here on a mission to retrieve for some very worried parents a child who the Church rescued from an unscrupulous baby-snatching ring. I will need an escort who knows the land and will be at my beck and call and will do exactly as I say."

He crosses himself. It's all I can do not to laugh. Combine Catholic guilt with a penis, and a mean man becomes a yelping puppy. I take the knife from his hand.

"How will you purify me," he says eyeing the knife, his hand falling protectively to his crotch.

I smile as I toss the knife to the floor.

"I will relieve you of the temptation to have sex with women. I will use my body to satiate your prurient desires."

He looks at me with confusion furrowing his dusky brow. He looks so darn cute I just want to—want to—want to fuck him.

I sigh, lifting up my dress so he can see my thonged sex. His eyes and parts lower bulge.

"In addition to paying your debts and some extra cash for your pains I will have sex with you now, and while you are in my service, whenever you feel temptation rising to purify you of all evil pressures."

I squeeze his cock. It's a hefty package. Yum yum. I'm in the mood for dick, and so is Lucretia. Yeah, I know I said I had no time for fucking, but that was a few minutes ago, and since then I've taken a nap, and I now feel we need an sexcharge prior to our next battle with pious, per-verted priests. And yeah, I'm horny.

"If you doubt my story we can go straight to the Church I'm to use as a base of operations. It is the Church of Our Mother of Guadeloupe."

Miguel's eyes light up and his dick twitches.

"It is not far from here."

"Good. There I will see Father Jesus Lopez and some fellow operatives and give you half the amount you owe up front. You'll receive the rest when my mission is complete and you drive me back to the airport. As a sign of good faith, I will drain your lust right now."

He puts his hands together, looks up at the roof of the Bug, screws up his eyes and mumbles a prayer of thanks. When he's finished he tears at his clothes, promising me that from now on he will stay away from gambling on cock fights, dog racing, bull fights and raping and robbing women.

You are wicked, my daughter.

I feel Lucretia stir inside of me.

Are you sure you don't want to punish him for his crimes?

Our eyes fall to his knife, to the crucifix hiding my knife.

I look at the golden brown Miguel sitting back in the carseat, his arms spread crucifixion wide across the rear of the Bug, his erection kissing his belly button.

No, my Guardian Angel, leave this one to me and enjoy the feel of his cock. He's not evil, just misguided and we don't have to kill everyone. Redemption has its plusses. We can use Miguel to help us get Luc back.

Our eyes fall to Miguel's cock, and I feel Lucretia salivate, our pussies moistening. I kick off my Mary Janes. No need for shoesex here. This has to be quick, and I don't have a spare pair of shoes.

I pull my dress over my head and turning my ass to Miguel, I shimmy out of my thong. I place my hands on the front seat headrests, spread my legs astride the center hump and lower my body into Miguel's lap. He angles his cock between my thighs and tries to stick it in my cunt but he misses the mark. His dickhead slimes up my asscrack so I reach around and hold his dick in my hand, sliding my slick hand up and down his pulsating shaft. The veins throb hot under my touch as his cock engorges with blood. It's an exciting feeling, but I restrain my desire to fuck his cock to mush because there's more at stake here than just a good lay.

"Hold my waist, Miguel and do as I say. I will determine where your penis goes and when. Your complete obedience is necessary if the purification rite is to work with God's good grace."

"Yes, Sister Lucretia."

Stifling a chuckle, I spread my pussy lips around Miguel's cock and slide the velvet hardness along my labia, from asshole to clit, pausing at both extremes to work his cockhead in tight circles around my sensitized flesh. Miguel squirms and thrusts and even though it's understandable it's important that he realizes who's boss if this arrangement is going to work.

"Be still, Miguel. I cannot relieve you of your corrupt lust if you give in to its impatient demands."

Miguel sighs and mutters what sounds like a prayer. His hands squeeze my waist. His touch feels good on me. My juices flow and my sticky opening parts as my walls melt. His mutter turns to words.

"Yes, Sister Lucretia, as you wish, but you are so sexy, you are driving me wild."

"I am driving the wild out of you. The exorcism is working."

I mutter some Latin mumbo jumbo straight out of *The Exorcist*, making the cross sign on my pussy with Miguel's cock. After three or four crosses I can't take the teasing anymore. Right when I'm at the center of the cross, right over my pussy hole, I sink down, taking Miguel's throbbing cock deep inside my cunt as slowly as my collapsing legs allow. I pull my hand out from underneath my crotch and sink down into his lap. My ass cheeks nestle on his thighs, and I squirm myself into him on the thin sheen of sweat between us, enjoying the wiry scrub of his pubic hair on my soft flesh, adding an incantation to keep the boy honest.

"Holy Father release this man from the grip of lust. Let flow his life force into me, your humble bride of Christ. Give me his lust so that I may free him to do your work, so that I may do yours."

I flex my legs up and down, sinking Miguel's cock deeper into me with every lunge. His erection swells and ripples in me, and now it's not just sweat lubing between us as my juices slick from my pussy in perpetual waves of tiny orgasms. In the cloistered confines of the backseat of his Bug taxi, Miguel's hands on my waist act as assistance to the up and down of my legs and hands, and even though I told him he must lie still it feels good to have this strength around my torso. I allow him the liberty because it frees my hands to fondle my tits, and there's something about fucking in this hot, sweaty, cramped space that just turns me on to max sex volume. I squeeze my nipples and pull them forward and around, making the tiny mounds shake with every thrust. I can feel my orgasm building with every tweak of my tits and every fuck of my cunt, so I slap my ass down into Miguel's lap. I love the sound of our skins colliding with such force, echoing around the lust Bug like we're center stage of a big sloppy orgy.

I think I've winded Miguel because I hear a gasp, but then I feel his toes arch under my feet as his dick tenses, and I have just enough time to reach up once and pull my juicing cuntlips to the tip of his erection before slamming myself down on his orgasming cockhead. Miguel's screaming like the Devil and God are buttfucking each other inside his dick and that noise takes me higher up the orgasm chart. I rip Miguel's hands from my waist and stuff them between my legs where I grab his balls and I pull the sacs up and rub them on my clit using his hands guided by my fingers. It feels fucking awesome, and the extra sensation on Miguel's scrotum sends him into a state of rigor where his whole body tenses and he lifts me up and I bang my head on the roof of the Bug.

It's kind of funny—the jolt from the impact of my head on the not-so-padded roof slams me hard into Miguel and his cock rubs right across my G spot, and I'm coming and it feels so good I'm thrashing his balls on my clit and Miguel is screaming more and more and the next thing I know he's passed out and I'm still fucking him until every bone in his body, including his boner, seems to melt.

She shoots, she scores.

Indeed she does my daughter, now let's get our son. I feel, and I feel you feel, rejuvenated by this wonderful sex.

Lucretia's right. I feel like a real Avenging Angel Sex Goddess able to leap tall buildings while fucking the shit out of any evil motherfucker who gets in my way. One problem. Miguel is out cold, curled up like a baby on the backseat. I look around. We're parked on a vacant lot surrounded by decrepit buildings.

So what the fuck if anyone sees my come-slicked ass.

Emboldened with the courage of the just fucked in the backseat of a car, I step naked out of the bug and don my nun's garb, not bothering with my thong. Miguel's still out cold, but the sun's going down and I don't want to waste any more time. Fuck checking into the hotel. I'm sex sweaty and skanky under my robes, and I don't fucking care. My blood—correction—our blood—

Thank you my daughter. We are one—

Yeah, Mom, and soon we will be one happy family. Where was I? The blood—oh yeah—our blood boils with the need to find Luc. I don't need the hotel as a base of operations. We can go by the church—Miguel said it was close by—get Luc and have Miguel take us right back to the airport before the local fuzz has time to count the bodies.

I give Miguel a prod. He doesn't stir so I reach between his legs and squeeze his balls. He yelps awake to find me in my nun finery. He crosses and covers himself almost in one confused movement.

"Get dressed, Miguel. Forget the hotel. I want you to take me to the church. You've earned your first install-ment. Any luck and all that God-willing shit and the final one's just a few moments away."

Miguel looks at me with a raised eyebrow like he's Mr. Fucking Spock. What the fuck is his problem? Then it dawns on me that I said God-willing shit and perhaps a boner-finder bride of Christ wouldn't take the Lord's name in such degrading vain.

Then again I'm no ordinary bride of Christ. I'm Sister Violetta Lucretia Valery Cutrero—Guardian Angel Avenging Angel Sex Goddess in nun's clothing. I stare down Miguel.

"What? Does my language offend or surprise you? Miguel, I've already told you I'm no ordinary nun. I just fucked the living shit out of you to purge you of demons. I speak to you in terms your body and gutter ears will understand. Now get the fuck off your sweaty ass and get me to the church on time."

I basically sing the last few words like I'm in *My Fair Lady,* but dressed up in nun's clothing I feel more like Julie Andrews in *The Sound of Music.* I'm so tempted to launch into a perverted version of "These Are A Few Of My Favorite Things," with Rodgering and Hammerstick music filling the ruined lot, but I stow my weirdness in favor of keeping Miguel in line. He already suspects I'm not a proper nun so I'd better play it straight, but fuck me to the convent, Mother Superior, it takes every ounce of self-control not to clutch my stomach with gut-busting laughter as Miguel reacts to my domineering by jumping out of the backseat, pulling up his trousers as he pogos to the driver's side, his floppy but still lengthy dick bouncing up and down.

CHAPTER NINETEEN

HAVING TO FUCK the shit out of a member of the Catholic Church to see if I've been lied to about my son is getting to be a royal fucking pain in the ass.

Father Jesus Lopez doesn't speak English worth squat, and he isn't cooperative in the way of getting out a phrase book. Thanks to my Guardian Angel I understand his Mexican mumble-jumbles, but I don't let on, content to let him think he has an advantage. The feet, apart from not being denied, also speak every language. I think he might have been expecting me because he sure seemed to drop too quickly into the arm-waving denials before he even knew what I wanted. I can only conclude that the Catholic Church Mafia have been hard at work telling the tail of what happened in San Francisco to all their minions and to be on the look out for the wicked shoesex mama Lucretia. Yeah, well, no matter what he'd heard about me and my bad other self I don't think he expected me to tie him to a chair with his sash, pull up his robes and jerk him hard then straddle him in my nun's habit and sink his erection into my cunt, bouncing up and down on his prick while pinching and twisting his nipples like he's an old car radio, and I just can't tune in the right station that'll play my request for "Blue Velvet" at the right damn volume.

Father Jesus and me, we're just on totally different wavelengths, and I don't think it's the language thing. He's being deliberately obfuscative—which is a fucking wordy way of saying he's prevaricating me, the bastard. He's yanking my chain. He's stalling because he knows I'm close, and he's buying time. Fuck, the truth is so damn elusive these days. What is truth, Pilate said. Damn fucking straight and it took a Roman pagan to say it.

Speaking of which, Lucretia's in control—as she has been since I walked in, leaving Miguel in charge of the bug taxi outside the shithole of a church—Our Mother of Guadeloupe—more like Our Motherfucker of Guadeloupe—Christ, is it a dump. Even the rats look ashamed to call it home. That they brought my son here really pisses me off. That they've left before I got here to rescue him pisses me off even more. That he left with his cajones intact is my only hope.

Father Jesus blabbers and tries to cross himself as I fuck him, but he can't do it right because I'm pinching his tits and batting away at his hands. When Lucretia's like this there's nothing we can't do. It's like we've got the strength of ten women. We'll get to the truth. The feet cannot be fucking denied.

"Come on, Jesus, fuck me good and tell me the truth. Your cock is so hard and so good. Doesn't that feel good, doing a nun. And I'm some nun, aren't I? I'm every nun you've ever wanted to fuck. Now where is my son? Don't make me stop. Tell me, and I'll make you feel so good you'll be in Heaven without having to die."

He blathers and gasps, and his cock burrows hard inside of me, so I reach around me, keeping one hand on tit pinching duty, and I use the other to apply some good old ball torture. Guys really dig this, especially when they're as old as Father Lopez. He looks like he must be ninety.

"Where's my son?"

As I ride his prick I twist his testicles, squeezing them tightly, rubbing them between my fingers, milking his load. I rub my finger across his asshole, letting my fingernail dawdle around his anus. He starts and shudders and I relax my grip. I need to make him want to be fucked so he'll let his guard down. The fucker's enjoying this too much. He's trying to shut out all thoughts of why I'm really here. Time to remind him this isn't a social call.

"Where's my son? Where's my fucking son? Where's Father Ritchie and Sister Maria?"

I pull on his ball hairs, cradling his balls again, pumping his cock ever so slowly to show him just how good I can make him feel. He closes his eyes as I touch him, but my fingers make him see that I won't be denied and neither will his feet. The old fucker opens his eyes and smiles, then his cock pulses like a cannon and he comes in a few passable spurts and there's a definite squelching around my cunt as the priest continues to ooze. I'm about to give him a good bitch slapping for premature ejaculation when he gurgles and his tongue sticks out and his eyes roll and he gasps and passes out, turning a ghastly purple.

I shake him, but it's no use. I'm not giving the old bastard mouth-to-mouth. He's dead. Probably had a heart attack. Well, at least he died of natural causes enjoying what the Church would call an unnatural act. Hopefully that joker God wasn't playing a trick on me by snatching Father Jesus before his feet could give me my answers.

I guess I'll have to find out.

I untie the dead dude and arrange his robes so it doesn't look like he died fucking, although half way through my tidying I change my mind. I pull up his robes to his pasty belly and clasp his hand around his dick so it looks like he died jerking off. Rigor mortis will set in, and he'll present a grand old picture of dedicated celibacy for the acolyte who finds the poor fucker. I grab his shoes, my bag and turn to head for a hiding place when I come face to face with a wide-eyed Miguel.

Oh fuck, I hope he didn't see it all.

"You're not a nun, are you."

Yup, he saw it all.

"Let's get out of here."

I walk towards the door. He steps in my way.

"All those fucks and shits you spoke weren't to talk down to me, were they. You're as much of a criminal as me."

He grabs my arm. He shouldn't do that while Lucretia's in control. At least she's not running free of me or Miguel would be dead by now. I feel her tense. She's ready to strike. Miguel waves his red cape at Lucretia's bull.

"I should call the police."

I'm trying to hold her back.

"What for?"

"You killed him. You tricked me."

"Bullshit. He had a heart attack, and you were gonna rape and rob me, so don't play all high and fucking mighty with me, Miguel."

I snatch my arm away from his grip.

"Go ahead, call the fucking cops, Miguel. They'll arrest you first."

Miguel lifts his hand to slap me, but my hand, that is Lucretia's, snakes to his throat and lifts him off the ground. The look on his face says it all. He sees Lucretia. He blubbers like a baby. I put him down, fighting hard to still Lucretia's desire to rip him apart.

"Listen, Miguel and listen good because your life depends on it and the decisions you make in the next few seconds. You have no idea who you're fucking with so don't threaten me, or do anything to piss me off, or I swear I'll snap you in two, tear off your dick and use it for a dildo until it shrivels up, then I'll stuff it up your dead man's ass. Now can we go before someone else—like you for example—gets hurt?"

Miguel nods and meekly leads the way to the car.

I feel Lucretia still pulsing to lash out.

"You should have let me kill him. He's trouble. He knows."

"We need him. Fuck knows where they've taken Luc. We need someone who knows the area to drive us around. Someone who doesn't mind being around strange shit. I can control him. Especially now you've shown yourself."

"Okay, Violetta, but don't get too attached. Once we're done with him, Miguel Cruz dies."

"Okay."

We're parked back at the vacant lot. Miguel's slugging down rotgut tequila. He's still paler than the full moon that's our only illumination.

"What happened back there?"

"Nothing."

"It wasn't you."

"Yes it was."

"You're not human. You are a devil."

Lucretia puts in her two cents worth.

"Don't tell him any more."

My head pounds from all these voices.

"Enough. Stop."

I'm shouting. Miguel's cowering. Lucretia sulks inside of me.

"Okay, listen."

I put my hand on Miguel's lap. With my other I reach for my bag. Miguel trembles.

"Don't worry. I have something you've earned."

He still flinches as I unzip my bag and reach in. I pull out a wad of pesos and toss it at him.

"There's your half. I'll give that and as much again when we're done. That's a hundred-percent bonus. Just drive me around until I find my son, and yes, I'm not a nun. I'm a woman whose son was stolen by the Church because I have a power they don't like."

Lucretia steams inside of me. I can hardly control her. My body feels like it's gonna explode, and she'll come ripping out like that *Alien* creature. The car feels very small and I feel very big. This is scary.

"Will you help me?"

It's all I can do to get the words out.

"Do I have a choice?"

"No. I could kill you right now with a flick of my wrist, and you'd be just one pathetic taxi bandit who robbed and raped the wrong chick."

"How do I know you won't kill me after you've found your son, and you don't need me anymore."

"You don't. You'll have to trust me. It's like I said. I could kill you now, so what's the big deal. You don't have much choice. Yup, it's a gamble on your part, but, hey, Miguel, you're used to taking gambles, right? Only I'm a much better bet than the losers you've backed recently. Look, it's simple. I find my son with your help, and you win bigtime cash and get tons of hot sex along the way. Fuck me over and you die. What'll it be? I don't have much time."

He shrugs with the ease of a young man who is used to making compromises to live.

"I will help you. But if you kill me promise me you'll

send my money to my mother. Her address is in my wallet on the back of her picture. She never thought I'd amount to anything. She kicked me out. I'd like her to know I was worth something."

"Deal, but you can give it to her yourself. I'm not going to kill you if you behave yourself."

Lucretia riles inside me—don't make promises I can't keep.

Shussh I silently pacify back. Let me handle this.

Be careful, Violetta, ordinary humans are never to be trusted.

I know, but there are ways to get them to do shit. We might be Avenging Angel Sex Goddesses, but we can't do it fucking all.

Just don't give too much away or get too attached. You'll regret it.

I won't—on all accounts.

Good.

Good.

Oblivious to our internal discord Miguel shrugs in that cute way he has.

"So where are we going?"

"That's the problem. I'm not sure."

"I don't understand."

"You know I said I had a power the Church didn't like. I can see inside people's souls and minds when they're fucking in shoes. I just have to put the shoes on, and I'm there inside them. Father Jesus' shoes will tell me what I want to know."

Miguel crosses himself.

"Watch, and don't try anything funny or you'll meet my mean half."

I slip on Father Jesus' sandals. Two people, one body, that old familiar feeling. Now where's my son, fucker?

CHAPTER TWENTY

WHEN IT COMES to sex, guys cannot be trusted to think beyond their genitals. It's true, just like the joke goes, men are dicks with life support systems, and as such, it's stupid to ask for any consideration beyond their getting off. No matter what you think or what they say, guys just can't be trusted when hormones are running high.

And for that matter, neither can Lucretia. She's a cunt with a life support system, and it's called me, Violetta Valery Cutrero.

I should have seen this coming. How many shoesex episodes have I enjoyed in my short life—thousands. You think I'd learn to watch out for rampant dicks and cunts, but noooooooooo. Yup, I sure am some slick kickass Avenging Angel Sex Goddess.

Here's the reason for my ranting.

I'm there in Father Jesus' soles getting fucked by me

and Lucretia and man I gotta say we're pretty fucking hot. This priest checked out in sex-to-the-max style.

My—that is, Father Jesus'—cock is aching hard to burst, and he's—I'm—feeling so good I feel bad. I'm thinking such nasty things. I'm imagining me doing some of those young nuns while the Pope watches and rubs off to the sordid spectacle. I shouldn't feel so much joy and excitement from these sordid spectacles, but I do. It's like being drunk on the blood of Christ wine. It's a sin, and I've got to remember she's a devil trying to rescue her evil spawn before we end the Cutrero curse for good with a few regrettable, but necessary cuts. Stop thinking about it. I must keep silent. I cannot tell her about Sister Maria and Father Ritchie. I thank the Heavenly Father that they left in time for—

—No, think of anything but them. Think of carnal pleasures and anything but—

"Come on, Jesus, fuck me good and tell me the truth. Your cock is so hard and so good. Doesn't it feel good, doing a nun. And I'm some nun, aren't I? I'm every nun you've ever wanted to fuck. Now where is my son? Don't make me stop. Tell me, and I'll make you feel so good you'll be in Heaven without having to die. It'll be the rapture starting deep down in your balls."

I blather about saving my soul, and I gasp for breath, but I don't want her to stop. Oh Holy Father, I haven't been this hard in decades. I'd forgot how good sex with a woman could be. Celibacy is such a waste. What's wrong with sex? Surely God would think it better that we have sex with women than force us to deny our urges and seek release with young boys or our colleagues—or worse—ourselves? God gave us the equipment and the will to use it. Sex isn't bad. It's good. Oh and is this devil good. She pinches my chest and it tickles. She pulls my nipples, and I feel like they're all hard and firm like they were when I was twenty and pulled on them when I played with myself.

Yes, yes, that's it, think about when I was twenty and didn't know any better or know anything about Father—

Stop with those thoughts. Think about the past. Not the present.

Yes, yes. How exquisite she looks. Such a temptress. Dressed like a nun, she is my fantasy come alive. I think of the many young women I've wanted to screw, and I've had to deny myself. It's ridiculous. I've wasted so much promising papal pussy. If only she were wearing stockings—black ones—or white ones—with seams and a garter belt to frame that sexy little furry honey pot that sucks me in. Oh how I've wanted such a cunt. Oh how many of them I've let slip by. So much tender, juicy, slippery, tight, pulsing, warm, come-sucking pussies I could have had with the snap of my finger-fucking fingers.

Did I think that?

Good, it's better than thinking about—

—how good her sex feels around my hard cock. How I'm going to come in this devil nun's pussy. How I'm going to fill her with my milky jism. How I'm going to deny her what she wants as she gives me what I want. What I have always secretly wanted—to fuck one of the nuns in my care—have her pull up her robes to show me her sexy stockinged legs and stiletto heels and the wetness of her cunt as she straddles my lap and bounces up and down on my cock, pulling on my nipples because she's so excited to be fucking me, to be fucking Jesus.

Oh, what's this now? She reaches around me, keeping one hand on teasing my nipple, and she squeezes my testicles and twists them, and I can't stand the pleasure and the pain. It hurts so much it feels amazing—now I know how Christ felt when he died.

"Where's my son?"

She bounces up and down upon my cock and twists my balls, squeezing them tightly, rubbing them between her fingers, milking my orgasm from me. Her fingers dart across my anus. Her fingernail probes. I spasm. She relaxes her grip on my balls and slows her pumping. Her finger backs away from my ass. She was so close. I'm so close.

She stops moving. She releases her grips on my chest.

I'm so close. So close.

So close to going soft.

No.

"Where's my son? Where's my fucking son? Where's Father Ritchie and Sister Maria?"

Her hands cradle my balls, pulling at the hairs. My shaft twitches. My erection renews. My come boils. Pump me, my naughty nun. Pump me. Make your holy father release his seed inside you so he stops thinking of Sister Maria and Father Ritchie traveling to the—NO—don't say it. Think of anything but the *Inglesis de la Sagrada Virgin Maria y* at—

A cock, a very hard cock, slides inside me from the rear, and for a moment I think somehow Father Jesus is fantasizing taking it up the ass, until I realize, the dick's not up his ass, but up my ass, that is, up Lucretia's ass as she's fucking Father Jesus.

Wait a fucking New York minute.

There was no buttplay when I fucked Father Jesus.

This is real sex blending with shoesex.

Through the fog of being Father Jesus I struggle for comprehension and the Inglesis de la Sagrada Virgin Maria y fades into Miguel Cruz humping into my ass in the back of his Bug taxi.

Goddamn it. It's gonna override Father Jesus' shoesex.

But it feels so mega-good. His hefty cock up my ass

and that priest's old wanker up my cunt is gonna take me over. I'm coming.

Inglesis de la Sagrada Virgin Maria y —the Church of the Sacred Madonna and—and what and where?

Oh fuck, I'm coming. Two cocks at once. There's nothing like double penetration. It's so long since I had two men inside me, both coming in my juicy holes, feeling their cocks rub together.

Fuck, get offa me, Miguel.

—the Church of the Sacred Madonna and—

Cupping my hand around the priest's balls, I twist them and pump into him, but I might be squeezing and twisting Miguel's equipment because I hear a screaming moan I'm not too familiar with, and there's a big flooding in my ass and then I feel Father Jesus let rip in my cunt, and I'm full of come and the priest is gasping as he thinks about the Church of the Sacred Madonna and what at where the fuck I have no idea.

I'm so pissed. I'm so close. This is like in old movies where the person who knows the identity of the villain has just been shot and tries to utter the name but expires with the name fading into a wheeze.

And Father Jesus is wheezing and turning blue and purple. Lucretia's still coming. Miguel is moaning what a good ass I have, and all I have to hold on to is the Church of the Sacred Madonna at fuck knows where.

I push Miguel off me and slap him around like I wanted to slap Father Jesus for a month of Sunday late night masses for coming too soon.

"Goddamn it, why'd you do that?" I say as I kick off the priest's sandals.

"You wanted it. You didn't object. You told me to fuck you in the ass."

"I did not."

"You did. You said it in Mexican."

"What else did I say?"

"You said that we should make for the Church of the Sacred Madonna and something at—"

"Where?"

"You didn't say."

"Well, we can figure it out. There can't be that many."

Miguel smiles.

"That's like saying meet me at the 7-11. There's hundreds of them. There's hundreds of Churches of the Sacred Madonnas."

"Then we're gonna visit all of them."

"You're crazy."

"No, you're gonna earn your money. And that ass fucking you just gave me, figure it's an advance on that bonus. Now drive before I rip your balls off."

"Yes, Sister Lucretia."

Miguel scurries to the front of the bug, pulling his pants up. I sink back into the back seat and let his spunk ooze out of my ass and onto the cheap vinyl.

I feel Lucretia come down from coming.

That was magical, my daughter. His cock is good. You were wise not to let me kill him. He'll provide much amusement during our quest.

You shouldn't have done that. We lost the location of the Church.

Poppycock my silly girl. Father Jesus never gave it up. I sense more than you. That's all the old fool let go. He took the secret with him to his death. That's why he came so well. Couldn't you feel it? The release, it was a rebirth, not a death. You gave him the wonder he'd been looking for all his repressed life. In that one moment of sexual bliss you made up for a lifetime of erotic neglect. Couldn't you feel it?

Yes, I did.

Then stop pouting and pull yourself together. We're off on our quest, so don't pout. Miguel will come in handy. Let's suck him off as encouragement.

Lucretia, you're wicked.

Indeed I am, my daughter. Now let's lick your shit and his sperm and my come from his still hard cock. It will taste so good.

I reach into the front seat and unzip Miguel's jeans.

"What are you doing?"

"Giving you another bonus, Miguel. Now take us to the nearest Church of the Sacred Madonna and don't get in an accident."

Lucretia was right. He does taste good.

CHAPTER TWENTY-ONE

WE SPEND ALMOST three weeks fucking priests, nuns and a variety of Catholic Church minions who get in our way.

We cut a wet and juicy and in some cases bloody swath through the Papal occupiers of Mexico. The Aztecs would have been proud of Lucretia, Miguel and me.

I'm not.

It's exhausting.

It's frustrating.

It's a fucking great big waste of time.

There are so many fucking Churches of the Sacred Madonnas and various combinations thereof that I'm beginning to think that Father Jesus Lopez was yanking my chain, knowing full well it'd be a goddamn wild goose chase across Mexico. I feel like fucking Cortez and his raping and pillaging band of pox-ridden conquistadors traipsing all over New Spain looking for my version of the golden city, only I'm on the other side from the Pope Squad, so it's even more of an ironic history belly laugh. I got a feeling that in the Old Deities Retirement Home looking down on my vain efforts are the one jealous Christian god and one of those old Aztec gods with unpronounceable names like Hzweckycoxyballszanarse and they're sharing a beer or something and having a darn good chortle at my expense.

Damn straight, and why not? It's funny the difference a bunch of centuries makes, but no matter the time that's passed, the song remains the same. I still haven't found what I'm looking for. And to add further soundtrack to my angst, I can't help thinking of that old Stones song— the chorus of which goes something like you can't always get what you want, but if you try some times, you just might find, you get what you need. Well, Mr. Richards and Mr. Jagger, I been trying all the fucking time, and I don't have what I fucking need.

My twenty-first birthday came and went on October 12 and I didn't get what I wanted. Lucretia and Miguel gave me a sexed-out tequila party with some cool presents and a cake, but the big one in the form of little Luc didn't show no matter how much I wished for the surprise. Halloween's come and gone, and it's the Day of the Dead, and I'm in my usual post-October three-one depression. Can you tell? If you're not sure why this date and all that comes before it in October is such a big deal to me, read the first two books. I don't have time right now to indulge your jumping in on the middle of my life and expecting the fucked-up mess to make sense. I'm in a funk, and I'm worried to puke that my kid has become a castrato at the sick, meddling hands of the Catholic Church. It pisses me off to think that they'll turn him into a permanent choir boy who takes it up the ass and can never give it in return because I, with all my Avenging Angel Sex Goddess powers and Lucretia with all her Guardian Angel mojo-wisdom, couldn't rescue him in time.

What the fuck. Maybe the Stones were right. Maybe I'll get what I need. Maybe Luc will get what he needs and never be bothered by the Cutrero Curse. Maybe losing the family jewels and scepter is a blessing. Maybe he'll want to transgender. Maybe he'll become a nun. Maybe he'll forgive me. Maybe I'll never see him again. Maybe Ellen was right.

Fuck that shit. Don't even go there. Don't think of the cunt that caused this whole mess.

A little anger does me good.

Maybe bay-bee, I should just quit with the maybes and get down to fucking business.

What the fuck am I doing here?

Here is some old run down hacienda down near Pátzcuaro in Michoacán about four hours and a month of Churches of the Sacred Madonnas out of Mexico City. It's humid. I'm exhausted. Our bedroom overlooks Lake Pátzcuaro. The locals are engaged in their yearly Day of the Dead observances. Hundreds of small flower-draped boats full of masked people holding candles, chanting, make their maudlin way to Janitzio Island. The sound of the waves and the boats and the chanting washes into our room adding to my funk. We've drunk a lot of tequila after yet another dead-end day of fruitless searching for Luc and the Church of the Sacred Madonna, and we're fucking ourselves into a stupor; it's our anti-festivity contribution to the Day of the Dead. Miguel is naked, a sheen of sweat coating his undulating olive body as he devours my cunt—actually Lucretia's cunt. One good thing that's come out of all this fucking to find Luc, especially Miguel's constant attentions and erections, is that Lucretia has the strength to exist beyond me for hours at a time without needing a threat or the Ripper boots to do her thang.

– 273 –

It's mega sexy to watch them and feel all that Lucretia experiences without having to worry about a murderer jumping out of the footy shadows. It's cool. It's relaxing. It gives me time to think while having sex without having to work at it. It's the best of all worlds.

Miguel's into Lucretia's pussy like she's a big old python swallowing her prey and he's it, and she's that really rare, exotic breed of python that feeds through her cunt. He holds his arms behind his back, fingering his ass-hole per Lucretia's demands. His mouth, courtesy of his weight and that he has no support for his body other than Lucretia, is full-on gnawing on her cunt. Her legs are spread wide, her toes carving into the bedsheets like they're digging furrows in wet sand for her ocean of come to drain away. Her hands grip Miguel's head by his long black hair as she works his face into her pussy, commanding him in raspy Mexican to eat her cunt and to lick her clit and all the things that go with a good slippery nasty. Man, is she working him and me over. It feels fucking awesome.

Sex is always the best funk antidote. Fuck away the funkaches is my motto along with the other one you've heard a bazillion times.

Miguel is a natural cuntlicker. He uses his tongue and his lips and his nose and that scraggly beard in all the right places. He knows where and how a woman likes to be licked. He's as good as any woman at cuntlicking and that goes for all the lesbians I've enjoyed, in realsex-time and shoesex-time.

He's so good because he takes direction well, and do Lucretia and I know how to give it. Thanks to our mouths and our hands and our orders Miguel becomes an extension of our bodies. It's like we're licking each other through him. I tell Miguel to lick harder. Lucretia says the same in Spanish, and she guides his head with her hands, and damn do I feel it as if he were latched onto my cunt.

"Suck on my clit."

Miguel fellates Lucretia's clit like a little cock. His lips purse into a tiny oh and he bobs up and down like a good homo should. He's so good at clitsucking I'm beginning to wonder if the boy isn't just a little bit bi. I wonder if he's sucked cock?

"You like that, Miguel, don't you."

He nods and, well, his whole body moves as he does, and that nod, oh my, how it travels up my pussy to my tits and bounces around my brain. This should fire my synapses into a bliss no funk can sour.

"Lick my ass, Miguel."

Lucretia pushes his face down to her butt, sliding his whole visage through her parted labia and juice-matted pelt, rubbing his hair into her pussy, fastening his long, angular Latin nose into her vagina as his tongue rims her butt. Oh, man, is this a lesson in how to pleasure a woman through the roof, to the stars, by way of Uranus.

"Fuck your ass, Miguel. Fuck your ass for us."

Miguel pounds his finger up his butt and the thrusts make his head jackhammer into Lucretia's cunt. His tongue burrows up her ass—his nose wedges into her cunt and his forehead bangs on her clit. It's something like giving birth.

As Miguel undulates his body he rubs his cock on the sheets against his flat stomach. I catch peeks of his dick as he moves. The tip is red, swollen, pulsing. His foreskin rolls up and down like he's jerking himself off. Sticky pre-come dribbles out of his dickslit and leaves a trail along the bed which smears on his golden skin and shines.

Lucretia bends her long leg at the knee and presses her foot against Miguel's cock, arching her sole around his pulsing shaft. She bends her other leg at the knee and presses down on Miguel's hands as they fuck his ass. She kicks her foot down, adding extra oomph to his thrusts. Miguel moans as his fingers push deep into his butt. I feel Lucretia's foot press Miguel's cock into the bed and rub it up and down with short, sharp, heavy attention. Miguel moans as best he can, his face muffled by my cunt and ass. His hot breath, the clustered suck of his lips, the gnash of teeth and the lunge of his body as he comes on Lucretia's foot lifts us both into a orgasmic Nirvana. Miguel's hot come flooding through Lucretia's toes is like warm massage oil that she uses his dick to rub into our soles.

We don't let him rest. We keep him moving up and down and licking at our pussies and asses as his dick grows soft through the mega-sensitive stage he finds himself trapped in. He's our living, breathing sex toy, and we're not finished yet. There's many more orgasms to go for us on this night of the Day of the Dead, and if Miguel's true to form then he'll be ready to go again in half an hour.

As my orgasm crests into a little lull, thoughts invade my mind. Negative shit, like am I ever gonna find Luc, and maybe it's the emotional rush of coming but damn if I don't start to cry.

Shit.

Enough of this feeling sorry routine. Fuck it. I'm sounding too much like Ellen the Whimpering Traitor.

Bad news. She's in my brain now, and thinking of Ellen deepens my funk because if we were still speaking I could ask her for help. She may not know what to do, but talking would at least be some comfort to my misery. Shit, I feel so alone. Even though I got Lucretia and Miguel they're too much a part of this to be real comfort. I need external, fresh view help, but not from Ellen. I can't call her.

So who ya gonna call, Violetta? Ghostbusters?

Maybe it's the way that Miguel's tongue works inside Lucretia, threatening to scoop out her gushing insides, but what I need to do comes through my consciousness in a blinding flash of clarity like someone turned on my lightbulb and the apple hit me on the head in one grand moment. Fuck, I must have been deaf, blind and stupid too for the last month.

I needed that orgasmic blast from my cunt to clear out the cobwebs.

Time to call in real heavy duty reinforcements and get the crap outta here with Luc like I should have done at the onset of this ordeal. Why it took this long to yell for help will probably be the subject of much boring Italian recrimination, but what the fuck, I never thought it would take so long. Fuck it, I'm gonna call the Lowest Soles in Rome and ask for help.

I pick up the phone.

At the sound of the phone being uncradled Lucretia's head turns towards me, and even though she keeps working Miguel's head into her nether regions, her distraction translates in to Miguel's face likewise turning my way. He's quite a sight. Cunt juice trickles from his nose. His eyes roll. His tongue bobs out like he should be in Kiss. There's a dent in his forehead where Lucretia's been banging her clit.

"Don't stop," I say. "Don't mind me. I gotta make a call. Keep fucking. Keep licking. It'll help me think us a way out of this mess. I need to come a lot, so fuck your best."

Lucretia shrugs and goes back to giving Miguel a Venus facial. Their answers to my encouragements becoming a crescendo of slurps and licks which feel and look oh so good between my thighs and Lucretia's.

Despite my assertion that all this sex will help me think, basic motor functions take a hit. It takes me a couple of orgasms to get through the combined idiosyncrasies of the Mexican and Italian phone systems and our joint climactic fog, but like the good little foot soldier that I am, I make it.

"Salvatore—it's Violetta."

"I've been expecting you. How are you? Is all well? Where are you? Are you in trouble? You should have called sooner. I—we—were all worried."

His barrage of good Italian questioning of my well-being is comforting. I expect him to say "Have you eaten? You look too thin. Let me cook you a big bowl of pasta," but before he continues I interrupt with the story of Luc's journal south of the border. He interrupts me back and we're off trading verbal fragments of information like we're gladiators trading blows in the Colosseum.

"I know all about it. We have our sources within the Vatican. Ever since you called me to tell me about the kidnapping we've had our ears to the ground and our soles. Your exploits have caused some consternation, but the details were sketchy. Rumors leaked wild but real facts dripped out. This has the highest level of Papal protection—they fear the repercussions of their kidnapping—especially in America."

"No shit. You got moles that deep in the Vatican—fuck me."

"Yes, not all of them are enemies. We learned enough to be worried, and then when your friend telephoned Johnny and confirmed our worst fears we—"

"Wait a minute. My friend?"

"Ellen."

"Ellen?"

"Yes, Ellen."

"Ellen's not my friend right now. What did she say? Why did she call Johnny?"

Salvatore dishes out a real buzz-kill story but Miguel and Lucretia keep on licking, although I feel my Guardian Angel tense at my discomfort. She tries extra hard to relax me by working Miguel's head into her thighs while he continues to do his butt with his hands, but I'm losing fucking focus, so Lucretia works harder, throwing Miguel around like a rag doll dildo. Dude, in the morning he's gonna be sore, and I'm not talking just in the sex department—I'm talking limbs in weird angles sore.

It's a shame that all Lucretia's sex efforts doesn't do me much good as I let the news that Ellen had told Johnny I'd gone off the deep end, and she couldn't help, rip my gut apart. I'm sure she's smiling somewhere, knowing that she's ruined another good fuck of mine. Fuck am I pissed off. Salvatore's words come through so real, as if I'd been there as Ellen the cunt pleaded her case to a gullible and in love with me and therefore do anything for me, Johnny.

I see and hear and feel Ellen say to Johnny "Maybe you could make Violetta see sense before she does more harm and the police catch her. I've covered for her before but I'm not sure I've got any favors left to call in. I'm really scared for her."

How the fuck did she get his number? She must have gone through my stuff in the beach house and found his phone number. Or looked at our phone bills. The fucking nerve. She didn't really know him. Where did she get off calling him?

Fuck.

She told him I was in New York, in keeping with my cover story that she didn't believe, but it was all she had to go on. She told him that the police had interviewed her about the killings because they bore such a macabre resemblance to the Dildo Killer's slaying. Ellen said she was worried that I'd gone crazy, believing this alter-ego, this other personality—Lucretia—inside of me was in control. She told him that we'd argued over the wisdom of letting the Church keep Luc—she didn't tell him that she engineered the whole fucking episode—and she liberally waved her "come help the poor damsel in distress" flag under Johnny's nose. What could he do? He got on the next plane to New York.

And so did Ellen.

Fuck.

It gets worse. Much.

After a couple of weeks in the Big Apple of being unable to find disturbed little me, Ellen tells Johnny that she doesn't think that she can keep quiet anymore because I'm clearly playing games, since no one anywhere in the usual foot haunts like Mistress Vamp has seen not so much as a little toe of me. Ellen's gonna go back to San Francisco and reach out to her contact at the SFPD and see if he can help me get well. Johnny bought time by saying that he'd go back with her and try and make contact. They should be in San Francisco right now.

I can barely speak through by boiling rage.

"Salvatore, please reach Johnny. Tell him I'm okay and not to trust Ellen. Tell him to do whatever he has to stop her from going to the police, but be careful, she's trigger happy. I'll be there as soon as I can get back to San Francisco. Tell him to stay at the beach house. Ellen has a key, but tell him to be careful. I've got to find Luc. That's my first priority. Use your contacts in the Vatican. They have to know where he's being kept, which Church of the Sacred Madonna he's holed up in."

"I will, and you, Violetta, you too be careful. Are you

sure you are all right? You know what I mean, with Lucretia."

I look over at my Guardian Angel and she smiles.

"It couldn't be better. We're like one. We bring out the best in each other."

Salvatore has me promise to keep in daily touch and we say goodbye, with him promising to contact me if he learns anything about Luc.

I slam the phone down. Lucretia feels me turn stone cold, full of anger as Ellen's interference eats at my soul. I feel Lucretia's reaction as an echo of my own, and it makes me feel worse. Lucretia feels this spiral and knows I need her inside me. I need her strength. This is Guardian Angel time. She pushes Miguel from between her legs and to the floor. He flops on the ground, his shocked expression betraying his confusion at being thrust away. His cock bobs and he continues to plunder his ass with one finger and jerks himself off watching Lucretia and I merge.

She wraps her arms around me and we kiss. It's a long, deep exploration of our tongues, wrapping and sliding over each other. Her hand falls between my legs and she rubs her two fingers up and down my cunt, parting the stickiness of my labia, circling my clit as one finger and then two and then three burrow inside, working in and out, around and around. She pulls me close, her leg sliding between mine as she presses her fingers deeper inside with the flex of her thighs. Bodies melting, our breasts slip and slide together, the hardness of out nipples feeling like hot little bullets in our respective bosoms. Her tongue circles my mouth, gliding over my teeth, and I bite her lower lip and I swear it feels like she's tonguing my cunt, and I feel her feel my tongue in her cunt and we both feel our teeth nibbling on our lower mouth lip and then on our labia.

We come, flooding each other's mouth with the pungency of a deeply born orgasm.

Lucretia's inside of me. I feel her strength surge with mine. We are one.

There's nothing we can't do.

The phone rings. It's Salvatore, and the news he brings severely tests that last statement.

CHAPTER TWENTY-TWO

"VIOLETTA, WE'VE FOUND where Luc is being kept."

"Salvatore, that's fucking awesome. You so rule. Let me get some paper—and a pen—and a map so we can plan our—"

"Violetta—"

"Don't worry. We'll zoom there right now—wherever it is—"

I put my hand over the phone.

"Miguel—get dressed—it's showtime thanks to Uncle Salvatore—"

I kick my foot out at Miguel. He sticks his tongue out and waggles it in sync with his dick. Come flies around. I dodge the splatters. "Get dressed," I mouth as I reach the table. Miguel snickers as he collects his clothes, still stroking his twitching cock. I think we've fucked him stupid. I ignore him, turning my attention back to Salvatore.

"Got the pen and paper—now which Church of the Sacred Madonna was it? I bet it was right under our noses."

"Violetta, it wasn't just a church."

I snap.

"What was it? A fucking young boy whorehouse for priests?"

I hear Salvatore sigh down the phone. He sounds exhausted and exasperated. I shouldn't be so bitchy.

"Look, Salvatore, I'm sorry. Go ahead. I promise I'll keep the editorial exclamations to a minimum."

He chuckles, knowing me well enough to know that I probably won't be able to be so restrained.

"It was a hospital. The Church of the Sacred Madonna and Hospital for Children of the Poor."

"And?"

Nothing but transatlantic static. I know well enough what Salvatore means with his silence, but I gotta ask.

"Salvatore, is Luc okay?"

"Yes."

"You know what the fuck I mean, Salvatore. I don't mean healthy. Have they cut his nuts and wanger off?"

Salvatore doesn't answer.

"Salvatore?"

"Yes, I'm sorry. They cut everything off according to ancient Catholic ritual. It was designed to prevent Luc from experiencing any sexual gratification and thus temptation. He is a full castrati."

It's my turn to go silent. There are no words for how I feel.

"Violetta? Are you okay?"

My resulting screams merge with the Day of the Dead celebrations still going on outside, rising until it's all there is—just that one single mandrakian explosion threatening to burst eardrums, shatter crystal and drive dogs crazy. Miguel cowers in the corner of the room, frantically pulling on his pants. Salvatore continues to speak, trying to penetrate my hysteria.

"Violetta? Violetta? Speak to me. Are you okay?"

It's moments later when rage turns to revenge. My scream quiets.

"Where is he?"

"If I tell you, you must promise to think things through carefully."

"I promise."

"Violetta."

"No, seriously, I'm calm. Really. Very calm. I won't do anything rash. Just tell me what you know so I can figure out what's best to do."

"Very good. The hospital is in Morelia, about an hour's drive from you. It's where the Michoacán state's Catholic bishop resides. Whatever you do, be very careful, Violetta. They are expecting you."

"Good, then we'll have us all a party."

"Violetta, don't blame yourself. Don't feel that hurting yourself will in some way make up for what has happened. You have everything to live for. There was nothing you could do for Luc once he was taken. The operation was performed immediately after he arrived in Mexico. He's been recovering ever since. Once he's well enough they plan to transfer him to Rome. They feel he'll be the safest in the confines of the Vatican."

No matter how much I try, my faux-calmness is a paper-thin mask.

"Well, we'd better not waste another second chatting or I might have to decimate the entire Swiss Guard to get my son back. Is there anything else I need to know?"

"We're all very sorry."

"Not half as much as some people in the Catholic Church are going to be, those fucking child molesting barbarians. You ever heard of an eye for an eye,

Salvatore? On the subject of retribution the Bible and I have something in common."

"What are you planning on doing?"

"Simple. I'm going to get my son and take him back to San Francisco, once I get there I'll have a darn good cry, and hopefully Johnny will be there to see me through the worst of it, and after that I'll raise Luc and try to give him the best life I can. Anyone who gets in my way of collecting him, taking him back home or raising him had better watch out. Lucretia and I are taking no prisoners."

"Violetta, Luc may need medical attention."

"He'll get it in San Francisco, once I figure out how to explain that someone has ripped his genitals off."

"If you could wait to attack then I and many of the Lowest Soles will fly over to help you."

"Thank you, Salvatore, but I can't wait. You said yourself that the papal perverts might ship him back to Rome. It'll be much harder to spring him from there. I have a feeling Lucretia and I can handle the locals here in Mexico."

"I have that feeling too. Good luck, my child. May the feet be with you."

I laugh.

"Now that's funny, Obe-one Salvatore. I'll call you once I've got my Luc Shoesexwalker back from the evil Empire."

"Excuse me?"

"Never mind, Salvatore. It's just a joke. That all happened a long, long time ago in a galaxy far, far away. Right now let's just remember that my feet cannot be denied."

It's a little before sunrise when we arrive outside the dilapidated hospital. Fuckers couldn't even send Luc to a nice, clean place to do their ritual mutilation. If he catches an infection in this flea bagplace I'll level the whole fucking building and for sure do lots of other poor kids a favor.

I'm in my nun outfit, but heeding Salvatore's warning that they might be expecting me I send in a very willing Miguel to do a look-see. I give him a photograph, which, I know isn't much good since all babies look the same, but I figure how many honky babies are there in there recuperating from being de-sexed.

Miguel says not to worry. He'll be back in a few minutes. About ten go by and here he comes, dressed in medical orderly clothes, running like the fucking wind and he's holding a bundle.

I throw open the door, and Miguel spins into the seat and hands me the bundle.

"What the fuck?"

"It's Luc."

"I guessed that you fucker. I didn't think you grabbed any old baby for me as a consolation prize. But how?"

Miguel guns the Bug out of the parking lot heading for the mountains as I cradle Luc tight to me.

Miguel sees me staring at him in adoration, expecting an explanation.

"I'm a good thief," he says, trying to control his smile. "And a charmer. It did not take me long to sweet talk a bored nurse into disappearing into a linen closet to wait for my romantic approach. I hope she is not too disappointed that I did not show."

I can't resist a laugh.

"You're a fucking good man," I say, and I kiss him on the cheek. Luc looks up at me and smiles. He's happy in my arms, so I pull off my wimple and give him a tit to suck on, and I let Miguel fondle the other one.

He's earned it, and so has Luc, the poor kid.

* * *

I don't have the nerve to look. It's still bandaged up. It being Luc's genital area. There's a little catheter for him to pee through and he seems to be able to do that well enough as my soaked nun's habit will testify to.

I cradle him so tight. I don't mind the pee dampness. He could poop, pee, drool and vomit all over me, and I'd be happy. I can't tell if it's Luc's pee or my tears that are soaking my gown, but once we're out of the town and in the hills we decide to stop at a gas station to clean up. Lucretia is bubbling over inside of me. I can feel how happy she is. It's strange. We suddenly don't feel the need for vengeance. We just want to get home and live our lives out in quiet. In the great Catholic tradition of castrating young boys so they would always have heavenly voices to soothe the Pope's guilty ears, maybe Luc will become a great singer like Farinelli. Or maybe he'll want to go the whole way and become a woman like his mom and Guardian Angel. We'd call him Lucretia. She'd like that. It'll all be up to Luc. We'll give him all the safety and strength and love he needs, and whatever he/she wants will be fine with us. Especially now we don't have to worry about the passing on of the Cutrero curse. Luc will be safe from all that, so maybe this ordeal wasn't so bad after all.

It's amazing the effect a mom's warm, cuddly gurgling baby has upon the angst machine.

Once we're de-peed, changed out of the nun garb and gassed up we go over our plans. Miguel will drive us to the airport where I'll give him all the extra cash I have stashed in the locker. That'll be more than we promised but the dude has earned it and more. He wants to have sex for old times' sake, but neither Lucretia nor I want to risk the distraction of even a quickie. We promise Miguel that we'll send him a ticket and he can come up to San Francisco for a wild time.

It's a date.

I just have to juggle Johnny and Miguel, but that's a complication I don't mind. It's nothing compared to dealing with serial killers and maniacal priests. It'll be fun to only have to worry about normal stuff like boyfriends and lovers.

And girlfriends. Yeah, there is the Ellen thing, but now that I have Luc back I kinda don't want to kill her. I don't want to even see her. Maybe one day we'll be friends, but for now she's gonna have to keep her distance and earn our trust back.

Luc's dozing in my arms. I'm feeling sleepy too. I feel Lucretia's energy drain. I lay my head down on Miguel's lap. It's still several hours to Mexico City and the airport, so why not grab my forty winks.

For Miguel it's forty wanks, the horny boy.

The road is rough so my head bounces up and down as I doze, and well, in all those bobble movements I kinda migrate my dreamy head into his crotch. The fleeting suggestive pressure of my head on Miguel's dick area makes him stinking hard. I'm dream-state aware of the protrusion, but I'm so out of it that it doesn't register as an erection-in-need. I just keep working my head into it kind of like it's a lump in my pillow I'm trying to work out so I can stay in my comfortable snooze zone. To make the whole little encounter all the more suggestive, I'm drooling, wetting Miguel's crotch, and in no time at all he's adding his own humps and bumps to the road vibrations when it all becomes too much stimulation for him so he whips his dick out and rubs it against my slumbering face.

What's a girl who's feeling kinda groovy to do.

I open my eyes in concert with my mouth and suck his cock so powerfully that it seems to me that if I could keep this suction up for more than a few seconds at a time his balls would shoot up his shaft and out of his cockhead like the really good tasting stuff at the bottom of a double espresso chocolate milk shake from the North Beach Italian Creamery.

It's not all suction either. It's pressure. I don't just pop his dick in my mouth. I tight cunt it through my pursed lips, peeling back the foreskin so the helmet shoots into the warm wetness of my mouth. Holding his cockhead at this precarious point, I arch my head upwards, pulling his dick along with it, tightening the skin so that every vein is magnified. I hold his cock there, defying its weight to pull it to safety.

I don't let gravity suck Miguel's cock from me, the jealous cockmistress that I am. I don't share with Mother Nature, just my Guardian Angel, who I feel stir at my oral attentions. Lucretia compliments me on my fellatio skill and our pussies moisten as she flows inside me. It's delicious, like she's rubbing against me as I suck off Miguel.

At her experienced urgings, I tighten my grip with just my lips, using my teeth inside my mouth to latch on to the taut flesh so that I can nibble my way down his length until his cockhead is nestled at the back of my throat, and I'm soaking his pubes with my saliva, taking his balls into my mouth with his dick. Miguel groans and says something in rapid fire Mexican. He strokes my head, careful not to make it seem like he's pressing my face down on his dick because he knows I don't like that. I'm the one in control here. Miguel's stroking of my neck is a reward, not a forcing.

I'm holding on to Luc through all this because no way would I risk putting him down. There's no carseat in this Bug, but I do trust Miguel to drive carefully over this windy mountain road, even with me latched limpet-like to his hard-to-bursting dick. Miguel knows that if he so much as brakes too hard or swerves too fast I'll bite his cock off. Nothing can harm my Luc now.

I suck up and down on Miguel's cock several times, using nothing but my mouth and teeth. Miguel continues stroking the back of my neck, and it feels so good the sensations make their way down to my clit. Luc's sucking on my tit, and Lucretia's grinding inside me, and I'm just so damn happy I can't help it I come. Lucretia comes too. I bury Miguel's cock as far down my throat as I can and let the gag reflex bring him off with the palpitations of my velvet rough tongue pattering his pulsing shaft.

He orgasms against the back of my throat, and I swallow, but I can't chug it all. My mouth fills. His come drains from my lips with every spurt and pulse. It's a big load. I can't help coughing, and that's even more of a mainline to Fuck Heaven for Miguel's come-sensitized cock. He moans, and then he screams some Mexican swear words even Lucretia doesn't know and his hand snatches from stroking the back of my head to the steering wheel as he spins the car and brakes to a swerving stop.

I figure he lost control when he came, and I'm about to give his cock a bite tattoo when he tells me to get the fuck up as he throws the car in reverse. Extricating myself from Miguel's cock isn't so easy when the Bug's going backwards because the motion throws me back into his crotch and down on his dick since I don't have my hands to brace me. My arms are locked around Luc who's crying like a baby should when his world is being turned upside down.

Miguel slams the brakes on again and he throws open the door after pushing me from him. He jumps out of the car, fists clenched, his dick still hard, protruding out of his pants. His fists unclench and his hands go upwards in surrender. I'm about to scream a what the fuck is going on when automatic gunfire makes Miguel dance like a demented puppet, slamming his body back into the open Bug door and to the ground. Blood spurts from the holes in his body, making me think of his moments ago orgasm in my mouth. His dick is still hard, pulsing, fading soft as Miguel's lifeblood puddles the dusty gravel.

I'm paralyzed, but Lucretia's out of me in a second. It makes no difference a Mexican cop rips open the passenger door and hits me square in the forehead with his riflebutt.

I'm blacking out, and I'm taking Lucretia with me, but I feel them snatch Luc from my arms, and I jolt awake. They hand him to two priests who speak to each other in Italian and run towards a dark, black SUV. I scream "no," and am rewarded with another riflebutt punch. I sink back into the seat. I feel so totally defeated, but even though I'm going down into this deep, filthy nothingness of despair, Lucretia fights through and my Guardian Angel takes control.

She kicks out at the cop with the offending riflebutt, sending him reeling backwards, but there are too many and they grab our legs and drag us out of the car. They hit us again and roll us over and put handcuffs on us and tie our legs together.

I taste blood and dirt, and I'm not sure if I'm going to live, since this feels like dying, especially when sweaty hands lift up my dress and a knife cuts through my panties.

CHAPTER TWENTY-THREE

I COME TO in a stinking jail. I'm handcuffed to the bars, my
hands held high above my head. I'm facing the bars. I'm
naked. I don't even have shoes on. My head pounds. I taste
blood. There's some gross lowlife on the other side of the
bars in another cell reaching between the bars to finger my
twat. As my vision clears I see another lowlife standing
next to the twattoucher. He's fingering my tits. They both
have their dicks out. They're hard and even though I'm a bit
dazed from the blows, it doesn't take a rocket scientist or
an Avenging Angel Sex Goddess in peril to figure out they
mean to fuck me through the bars.

Not a good situation.

My fight or flight response kicks in. I push myself
away from titfeeler and twattoucher. I'm aware enough of
my surroundings to know that I'm handcuffed to the bars,
but if I can back away far enough—the lowlifes' dicks

aren't that big, and with enough of an angle I can launch some nasty kicks at them to keep them away from me.

I step away from the lowlifes but I'm pushed back into the bars by a rough hand into the small of my back and another hand squeezing my neck. Sour breath burns my ear.

"Aaaaah, you are awake. That is good. Now we can begin the last fuck of your life. My men and our guests were growing impatient."

Definitely not a good situation.

I push backwards, but it's no use. This asshole cop is too big. He laughs as he grinds me into the bars with his weight. I feel the throbbing outline of his cock against my back. I hear other cops behind him urging him on. He responds with more sour breath in my ear.

"Don't waste your time struggling, senorita. You have no choice but to be fucked by me and my men and my prisoners, and when we are done we will shoot you and put you in the stolen taxi with your dead accomplice and a terrible accident will happen. The roads are so windy. You were perhaps having sex, sucking his cock like the whore you are, and he lost control and went over the hillside as he came. The car burst into flames and you were both burned beyond recognition."

I'm smart enough to know that saying something stupid like "you won't get away with this" is just a squandering of effort I need every ounce of. I gotta think calmly. Fuck that. I need Lucretia and we need to kick some Mexican cop ass.

"Spread your legs," the asshole cop commands to the rape soundtrack of an undoing zipper and unfastening belt and the rustling fall of trousers around ankles.

I spread my legs—no useless energy being my mantra. He spits on his hands. One coats my anus, his fat finger probing in. From the slippy-slappy sound and my experience, I deduce the other hand is busy soaking up his hard cock.

"Once I'm inside her ass you two can take turns."

The lowlifes grin their thanks.

"And once I'm done, while you two are enjoying her from the front, my men will finish her off from the back."

To the cheering laughs of his asshole cop buddies, asshole cop parts my ass cheeks and nestles his cockhead at my back door. I brace myself against the bars. The lowlife who'd been fingering my pussy stands, moving titfeeler to the side, but titfeeler stretches and keeps on pinching my nipples. Twattoucher squats and settles his cock between my pussy lips, finding the cunthole. He lunges, but stumbles and his dick slides under my pussy and bashes into the asshole cop's dick and balls. This prompts a burst of rapid-fire Mexican and a through-the-bars punch at twattoucher. Titfeeler and I get a good chuckle out of this. Then asshole cop tires of our jocularity at his expense and lunges into my ass, thudding me into the bars, knocking the wind out of me. Twattoucher lashes out at the giggling titfeeler before resuming his attentions to my cunt. This time he penetrates me just right, and I become an asshole cop and twattoucher sandwich with titfeeler and more asshole cops waiting around for their turns.

My rapers's cocks burrow inside me with rough lunges and, yeah, I'm such a whore it doesn't feel too bad. Through all my shoesex experience I've learned to enjoy every degradation because it's fear and hurt that these bastards get off on. Enjoy it and they don't win.

Yeah right.

That's the spirit my daughter. That's how I beat Rictius Varus. It's how we will beat these vile creatures.

Lucretia. Where have you been?

Gaul—Soissons—several thousands of years ago— reliving and relearning how I dispatched Rictius Varus. The pagan spells will still work, and more so now, my daughter for we are one, together, stronger, more powerful.

Okay, well, I'm waiting. I don't feel so strong.

Concentrate, my daughter. Focus on the feel of their cocks as they thrust inside you. Let your juices coat their cocks. Enjoy this fucking, for from your juices will flow the power needed to destroy your captors. Thousands of years ago I only had myself, and that ordeal made me stronger, created the power, the curse, that has brought us together. Now we are one this attack will not be our death but our birth. The two of us are unstoppable—the ultimate Avenging Angel Sex Goddess—what we were always destined to be, and these fools will help us in our quest.

Lucretia's thoughts—words—are hypnotic. I find myself reciting them in a language I don't know. I feel so sexy. It's as if I wished this rape to take place. The handcuffs are a turn on. The jail bars are hot against my skin. I lick one and feel the steel dissolve in me, like the steely hard cocks that rape my pussy and ass, steeling me with the power I need. My hips move from side to side. I clench the tightness of my cunt and my ass on my intruders' cocks. I enjoy feeling these two plundering weapons rubbing against each other through the thin juicing walls of my body.

Titfeeler squeezes my nipples. My breasts smolder, lighting fires through my skin. The air crackles around me.

Lucretia's excitement cannot be contained.

It's working my child. When they come, as they soon will, place your feet on theirs. One on the cop—one on the lowlife. I will do the rest.

My rapists lunge in and out of my cunt and ass. Their sweat drips on my skin and it sizzles and evaporates. The jail bars press into my body, making me feel stronger. Asshole cop's cock bulges in my ass. He groans. His cock stiffens. He's ready to explode in my butt. I angle my body, shifting my foot onto his boot. I slide my other foot through the bars and press down on twattoucher's bare foot. Titfeeler is so engrossed in squeezing my nipples that he crowds in and steps on my foot. I enjoy the sandwich of their feet around mine. Titfeeler's cock angles towards the bars and with a slight shift of my body I trap it between my hips and the bars, jerking him off through the motions his comrade-in-rapes' thrustings cause in my body. They all come together. Their sperm floods my pussy and ass and skin, and as they pulse their warmness in and around me I come too, a powerful, full body orgasm erupting not from my cunt but from my feet upwards, swelling my entire body into one pulsing pussy of female sexual power.

That's when all hell loose for them. For me it's pretty cool.

Lucretia erupts from my body, using the footsex energy of the combined orgasms to materialize behind the asshole cop's other asshole cops waiting their turn. It doesn't take her long to bash their heads in, rifling them with bullets from their own guns so it looks like they shot each other. Her pagan spell has the same effect upon asshole cop and the lowlifes as her two-thousand year previous spell had upon Rictius Varus. Asshole cop falls from me possessed by demons sucking at his body, devouring his flesh. He clutches at himself, babbling, begging for mercy, tugging at his cock as if pulling it off will stop his torment. Titfeeler and twattoucher are similarly writhing on the floor, assaulting each other's bodies, their vision distorted by Lucretia's spell such that they think that each is a vulnerable woman ready to be raped. We laugh at our erstwhile attackers. Lucretia takes asshole cop's keys from him and unlocks my handcuffs. I turn and throw my arms around her. We kiss. It's a deep, throaty tongue entwining in which we feel every cell of our different beings become one as our feet touch.

We stay linked like this for eternities—as it seems for

the cursed beings at our feet—although for us it seems like only a few seconds. As our lips slide apart, our feet separate and we know what to do.

I take the asshole cop by the scruff of his neck and drag him from the cell. Lucretia grabs the two lowlifes who remain busy fighting and fucking each other. We emerge from the dingy jail to find Miguel's taxi in which he sits bullet-riddled in the back. We toss our rapists into the back with him and drive away to find a nice, quiet spot to exact our final punishment.

Lucretia pulls on some clothes from my suitcase as I drive, and I find I've somehow dressed as well. What she does, I do and vice versa. We're separate and one. She takes Miguel's wallet from his bloodstained pants and finds the information we need. I immediately know what she's looking at without her having to tell me.

This is a good spot, and I think the same thing as she thinks it.

I stop the car and carry Miguel's body to the banks of a small stream. Lucretia follows with our three victims. At her command they dig at the ground with their hands until they have nothing but bloody nubs left for the fingers which once molested us. We place Miguel in the grave and our victims fill in the dirt with their bleeding palms as shovels. We walk up the hillside and get back in the car, our three stumpy fingered stooges battling with each other in the backseat. We drive for a few more miles.

This is a good spot. Yes, it is.

We get out of the car. We sit asshole cop in the driver's seat. The lowlifes remain in the backseat fucking and fighting each other. Lucretia kisses asshole cop on the ear, whispering one final curse. He screams, guns the car and rockets it through the barricade, plunging down a hillside until it bursts into flames. We watch it burn. We hear our rapists scream, and we feel good.

We feel powerful.

We kiss, our mouths talking through our brains as our pussies juice with sexual gratification.

There's much to be done.

Yes, there is. Time is short, we must make our way to San Francisco and on to Rome.

Johnny and Luc will be waiting for us.

CHAPTER TWENTY-FOUR

BEFORE WE LEAVE Mexico we take care of one last item of business. We send the airport locker key to Miguel's mother with a note that tells her how her son died a hero fighting police and Catholic Church corruption, and he did amount to something. We include a map as to where we'd buried him, and suggest that with a little of the reward that she'll find in the locker that she might want to give him a decent burial.

Or perhaps not. Spend it on the living.

Speaking of the living, we call Salvatore and tell him what happened. After expressing much relief that we're still alive, he confirms that Luc has been transferred to the Vatican. I ask him to tell Johnny to stay put in San Francisco and keep Ellen occupied. We end the call by planning a Lowest Soles reunion in Rome to figure out how we rescue Luc.

                              *   *   *

It takes us almost a week to get back to San Francisco. We
don't risk the traditional routes, avoiding the airport, going
through as one on a bus across the Tijuana border as
Violetta Valery Cutrero. I—we—arrive in Marin on the
early evening of November 8.

Just in time.

Johnny's at the beach house looking mighty concerned.
"Violetta—we were so worried. I'm so sorry about—"

"Sssssssh."

I put my finger to his lips and they pucker and kiss my
digit. It's all we need. He sucks my finger, and I wrap
myself around him, lifting myself off the ground by my
arms, my legs around his waist, my cunt grinding into his
bulging hardness, like when we first fucked on the plane
from New York to Rome.

We kiss in between those wonderfully sexy protestations of eternal love uttered in dripping Italian. Hands
occupied, he gesticulates with his dick. It moves and
flicks under the constraint of his tight jeans, illustrating
better than any other gesture how excited he is by me. He
nibbles at my neck, and I arch backwards, wetting my
pussy with every up and down squirm along his hardness.
He carries me to the boudoir, bumping into walls,
knocking over chairs and general household crap.

Spykes runs for cover.

When Johnny and I are in range of the bed he falls on
top of me, launching us with a crash into the covers. We
don't take time to undress. He pushes my dress up and
pulls aside my panties as I push his jeans and underwear
past his hips. We make love half-clothed with an urgency
that Johnny thinks is because we haven't seen each other
for so long, but I know it's because we may never see
each other again.

Smothering me with a deluge of kisses, he drives into me, burying his cock deep, holding it for a few seconds against my pulsing, dripping walls, pulling its pulsing length out slowly such that my cunt tries to suck him back in. He tears open the front of my dress with his teeth so he can kiss my breasts, squeezing the small cleavage together with his arms as he holds himself above me, burying his face between them, alternating sucks on each nipple. He make me feel beautiful, voluptuous.

He comes inside me just after holding himself still for a few seconds as deep as he could. His orgasm erupts as he pulls slowly away, interrupting his withdrawal, inspiring him to plunge deep as he comes. His cockhead is so sensitive that he moans in delight as his eruption pulses against my walls, and he batters into the roof of my cunt. He holds himself full inside me, twitching, moaning, staying hard for me, and I hold him tight, enjoying the feel of his heart beating in time to the pulse of his cock.

Ever the gentleman, Johnny reaches between our compressed bodies, inserting his hand between my cunt lips and his abdomen. He finds my clit with an instinct for the female body I'm always amazed at. He slides two fingers up and down, working my clit between them as he grinds his still hard cock into all the right places in my cunt. It doesn't take me long to come, and I cry real tears for him, for Miguel, and I vow I'll damn well make sure that nothing like that happens to Johnny.

We're forever.

Lucretia stays hidden inside me. She keeps quiet. She doesn't say anything to me. She knows this is just Johnny and I—for now.

I run my hands over his chest.

"Johnny, I want you to do something for me."

"Yes, anything, other than let you out of my sight."

"That's what I need you to do. Just for a few hours."

"You ask the impossible."

"No, you must let me have this space. There's something I must do."

"Then I'll do it with you."

"No, I have to say goodbye to Ellen. You can't be there. It wouldn't be right. I want you to get Spykes, put him in his pet carrier and go to the airport. We have tickets on the late night flight to Rome by way of New York."

"What? You've just got home."

"This is not my home anymore. I want to make a new home in Rome with you, but I can't have loose ends here."

"Will you be okay with Ellen? I could wait out in the street or on the beach and we could go to the airport together. I don't trust her."

"Thanks, but no thanks. This has to be just Ellen and I. She won't hurt me. If anyone's going to be hurt by what I have to do it'll be her."

"Violetta, I must ask. Forgive me. Are you trying to get rid of me? Will you show up?"

I kiss Johnny.

"Of course I will, silly, and if I wanted to get rid of you I'd be straight with you. You know me well enough by now. So don't even bother showering because we're going to fuck in the airplane's bathroom to celebrate our new life just as soon as those unfasten seatbelt signs are illuminated, just like the first time."

Johnny leans over and kisses me.

"I'll pack my bags and grab Spykes."

"Thanks, and Johnny, I do love you."

"*Ti amo*, Violetta. *Ti amo*."

It's all I can do to keep up the brave front as I wave bye to Johnny and Spykes. Once the taillights have disappeared I run into the house, glancing at every clock as if one of them will give me more time.

They don't.

I have just enough time.

I dial Ellen's number.

"Hi."

"Hi."

"Has he gone?"

"Yes."

"How do you feel?"

"Sad. I want you. I need to see you."

Ellen's response is predictable.

"I'll be right over. We can talk and set things straight. I can get you the help you need. I love you."

"Thanks. I love you too. Just hurry. I don't want to be alone much longer."

Ellen clicks off the phone. I lied. Of course, I'm not alone, and I don't love her after what she caused to happen to my son, our son—our as in Violetta and Lucretia. My Guardian Angel's with me. She looks at the clock.

"It's time."

"Yeah."

She kisses me.

"I love you, Violetta."

"I love you, Lucretia."

"Do you trust me?"

"Yes, like I trust myself."

We laugh at our inside joke. Lucretia retrieves Jack the Ripper's boots from the closet. I lace them on for her. There are tears in our eyes as we fall together on the bed, kissing and finger fucking. It's frenzied and passionate. We roll around, neither one of us on top for very long. The dampness from Johnny's lovemaking touches my body and far from making me sad it gladdens me, as if he were here helping me in what I have to do.

I hope he understands. There was no choice. It is my destiny. Our destiny. His destiny.

I look over at the clock near the bedside and watch it change to eight p.m.

Four in the morning in Victorian England, the ninth of November. I hear the chimes of a distant bell.

Lucretia's inside Jack's boots experiencing what Tumblety felt as he sliced apart Mary Jane Kelly in the most horrible of all Ripper crimes. Beautiful little Mary, the fifth victim, most recently of the Providence Row Convent and Night Refuge, appropriately enough to be found in Crispin Street, until the nuns sent her out into domestic service and Mary fell into service of a different kind. I can't help feeling how strange it is how history works in small circles and how shoes and all that they're associated with pepper my life. Crispin Street—Crispinus and Crispinianus—the patron saints of shoe repairers. It's the last piece of the jigsaw puzzle of my life that started falling into place when a couple of weeks before Halloween, just after my tenth birthday, my dad sneaked into the bedroom and fucked me, the experience courtesy of my mom's sparkly high heels which I'd put on to complete my Bride of Frankenstein costume. And now there's Crispin Street leading Mary to her death and all those years later to me. Crispin Street—Crispinus and Crispinianus—the patron saints of shoe repairers—Lucretia's brothers who started all this battle between good and evil that has been the story of my short life.

And Lucretia who will end it.

In those boots at this time she's Jack the Ripper.

And under her, lying on a bed in 13 Miller's Court, I'm Mary Jane Kelly.

She ruts into me with an angry penis, strangling me with one hand, coming inside me as the knife comes down and splits me apart.

CHAPTER TWENTY-FIVE

I HEAR HER come in the house. The door bangs like it always does when she breezes in.

"Violetta?"

"In here, Ellen" I say. "In the bedroom."

"Traffic was horrible across the—oh my God."

She falls to the floor and gags. For an ex-cop she doesn't have a strong stomach, but then again, many of the stiff-upper-lip British cops who investigated the Mary Jane Kelly crime scene also lost their cookies.

The beachhouse bedroom is a ghastly reproduction of the horror of 13 Miller's Court. There's not much left of Violetta Valery Cutrero.

It dawns on Ellen that someone with Violetta's voice invited her to the bedroom. She looks up and sees me standing there, naked except for my Jack the Ripper boots.

I offer Ellen my hand, speaking in my Italian accented voice.

"Pleased to meet you. I'm Lucretia—"

I change my voice to Violetta's.

"—Violetta Valery Cutrero."

Ellen scurries away, but I don't let her get very far. I lift her up by the neck and hold her in the air. Her legs kick, but she's no threat. Soon enough her protestations wane. Her eyes bulge.

"From the beginning you were jealous of Luc. You couldn't stand that he was created by Violetta having sex with Tony, who you killed out of your jealous, over-protective rage. You schemed with the Catholic Church to trap us when Violetta came back to save you. You could have left well enough alone, but you couldn't trust me," I say. "You sold my baby out to the Church so you could have your concept of a nice, peaceful life with me. You wouldn't listen to me."

Through sputtering gasps Ellen can't resist arguing, the stupid woman.

"Not—your—baby—Violetta's—"

I can't resist a laugh.

"You silly idiot, Ellen. Can't you see what's before your eyes?"

I roll through several Violetta/Lucretia transformations. It's obvious from her expression she still doesn't believe the obvious.

"You thought Violetta was crazy, imaging her Guardian Angel Lucretia, but you were the crazy one, Ellen, for not believing more in the Cutrero power. After all you'd seen Violetta do and endured together, did you think she possessed just some little parlor trick—something like fortune telling or the Psychic Friends Network? Come on, Ellen, you saw Violetta at work. You knew her power was something special, fundamental, supernatural, yet you chose to fuck with it and you cost our baby his sex. You know what they did? They cut off his genitals, kind of like what Jack the Ripper did to Mary Jane Kelly. Look—take a good fucking look at the crime scene you caused with your sick alliance with Jack the Ripper's boots and the Catholic Church."

I throw Ellen onto the bed. In her panic she wrestles with the shell that once housed my spirit and soul and most importantly, my soles. She covers herself in the blood and gore, and as I expected she finds the shoe trimming knife I used to set myself free and lunges at me. I allow Ellen several good thrusts to get her prints all over the weapon, and then I bore of her antics. I take one of the bloody sheets that's lying on the floor and pull it, sending Ellen toppling to the ground. I step on her wrist. She lets go of the knife. I wrap the sheet around her neck and loop it into a noose, hanging it from the ceiling light fixture. I rub Ellen's pussy as the sheet tightens.

"Rejoice, Ellen. You'll die using my favorite means of dispatching serial killers—strangulation from hanging. I prefer it because it adds a sexual charge to the departure, and indeed, we've used it ourselves to take us to the next level of our evolving existence. It's also so easy to make it look like suicide. I used it to off the couple I fucked to bring me back. Don't look so hurt and surprised. You know the time when I left because you wouldn't have sex with me to bring Lucretia back, and I came back to you and I said I couldn't go through having sex with someone else. Well, I lied. Big deal. You're used to lying, right. I did have sex with a hot couple and that's how Lucretia came back. They were great. We got stoned and fucked some of the best fucking I've ever enjoyed, and then Lucretia offed them because they were going to kill me. You almost got me killed by the Kama Sutra Killers, Ellen, in addition to selling out my son, but Lucretia saved me and we fulfilled our destiny as the serial killer of serial killers, and now it's your time to die."

Ellen struggles, and I tire of making her pussy feel

good. I give her a push, and under her swinging weight the fixture gives away from the plaster with a jerk, but the cord holds Ellen, snapping her neck with a whip-like crack. As Ellen dangles lifeless I arrange a toppled chair under her to complete the murder-suicide pact.

Almost.

Now comes the suicide note. I hold Ellen's hand and guide her through the motions of confessing all.

"Dear Michael—you'll probably be one of the first on the scene. I'm sorry to have misled you all these weeks. I couldn't stand Violetta's love for others. I expected us to be happy after she helped set me free, but she'd fallen in love with another—a man—after all I'd done for her. She was going to run away with him tonight but I couldn't let her. There was nothing I wouldn't do or haven't done for her. I couldn't let her go. I couldn't let anyone have her sex so I took it away, and now I can't live with myself. Forgive me. You deserved better from a friend and Violetta deserved better from a lover.

Ellen."

CHAPTER TWENTY-SIX

"EXCUSE ME, I believe that's my seat next to you."

"I'm sorry, excuse me."

He shifts his long legs so that I can step over him in my Yves Saint Laurent stilettos and into my window seat. I notice he's wearing the purple suede Cuban-heeled short-height boots with side zippers that he wore when he first met me, as well as the same orange silk pants. As I step over him I encourage my Gucci miniskirt to ride up to make sure he sees enough of my dark Wolford stocking tops so he'll appreciate I'm wearing stockings and the attendant promise that my unclad thighs tensed to perfection in fuck-me heels offers. He looks up from staring at my legs and smiles the eternal Italian male beauty worship compliment before looking away a bit too fast than he would under normal circumstances. It's clear he's still recovering from the shock of finding my body and having to testify at the hearing of the tragic murder-suicide case of Ellen Stewart and Violetta Valery Cutrero. In the few moments that our eyes connect he doesn't show much recognition, but that's to be expected, since there's no reason why he should recognize my Sophia Lorenesque long raven hair, larger bosom, skyscraper legs and overall more of a Lucretia dark sexbomb va-va-va-voom appeal than I had in my Violetta punk days.

It's been tough all this time for Johnny, having to deal with the guilt of having left Violetta to that mad Ellen woman. It's been no breeze for me also, hiding away, waiting for him to make his reservation to fly back home with Spykes, but now my patience has been rewarded. We're here awaiting take off and the reunion he has no idea about but which will soon follow is only a few moments away.

"You're Italian," I say. "Me too." I introduce myself.

"Nicola Anacapa," I say with a smile, snapping my suspender strap brazenly against my ass through the material of my miniskirt. I enjoy the fleeting look of recognition and bewilderment on Johnny's face as I imagine him remembering the fake name I used when he first met me combined with the abandoned restaurant in New York where we fucked, and I wore stockings like I'm wearing now and he enjoyed snapping them against my butt.

"Johnny Gianni," he says, shaking my hand, bending to kiss it with a smile, staring at my legs. I feel the electricity between us. So does he.

"Where are you from?" he says, adding "I feel like we've met before." I let my Violetta voice answer.

"In another life, Johnny. I'm from Rome, like you," I add even though he hasn't told me. He looks puzzled. I continue as if nothing's amiss and his gorgeous mouth isn't gaga wide open. "I've been in the States visiting relatives for quite some time but now I'm going home to find my son. I lost him in—shall we say—a custody battle with the Catholic Church."

Johnny stares at me. I can tell he thinks he's going crazy. I grab his hand before he can cross himself and kiss his cheek. I whisper in his ear.

"Johnny, it's me, Violetta. The feet cannot be denied."

He crosses himself, pulling my hand along with him. I stop the silly ritual right above his heart where I press our hands together firmly against his chest. I look into his eyes and I can tell he knows who I am.

"Mamma mia."

"You might say so, Johnny. Guardian Angel mother Lucretia and Avenging Angel Sex Goddess Violetta are one, and we are yours and you are ours."

I kick off my high heels and rub my stockinged foot up his leg underneath his baggy silk trousers. Despite the excitement his body exhibits, Johnny can't help but be bewildered and angry.

"Why didn't you tell me? Or send me a message. These weeks have been horrible."

"I'm sorry you had to go through all that, but I couldn't involve you any more than you were. I couldn't tell you what was going to happen because you'd have tried to stop me, or worse, contact me while there were still so many police around you. At least this way you didn't have to lie for me, just grieve, and now be happy."

"I knew you were getting rid of me that night."

"I knew you knew, and I love you for trusting me enough to let me be me and do the things I had to do."

"I waited at the airport. It was horrible when Violetta—you—didn't show. My heart broke. The ride back to the beach house was hell, then I found you—that—that mess. And now you're here and ask me to believe it's you."

"Like I said, Johnny, I'm sorry for what you went through, but it's over now."

"But how? That mess—"

"What you saw in that beachhouse bedroom was just

the chrysalis from which this beautiful butterfly has emerged. You'll see that it's still me, and more. Just wait for the unfasten your seatbelt sign to illuminate and in addition to fucking your brains out in the bathroom, I'll also explain how you'll come to spend the rest of your life with Lucretia Violetta Valery Cutrero."

For once Johnny Gianni is speechless. I kiss him on the lips, probing his mouth with my tongue. As the 747 rumbles down the runway I grab his cock and squeeze it in exactly the way I used to. There are tears in his eyes and his cock is rock hard.

I whisper in his ear.

"And this time we will all live happily ever after."

Romance of Lust
Anonymous

The Romance of Lust is that rare combination of graphic sensuality, literary success, and historical importance that is loved by critics and readers alike.—*The Times*

"Truly remarkable. All the pleasure of fine historical fiction combined with the most intimate descriptions of explicit lovemaking."
—*Herald Tribune*

"This justly famous novel has been a secret bestseller for a hundred years."

The Altar of Venus
Anonymous

Our author, a gentleman of wealth and privilege, is introduced to desire's delights at a tender age, and then and there commits himself to a life-long sensual expedition. As he enters manhood, he progresses from schoolgirls' charms to older women's enticements, especially those of acquaintances' mothers and wives. Later, he moves beyond common London brothels to sophisticated entertainments available only in Paris. Truly, he has become a lord among libertines.

Caning Able
Stan Kent

Caning Able is a modern-day version of the melodramatic tales of Victorian erotica. Full of dastardly villains, regimented discipline, corporal punishment and forbidden sexual liaisons, the novel features the brilliant and beautiful Jasmine, a seemingly helpless heroine who reigns triumphant despite dire peril. By mixing libidinous prose with a changing business world, Caning Able gives treasured plots a welcome twist: women who are definitely not the weaker sex.

The Blue Moon Erotic Reader III

Once again, Blue Moon presents its unique collection of stories of passion, desire, and experimentation

A testimonial to the publication of quality erotica, The Blue Moon Erotic Reader III presents more than twenty-five romantic and exciting excerpts from selections spanning a variety of periods and themes. This is a historical compilation that combines generous extracts from the finest forbidden books with the most extravagant samplings that the modern erotic imagination has created. The result is a collection that is evocative and entertaining, perhaps even enlightening. It encompasses memorable scenes of youthful initiations into the mysteries of sex, notorious confessions, and scandalous adventures of the powerful, wealthy, and notable. The Blue Moon Erotic Reader III is a stirring complement to the senses. Good taste, and passion, and an exalted desire are all here, making for a union of sex and sensibility that is available only once in a Blue Moon.

Beauty in the Birch
Anonymous

Beauty in the Birch is a remarkable description of exotic Victorian sexual episodes. Reportedly first published in Paris in 1905, the letters reveal the exploits of the handsome thirty-year-old rake Charles, who finds employment in a country mansion for wayward girls, and the impetuous and mischievous Lizzie, who, as the daughter of Britannia's plenipotentiary in an Arabian territory, makes herself privy to all the pleasures and punishments of the royal harem.

Addicted
Ray Gordon

Housewife, Helen Hunter, has it all. An attractive, successful husband. Money. Looks. However, things go wrong when her husband leaves on business. She becomes tired, nervy and anxious...panicky even. But on his return—after a hearty 'welcome'—the symptoms disappear. Something bizarre is happening—she has become addicted to sperm.

The supply from her husband soon becomes insufficient. She embarks on an incredible sexual journey to satisfy her desires. Unfortunately it soon becomes apparent that too much is never enough...

_____

Slave Girls of Rome
Don Winslow

Master eroticist Don Winslow takes an erotic look back on the Roman Empire during its ascendancy in the world. This is a tale of power and pleasure. Never has a city been as depraved as Rome—and never have women been so relentlessly used as were Rome's voluptuous slaves! With no choice but to serve their lustful masters, these captive beauties had to perform their duties with the passion and purpose of Venus herself.

_____

Lusts of the Borgias
Marcus Van Heller

Italy, during the Renaissance, was a time of culture but also of uninhibited corruption. And no powerful family of the age was more depraved than the infamous House of Borgia. Here is the story of their cruel, passionate, erotic adventures.

"One of the few historical erotic novels worthy of being called a classic. [It is also] a novel of outrageous sexual indulgence."— *Evergreen Review*

The Intimate Memoirs of an Edwardian Dandy
Anonymous

Raised in the English countryside, fifteen-year old Rupert is ready to savour the traditional sporting delights of privileged English gentleman—and to master the equipment needed for them. Who better to introduce him than lusty, libidinous country girls? A fine upstanding young man and a quick learner, Rupert is soon au fait with the hidden talents of parlor maids and damsels in delicious distress. He attends a revealing hypnosis sessions, and indulges in team games they don't teach at school...

Jennifer and Nikki
D. M. Perkins

From Manhattan's Fifth Avenue, to the lush island of Tobago, to a mysterious ashram in upstate New York, Jennifer travels with reclusive fashion model Nikki and her seductive half-brother Alain in search of the sexual secrets held by the famous Russian mystic Pere Mitya. To achieve intimacy with this extraordinary family, and get the story she has promised to Jack August, dynamic publisher of New Man Magazine, Jennifer must ignore universal taboos and strip away inhibitions she never knew she had.

Burn
Michael Hemmingson

Nicholas Wilde is a 50-year old painter shunned by the art elite for his unflinchingly representational depictions of the female form. Rose Selavy is the 24-year old muse who refuses to let him own her. When they meet, their passions burn red hot, then bloody and inspire one another, but when Rose leaves Nicholas is left impotent, unable to seduce the slew of women he encounters because none can stimulate him with the heat that Rose had provided.

Wet Dreams
Anonymous

A collection of vivid tales to spur the imaginations of uninhibited men and women. These stories offer a cornucopia of sexual delights. In Wayward Venus, a young man is seduced by his governess. Another is initiated by a countess and her maid. In the merry ménage a mother and daughter invite the attentions of a gentleman of dubious reputation, and a girl is taught the pleasures of spanking.

"An intoxicating sexual romp." –Evergreen Review

Emily Insatiable
by Anonymous

In this dream-like tale of erotic pursuits, a young English lady at the turn of the century delights in every act of debauchery imaginable. In the tradition of *Laura* and other fine novels from the Victorian underground, the insatiable Emily experiences new and exciting exploits that leave her wanting more.

Haunting Lust
by Ray Gordon

When twenty-year-old Tina Wilson moves into the old Victorian house that had been left to her, she suddenly becomes aware of a heightened new sexuality flooding through every fiber of her being. The mystery of what had triggered this powerful change is discovered in the attic, where she finds a hidden torture chamber and old diaries that reveal the true nature of the occult force that has possessed her with this haunting lust.

The Ravishing of Lesley
by Anonymous

Lesley, a beautiful young English woman who has left behind her husband and children, makes a strange, dream-like journey to a beautiful summer villa in Florville. There, under the guidance of her mentors, she gives herself over to total sensual abandon.

Gardens of the Night
Felicia Plessey

"So self-conscious, Lesley?" he asked, "Do you imagine you are made differently in that area to a thousand other girls who have bent over before their masters? You see? You flinch at the touch of a finger there! Ah, I think it is because you envisage what will be done to you in that part by the men who possess you!"

Best of the Erotic Reader, Vol. II
by Anonymous

Companion to *Best of the Erotic Reader*, this historical compilation contains extravagant samplings from classic works of the erotic imagination. In abundance are memorable scenes from ancient Roman orgies to scandalous confusions in Victorian England, from aristocratic seduction in eighteenth century France to modern sexual adventures.

"Frank" and I
Anonymous

The narrator of the story, a wealthy young man, meets a youth one day—the "Frank" of the title—and, taken by his beauty and good manners, invites him to come home with him. He quickly discovers that his charge displays an unacceptable lack of obedience and consequently he commences to flog him in the traditional and humiliating English manner. One can only imagine his surprise when the young man turns out to be a young woman with beguiling charms.

Eveline II
by Anonymous

Eveline II continues the delightfully erotic tale of a defiant aristocratic young English woman who throws off the mantle of respectability in order to revel in life's sexual pleasures. After returning to her paternal home in London in order to escape the boredom of marriage, she plunges with total abandon into self-indulgence and begins to "convert" other young ladies to her wanton ways.

Best of Shadow Lane
Eve Howard

Here at last are the very best stories from Eve Howard's ongoing chronicle of romantic discipline, Shadow Lane. Set in the Cape Cod village of Random Point, these stories detail submissive women's quests for masterful men who will turn them over their knees. At the center lies the mischievous Susan Ross, an Ivy League brat who needs a handsome dominant to give her the spanking she deserves.

Slaves of the Hypnotist
by Anonymous

Harry, son of a well-to-do English country family, has set out to "conquer" all the females within his immediate reach. But no sooner does he begin his exploits than he encounters the imperious beauty, Davina, who enslaves him through her remarkable power of hypnotism. Thus entranced, Harry indulges in every aspect of eroticism known to man or woman.

The Sleeping Palace
M. Orlando

Another thrilling volume of erotic reveries from the author of The Architecture of Desire. Maison Bizarre is the scene of unspeakable erotic cruelty; the Lust Akademie holds captive only the most debauched students of the sensual arts; Baden-Eros is the luxurious retreat of one's most prurient dreams. Once again, M. Orlando uses his flair for exotic detail to explore the nether regions of desire.

"Orlandos' writing is an orgasmic and linguistic treat." –Skin Two

Venus in Paris
Florentine Vaudrez

When a woman discovers the depths of her own erotic nature, her enthusiasm for the games of love become a threat to her husband. Her older sister defies the conventions of Parisian society by living openly with her lover, a man destined to deceive her. Together, these beautiful sisters tread the path of erotic delight—first in the arms of men, and then in the embraces of their own, more subtle and more constant sex.

———

Drama
Michael Hemmingson

Drama tells the titillating story of Bad karma and kinky sex among the thespians of The Alfred Jarry Theater.

The story kicks off with Jonathan, a playwright associated with The Alfred Jarry Theater, living with his director and lover, Kristine. But soon this stable arrangement collapses. He has an affair with a deviant actress, Karen, who has just left her husband and is seeking sensual experiences of extreme debauchery wherever she can find them—no matter who she destroys, including herself.

———

Tropic of Lust
Michele de Saint-Exupery

She was the beautiful young wife of a respectable diplomat posted to Bangkok. The permissive climate encouraged even the most outré sexual fantasy to become reality. Anything was possible for a woman ready to open herself to sexual discovery.

"A tale of sophisticated sensuality [it is] the story of a woman who dares to explore the depths of her own erotic nature."—*Avant Garde*

Oyster Redux
Anonymous

This is an expanded edition of the infamous novel *The Times of London* labeled "naked and unabashed in its eroticism."

The original edition of *The Oyster* was privately printed and circulated. It enjoyed an even greater popularity than *The Pearl* because of the robust sensuality of the memoir *A Frank Recollection of Youthful Days* reprinted here in its full unexpurgated form.

The Autobiography of a Flea
Anonymous

The Autobiography of a Flea contains, in abundance, all the elements of great nineteenth century erotic literature: innocent maidens, lusty, unscrupulous clerics, wayward wives and duped husbands. These are the ingredients that have made this classic French work of erotica justly famous.

The Captive's Journey
by Richard Manton

At the Fortress Ben-Abar, Miss Caroline Martin, the abducted English debutante, continues her erotic education under the stern tutelage of Jason and the Countess. At the completion of her training, she is sent to London to her new master, Sir Basil Rothberg. There she is introduced to more debauchery, and begins a new journey to personal erotic fulfillment.

Love for Sale
Celia St. Gogarty

Like many another ingénue before her, Mae Li has traveled a treacherous path to the city, arriving with only a dream of a better life and a fantasy of life as a pop singer. Speaking little English and betrayed by her unscrupulous cousin, Mae Li is soon the prey of pimps, pornographers, and one woman, with a desperate secret of her own, who may be Mae Li's rescue.

The Memoirs of Josephine
Anonymous

19th Century Vienna was a wellspring of culture, society and decadence and home to Josephine Mutzenbacher. One of the most beautiful and sought after libertines of the age, she rose from the streets to become a celebrated courtesan. As a young girl, she learned the secrets of her profession. As mistress to wealthy, powerful men, she used her talents to transform from a slattern to the most wanted woman of the age. This candid, long suppressed memoir is her story.

Jennifer
D.M. Perkins

His touch released a dark flood of sensation in Jennifer. It coursed through her body and changed her from a rational, intelligent, career woman into someone else: a woman who would do anything—move to any primitive sexual level—when she was aroused. She'd always had an active fantasy life. One of her earliest sexual scenarios was a daydream of being kidnapped by a strong ruthless man.

Mistress of Instruction
Christine Kerr

Mistress of Instruction is a delightfully erotic romp through merry old Victorian England. Gillian, precocious and promiscuous, travels to London where she discovers Crawford House, an exclusive gentlemen's club where young ladies are trained to excel in service. A true prodigy of sensual talents, she is retained to supervise the other girls' initiation into "the life." Her title: Mistress of Instruction.

House of Lust
Ray Gordon

Lady Hadleigh likes to think she can abuse anyone on her estate at will. But when she seduces Tom, her ambitious stable boy, she discovers an adversary determined to rise by mercilessly exploiting his tremendous sexual prowess at every opportunity. 'Breaking in' Lady Hadleigh's two teenage daughters is just a step in Tom's rapacious progress. There's a lot more to come as he thrusts his rampant way to the top.

Incognito
Lisabet Sarai

By day, Miranda Cahill is pursuing her doctorate in English literature. But at night, compelled by a hunger she barely understands, she
haunts the streets, bars and clubs of the city, engaging in anonymous,
outrageous sexual liaisons. The line between these two selves begins
to blur when she discovers that her masked partner in a fetishistic
orgy and the attractive, bookish colleague who has been wooing her
are the same individual.

Dark Star
Michael Perkins

Dark Star explores an underground Californian sex world that
ranges across San Francisco's "sacred prostitutes" and pagan play
parties to Los Angeles's world of extreme porno video. The plot follows adult video star China Crosley who uses an admiring stalker
named Buddy Tate to help her escape a complex Bondage and
Discipline marriage to erotic dream entrepreneur Jack Blue. This is
a novel of radical sexual relationships that spin passionately out over
the edge.

The Ironwood Reader
Don Winslow

The master of erotic discipline and instruction gathers the very best
from the Ironwood series.

Ostensibly a finishing school for young ladies, Ironwood is actually
a unique enterprise, that singular institution where submissive young
beauties are rigorously trained in the many arts of love. It is narrated
by James, an instructor for whom Ironwood is a fantastic dream
world where discipline knows few boundaries, and where his role as
master affords him free reign with the willing, well-trained and submissive young beauties in his charge. *The Ironwood Reader*
presents carefully chosen selections from the notorious saga: choice passages
written in elegant style, with formal opulence and erotic sophistica-
tion. Vibrant with raw sexual imagery, they reveal the essence of the
Ironwood girl—that consummate blend of sexuality and innocence.
These are leisurely passages that dwell on those exquisite young
women with their unaffected air, as though they were unaware of the
powerful erotic attraction they hold for those around them.

Order These Selected Blue Moon Titles

Souvenirs From a Boarding School . . $7.95
The Captive $7.95
Ironwood Revisited $7.95
The She-Slaves of Cinta Vincente . . . $7.95
The Architecture of Desire $7.95
The Captive II $7.95
Shadow Lane $7.95
Services Rendered $7.95
Shadow Lane III $7.95
My Secret Life $9.95
The Eye of the Intruder $7.95
Net of Sex $7.95
Captive V $7.95
Cocktails $7.95
Girl School $7.95
The New Story of O $7.95
Shadow Lane IV $7.95
Beauty in the Birch $7.95
The Blue Train $7.95
Wild Tattoo $7.95
Ironwood Continued $7.95
Transfer Point Nice $7.95
Souvenirs From a Boarding School . . $7.95
Secret Talents $7.95
Shadow Lane V $7.95
Bizarre Voyage $7.95

Red Hot $7.95
Images of Ironwood $7.95
Tokyo Story $7.95
The Comfort of Women $7.95
Disciplining Jane $7.95
The Passionate Prisoners $7.95
Doctor Sex $7.95
Shadow Lane VI $7.95
Girl's Reformatory $7.95
The City of One-Night Stands $7.95
A Hunger in Her Flesh $7.95
Flesh On Fire $7.95
Hard Drive $7.95
Secret Talents $7.95
The Captive's Journey $7.95
Elena Raw $7.95
La Vie Parisienne $7.95
Fetish Girl $7.95
Road Babe $7.95
Violetta $7.95
Story of O $5.95
Dark Matter $7.95
Ironwood $7.95
Body Job $7.95
Arousal $7.95
The Blue Moon Erotic Reader II . . . $15.95

ORDER FORM
Attach a separate sheet for additional titles.

Title	Quantity	Price
_____	____	_____
_____	____	_____
_____	____	_____
_____	____	_____
Shipping and Handling (see charges below)		_____
Sales tax (in CA and NY)		_____
Total		_____

Name _____

Address _____

City _____ State _____ Zip _____

Daytime telephone number _____

❑ Check   ❑ Money Order   (US dollars only. No COD orders accepted.)

Credit Card # _____ Exp. Date _____

❑ MC   ❑ VISA   ❑ AMEX

Signature _____

(if paying with a credit card you must sign this form.)

Shipping and Handling charges:*

Domestic: $4 for 1st book, $.75 each additional book. International: $5 for 1st book, $1 each additional book
*rates in effect at time of publication. Subject to Change.

Mail order to Publishers Group West, Attention: Order Dept., 1700 Fourth St., Berkeley, CA 94710,
or fax to (510) 528-3444.

PLEASE ALLOW 4-6 WEEKS FOR DELIVERY. ALL ORDERS SHIP VIA 4TH CLASS MAIL.

**Look for Blue Moon Books at your favorite local bookseller
or from your favorite online bookseller.**